I0664197

AMBUSHING THE VIGILANTE
A Rose Brashear & Savio Mendes Novel

Lesann Berry

Isinglass Press
SILVERLAKE, WASHINGTON

Isinglass Press
PO Box 1731
Castle Rock, WA 98611
www.isinglasspress.com

Publisher's Note: This is a work of fiction. Names, characters, places, and incidents are a product of the author's imagination. Locales and public names are sometimes used for atmospheric purposes. Any resemblance to actual people, living or dead, or to businesses, companies, events, institutions, or locales is completely coincidental.

Cover Design by www.HumbleNations.com
Interior Design by www.BookDesignTemplates.com

Ordering Information:
Quantity sales. Special discounts are available on quantity purchases by corporations, associations, and others. For details, contact the "Special Sales Department" at the address above.

Ambushing the Vigilante/ Lesann Berry. -- 1st ed.
ISBN 978-1-939316-16-5

For my Dad.
It's not quite what we talked about but it's finally done.

"Adventure seeks me out."

~MEDE BANNION

Chapter One

T HE TRUTH IS some roadkill is better than others. Rose Brashear evaluated the dead deer through critical eyes. The Montana sun fell warm across her back as she assessed the bundle of dry bones. She squatted to poke at the remains just as a tractor-trailer burst over the incline and roared past. Dust and dried plant debris swirled over the roof of her car to settle on her shoulders. With one hand she scooped her long hair into a twist and hooked the mass under an arm as she bent forward.

On closer inspection she decided that carcass was too generous a term given the deer's desiccated condition. Threads of tight sinew and bits of hardened cartilage stretched beneath a dried hide decorated by tufts of patchy hair. Even the insects had abandoned the young buck as a done deal. For purposes of taxonomic comparison, this one just wasn't good enough.

She stood and stretched until her thighs shook with the effort. Arms spearing the cloudless sky, she rotated her head and tried to loosen muscles atrophied from too many hours in the driver's seat. Hands lowered to her back, she applied her palms to her lumbar and twisted. The waistband of her jeans slid loose against her hipbones as her spine popped. She'd lost twelve pounds during the previous year. The combined impact of two semesters of adjunct teaching while finishing her dissertation and competing for a faculty placement had drained her energy stores.

She aimed one final glance at the remains. Compared to the prime examples of western fauna she'd already stowed in the hatchback of her car, the deer was not a worthy addition. She'd run out of storage space long before the pool of potential highway victims was depleted. At any rate, as much as she enjoyed procuring new taxonomic materials for campus, right now she needed to focus on other professional matters. A mere ten weeks remained to complete her field research, reduce the results into a flawless summary, and submit her article for publication.

Her career might very well hinge on the success of this summer. Meeting that deadline might propel her ahead of the other candidates and earn her the coveted appointment of Assistant Professor.

She walked to the rear of the car and popped the hatch release.

Two boxes filled with skeletal elements sat stacked in the center of the trunk space. She pushed those aside to make room for the books that kept sliding off the passenger seat onto the floorboard. Unsure what might prove useful once she arrived, she'd thrown in a lot of extra source material. Folders were crammed with maps of the region and articles about identified historical sites. Copies of government records and print-outs from internet sources were stuffed inside the covers of books. That mess, along with the compact duffel bag that held her clothes and toiletries, cluttered the interior of her vehicle.

She dropped her knapsack on the driver's seat, the worn canvas bag hiding her granddad's Luger handgun. Ever since the vintage leather holster had disintegrated, she'd hesitated to stow the gun in the trunk. She needed a safer place than between the seats but over the last five years she'd learned a firearm had practical uses for a woman alone in the wilderness.

After driving all day, she ached to check into her lodging and stretch out on a horizontal surface. She'd booked a room in the small town of Riverside, a luxury afforded by the stipend she'd received from her mentor, Dr. Wilcox. A soft bed and a flush toilet were atypical during a field exercise and she planned to enjoy both. That nice little dividend had come her way as a result of the faunal contributions she'd sourced for the department's anatomical collection. With careful management the unexpected windfall would cover her expenses for the entire six weeks.

For the price, the White Horse Inn better deliver.

She transferred her research materials and slammed the hatchback shut. A breeze kicked up and she took a moment to admire the scenery. The road stretched away until it met the horizon. In the time she'd been parked along the highway, only a handful of vehicles had driven past. No wonder people called this Big Sky Country.

A white sedan popped over a hill and sped toward her.

A second car lurched into view a short distance behind it and caught her full attention. The rack of lights on the roof provided instant identification. Sure enough, the cop slowed and began to ease off onto the shoulder just as the white sedan blew past. She closed her eyes as a precaution but only a minimum of dust stirred up. The patrol car rolled to a halt twenty feet behind her.

Rose leaned against her fender, arms crossed over her stomach and her hands linked to the opposite elbow.

A man about twice her age emerged and slapped a broad-brimmed hat on his head. He wore dark blue jeans creased down the front like trousers. Square-toed cowboy boots adorned his feet. His long-sleeved dress shirt and narrow black tie were a formal contrast to the denim.

The countrified uniform fit her image of Montana.

An embroidered patch sewn to either shoulder indicated jurisdictional affiliation, as did the glint of the shiny chrome badge on the left pocket of his chest. A small handgun rode his hip, the dark carbon grip blending into the hard leather holster.

Despite the deputy's undeniable authority, she liked the effect of his casual attire. Clothes made the man, right? At the least, the blue jeans radiated a sense of approachability. Rose knew the sheriff of a small town in Nevada and his stiffly creased uniform and constant glower always got her hackles up.

As the deputy approached, he raised a hand and tipped his hat with two fingertips. The action appeared so ingrained Rose bet he was unaware of offering the habitual greeting.

"Afternoon, you have car trouble?"

She waved toward the bleached skull. "Just taking a stretch and looking at the local fauna."

Following her gesture, he surveyed the scene for a moment before swinging his gaze back to her face. "Weather's warm today. You need help with anything?"

She shook her head but he still looked skeptical so she smiled. "Honest."

He nodded, not returning her smile.

Up close, she revised his age. Younger than she'd first thought but definitely part of her parent's generation. His skin was weathered and though grey streaked his hair, he moved with smooth muscle tone.

The lawman studied her before he turned to scan the empty landscape. "Bad place to get stranded. This is deserted country."

"I appreciate you stopping to check on me, especially if my car had broken down." She patted the quarter panel, her hand leaving a smudged print in the dust. She swiped her palm down her thigh.

He looked back at her, "You headed to the park?"

"Yes," she nodded, "I'm conducting research there this summer."

"You must be staying with the group at the Porcupine Bluff Research Station."

It didn't really sound like a question but she answered anyway. "I'm solo. My study involves historical archaeology." Usually, that was enough to bore even the curious and it did the job again.

"Well, best get going. The exit you want is a few more miles down the interstate. Enjoy your visit." With a polite nod of dismissal, he strode back to his vehicle.

Rose sidestepped until she could reach through the open driver's side window. She grabbed her digital camera off the dash, clicked the button and took a picture as the man climbed inside his car. Then she snapped shots of the scenery before she concluded the sheriff wasn't going to depart until she left too. With no reason to dawdle, she slid behind the wheel and pulled back on the pavement.

The cruiser followed.

A few minutes later she reached the numbered exit for her route and flicked on her turn signal indicator. The lawman took the same ramp behind her as she entered the two-lane county highway. She carefully eyed the speedometer but at the next fork the cop car turned north while she continued east toward Yellowstone National Park.

Evergreens pushed in from both sides. They choked the shoulders of the road, crowding against the narrow strip of gravel that ran along the ribbon of pavement.

Excited to finally arrive at her destination, she rummaged in her bag and withdrew a Park Service envelope. Inside was a packet of papers, the official documents which granted her permission to conduct surface surveys of nineteenth century mines in a specified portion called the West District. The three pages represented months of planning but in truth, she'd selected this locale over others because of crass commercialism. The people who typically sat on hiring committees were impressed by name recognition and Yellowstone was an Ivy League member of the National Park system. She hoped that played in her favor.

There was another reason Montana appealed to her. She relished the idea of revisiting any place her granddad had spent time. That association was why she'd chosen Riverside instead of the more populous eastern edge of the park. Chewing on her lower lip, she grinned when the stone archway slid into view.

CHAPTER TWO

SAVIO MENDES KNEW he needed to get his ass back to Los Angeles but still he procrastinated. He'd reached no conclusive decision about the source of the breach in security that had driven him from Mexico City. Riding the collapse of the Almeida Cartel, he'd decided to remain incommunicado until he determined exactly who he could trust.

Now that he'd landed in the quaint community of Riverside, Montana and achieved successful contact with the cartel's local client, he felt compelled to stick around and see what happened. Besides, after spending months playing cat-and-mouse with the criminal head of the Mexican crime family, he liked being off-grid. Too many hours cooped up in the dusty sedan had provided plenty of preparation for taking on the role of courier.

A twinge of guilt made Savio shift on the hard wooden bench.

Upon learning his employer had been arrested, Benito knew Savio had lied to him. The man panicked and threw himself from their moving vehicle in an effort to escape. He'd broken his neck. An event such as that might make a man introspect, make him assess why a stranger opted to take such a risk but Savio refused to dwell on the subject. Guilt was a luxury he couldn't afford.

At any rate, he'd managed to represent himself as a mouthpiece for the bad guys and pulled off the meet-and-greet with the drug-producer who'd been impatiently awaiting Benito's arrival.

Events had not gone well. The two had shared an instant and mutual dislike. Even so, delivery was imminent because, in the end, business was business.

Guys like Kurt Mackenzie fulfilled the role of middle men. They were mid-level distributors, the ones who received raw compound from the cartel, which they then cooked into marketable product and sold to the next tier of salespeople. Cooking narcotics required time and a secure location. Mackenzie didn't transport the methamphetamine directly to a wide customer base; instead, he turned a concentrated solution over to merchants who diluted each batch with an agent to increase the quantity and raise the value. Once delivered, the drug moved down the line until little plastic baggies slipped into sweaty palms in exchange for folded cash.

Savio knew that meant the distribution agents were probably close by. The wilderness landscape limited his options by simply being so vast. Park facilities, campgrounds, and nearby towns provided the most logical possibilities for buyers engaged in the hurry-up-and-wait process of drug production.

Finding them might be a wasted effort if Mackenzie broke and ran but Savio couldn't help but amuse himself at the man's expense. He enjoyed how nervous he made Mackenzie. The guy responded especially well to blank stares, going still and then twitching and jerking until he erupted in a burst of foul language. Maggots like Mackenzie generally avoided conflict. Aggression drew the attention of authorities but, they were also the first to spew with outrage whenever they had a ready audience. Besides, pushing the man's buttons helped defuse Savio's own frustrations.

The manipulation of violence was a primary difference between U.S. and Mexican treatment of pharmaceutical trafficking. In America, avoiding public notice contributed to the success of commercial narcotic and stimulant trade. In Mexico, savagery regulated most interactions.

His summer had kicked off with the largest inter-agency drug bust in the history of Mexico City. For a fellow in Mackenzie's line of business, the crash of the Mexican Syndicate and the collapse of the Almeida Cartel signified potential disaster. Faced with being forced to rely on other suppliers for raw materials, Mackenzie had opted for the next best thing by agreeing to meet with Savio even though Benito was his expected courier.

Changes in legislation and public accessibility made the unprocessed components of methamphetamine increasingly difficult to procure. When sources dried up, so did revenue. Risks increased.

Mackenzie enjoyed success primarily because he hovered under the radar. His production rate, though minor compared to the big operations, still funneled millions of dollars' worth of contraband into the system. Closing down his operation was like pulling the plug on a bathtub rather than a lake, but in Savio's opinion, fewer drugs on the open market was always a good thing. And, Mackenzie was an asshole. Savio intended to add to the man's challenges in any way he could manage.

Until the cartel recovered from the havoc created by recent arrests, Mackenzie needed to capitalize on every contact available to him. In time, a successor to the Almeida family business would be appointed and the infrastructure rebuilt. Cartels always lived again.

In the meantime, Savio had a backpack filled with medical grade ephedrine, the key ingredient of methamphetamine, and he was prepared to hand it over if his conditions were met.

"Surely, you realize I cannot just let you take it, senor? I will accompany you."

Mackenzie balked at the suggestion. "That's not how this works, Mendes. I get the raw material on account. Your people know I'm solid for it."

His words rang true. Eduardo Almeida extended credit to many of the lower-level functionaries in his business. With the recent upheaval in upper management, Savio was banking on Mackenzie being desperate enough to recoup as much cash as possible that he would cave under pressure.

He applied more pressure. "While the company is in transition, we must operate on a currency basis. If you cannot pay up front, you will have to allow me to accompany you."

The maneuver was a calculated risk but Savio's reluctance to let the expensive ephedrine walk away was to be expected. From Mackenzie's point of view, he was just another courier drawing a paycheck from the Almeida family enterprises.

In the end, the man buckled, telling him to stay out of the way and keep out of sight.

The remote manufacturing location was situated on the western edge of Yellowstone Park. They hiked in from a turnout off a public highway, traveling thirty minutes by foot through a densely wooded area until they reached the top of a ridge where the trees thinned. Another couple hundred yards and Mackenzie led him behind a screen of immature evergreens where an oval of blackness appeared on a steep hillside.

Savio slowed. He surveyed the area and realized the hole was the entrance to a tunnel, the mouth of a mine.

"Very clever, senor." He glanced around, "but this location is not remote. How do you avoid the interest of hikers?" He'd been prepared to walk a much longer distance.

"This used to all be restricted, a habitation zone for black bears. Rangers never let anybody near the place. Damned bear died last winter and the ban got removed this season. Screwed up everything."

Savio nodded. That certainly escalated the possibility of discovery. That also meant the production site had been served its final curtain call.

Mackenzie's voice muted as he ducked inside the entrance of the mine. "Now fuckers are crawling around photographing each bug and tracking every weed."

Savio followed him. He explored the shallow interior depths with interest. Only two lines branched off the main trunk and neither extended far. If Mackenzie had used this place for nearly a decade, he saw no visible signs of it anywhere. The rough walls showed nothing unusual. The interior was dry, the floor powdered silt, and the temperature chilly.

After another terse exchange, he turned over the backpack and left Mackenzie to set up the drug production apparatus. He returned outside to continue his survey.

Mackenzie's prized location, cultivated over many annual visits and hidden behind a screen of carefully transplanted saplings, served him no longer.

Not bad though, Savio thought. The ruse had worked for *nine years*. That kind of longevity made Mackenzie a veteran in this business and it indicated he was smart. Savio filed that fact away in his memory.

The Yellowstone landscape lay littered with noxious pockets of water, an excellent cover for the copious stinking waste of methamphetamine production. For a guy in Mackenzie's profession, by-product sludge could be dumped anywhere with impunity. Pushing through the trees, Savio realized the ridge also provided clear visual access down the incline to one of the thermal features for which visitors flocked to Yellowstone.

He skidded to a halt and stared.

Though it was a fair distance away, he recognized a human figure sprawled at the edge of a pool of steaming water. At least a couple hundred yards stretched between them. Savio thought the individual might have stumbled and fallen. He waited for a count of twenty but the figure did not move. Either the man was unconscious or dead. Based on the awkward position of the limbs he bet on the latter.

Spurred into action, he trotted down the hillside, picking his way between stunted trees and clumps of scrubby brush. In a few minutes he was close enough to confirm it was a body.

Not one to pass up an opportunity to complicate things for the bad guy, he improvised with the materials at hand – in this case, the dead man.

Savio wanted a shocking tableau, something that shouted unnatural death, and he had to hurry. Not taking the time to shuck his boots, he put his athletic and artistic experience to good use and leaped across the muddy ground, leaving what he hoped proved to be incomprehensible prints. A few quick alterations to create a fuss among local authorities and he was on his way back up the hill.

Soon enough Mackenzie would feel the bite of panic.

In and out of the scene in minutes, Savio returned to the mine short of breath, exhilarated from racing up the rough hillside. Back outside the entrance, he waited, letting his breathing slow and his pulse return to normal. He tapped a small cigar out of a pack, his shoulder leaned against one of the larger trees and lit the thin cigarillo. He inhaled and blew out a stream of fragrant smoke.

Eventually, Mackenzie came to hover near the entrance. "That shit smells foul."

Amused, Savio smiled. "There is no one here to smell it. While you have been occupied with our enterprise, I have reduced our risk, my friend." He made the comment with casual disregard like someone mentioning a quick stop for a cup of coffee.

Mackenzie went still. "What are you talking about?"

Savio pointed through the trees. "The man who takes the water samples will be no more trouble."

Mackenzie's face blanched. He scurried down the path.

Savio waited. After a few seconds, he guessed Mackenzie had progressed far enough along the ridge to have a clear view of the downhill slope. The open expanse of terrain rolled down to the thermal pool and offered what he hoped were two obvious conclusions.

One, someone was dead.

Two, Savio must have killed him.

Hopefully, Mackenzie considered cutting his losses and ditching out now. With research personnel wandering all over this part of the forest, he risked routine exposure on a daily basis. This might just be enough to make him turn tail.

The man's return passage was marked by the sound of him crashing over the rough trail. He charged back to the cover of the mine and skidded to a stop near the entrance.

Savio turned to face him, displaying features absent of emotion. Despite Mackenzie being half a foot taller and outweighing him by at least sixty pounds, he looked wary.

He stabbed frustrated fingers through his hair. "Are you crazy, Mendes? A corpse will have law enforcement stumbling all over this place."

Savio pushed off the wall. "I have removed a potential obstacle, you should be pleased, Senor."

Distant screams broke the silence. *That was fast.* He assumed they came from the thermal site.

Mackenzie backed up a step, clearly unnerved. "We need to get out of here. I'll come back later tonight and check progress." He pivoted sharply and scrambled away.

Savio followed, melting into the forest like a ghost. He let Mackenzie pull ahead as he considered what new challenges his transition from sneaky observer to cartel courier faced. Spur-of-the-moment game plans allowed no time to strategize and with events moving this fast he needed to manipulate Mackenzie in the correct direction.

The discovery of a dead man at the nearby pool might not have jarred the drug dealer's self-assured composure but believing Savio had killed a complete stranger had produced the desired reaction.

Next on his agenda was identifying the pusher's compatriots.

He traversed the narrow path with ease, picking his way along a route no more traveled than a game trail. After twenty minutes the trees thinned and the sky grew brighter as he left the heavily wooded area. The density of overhead cover lessened. Undergrowth surged up. The terrain became difficult to travel, tangled roots grabbing his boots and loose rocks turning underfoot.

Hunger clutched at his gut but eating must be postponed again while he considered his next move. Many months of carefully orchestrated observation had finally produced results in Mexico City, only to have the situation explode. His sudden departure left him disconnected. Isolated. But that was okay. Before he worked through those issues, he'd snip this final thread in the fabric of Almeida's drug distribution tapestry and consider his job complete.

Then he had no choice but to face the possibility his cover had been compromised.

In the weeks before he fled Mexico, a pattern had taken shape. One which continued to make him uneasy. He had no idea if he still trusted his immediate superior. As his handler, Henri was tasked with making his undercover work safer. His tasks were to provide support to Savio in the form of critical information and immaculate cover stories. The system had worked flawlessly for years.

Until Mexico City.

Until Henri had broken protocol, withheld important intelligence, and approached him in an unsecure café where anyone might have observed them together.

Things sometimes went sideways on the job.

Shit happened.

But not like this.

Savio stopped to admire an ancient fallen tree. He laid a palm against the cold surface. The granulated bark crumbled underneath his hand, turning to aged compost as it fell to the ground. All around him lay an alien landscape, unlike anything in his experience. He'd slithered across swamps, hacked apart thick jungle foliage, and disappeared into the hum of thriving cities, but this sort of wilderness was an unknown quantity to him.

It intrigued him.

He continued on his way, his train of thought returning to the present puzzle. Life in the field required fluid responses. Sudden events often forced awkward split-second decisions. Results could prove perilous. Wrong choices ended lives.

He loved the adrenalin rush. Unexpected danger fed his craving for action and was half the reason he enjoyed his work. Once, he'd been a career soldier, following orders without question, the product of a strictly maintained discipline he'd wholeheartedly embraced. Instinct had saved his life on more than one occasion and he trusted his gut. People who made careless decisions in the trade didn't survive long.

Shaking off his musings, he picked up his pace.

Mackenzie was somewhere ahead of him on the trail and he wanted to know which direction the man went when he drove away.

CHAPTER THREE

ROSE ROLLED UP to the entrance with the map draped over the steering wheel. She looked at the tentative locations of mine sites she'd identified. Each one was marked by a small cross. Only one was close to this edge of the park. No one had done a complete survey but the number of records she'd requested copies of from the archives had assisted in narrowing the gap.

The warmth of the afternoon sun dissipated fast as the glowing ball approached the horizon. Cold air poured through her open window as she braked her car to a standstill beside the small wooden kiosk. The tiny structure hunkered between the eastbound and westbound lanes.

A ranger, smiling with practiced enthusiasm, leaned down on his elbows and peered at her. "Welcome to Yellowstone Park. Just you today?"

Rose nodded and thrust a paper through the window. "I'm here to pick up my research permit."

He accepted and scanned the page before handing it back. "Sorry, but I can't help you." He checked a clip board thick with bent-cornered pages and aimed an apologetic smile in her direction. "The folks at the Regional Office issue the tags and permits. They're closed on Sunday but are open between ten and four tomorrow. They'll provide you an entrance pass. In the meantime, I can let you drive in tonight to find your way around."

Rose wondered sourly why they couldn't send all the necessary stuff with her letter of approval. She'd really wanted to get in the field early in the morning – like the second after dawn broke. Leave it to the bureaucrats to roll in at ten o'clock to check the redundancies in the paperwork.

She thanked the man as she slid the folded paper back into the envelope and tucked the letter inside her knapsack.

"How far is it to the Regional Office?"

"About twelve miles. Take the main road to the fork, turn left and follow the signs from there." He pointed with two fingers. "Let me give you some information. Understanding the geologic features of the park and the overall environment will make your stay that much safer." He pushed a large stack of pamphlets into her outstretched hand and scooted her away with a gesture.

Rose left as directed.

She dropped the literature on the passenger seat and depressed the accelerator. A short distance down the road was the first turn-off. Rose spied a paved lot and switched on her turn signal. Based on her less-than-scientific calculations, this offered the closest proximity to one of the crosses on her map. She turned the wheel and coasted into a slot near the start of a trail. She let the engine idle and flipped through the materials from the ranger.

She fanned apart the pamphlets. The glossy covers evoked a memory. Held captive at a college fundraiser last winter, she'd run out of small talk and inquired into a colleague's research, a surefire method to instigate one-sided conversation. He'd ignored her glassy-eyed stare and waxed poetically about Yellowstone being the establishing site of the National Park System. She should probably add him to her Christmas card list since that discussion had planted the seed for this adventure.

She plucked the topmost pamphlet off the stack and read, alarmed to learn the entire geography of the terrain sat atop the largest supervolcano on the North American continent. Not just a volcano but a *super*volcano. She slumped, open-mouthed for three minutes, engrossed in the tri-folded paper. The shiny high-resolution photographs illustrated colorful steaming reservoirs of water and bubbling volcanic thermal features.

Shit. No wonder nineteenth century settlers scribbled in their diaries about arriving at the outskirts of biblical hell.

Although she already knew a full half of the world's superheated groundwater displays existed within park boundaries, the images sparked her imagination. This wicked mass of energy bubbling up from beneath the rocky soil created amazing panoramas. The literature claimed the region a biological oasis of plant and animal life inside a rare almost-intact chunk of ecosystem in North America's northern temperate zone.

That explained the hundreds of annual research studies.

She tossed aside the pamphlet and turned off the engine. She tumbled out of the car and bounced up and down several times to shake off lethargy before turning her attention to the path. The trail angled from the paved lot up a gentle incline and disappeared around a corner. Based on the position of the road, she calculated the possible location of her potential research site.

A thick growth of conifers blocked her view.

Hopeful for one of the park's famous geothermal features, she locked her car, tucked the key in her front pocket and started up the trail.

Rose felt like she'd plunged miles deep into the wilderness. The silence was complete save for the birds and the breeze. Chickadees flitted between small branches. Dark blue Steller's Jays soared among huge beams high overhead. A soft wind shivered the trees and carried the fresh tang of wood sap. She paced forward, pine cones crunching underfoot. The air tasted crisp, a reminder of winter's recent departure.

Asphalt gave way to a wooden platform. She raised a foot and stepped up, tensing when she saw a pair of muddy boots sticking out from behind a pine tree.

Rose stumbled forward but managed to recover her balance.

She'd found one of the geothermal features that attracted droves of visitors to Yellowstone. Unfortunately, it was occupied.

A man sprawled in the shallows of the large pool.

Her gaze locked on the body attached to the boots, she still registered the patchy steam lifting off the surface of the water in her peripheral vision.

Lungs reminding her she needed to breathe, Rose sucked in air. She tried to focus on her surroundings but failed, unable to look away from the dead man. Mud curved along the visible curve of his brow, the vibrant smear the result of contact with resident microorganisms.

She shuddered at the sight.

A rapid glance around the empty space did nothing to slow her pulse. Steam drifted in currents. At least the pond didn't bubble like the turbulent mud pots displayed in the vivid pictures of the pamphlet. She noticed a lingering unpleasant odor and hoped it came from the pool and not the occupant.

He lay on his belly, face turned toward the walkway. A wisp of steam curled over his left boot and the heel of his right twisted at an awkward angle. Potent indicators of death were revealed by the contorted torso and splayed legs. She checked her impulse to rush over and search for signs of life.

One chilling detail shouted out the wrongness of the scene. Something stuck out of the side of the man's head. She peered intently and realized a piece of deer antler impaled the victim's exposed ear. The antler tine protruded five or six inches. Attached to the blunt end hung a metal ring with a cluster of keys.

Rose blinked.

A small movement drew her attention. She focused and saw that a salamander sat on the dead man's shoulder. The amphibian's skin stood in vivid contrast to the dark navy of his jacket. The color of cola splotched with mustard patches, it lifted one front foot and took a creeping step forward. The presence of wildlife, no matter how small, introduced the idea of food chains. Rose swallowed hard, fighting the sudden rush of fluid in her mouth. She whistled air between her teeth and pushed five repetitions out her nostrils until the nausea passed.

Paralyzed by the scene, she looked for blood or evidence of overt violence. Other than the freakish antler, nothing stood out on the motionless form.

Cold wind gusted. She shivered.

A trail of human footprints punctuated by three deep narrow depressions led to the figure. Maybe the man's own tracks? She scanned the surrounding area, half expecting to find the marks of a hunger-wakened bear. Experts estimated a thousand bears roamed inside Yellowstone. To her way of thinking that was a pretty substantial crowd when compared to a like number of humans at a concert. No evidence of sharp-clawed attack existed though. Just a dead man, half in the water, with a deer antler stuck in his ear.

Rose closed her eyes. She'd found a corpse. Not bones, but a fresh body. *Ick.*

A poster stapled beside the fee window at the entrance kiosk had claimed the odds of a four-legged attack on a human approximated one in two million. The statistics, intended to calm tourists, served to remind her that with millions of annual visitors a few bears must still get in the occasional lick. On a statistical basis, murder should occur even less often.

She shuffled closer.

Freshwater geothermal hot springs had renowned odors. Such stink pots once garnered the reputation to impart medicinal properties. Many pioneers considered them desirable commodities. Rose knew mud baths remained popular in the California wine country. People paid exorbitant amounts of money to soak in one of the mineral-rich thermal destinations.

Since the dead man wore clothes, she ruled that out.

Of the more than 10,000 geothermal attractions boasted in the pamphlet, springs like this one numbered among the most plentiful and the least dangerous – which just proved the information in the park supplement was suspect. The proof was right there in front of her.

Dead.

If someone had murdered him, the killer might still be close.

She looked around again.

Natural death was possible too. People had seizures, accidents, overdosed, got mugged, or made poor decisions while inebriated. Unless the damage appeared on his front, she could rule out animal attack. A single gunshot to the forehead still figured in the realm of possibility though. Of course none of this explained the deer antler but her brain wasn't processing information clearly.

She should call 911.

Spooked by the litany of potential explanations she backed up a step. Her momentary impulse to abandon the scene revived but she quashed the idea. She pulled her cell phone from her pocket. A quick check showed no signal. *Damn.* She'd have to go for help.

Her analytical mind took note of physical details while she slowly reversed. The man would tower above her on long legs. He lacked a heavyset frame but the way the denim fabric cupped against his muscular calves and thighs demonstrated he was fit, like someone who worked out. The portion of his visible profile didn't make her think handsome. He carried the pronounced brow ridge and heavy facial structure that turned people ugly with age.

A scream shattered the afternoon quiet.

Rose jumped. She scanned the area and located the source of the noise on the other side of the pond.

Hysterical yells issued from a woman dressed in crimson shorts and a white shirt. The stranger pointed a finger at the water and screeched out one long wail after another.

The distance was too far to make meaningful eye contact so Rose started up the path, continuing around the pool. She trotted along until she discovered she could go no further. The trail ended at an overlook displaying a vista of thermal pools, trees and stunted weeds that led up a steep hill to where the woods became denser.

Feet pounded the boards behind Rose.

The heavy steps reverberated up the soles of her boots. Shouted voices indicated the arrival of still others. Rose turned on the slick wood but her foot slid sideways and she crashed to the ground. She glimpsed the khaki and olive of a park service uniform before her head snapped against the plank and a starburst of light blinded her vision.

She sucked cold air into her lungs. Her breath caught and her heart started slamming inside her chest again. She forced her eyes open and immediately clamped them shut again in reaction to an accompanying head spin.

The rhythmic pounding of heavy feet stumbled. Somebody swore.

The sensation of the world rotating wildly on its axis was worse than the morning after she drank too many Mai Tais. Struggling to sit up, Rose failed and fell back.

A man came over and squatted beside her. She peeked out one eye and registered his uniform about the same time he spoke.

"I'm sorry, are you okay?"

"Unh," she said.

He gently grabbed her shoulder as she tried to roll over and assisted. "I'm Rob Saxton. I'm a ranger here in the park."

She whispered her name.

"Well, Rose, it's a good thing you dove out of the way or I'd have run you over. I couldn't stop on these slippery boards."

Rose responded to his hulking presence by flopping over on her side. *Damn that hurt.* She ran careful fingertips over one temple. *Talk about getting her bell rung.* The tender exploration revealed a bump. Gently depressing the spot rewarded her with a tiny burst of pain.

"Are you okay?" he asked again, not removing his hand from her shoulder.

Rose blinked. Her vision improved. "Yeah, I think so."

A second ranger joined the first.

Rose didn't complain although they crowded in too close. Her brain ached as she tried to recall the signs for concussion. She was still staring at the woman's uniform collar when a finger poked at her wound.

"Ouch!" Rose recoiled with a glare and jerked her head back, breaking free of Rob's grasp.

He didn't touch her again.

"Good, you're alert," the woman said. Then she proceeded to ask questions and poke at Rose some more.

Her responses must have proved satisfactory because the queries subsided. Rose sat up, swaying back and forth in fair imitation of the swishing tops of the surrounding pines, and waited the buzzing in her head to clear. Her butt went numb.

"The ground is friggin' cold."

The ranger was built like a brown bear. He held out his paw and asked, "You want help standing up?"

Rose decided she'd wait until the cyclone in her head ran down. "In a minute."

Soon both rangers were squatted in front of her, green trousers drawn taut over their thighs as they balanced and tried to assess her condition.

"Hold still now, it's hard to do an exam while you weave and bob." Someone pressed fingers over the sore spot again.

Rose grunted a warning.

They ignored the sound. The person continued to palpate the site.

"Gonna have a bump," the female ranger announced.

Rose thought she sounded awful cheerful about that fact.

A hand manacled Rose's wrist and pulled. "Let me help you up and we'll walk to the parking lot."

Hauled to her feet, Rose was steered back down the path.

She pointed in the direction where she thought the corpse was located. "I found a dead man."

"How do you know he's deceased?"

Rose hadn't realized the other ranger had followed them until that moment. "Because half his face is under water."

Without taking a perceptive breath, her guide spoke. "Watch your step. You took a pretty hard knock. Feet slipped right out from under you on these slick boards didn't they? The weather warms up just enough to turn the shady parts into an organic slip-and-slide. First week on the job I did the same thing. Embarrassed me, but I got over it pretty quick. My name's Ranger Neet, by the way. I work here too." She arched her elbow to flash the patch on her sleeve. "You still doin' all right?"

Rose nodded.

"It appears there may have been an accident." The woman peered intently at her. "Did you touch the body?"

The body.

That kind of question just put the icing on today's cake. After crawling out of bed at sunrise, driving almost five hundred miles and discovering a dead guy, Rose figured she'd had enough strain for one day.

"No, I never left the path."

Ranger Neet adjusted her grip with the dexterity of a professional wrestler. "Disorientation is normal after a blow to the cranium. I'm going to let you sit down for a few minutes and then you can tell me what happened."

They reached the paved lot and found a congregation of people. Several cars sat parked near her Ford Focus but she was steered to a white truck and instructed to open the passenger door.

"I'll find something for your head."

Allowing herself to be shoved down on the cold vinyl bench, Rose leaned her pounding skull back into the corner. The other woman extracted a case from under the seat, rummaged through the contents, and a moment later handed over a couple of tablets. She offered a plastic bottle sporting a label with a picture of a gushing geyser.

Oddly appropriate, Rose thought, and accepted both.

She stuck the aspirin under her tongue and tucked the unopened water bottle between her thighs. The acrid flavor of the medicine stung but the sensation chipped at the numbness buffering her awareness.

Maybe she was in shock?

"I'll be right back." Ranger Neet patted her on the arm and walked away.

"There weren't any other cars when I parked," Rose called after her, not even opening her eyes.

The woman failed to acknowledge her comment.

It was a significant observation, Rose thought. If the dead man didn't have a car in the lot, how had he come to be here?

4 CHAPTER FOUR

R OB FOCUSED ON the incongruous antler and grimaced. The visual disturbed him but nothing else
about the scene suggested violence. During his years in
the park he'd seen a number of bodies. None of them had been
murders, even when they looked that way at first glance. Just
because a keychain was stuck in the man's ear didn't make that
the cause of death.

What a way to start summer.

He positioned himself on the path in order to view the entire
scene from a different perspective and began another survey.

They already had a tentative ID on the deceased. Ranger
Neet thought she recognized him as one of the regular researchers from Porcupine Bluff. If he considered this information and
estimated the distance between the field station and where the

body lay, he wouldn't consider it too far to walk and the victim probably hadn't either. Coming through the woods was risky but not so dangerous with the small amount of thermal steaming in this area. If the guy returned to Porcupine every season, he'd know that too.

Rob's radio crackled. His request for a transport vehicle had been processed. He huffed out a sigh. Until he knew what had happened here, he would have to shut down all the active studies in the area. He rubbed a hand across his forehead. Cancelling field permits created headaches for everyone but it was better to be safe than regretful.

Recent outbreaks of norovirus and hantavirus in various locations within the park system had made top-level officials nervous. Nothing discouraged visitors like screaming media headlines punctuated with images of vomiting children – he glanced over at the dead man – well, this would be worse. Once the medical results ruled out the possibility of something easily transmitted, he'd re-open access. After the wildlife restriction had been lifted, researchers eager to get into this section of the landscape had flooded the permit office with a surge of requests. There'd be plenty of fallout but at least the coroner should determine the cause of death relatively quickly.

He studied the scene again, trying to view everything from a fresh perspective.

Swirls of cobalt blue and peridot green algae created a colorful contrast against the dead man's dark clothing. His lower extremities were encased in denim pants and heavy waterproof boots, his torso wrapped in an aqua and navy all-weather jacket. A sodden knit cap lay nearby. He was dressed for the setting, another indication that he was a member of the transient seasonal population that descended on Yellowstone as soon as the deep snow receded.

He felt no need to search for a pulse, the man was dead. Still, he decided, he should be thorough and check. Rob glanced at the sky, estimated the amount of light left in the day, and then stepped down from the wooden planks. With careful movements, he crossed to the body. Pressing the toes of his boots into the damp ground, and cautious of the slippery quality of the mud, he squatted on his heels and made a close-up study.

His park-issued satellite phone vibrated. He slipped it out of his shirt pocket and recognized his uncle's number.

The text message was brief. *On my way.*

Relief shivered through him. Harlan Groates might be a small-town cop but he was the most observant man Rob knew. He wanted a second opinion about this off-kilter scene. As sheriff of Riverside Township he was technically outside the jurisdiction of the park but Rob considered it a professional courtesy to apprise local law enforcement of any situation that potentially impacted folks.

Rob swept his gaze around the pond and came back to the dead body. He pocketed his phone and hefted the camera to begin snapping shots. He compared this angle with the ones he'd already taken from the path.

His legs were going numb, the circulation pinched by his tightly laced boots, when the sound of thumps indicated someone approaching on the plank walkway.

Harlan rounded the stand of lodgepole pines, pushing aside the lowest branches and calling out a greeting.

"Over here. Thanks for coming." Rob rose and stretched his legs, limbering them up before he attempted to pick his way back across the slick ground.

"There's a landslide on the highway between us and West Yellowstone."

From his vantage point next to the corpse, Rob raised a brow and grunted at this new information. His uncle's voice sounded as if his mouth overflowed with sharp gravel and he recognized the tone of frustration. A road closure meant the transport vehicle had to circumvent the blockage and route through the park. His lips clamped down. Instead of a thirty minute drive, he was looking at several hours. The distance wasn't so far in mileage but tourist traffic slowed everything.

His gaze dropped to the body in front of him. Not that the poor bastard was in a hurry now.

"Probably be tomorrow before the road crew finishes clearing debris. I sent someone to borrow the wagon from the undertaker's widow just in case you end up with the deceased in your digs overnight."

Rob hunched his shoulders. He did not want the dead man parked outside his office.

"Appreciate that. If West Yellowstone can't get the transport here tonight, I suspect we'll figure something out."

Harlan raised a grizzled eyebrow. "You got someplace to keep him?"

Rob waved an arm. "Not really. If nothing comes through, we'll use the hearse." He finished retracing his route to the boardwalk and grasped Harlan's waiting hand. "Let's record and sample the scene. I'd like to get home and see my wife some time tonight."

Harlan grunted agreement. His eyes never strayed from the edge of the pond as he moved slowly up the path.

Rob jerked his head in the direction of the dead man. "No obvious signs of violence."

He described the sequence of events, his voice increasing in volume as they separated and moved in opposite directions.

Harlan disappeared from view as the path curved.

Rob used the evidence camera to continue making a systematic photographic record of the extended area. He snapped pictures, focusing the lens and framing each snapshot to locate reference information for the viewer.

Before long, the sheriff returned, working his way close before he spoke. "This is the second time this year that damn mountain has dumped a load of rock and blocked Jasper Pass."

Rob grinned from behind the camera. He adjusted the zoom and snapped a series of vertical and horizontal photographs. "Cite the work crews. Town could use the revenue."

Harlan pushed a crushed pinecone off a slippery uneven board. "Sure he didn't slide off this slimy surface?"

No marks indicated such an event but it was possible. "Not a hundred percent certain. Still doubt it." Rob took another series of pictures, adjusting the close-up focus on the brass key ring. He was losing the light. "Think the antler's an artifact of a fall?"

The older man's eyes moved across the environment. He snorted out a short harsh sound. "Hardly."

"Yeah, me neither," Rob agreed.

After issuing explicit instructions to have the area cordoned off, Rob motioned for Harlan to join him. "Let's find out what Ranger Neet got from the witness."

Harlan frowned once more at the bizarre scene before he followed. "Dammit, I hate dead bodies."

5 CHAPTER FIVE

ROSE SAT IN the truck and reflected. In the past she'd made plenty of bad decisions. She'd failed to avoid a number of difficult moments in her life because she hadn't thought about repercussions before springing into action. The tattoo on her left butt cheek offered one prime example. Hopefully the decision to come to Yellowstone didn't turn out the same way.

With a determined shrug she thrust aside her doubts. In a few months, looking back on this event with the beauty of hindsight, she'd see it in the context of a much bigger framework. She supposed finding a freshly dead body should be unsettling but she couldn't quite suppress her excitement about getting started on her research tomorrow. Monday promised to kick ass. So would she.

She yawned. Not only did she suffer from traveler's fatigue, she'd toiled too long in academia without a break. Locked in the ivory tower and burrowed deep into the stacks, she'd been unprepared for such a shock in the real world. No wonder she felt weird.

Ranger Neet returned and parked herself near the open door, her feet splayed wide in a balanced stance. "Head better? The swelling's already gone down."

In point of fact, Rose thought her discomfort subsided in direct proportion to her worsening detachment. She shifted position and pushed a foot against the doorframe.

"Still a little fuzzy?"

Rose nodded.

"Drink more water, it helps with shock." Nellie pulled a small notebook and pen from an inside pocket of her jacket and prepared to take notes. "Why don't you tell me what happened?"

Rose didn't hesitate. Relating the events of her discovery without fancy details only took a minute.

Ranger Neet scribbled furiously on her notepad. "Repeat that last part again, please."

Dedicated to duty. Of course, for all she knew the woman was making a grocery list. Rose said, "Footsteps pounded up behind me, I spun around and lost my balance."

The ranger raised her eyebrows in response.

Rose concluded the woman must pluck. Nature simply did not form arches with such perfect proportions – which only served to remind her of her own misshapen brow. She lifted the water bottle to set the cool bottom against the bump on her forehead and heard someone cough.

The sound carried from a distance.

Rose listened but the echo was drowned out by the rumble of a large vehicle on the main road. As the reverberation stretched out and faded away, she recited the Doppler effect under her breath. The shock of her discovery began to wane. In a sense, she was accustomed to death, being an archaeologist and all – but bones and corpses differed significantly. In important gushy, wet, spongy kinds of ways. Her stomach flipped over and she tried to avoid thinking about the scene, blocking out images of the pool and the sprawled occupant. She failed.

The big ranger stepped into view and approached the truck.

She recognized the second man with him as the cop from her earlier roadside encounter. She waved at him a little too enthusiastically, happy to see an almost-familiar face.

He returned a polite nod.

Formal introductions were offered and she immediately forgot men's names as she concentrated on stifling a smirk over the fact that Ranger Neet went by Nellie.

Nellie Neet.

The woman should have her own nursery rhyme, she thought and snickered inside.

Rose's account of events was once again requested. She pressed the cool bottle against her head and summarized.

The series of questions might have been designed to elicit information but they made for stilted conversation. The exchange rapidly reduced to brief jerky statements being fired back and forth. By the third repetition, she felt like she was delivering a recitation.

Hands folded in her lap, she went through it again. "I saw the dead man from the boardwalk."

The ranger wrote down her response. "Why were you standing there?"

"Because that's where you're supposed to stand."

Another notation went into the book. "Can you explain how you came to be on-scene?"

"I wanted to find a thermal feature."

"Why choose this locale?" Expectant eyes looked at her.

Rose shifted her gaze to the sheriff but he offered no help. "This was the first place to pull off the road after I entered the park. Lousy luck, if you ask me."

The ranger wrote something down. "What did you plan to do?" He glanced over at her when she didn't immediately answer.

Rose spread her hands in a frustrated motion. "You're kidding, right?"

He wasn't.

"I had no explicit plan."

"Do you have any relationship with the deceased?"

Rose stared until he prompted her again. "None."

He ignored her overemphasized articulation and reversed direction. "Ms. Brashear, please explain your location at the time you made the discovery."

She let the sarcasm flow. "I walked up the path. The man's feet were visible as I stepped onto the wooden walkway. I was surprised and almost lost my balance but recovered. Uncertain what to do, when the woman on the other side of the pond started screaming, I decided to go around and join her." She clasped her hands in her lap and frowned. "I kept going until the trail ended and that's when you guys arrived and I fell down."

Harlan Groates rumbled in his throat. The vocalization distracted Rose though she couldn't tell if the noise indicated amusement or frustration.

"We're just fishing for routine information here," he said.

She nodded. "So, I parked the car, walked up the path a bit and found a dead guy. I continued up around the pool and heard footsteps, turned too quickly and fell down. Now my head hurts and you're treating me like I'm withholding information." She scowled for added emphasis. She hated being the center of attention unless she'd initiated it for her own purposes.

"All right, so you walked up the boardwalk." The ranger arranged his stub of pencil on the notepad he'd yanked out of his shirt pocket.

Rose sat in silence. *Let him wait for a response.*

After a moment he looked up at her.

She smiled at him. "That wasn't a question. It isn't my turn to answer."

Ranger Neet's lips twitched.

The sheriff turned away but his shoulders shivered.

A hint of amusement softened Rob's mouth.

Rose decided to take the direct approach. "I know you're doing a job but I've given you name, rank and serial number. I've answered questions and been as forthright as possible. What else do you want from me?"

"Look, I understand your frustration, I really do. The information we collect, even if it sounds useless, might help us comprehend the bigger picture. The more people we rule out of the equation, the easier and faster we'll be able to determine the actual course of events leading to this man's death."

The words were delivered with what sounded like genuine sympathy and the fuse on Rose's temper burned out. She responded on an emotional level, visualizing the crumpled form in the water. The people who cared about the deceased man were going to receive a terrible phone call. Her having a bad attitude didn't help anyone.

She straightened her shoulders. "You're right."

He took her at face value and started over with his questions, asking again for her reasons in visiting the park.

Tamping down her impatience, she explained the details of her permit to inspect historic mines.

He wrote down every word. "What will you do with the results?"

Rose felt a shade pretentious talking about her work but no one seemed to notice her discomfort. "I'm writing an article for publication next winter. My research compares lifestyle differences between nineteenth century sites in Nevada with contemporaneous locales in Montana." Actually, that stretched things a bit. She needed comparable data and hoped Yellowstone offered enough of a match to make it more than just sound good.

Rob scribbled for another thirty seconds. "How long will your project take?"

She exhaled heavily. "I hope to finish by the end of the month."

"You staying in park housing?"

"I should be so lucky." Rose rubbed her thumb and two fingers together. "I'm paying up front. I have a room booked at a place called the White Horse Inn in Riverside."

Rob smiled at her with genuine amusement. "I think you'll prefer the inn over an employee bunkhouse."

A long ebony station wagon turned into the lot, its headlights glowing although dusk had not yet fallen.

Rose recognized the vehicle as a hearse.

Harlan muttered and stepped away. He paused and held his hat against one thigh, his face cast down to the ground. After a moment he raised his eyes to meet hers. "We appreciate your patience and apologize for taking up so much time. Since the event occurred within the confines of the park, Ranger Saxton will be the one to collect and file reports. I'm only here as a professional courtesy." He gave a stiff nod in her direction, said goodbye, and left.

Eventually the notes were transcribed on official printed forms, the kind with three different colors of thin paper, and she was asked to read and sign if she approved the content. Rose quickly scanned the information and scribbled her name at the bottom.

The rangers proffered more apologies and shook her hand, and then she was free to go.

Rose yanked open the driver's side door of her car. The cotton fabric of her shirt offered scant protection in the biting wind. Summer had vanished with the sun. The locals appeared unaffected by the temperature drop, further proof of how far outside her element she'd landed.

"If you want a good meal, the diner next to the inn has the best food in town," Ranger Neet volunteered.

Rose thanked the woman and pulled the door closed. She cranked up the heater and waited impatiently for the engine to warm up. Reminded she hadn't eaten since mid-morning, her stomach growled.

CHAPTER SIX

SAVIO DESPISED MEN like Mackenzie. The guy struck him as another narcissistic asshole who believed he was entitled to a life of ease and comfort because he challenged the rules of society. He was the kind of jerk who bragged over a beer at a local watering hole about how he'd escaped the doldrums of dead-end jobs and the endless grind of corporate-controlled America with his entrepreneurial spirit. The bastard actually took pride in his status as a purveyor of drugs. He believed himself a pioneer, a true blue-blooded American. His attitude offended Savio.

In truth, Mackenzie's comfortable lifestyle was built on a foundation of addiction.

Savio knew the specious arguments. These guys claimed they manufactured goods for an open-market economy like anyone else. If legislation changed in order to restrict the product, they simply circumvented the laws. Money just waited to be made and he might as well be the one to benefit. The really delusional ones spouted rhetoric about how one day the government would abandon its fight against the buccaneers and legalize the hell out of the substances. They never seemed to grasp that if such an event happened, all the profit in the process was guaranteed to bleed out and leave the feds holding the primary position in town.

Savio had his doubts about this grim possibility. Right now he'd managed to make Mackenzie worry that his business prosperity was headed due south. He intended to keep applying pressure while he waited for something new to break.

As a one-man operation, Mackenzie had limited distribution reach but Savio didn't underestimate his range.

Recent laws had impacted the American drug exchange. The new limits restricting access to the chemical components required to complete large-scale batches of meth had forced everyone, including the addicts, to figure out how to cook small quantities with easily-obtained materials.

The loss of future shipments of raw supplies from the Almeida source created a vacuum not easily filled.

The good news was that greedy people proved easier to control.

Savio raised the field glasses and peered through the branches of a tree. Cloistered behind the pine boughs, he stood far enough away from the thermal pool to remain hidden from view. The drama unfolded quickly, the authorities appearing onsite with surprising speed.

Superb.

Now there was no chance for Mackenzie to move the corpse. The proximity of the dead man and the subsequent investigation might crash and burn the drug production effort in one fell swoop. He shifted his gaze and tried to follow the logic of park service personnel as they went about investigating the macabre scene.

He'd left the mine when Mackenzie did, following him back to where they'd parked. But Savio had returned, retracing his steps through the woods to make certain he could find the place again.

Then he'd decided to wait for dusk before hiking out. No sense being sighted by an alert park representative. Stumbling over his feet in the deep twilight seemed a small inconvenience in exchange for knowing what was happening. Perhaps he'd even mimic forestry personnel and brush out his tracks to remove any obvious signs of human intrusion.

He checked the interior of the mine, surprised to find the noxious smell had noticeably increased as the drugs cooked. Fumes built up until they became intolerable. More than once he'd seen fires and explosions result from an accumulation of dangerous vapors. If precautions were not taken, a stiff breeze might attract attention.

Intent on staying under the radar, he suspected Mackenzie would return before dawn to dump the waste bucket. Savio had to admit, the smelly geothermal pockets provided excellent cover.

Once their business concluded, they would part ways. In the meantime, if things went downhill too fast, Mackenzie might cut his losses and bolt. Savio was betting the man would opt to harvest all the cash possible before he walked. Waiting another couple of days could prove very profitable.

He sucked in smoke and rolled it back out in a fragrant cloud, cupping his hand around the magenta glow of the cherry on the thin cigarillo so it couldn't be seen.

The operation was simple but brilliant.

So far he knew that every year Mackenzie had arrived in Yellowstone for a two-week stay. To the public, he appeared to be the epitome of a hard-working blue-collar all-American male, a carefully cultivated persona.

Under the guise of spending his hard-earned vacation by relaxing in the great outdoors, Mackenzie chatted up the locals with his good-old-boy demeanor, bought his goods from town merchants, and tipped with generosity but not extravagance. Behind the wheel of his jacked up truck his closely-cropped beard fit the expected masculine stereotype. Townspeople didn't look at him twice. In certain company, he made a point of mentioning the .45 handgun he kept to protect the things he'd worked hard to earn. Casual listeners nodded with approval.

The truth produced a more ironic image. A veritable one-man plague, Mackenzie drove into Riverside every summer and cooked up enough methamphetamine to kill off the entire town population.

He was clever though. Curious ears only half-listened to stories of his three and four day junkets through the back country, hiking rough wilderness trails, fishing remote streams, and photographing the renowned volcanic sights. The locals dismissed him as just another solitude-seeking nut from the city.

In reality, the man camped out somewhere, spending his time manufacturing illegal substances in the mine. Pretty good quantities of stuff cooked from premium ingredients, too. Each batch of finished drug sold for around one hundred thousand dollars and in a two-week period the man could churn out at least five batches.

Savio considered that a fine return on the investment cost.

The entire set-up offered a minimal amount of risk for maximum results. Mackenzie worked hard. Neat and tidy, he carted supplies in and out by hand, the meticulous removal of debris working in his favor. The obscured evidence created an identity difficult to trace.

Reluctantly impressed by the ingenuity of the set-up, Savio liked the man even less.

Mackenzie admitted that when he didn't deliver in person, he shipped consignments to his clients with flair. The drugs were uniquely packaged to avoid detection, sometimes with breathtaking simplicity. The most recent batch he'd poured into microbrew bottles in a liquid state. Re-capped and sealed, he sent them off to an anxious customer via standard overnight courier. So you weren't supposed to mail alcohol, but it looked like a six-pack of beer. Not worth the paperwork if a curious employee took a peek. It was easier to let it slide. Except Mackenzie's special brew held greater value than most honest folks earned in several years of salary.

Yes, in the big scheme, the volume was small-time. But a dozen guys like Mackenzie could feed a big chunk of the insatiable monster that was America's meth addiction and they did it while floating right under the nose of the law. Product got diluted the farther down the line it progressed; a brew became a barrel, then a vat and eventually it left a swathe of devastation through a community.

Savio took one last toke, exhaled the smoke and crushed the little cigar underfoot, retrieving the butt and folding the flattened filter inside a scrap of paper. He tucked the tiny package into the coin pocket of his jeans. He too could be meticulous and precise.

During his two-week vacation, Mackenzie produced methamphetamine worth roughly half a million dollars. Money like that equaled a lot of incentive. And the man had been doing this for years.

Savio wondered how many other locations Mackenzie used for exactly the same purpose?

With sites scattered across the country, an enterprising and dedicated worker might repeat the same stunt in an endless cycle, living a lifestyle of perennial vacations spent in illegal pharmaceutical production.

He stretched his left leg and worked at loosening the site of his old injury. His entire body felt too tight. One hand braced against a tree for balance, he ran through a simple routine. Protracted muscles relaxed and the strain on the scar tissue eased.

Driving two thousand miles from Mexico City to the western side of Montana had exhausted him. The final leg of the journey had been particularly grim with the dead courier tucked in the trunk. He'd done his best to make sure Benito would be discovered, just not right away.

Dusk fell. Savio prowled toward the woods, his progress slowed by the sudden lack of light.

The clock was ticking.

The drug apparatus sputtered in the mine, steadily distilling powdered chemicals into potent slurry. He refused to make any more decisions tonight. Exhaustion pulled at him. He needed rest. He rubbed a hand across his flat abdomen and his stomach growled. But first, he must eat.

CHAPTER SEVEN

RIVERSIDE WAS A narrow picturesque community nestled into the landscape. It sat a dozen miles beyond the Yellowstone boundary, the geography of steep buttes on one side and the wide river on the other, constricting the town. A billboard at the outskirts advertised the area's renowned fly fishing but a quick glance at the map showed how the road linked the park to the interstate and bypassed Riverside. This secondary side access lacked the popularity of the West Entrance in nearby West Yellowstone and Rose suspected it served more of the local crowd. She bet they preferred it that way too.

She'd read that Yellowstone had been established as a wildlife preserve back in 1872. Today, the boundaries encompassed almost 3,500 square miles of lakes, canyons, rivers, and mountain ranges. By contrast, she'd wager Riverside Township covered a single residential mile at the river's edge and only then if she included the homes stretching up the hillsides.

She saw none of the ramshackle ambience she associated with western towns. Every structure appeared in good repair. Straight neat fences bordered yards and mailboxes mounted next to front gates like name badges. Light posts stood before each house, soldiers at attention. The manicured properties provided an unexpected note of prosperity.

Rose missed the census sign but the number of kids on bicycles and the frequency of play equipment in yards spoke to a thriving community.

Two high buttes sheltered residents from the worst of winter storms. She followed the main route through the center of town where structures set back from the road on generous lots. Streets crept up the hillsides, a network of switchback lanes whose exterior lamps twinkled in deep groves of pines. Rose glimpsed modern log cabins interspersed among the more common clapboard houses. From her vantage point, a montage of smoking stovepipes poked out of the trees. The spice of wood smoke brought back memories of childhood campouts, an echo of pleasant nostalgia.

To her mind, Riverside felt content.

Homes gave way to a central district lined with small shops. Continuing down Main Street, she guessed tourism was responsible for the great variety of businesses, more than just a local population would sustain without the nearby national attraction. Even so, she sensed an atmosphere of legitimacy rooted in the place, as if the town existed despite the proximity of the park. The view down side streets showed a parallel avenue with what looked like schools and civic structures.

Rose had no difficulty imagining the entire shopping district ablaze with Christmas lights. Sorry to have missed the spectacle, she bet they celebrated the Fourth of July with an old fashioned parade and banners featuring the stars and stripes.

She slowed down to read signs. Halfway down the third block she spied a massive Victorian structure. An iron picket fence studded the property frontage, the dark line stretching from a paved path on one side of the lot to a row of dense shrubs on the other.

Two driveways ran side-by-side, separated by a difference in height, which created a curb. Rose assumed the left lane led behind the house and the right one to the rear of the adjacent restaurant.

An aggregate concrete path flowed from the sidewalk up the wide steps to the porch, crossing a vast expanse of yard filled with dead grass just beginning to brighten with a hint of green. Small ornamental trees grew close to the house but a stand of large pines towered behind, peering over the roof like alert sentinels. At the front of the property, near the open gate, stood the sign, an iron post from which suspended a whitewashed wooden cutout in the shape of a large horse. The name of the White Horse Inn was lettered across the surface in stark script against the body of the animal. A small vacancy sign hung underneath.

She pulled in at the curb and stared.

At first glance, the inn appeared one of the more ornate architectural specimens from the late Victorian era but closer inspection revealed clever additions stuck on an old farm-style home. The house boasted one full corner rounded into a circular turret and Rose took a moment to admire the graceful lines. She'd first seen the features as a child when her parents visited San Francisco to tour the grand painted ladies of the nineteenth century. The tall pointed roof lines on some of the houses had reminded her of witches' hats, and for years she had coveted such a space.

Gingerbread detail covered the exterior and decorative trim filled out the eaves. A large porch echoed the façade of the house, banding the turret room like an apron. The front corner bulged out big as a pregnant woman in her third trimester, round and ripe and thick. Leaded windows with stained glass panels filled even the third-floor dormers. The details glinted like large jewels in the sunlight.

A colorful display of flowers spilled from planters placed at regular intervals along the wide rail of the porch. The extra tall double front doors featured narrow intricate colored glass patterns in their upper halves. Period appropriate curtains hung over the windows and contributed to the polish of the place.

Rose drank in the exquisite façade. Now she understood the rangers' collective amusement about her staying here. By contrast to the typically rugged conditions in research stations, the opulence of the inn overwhelmed her.

She jammed her car into park and climbed out, hurrying up the walk.

As her hand reached for the knob, a man loomed up out of the shadows. He politely ignored her surprised yelp and palmed the door open with a gallant flourish.

The pewter-haired stranger introduced himself as Anton Ingram, the owner. He followed her inside.

The entrance, framed by the brilliant stained glass panels, led into a spacious foyer. Beyond the entry she admired a parlor stuffed with comfortable looking upholstered chairs arranged to encourage intimate conversation. To the right squatted a round oak table, which required no stretch of her imagination to visualize a host of poker players gathered around it in a smoky saloon. Now the surface sat filled with beverage and snack options in what appeared to be hand-painted porcelain dishes.

Along the back wall, a wooden counter served as the concierge desk. Rose announced she was there to check-in and the man slipped behind the length of polished wood and requested her name.

He reeled off a spiel so well-rehearsed he sounded like a professional tour guide. She learned about the suites on the ground floor and singles on the second level, and though tourist season approached full throttle, he confessed they had only three rooms occupied because he and the missus had decided to semi-retire.

His wife Lily appeared through a door behind the counter and insisted on introducing her to the other guests. While her husband discreetly processed the credit card, she spirited Rose around and showed her the amenities.

A retired couple from Minnesota inhabited a suite. They greeted her with enthusiastic smiles and Rose pegged them as the sort of people who relished pumping total strangers for information. The upstairs guest was a stoop-shouldered young man with the remarkable name of Remy Boothe. He held onto her hand a moment longer than necessary, a sensation Rose found uncomfortable since his palm sweated.

Her grandmother would have termed Remy's expression a smoldering look and fixed him with a steely stare. His attention did not escape Mrs. Ingram's notice. Avoiding the guy's torpid gaze, Rose scrubbed her palms down the front of her jeans as she returned to the reservation desk. She didn't much care for the tousled Byronic look but he sported a mop of red hair in that luxurious natural shade of burgundy most women paid their hairdresser to mix up in a bottle. That was something she could appreciate.

Upon their return to the counter, the Innkeepers held a brief whispered conversation that ended with her host replacing the key he had selected and choosing a different one.

He slid a large heavy book across the polished wood and handed her a pen. The old-fashioned register lent a touch of authenticity Rose much appreciated. Feeling a shade more proper than normal, she penned her full name at the bottom-most line on one of the hand-written pages. She'd spied a modern laptop computer on a narrow desk inside the host's private quarters, which suggested the ledger was a prop more than a relic, but Rose appreciated the detail. Mr. Ingram inspected her signature on line forty-one of the register and rolled all the r's in an exaggerated accent.

Rose almost suppressed her grin.

Her hand resting on his forearm, he escorted her up the wide staircase. In a conspiratorial whisper he admitted he'd moved her to the larger corner room with a private bath for the original rate she'd been quoted.

Rose agreed enthusiastically. The idea of bumping into Remy outside the upstairs communal bathroom was an awkward possibility she'd rather avoid. Propriety in Montana might be observed with more dedication than in California but she could get in line with that reasoning.

As they climbed, she mentally deducted the cost of breakfast from her daily budget. A continental breakfast was included in the price of accommodations, thank god. Free meals helped a lot when it came to paying the long-term expenses of doing fieldwork. When she added in the value of the tea and snacks served for guests between four and six each afternoon, she concluded bankruptcy might be avoided after all. If she exploited the amenities and saved money on restaurant meals, she could manage the rest of her stay without dipping into personal savings. Good news since academic salaries encouraged frugality.

At the top of the stairs, Mr. Ingram identified Remy's door as the last one on the right before promenading her to the opposite end of the corridor.

Based on this quaint courtesy, Rose gathered that a pair of unmarried individuals housed at the inn risked a breach of respectability. Or maybe her host's protective instincts had been roused by the warm admiration in Remy's eyes. Not having to scamper down the hall to the shared facilities every time she had to pee sounded marvelous to her.

They stopped in front of the last door. A small metal plaque nailed to the surface read *Clementine Room.* Her host inserted and turned the heavy brass key in the massive antiquated lock, bowed in a quick gesture, and stepped away.

Rose thanked him and pushed opened the door. Her breath caught. The space encompassed the upper level of the turret, including a bank of five tall curved sash windows rounding out a panoramic view of the street. She had the witch's hat.

Everything glowed in tones of cream and ivory. Wheat and gold hues offered a warm contrast to the wood trim, which shone a deep burnished walnut. A colossal high queen-size mattress faced a small marble-fronted fireplace. A pyramid of compressed woodchip logs stacked to one side of the raised stone hearth. The Victorian-era settee positioned at the foot of the bed provided the perfect place to sit and admire flames. Two wing-back chairs filled the center of the turret, a petite table separating them. A large braided rug of soft calico colors flowed over the open floor. A peek into the powder room revealed a footed cast iron tub with clawed talons. The delighted squeal she produced didn't even embarrass her.

Ignoring the grumbling of her stomach, she committed to hauling up essential supplies from her car. No matter how late she arrived somewhere she'd rather finish the task then than face it in the morning. Research materials and luggage required three trips. The other friendly guests had mysteriously disappeared, so she huffed and puffed up and down the stairs alone. She ventured back out for the sole purpose of getting take-out, after which she planned a long soak in the antique tub. She jumped off the outside porch, darted across the lawn and bounced up the steps to the restaurant.

CHAPTER EIGHT

S AVIO DRAINED HIS coffee and set the empty mug near the table edge. Instead of upping his caffeine intake he should be out searching for answers but he needed time to decompress. The smell of the grill made his stomach clench. Even if the restaurant interior didn't offer confidence in the quality of the fare, his hunger was willing to ignore it.

The bell clanked above the door.

Out of habit, he glanced up to scan the arrival. The last time an aged couple had departed and a pair of teens entered. Now a small female stood framed against the glass backdrop.

He caught a glimpse of delicate features and large eyes before she turned toward the counter.

Savio's mind blanked.

The woman's hair was pulled back, displaying the sweep of her jaw and throat. Focus riveted, he traced the lines of her body, his gaze lingering. She dressed in jeans so faded they appeared to have been soaked in bleach. The denim shone with a soft threadbare sheen and caressed her curves like loving hands. His fingers curled at the thought of sliding his palms down her thighs. Heavy black steel-toed boots encased her feet. The awkward footwear looked both wicked and sensual. She wore a man's plaid flannel shirt as a jacket, the cuffs folded back to expose her forearms.

Short and curvaceous, she bore no resemblance to the women he usually found attractive. That didn't deter him from shifting his weight on the seat or scooting to the edge of the booth for a better look. Once she was in his direct line of sight he slouched down on the maroon upholstery and propped a foot on the opposite bench, getting comfortable in order to admire the view.

The woman exchanged words with the cook before following his pointing finger and turning toward the menu board.

Intrigued, Savio studied her profile.

Her smooth cheek drew into a strong chin line. A straight nose rose above pouting lips. She opened her mouth to speak and heat pooled in his abdomen, provoking a rumble of self-conscious laughter at his visceral physical reaction. The busboy came over and refilled his coffee cup but Savio's attention remained on the woman.

She stood with one knee bent forward in a relaxed stance, the toe of her boot balanced on the scarred floor. One thumb hooked in her front pocket, the side of the flannel shirt bunched behind her wrist and displayed the form-fitting t-shirt she wore underneath. He followed the curve of her rib cage down to her waist where the flare of her hip jutted out and found it erotic.

He shifted on the seat.

She might be dressed as a boy but in no way resembled one. Too many lavish curves. He wondered if her mass of dark hair, rolled and clipped at the rear of her head, would spill loose once relieved from its confines.

A server delivered his plate of steak and eggs, setting the dish on the Formica tabletop with a thump. He murmured thanks and leaned back in order to keep the enticing female in sight. Savio tore into his meal, averting his eyes long enough to slice off hunks of medium rare steak. He watched steadily for several minutes until the cook engaged the woman in conversation again. She responded by leaning on her elbows, one hand propped under her chin. The stance curved her spine and Savio forgot about food.

She stretched.

He swallowed hard.

The waitress set a package next to the register and slid a receipt across the counter. The dark-haired woman shifted her hips to one side and dug in her back pocket.

Savio gripped his fork. He craned his neck to catch a glimpse of her left hand.

No rings.

She handed across some cash and picked up the package of food, turning away. The bell clanked as the door opened, held wide by an old mestizo man.

Savio tensed, seized by an inexplicable urge to follow her outside. With a frown, he squelched the desire and watched her descend the steps. He fought the impulse until the graceful senorita crossed the driveway and stepped over the low fence.

She's right next door.

This fact was profoundly agreeable to him since the White Horse Inn was also his destination tonight.

9 CHAPTER NINE

WINSLOW DEVERAUX HELD open the door of Vic's Restaurant and stepped aside as a young woman exited. Every Sunday he met the others for pie, coffee, and companionship. He slapped his pants pocket to make sure he hadn't forgotten his wallet again. This was his week to pay.

Vic called out a greeting as the bell clanked overhead. The dinner crowd was thin, only a few latecomers finishing up as Winslow crossed the room and slipped into the corner booth. The table seated five and offered the best view of Main Street. From this vantage, they'd spy every car passing through town although traffic would be slim tonight because the road to West Yellowstone was blocked by another rock fall.

He flipped the pages of the *Bozeman Daily Chronicle* abandoned by a previous customer. The others razzed him for always being the first to arrive but he hated being tardy. Thirty years of military service backed up by a lifetime of regimented behavior taught him to value promptness. He erred on the side of punctuality.

The server brought boiling water and a tea bag wrapped in a colorful paper envelope. Winslow moved the newspaper so she could slide the dish in front of him. "Evening Annie. How's Rob?"

"Working late. Someone found a body in the park today."

Winslow had already heard about the dead man of course. "You don't say."

"Terrible thing," Annie said. "Harlan should be along shortly."

Winslow nodded.

Annie flitted away.

The unfortunate death *was* abhorrent but as Delmar Johnston had confided on the telephone, a possible murder victim was also darn interesting.

The last patrons left while Winslow waited for his friends to arrive. He paid little attention to the foot traffic. Strangers were nameless entities in an endless stream of unfamiliar faces that flowed through town.

Two minutes before eight o'clock his partners showed up.

Delmar set down a dirty ivory clutch handbag. The purse, covered with garish multicolored plastic beads, had belonged to the man's wife. He scooted across the curved vinyl bench, pushing it along with a gnarled hand. Already a widower before Winslow returned to town, the tight-ass still used the battered pocketbook to cart around his cash stash.

The door clanked and indicated the final arrivals. Nelsen Orvik carried a plastic sandwich container filled with coins and folded bills. The sheriff held a flat zippered pouch sewn from canvas.

Winslow dropped the deck of cards next to his tea and cleared away the tabletop debris.

Vic turned off the open sign and threw his stained apron behind the counter. The men converged on the booth and settled in as Winslow announced the stakes.

"Tonight's ante is a quarter, gentlemen. The game is Five Card Stud, original style 'cause we're old guys."

Vic lit one of his foul cigars and blew a stream of bluish smoke above their heads. The ceiling fans spun in slow asynchronous revolutions, catching the cloud and dispersing the fumes inside the restaurant.

The busboy wiped tables.

Winslow dealt the cards and tossed a coin in the center of the table. "So Harlan, tell us what happened today."

"Not much to share." The sheriff scratched his chin. "Someone found a dead man at one of the thermal pools. Think he's one of those researchers from Porcupine but we won't know for sure until the poor bastard is officially ID'd."

Nelsen's face was troubled. "You got a pending identification?"

Harlan nodded.

"How'd the bugger check out?" Delmar asked.

Harlan pursed his lips and frowned. "Not sure."

Winslow threw in a dollar bill to finish the round. He eyed Harlan.

Vic exhaled another cloud of smoke. They gamed here because no one wanted the stench of his Havana tobacco.

Nelsen increased the bet.

Winslow folded on the next turn.

Nelsen raised again on the final round and collected a decent pot for his trouble.

Winslow narrowed his eyes. He believed Nelsen bluffed half the time but on every instance he called, the man revealed winning cards.

Vic grunted and opened high.

Harlan and Nelsen folded right away and let him take the pot in the second round.

He cackled out a rude comment in Italian.

"You make that shit up." Delmar's tone sounded offensive. "It's not like any of us can tell the difference."

Vic followed up with a lewd gesture.

The others ignored the byplay.

"Where'd the body end up?" Winslow asked.

Delmar peeked at his hole card and raised the bet. "They can put it in the cold room at the market if you need a place."

Winslow turned his gaze to the J&L Market across the street. "You're kidding, right? Best not let the health inspector catch wind of that."

"Hallie Nesbit is in Syracuse visiting her grandkids till the end of the month. As long as he's gone before she gets back, the county health department won't know about you keeping corpses in with the cabbage," Nelsen explained.

"Rob's taking care of the body. The park has jurisdiction," Harlan said.

Vic flipped over his cards with a flourish. "Full house, gents."

"Damn dago," Delmar barked.

The conversation continued until the game broke up at half past nine. The crew clambered down the steps and went different directions.

Winslow lived on the far side of the tracks in the house his mother had purchased when he was twelve. Times had changed. The train no longer ran on the sidetrack to Riverside. Shrugging deeper into his jacket he quickened his pace. He'd never married, had been a career Navy man. Mostly he liked being a bachelor. But some nights, like tonight, he wished he wasn't going home to an empty house.

CHAPTER TEN

A FTER LEAVING THE diner, Savio drove to West Yellowstone and ditched the sedan – picking up a motorcycle he found in the local want-ads. Directly upon his return to Riverside, he checked into the White Horse Inn, handing over his ID to confirm a night's stay. He paid cash, signed a brand new page on the register, and accepted a key for a room on the second floor.

Food and a hot shower made him human again. Though he listened intently, no sound came from the other guests. As curious as he was about the pretty woman from the diner, he was there for intel on a man named Remy. Mackenzie had phoned the guy twice that afternoon. In a town this size, and with only one inn listed in the local directory, it wasn't difficult to piece together the clues.

Savio yawned. The pillow whispered to him. Instead, he climbed out the window. The shingles sloped but not so steeply he couldn't creep along the expanse. The porch ran the entire front of the house with a fifteen foot drop to the ground. On his left curved the glass panes of the turret but no light came from the interior. To the right, a golden glow shone from the single casement.

A car accelerated down Main Street. He went still, holding his position. Once the vehicle passed he moved stealthily on toward the lit window and peered inside. From his vantage point he could view only one corner of the interior but hear the sound of snoring. Balanced on the balls of his feet, he leaned forward and risked a peek inside. A man with dark red hair sprawled across the bed.

Savio retreated.

The old house sat silent under the shine of the cold moon. At this hour the town appeared deserted. The temptation to peer into the turret room intensified. Was *she* within? The moon approached full, casting a silvery sheen across the landscape and he'd be backlit if he stepped too close. A feminine scream in the quiet dark would wake the dead. Despite that possibility, the thought of seeing her spurred him on. He couldn't stand out here till dawn.

Now or never, he chided and moved.

Stepping up beside the rounded turret, he peered inside. The panes bulged out to provide an excellent view. Flames flickered in the fireplace and washed the space in a pale gold. Just enough illumination showed the bed positioned against the shared wall of his room. His eyes focused and the surge of his pulse identified the figure on the mattress as the woman. He traced her outline. Undeterred by a touch of guilt, he eased forward through the shadows and froze halfway into view.

The casement sat raised at least four inches, more than enough to slip his hands under and lift. He imagined the frame sliding upward, smooth and silent as a gust of wind, and shook his head. Fans of fresh air made life too easy for the bad guys.

The woman shifted position on the linens, turning in her sleep, rolling over and leaving a broad wave of dark hair cascading across creamy sheets.

A sigh escaped his lips. She looked glorious.

The log in the fireplace collapsed in a fountain of sparks, the vestiges of fuel burned down to a pile of embers. A lone small flame danced atop the grate, emitting little radiance. Then the spark died, fading out completely.

Savio felt exposed. Desire twisted through him in a raw torrent. Confused by his reaction, he stood silent and immobile in the darkness.

He retreated one step at a time, hoping no telltale creaks alerted an insomniac guest. Nocturnal footsteps in an old house were sure to be noticed. He climbed back into his room and dropped down on the side of the bed, tried to relax. His body hummed, his thoughts centered on the woman in the neighboring space. A flimsy barrier divided them, less than a foot of wallboard and plaster separating their heads. Closing his eyes, he forced his mind away from this fledgling obsession and counted down from one hundred, starting over with added determination when he reached one and found himself still tense.

Hours later a sound jerked Savio awake. He listened. The creak and groan of old floor boards announced furtive movements. After a minute he crossed the room. Balanced on the balls of his stockinged feet to reduce any whisper of his passage, he grasped the knob and placed his ear near the doorframe. The telltale flush of a toilet indicated the prowler had a perfectly good reason to be up and about. He released his grip but strained to listen through the wood panel.

A minute ticked off. The nighttime wanderer had not returned. He glanced at his watch. By this time even the rowdy crowd had called it a day. Everyone slept except him and a fellow guest with a full bladder.

Savio grimaced. Perhaps he made mystery where none existed. It was altogether reasonable for someone to rise and use the facilities, even take a stroll if unable to sleep. But still, he kept an ear cocked. Soon the sound of soft footfalls came back from the far end of the hall. With only three bedrooms on this level, what had Remy been doing down there? Savio crossed to peer through the curtains.

In the hours before dawn the town huddled in a hushed silence. Little had changed. Her room featured nothing but inky blackness while a glow came from his other neighbor's window. The soft click of a latch closing sounded and seconds later the light switched off.

Savio waited five minutes before stepping out. He moved in a quick burst of speed, his footfalls unheard as he slipped down the wall, keeping to the steep shadows thrown by the dim bulbs in the old sconces. The moon angled a wash of dull illumination through the stained glass at the end of the corridor. As he'd expected, no other access existed, only the door to the pretty senorita's room.

Remy might have walked down here to admire the intricate patterns of the art glass but Savio didn't think so. For argument's sake, and because being thorough was his nature, he looked out the window. Distorted through the color and the age of the panes, he saw the back of the neighboring restaurant contained nothing of interest. If a bulb ever burned over the aged loading dock, it had long ago disappeared.

He returned to his bed. Toes curled in a stretch, he surveyed the ceiling. Despite his best effort, his attention focused on the woman again. He drew up an image of her, startled by the clarity of his recall. He liked her dark curls, the way they waved over the pillow. The narrow straps of her nightgown, some slick material that shined even in the dim illumination, sent his mind skittering down a path of imaginary exploration. In his fantasy her smooth skin, warm from sleep, compared to the sleek texture of silk.

He frowned. This lingering interest was unusual.

He mentally retraced Remy's route, his hackles rising. This proprietary reaction to a total stranger was a novelty and it had to end. He had no time to indulge an infatuation. The faint scratching of a mouse in the ceiling reminded him of the late hour. He slid under the covers but long minutes passed before sleep claimed him again.

11 CHAPTER ELEVEN

S
UNSHINE FLOWED OVER the tops of the trees outside her windows when Rose finally woke. She'd slept like the dead. Blinking against the brightness she liked how the beams streamed through antique panes of glass rippled by the slow creep of years. The golden richness reflected off the ivory and cream tones of the interior, generating a sense of cozy warmth. She hopped out of bed and crossed the braided rug. With a single tug the casement slipped the rest of the way up and she leaned out to breathe in the fresh air.

She felt renewed.

After finding the body yesterday, she was grateful for her lack of dreams. The half bottle of wine she'd consumed probably had as much to do with that as the exhaustion of the day.

Touching her temple she barely registered a raised bump but she wondered if the bruise had darkened.

A montage of evergreens blanketed the steep hillsides, their delicate tops swaying high above the town. The scenery exceeded her expectations. Much of the region's beauty stemmed from the heavy glaciated ruggedness of the Bitterroot mountain range. She'd read about the picturesque back-country trails and the thought of hiking brought another surge of energy. Wispy clouds floated over the peaks of the lodgepole pines and the sheer immensity of sky and landscape created a powerful sense of wilderness.

The Continental Divide occurred here, separating the flow of waters to the east and west of the land, forming the literal backbone of the nation's topography. The idea fascinated her. She imagined a skeletal spinal column erupting from the soil, bony protuberances poking into the endless vault of blue.

She stretched farther out to look up and down Main Street. Almost every business had propped its doors open to welcome the fresh air. Busy residents sauntered along the sidewalks, stopping to chat and greet each other. Across from the White Horse Inn, two elderly men sat on a bench below a flutter of public notices pinned to a bulletin board on the deep green wall of the market. A high-pitched squeal of childish laughter carried from a neighboring lane.

Postcard Americana at its best.

A battered rusty pickup clamored into view. Dilapidated fenders shook and rattled until the relic passed. A ricocheting crack of sound echoed as the driver shifted gears. The spatter of backfire made her jump and leaning so far over the sill, she almost lost her balance.

Flipping ass-over-end seemed a poor way to start her day so she pulled back inside and closed the window.

Nature called.

She hurriedly took care of business and bathed, trying to dress while brushing her teeth. Anxious to begin work as soon as possible, she rushed through her preparations. Less than an hour later, her damp hair coiled into a lump on the back of her skull, Rose paused in the parlor on her way out.

A heaping plate of pastries sat next to a coffee urn. Both drew her like a beacon. She bit into the perfect balance of light flaky crust and fruit jam covered in icing and experienced a knee wobble. Two Danish later she refilled her travel cup, snapped on the lid and wandered out the rear door.

Behind the house she discovered a petite paved lot with three empty parking spaces. Remembering that she'd parked in a limited time zone, she headed around to the front. As she rounded the corner and spied her car still sitting at the curb she exhaled with relief.

Yep, right beneath the sign with a dire warning against overnight vehicles.

Last night she'd been too exhausted to worry about it but this morning the prospect of getting towed worried her. Either she'd gotten off easy because the Sunday nightshift was lazy or nobody bothered to enforce the law.

Rather than perform a complicated and probably illegal three-point turn on the thoroughfare, she reversed and backed up until she could swing into the driveway. In the lot behind the café a sleek motorcycle sat beside a van which – judging by the four flattened tires – hadn't moved in years. She swung into the last open slot, backed out, and guided her vehicle down the asphalt strip. Her car was small but it filled the narrow space between the Inn's driveway and the diner's steps.

A man exiting the restaurant caught her attention. She slowed to watch as he gracefully descended to the sidewalk.

Musculature displayed the athletic fluidity of someone in prime physical condition. His trim frame moved with an innate elegance impossible to emulate if naturally lacking.

She braked to a stop.

A purr of appreciation rumbled up from her chest. She crept forward as he continued toward the street. Gaze riveted to his ass, she appreciated the contrast of the plain black jeans and long-sleeved chalk white t-shirt. His every motion meshed energy in smooth alignment with the limbs under the fabric of his clothes. The man's hair was true obsidian with lapis highlights that glinted in the sun. The dark strands and his streamlined physique attracted her like a moth to flame.

She emitted a sigh.

The man became aware of her vehicle and turned.

Rose admired his clean-shaven cheek as he rotated, but the vivid sapphire eyes startled her into stabbing the brake. The car jerked to a stop. She gawked unabashedly.

He returned her interest, even took a step forward.

Piercing her with an intense stare, she noted how his vibrant eyes contrasted with his tan. Black hair framed his features in a perfect foil. Inky slashes of eyebrow added punctuation to a hawkish face. A compact trim goatee and mustache did nothing to disguise well-formed lips.

She liked his fine-boned jutting cheekbones and the hollowed grooves that planed along each cheek and emphasized the angularity of his jawline.

His lips curled, pleased by her obvious study and his head canted to one side. A wide smile revealed excellent dentition.

Rose stared. She found an utter lack of flaws. Even his mouth was sexy.

If it weren't for her pressing appointment with the park service, she'd be tempted to throw the gearshift in neutral and ask the hottie his name. She ogled her way up his physique until she met his eyes and matched his smile. No reason he shouldn't know she found him handsome.

They shared a long moment.

Her breath shallowed, lips parted. Body temperature climbing, a minor solar flare exploded inside her belly. The attraction was provocative. Finally, she let the car idle forward but she never broke eye contact with him.

He swiveled as she came even to his position. His crooked grin twisted something in her chest. She fanned her cheek with one hand and puckered up, blowing him a kiss.

His eyes narrowed and tightened as she rolled past.
She managed the left turn onto the street without causing a wreck but it was sheer luck since her attention remained on the sexy pedestrian. It was totally unfair that a man like that never wanted to hold her hand longer than propriety allowed.

12 Chapter Twelve

FEET CEMENTED TO the sidewalk, Savio stared after the car.

Merda!

His heart pounded out a frantic cadence. A casual observer might assume nothing of great interest had just occurred but they would be wrong. The senorita's bold gaze intoxicated him as she checked him out.

The California license plate receded down the road and his memorization of make, model, and tag number was automatic.

Heat thrummed through his body as he relived the scene. Her passionate attention sizzled inside his bloodstream and rocketed directly to his cock. Christ, the seductive image of her mouth puckered in invitation might haunt him for the rest of the day.

Last night he'd been intrigued. Today he'd been struck by lightning.

The oval of her face framed features highlighted by the curve of high cheekbones. Her eyes were wide and deep, not the black he'd imagined but dark and rich as strong brewed coffee. Again she wore her long hair pulled tight, drawing his attention back to her graceful throat.

Scratch his plan to check out of the White Horse Inn today. It seemed that fortune had favored his interests after all. He was not fool enough to deny himself the pleasure of pursuing what promised to be a most satisfying sexual release. With a little strategic planning he could enjoy getting cozy with one neighbor while he spied on the other.

He went to pay for another night's accommodation before turning his focus to different matters.

Three men entered the inn as he started up the stairs to his room. He paused on the bottom step and listened for a moment. He'd noticed the old guys sitting on a bench in front of the market and suspected they were locals.

The one in the overalls flipped a gnarled hand. "Morning, Anton. Thought we'd come over and see if Lily baked any more of her famous pastries?"

The Innkeeper emerged from behind the counter and greeted his friends.

Savio dismissed the rest of the exchange and continued upstairs. His half-hearted plan to scope out the living quarters of the remaining second-floor occupants was abandoned when he discovered the cleaning crew already active.

He grabbed his jacket and helmet and returned downstairs.

The men were deep in conversation in the parlor so he slipped out the back door. His sudden departure from Mexico

City had disrupted his normal cycle of check-ins. Now it was time to fire up his phone and listen to messages.

An hour and a half later he found Mackenzie at the mine. The man stood with his booted feet spread wide, waiting near the entrance. As soon as he caught sight of Savio his hands clenched into fists.

Savio ignored the aggressive stance.

Tilting his head, he applied flame to the end of a thin cigar before swiveling his gaze to the other man. He inhaled a deep breath and enjoyed the rush of smoke. He tapped the tip of the cigarillo with a practiced gesture.

"*Buenos dias.*"

Mackenzie brushed aside his greeting. "This batch is almost done. I'll have the money to pay for the delivery. I'd appreciate if you told your contacts that I'll be ready for more in a couple of weeks. I'll let them know where to deliver."

Savio shrugged.

Casually relaxed, cigar clamped between his thumb and forefinger, he decided to probe for information. "Business is moving along well, then?"

Mackenzie crushed a pile of debris in his hands, flattening the trash with meticulous attention. He finished folding the compact bundle and stashed it inside his backpack.

"Everything is on schedule." His intonation cut each word off with a sharp edge and his lips compressed into a thin line.

Still sulking, Savio decided. He hadn't really expected an answer but it never hurt to ask. "Excellent. I am in no hurry, senor."

CHAPTER THIRTEEN

ROSE FUMBLED HER cell phone out of her back pocket and checked the battery life. She groaned. Only two of the five bars glowed green.

Crap.

She needed to remember to plug in the charger tonight. Signal strength indicated enough connectivity to do her duty so she pressed and held the number three button to auto-dial her parents.

The phone rang a long time before the answering machine picked up and her mother's voice directed the caller to leave a message.

"Hi Mom. I'm just checking in with a survival update. I'm in Riverside, Montana. I found a dead guy. Call if you want details. Love to Dad."

She disconnected and tossed her phone on her bag. Experience had taught her that unorthodox messages produced faster response times.

A different ranger manned the kiosk at the park entrance today but this one was just as perky and chipper as yesterday's model. She pointed Rose in the right direction.

Distracted by thoughts of the sexy stranger, Rose drove right past the turn-off to the notorious parking lot without realizing she'd done so until already a mile down the road.

Now that was impressive, the hot guy made her forget the dead one.

At the regional office, she received her first major check of the day.

Rose flattened her palms on the counter and tried to control her temper. She inhaled and counted to three before exhaling. It was the same method she used in class to keep from yelling at hung-over coeds.

When she believed she could speak without her voice screeching, she asked for clarification, "Why is *my* permit on hold? I can conduct research and easily avoid the area where the body was found." She lifted her arms in a display of entreaty.

"They're all sidelined. Sorry."

Rose glowered at the reply but Ranger Burnside ignored her anger.

He bent close like he was about to share a confidence. "The park service has suspended permits in the West District until further notice."

"How does that even make sense?" she demanded.

He pressed his lips together as though commiserating with her frustration. Then he tilted his head forward, demonstrating remarkable flexibility for a man with no neck.

"The delay will only last a couple of days. Probably."

He stepped to one side and pointed at a large square of paper pinned to the wall. The map displayed the whole of Yellowstone Park parceled into geographic chunks like a state broken into counties.

"This entire area," his thick finger swirled over one section, "is locked down until cause of death is established."

She huffed out a breath.

He offered her a stern frown. "Now then, it's for your protection. Until we determine the chain of events, we must restrict movement in areas accessible to the general public."

Rose raised her palms in defeat. She'd get nowhere with this automaton.

This was so frustrating. Lord knew, if the victim had expired as a result of microbial invasion, she was already contaminated. Despite that obvious fact, the knuckle-dragger in front of her refused to negotiate. She took a moment to run her hands over the objects within easy reach.

Just sharing the wealth, she thought and cast him a grim look.

"Better hope it's not a homicidal maniac. Since you're inside the quarantine area, he might come find you when no convenient victims are scrambling around in the wilderness." Even her smile felt bitter.

Ranger Burnside frowned back.

Barely able to control the urge to slam the door, Rose stomped out of the office and across the gravel lot. Her tires sprayed pebbles as she pulled onto the paved road. Belligerent and frustrated, she steered along the banked turns of the highway at a speed exceeding the posted limit.

Her mind processed.

She needed a work-around. Logic dictated that if park personnel wouldn't let her work until they knew what happened, they couldn't be pissed off when she nosed into their business, right?

She arrived at the proverbial 'scene of the crime' surprised no barrier blocked the lot. Parked in the same space, she ignored the brief echo of déjà vu and in conscious replication of the previous day, trudged up the rise and pushed past the trees.

Caution tape surrounded two-thirds of the hot spring. The yellow and black strip of plastic, reminiscent of a wasp's carapace, had collapsed across the width of the pool and floated over the surface, a warning to trespassers.

Uneasy to be alone in the place, she squatted to study the muddy stretch of ground.

She'd never fancied herself a sleuth but plenty of childhood hours engrossed in reruns of Hercule Poirot and Miss Marple had provided the basics. Everyone knew the first step of investigation involved making observations, especially at the death site.

She didn't have much choice in the matter. The rangers wanted a resolution and she needed to get to work.

Things looked oddly normal.

Yesterday, the discovery of the body had shocked her but the scene hadn't struck her as macabre. Even though wisps of steam curled around the corpse and gave off a Halloween spooky ambience, the sight seemed more surreal than frightening.

Today the memory was sad.

She considered if death might have occurred as a result of natural causes. The odds against a healthy fit young person toppling over dead tipped the scale toward the unlikely side, but weirder stuff had been known to happen.

As she perused the setting, two things bothered her.

The first one had to do with the fact she'd parked in an empty lot yesterday. Where was the man's car? For all she knew, paved parking areas sat at measured intervals throughout Yellowstone. Camp sites too, for that matter. But whatever the explanation, it needed to be within walking distance.

She scribbled a mental memo to drive around and check for both.

The second discordant note resulted from the pattern of distinctive footprints in the area near the pool. The imagery tapped at her subconscious like an insistent woodpecker. There was no chalk outline depicting the location of the remains, something which genuinely disappointed her. She supposed the water complicated the process.

Curious, she squatted and angled her foot sideways off the wooden platform and stuck her heel in the mud. The Vibram sole left no impression. Puzzled now, she scrutinized the ground. She jabbed the tread against the surface again. The muck appeared soft but proved surprisingly solid underfoot.

She contemplated for a minute. The angle of the foot in the prints indicated a person with an odd gait. She tried to imitate the posture and discovered she needed to twist in order to bend her ankle in such a strange position. When she tried to walk, she discovered she couldn't stand upright without a noticeable back arch. But if she didn't contort her body, she couldn't come close to replicating the prints.

A quick mad image blossomed. She visualized an ancient hominin gamboling through the woods of North America. Her brain rejected the idea but other equally ridiculous scenarios continued to cycle in her grey matter.

Gracile and short, early human ancestors might clean up more like the guy next door than a modern ape but not by much. Once arboreal in the collection of foodstuffs, they moved in the branches of trees and sought shelter in the treetops to escape dangers on the ground. She looked and found a lack of forest where the body had lain. A killer throwback made an awesome theory, one that encouraged supermarket rags to run screaming headlines. The thought even accounted for the weird footprints. Too bad it was ludicrous. Sometimes, she missed the days when evidence hadn't seemed necessary to support conclusions.

Rose shucked her boots and peeled off her socks. Cuffed together, she rolled them into the middle of the walkway and flexed her bare feet. The ground squelched like wet sand under her naked toes.

She slipped under the rail and stood upright. The surface felt solid but she tested each step with caution as she moved away from the safety of the walk. A trail of debris showed where the emergency crew had recovered the body.

She stayed outside the string of tape and searched for an expanse of softer mud. Closer to the edge of the pool, the surface softened and grew slick. She tried an experimental tap and pushed her toes into the muck. It gave. Empirical reasoning suggested she leap and jump to see if she could reproduce the prints. The act was more challenging than she'd expected. She found by balancing most of her weight on one foot, that if she swung the other one up high and pushed down as she stepped forward; she replicated the marks with reasonable accuracy. But her prints still looked different. The original ones were rounder. It wasn't the odd angle, she'd gotten pretty close to approximating that – but no matter how she twisted her ankle, she could not produce the same impression.

She rinsed her feet in the shallow edge of the thermal feature, appreciating the warm water.

A sulphurous odor permeated the area. The soil near the perimeter displayed cracks and discoloration, like a crust of mineralization covering patches of heated water. When the wind kicked up, a plume of steam rose from the aquamarine surface, reminding her of an antique illustration of a malevolent genie rising out of a battered lamp. The sight spooked her.

She flat-footed a path back to the boardwalk and crawled under the guard rail. Most of the dirt had rinsed away but the mineral rich deposit left a dark residue ringing the underneath of her toenails.

Lovely.

She wiped her soles on the cold wood before she struggled back into the socks. Toes aching from the chill, she shoved her feet in the boots and stamped the ground in the heavy footwear until circulation returned.

As much as she liked her hypothesis, she assumed the person who killed her dead guy – assuming he'd actually been murdered – did not fit the profile of a long-extinct hominid.

She flexed her fingers and theorized. Ground consistency probably changed with the weather, certainly with the moisture content in the surface, but it seemed safe to assume the killer weighed more than her buck and loose change. By necessity he featured agile feet and she attributed this in part to someone with a taller and heavier build. She failed to explain the awkward angle of the impressions.

An ache sprouted in her temples and she retreated to the car.

Cranking up the heater she let the engine idle while her toes defrosted. Slumped down in the seat with the tips of her shoes stuck against the vent she admired the snow-capped tops of the Grand Tetons shining in the bright sun.

Heat blasted the interior until Rose simmered. She grunted in desperation, she could think of nothing to do. She'd replayed the minutes before and after the discovery of the body so many times they'd taken on the semblance of a film she'd seen long ago and too often.

The dead guy had been removed by park officials. Not much remained to work with there.

She moved on.

The man must have arrived at the pool on foot. Which way had he come? The distance she'd driven from the entrance made it seem unlikely he'd left a car somewhere else and hiked in. Considering this angle, she mentally retraced her route until she reached the end of the path the park service had installed to safely navigate around the steaming water feature. She imagined herself leaning against the top rail.

In the months prior to her visit she'd reviewed the history of Yellowstone, watched a couple of televised documentaries, and read news accounts of local events. Recent headlines had featured a story about a main road within park boundaries that had literally melted as a result of underground shifts in thermal energy. In a place with such constant seismic activity, she reasoned, alternate routes must be common. Had an older trail once existed, one she'd missed because it was no longer in use?

This was a question warranting investigation.

She killed the motor.

Two minutes later Rose paused at the edge of the board-walk where she'd smacked her head. Other than some skid marks on the boards and the faint bruise above her brow, there were no traces of the event. Though she was engrossed with studying the ground, she wasn't so distracted that she failed to notice a man dive behind a screen of low silvery-green bushes.

She froze but her pulse rocketed. The spare physique sparked an instantaneous recognition.

His sable hair shone in the bright light just as it had out in front of the restaurant. The figure disappeared halfway between the distant tree line up-slope and where she stood. She sputtered out an uneven breath. At least she needn't admit to anyone that her increased heart rate wasn't entirely the result of fear.

Rose tamped down her rush of excitement. Mr. Hottie's presence suggested he was a participant in this drama but the fact he'd hidden didn't bode well.

Disappointment flooded through her. She had no business being here either but it should be noted she wasn't concealing herself in the landscape. It was just her lousy luck he'd turn out to be one of the bad guys.

Her libido insisted she must be mistaken.

Lunatic as the idea sounded, the temptation to shout out some questions occurred to her.

True, she was in an isolated place where one person had already died. Oh, and yeah, she was not alone. Maintaining a reasonable distance might be wise. She vacillated about hightailing it back to the parking lot and leaving. With a lack of defensive options, and surrounded by desolate landscape, she considered what to do next.

Her gun was stowed inside her bag on the passenger floorboard of her car. She rarely loaded the thing anyway. She used it mostly for scaring off curious rattlesnakes when she worked in Nevada. She did have a handful of bullets in her pocket. Fat lot of good they would do her. She could pelt the man with 9mm projectiles but what if he caught the bullets and returned fire?

Puckering her lips, she debated.

Her grandfather had lived a reckless life. He'd done dangerous acts, taken incredible risks, and gone on magnificent adven-
tures. He'd also been well over six feet tall, physically imposing,
and a man. Sexist or not, she believed that made a difference
when trying to intimidate others.

She'd ventured into deep water and was out of her depth.

On the other hand, she was desperate, obviously in more
than one way.

Attractive men were so absent in her life, she questioned if
she'd remember what to do with one. A hiccup in her respiration curled her mouth into a smirk. No doubt sex was like riding a horse, once you hiked your leg back over the saddle,
instinct took control.

Rose traced a visual path up the gentle slope of the hill. The
incline was steady rather than steep. She'd heard about people
crashing through ground that appeared solid but was actually a
thin crust concealing a geothermal feature filled with boiling
water.

She shuddered. Staying on this side of the split-rail fence
seemed smart. The landscape was littered with small steaming
calderas. They reminded her of bowls of hot soup.

What about the guy? She peered at the scrubby hiding
place where her sexy admirer had disappeared and studied the
terrain. With one eye on alert for the concealed man, she
searched for a path or a trail. If he popped out to threaten her,
she had a vague plan to sprint for her car.

She saw nothing, not even one of those thin trickles of dust
indicating the passage of deer.

14 CHAPTER FOURTEEN

S AVIO CRANED HIS neck to keep the woman in sight. He cursed the barren landscape that kept him from creeping closer. He missed the tropics. Jungles made it so much easier to sneak up on people.

What was the senorita doing here?

His current position placed him halfway between the mouth of the mine and the steaming pool of water where he'd discovered the dead man. If she continued straight up into the tree line it couldn't be more than a few hundred yards to the patch of saplings which screened the entrance of the mine. Mackenzie's carefully constructed enterprise was weakening like a faulty dike. He sensed a breach and imagined the walls letting go, water flooding out to cover the land. That meant he must decide how to play things out, and soon.

Now he had a valid reason to meet this woman. Tempted to reveal himself, he decided against doing so. Since he'd initially hidden, his sudden appearance would be suspect, to say the least.

Reliving their fiery eye contact, he frowned.

A chance encounter on an empty isolated plain seemed unlikely to work in his favor. The specter of the recent dead loomed nearby. And no matter how brave, facing a stranger alone in the wilderness should give any woman pause. His attention stayed with the girl. The senorita piqued his curiosity.

In his experience, chance encounters seldom occurred. With limited accommodations and restaurants to choose from in town, the odds of crossing paths increased. But repetitive intersecting events indicated a common interest. They were both at this thermal pool for a reason. His was base curiosity. What about her? The larger the number of intersections, the closer each individual's involvement usually proved to be. In less than twenty-four hours he'd experienced multiple connections with the petite beauty.

Her bizarre activity at the death scene had drawn his attention. Squatted in the cover of dense growth, his military-grade field glasses focused on her, he'd studied her actions with fascination. Puzzled by her barefoot antics in the mud, he finally realized she was experimenting, trying to figure out the strange prints he'd left behind. After a particularly energetic pounce tipped her off-balance, his legs had clenched in sympathy.

She'd recovered without falling and he grinned.

Her capering romp beside the water drew him from the safety of deep cover. Now Savio sat on the cold ground and peered through tree limbs that provided scant coverage. Surprised she hadn't caught him in clear view as he traversed the open expanse between the mine site and the thermal pool, now he wished she had.

With a last survey of the landscape, she turned away.

Savio kept the glasses trained on her until the muscles in his arms burned. His leg ached, the muscles in his thigh sending out an alarming twinge. He set aside the lenses, positioned his legs straight in front of him, and rolled his body down against his thighs, tucking his palms under the bottoms of his boots. He stretched three times to force major muscle groups to expand and retract. Then he picked up the binoculars and resumed his study, drawing up his knees to rest his elbows for balance and reduce arm strain.

Disappointment swelled when he didn't find her. She must have returned to the parking lot. He caught her on the second sweep, his breath catching in his throat.

She sat perched on the end of the wooden walkway, legs dangling over the edge, her face directed toward the pond. Wind whipped her uncoiled hair in a tangled maelstrom of strands.

Fingers clenching in reaction, he jabbed the field glasses against his eye sockets. He wanted to fist his hands tight in that long mass and pull her close.

He gave himself a mental slap. He desired information.

More than a decade of training shifted into action. First, he needed to determine if the woman knew the dead man. Perhaps they worked as colleagues. In the news, scientists always spouted rhetoric about working together for the common betterment of the world. He pondered what conventional knowledge researchers gleaned from study of the sparse flora and fauna in this place.

He shifted to the next idea.

She might be a specialist in crime scene analysis. Unlikely. She neither acted nor moved like someone with law enforcement experience. She was observant and adept in the environment but no one skirted legalities or fought criminal elements without developing a strong sense of self-preservation, at least not for long. They didn't survive. This woman lacked instinctive impulses.

Even from this distance he saw she appeared oblivious to her blind areas, unaware of how easily danger might appear from nowhere. He could walk up behind her, wrap a thin cord around her neck, choke her unconscious or worse, and depart in under a minute. His shoulders tightened again, his hands gripping the binoculars with intensity.

This was absurd behavior.

He forced himself to consider another option. The man who took the water samples might have been her lover.

He rejected this idea immediately. Last night she had slept with ease, alone in the large bed, a woman unaccustomed to a nighttime partner. No rings adorned her fingers but the lack of visible promise markers in today's culture meant little. Most conspicuous, she portrayed no tears or sorrow. In his estimation a lover, even a poor one, who expired under such circumstances, should wring at least a tear from his intimate.

Pleased with his deductions, he was unable to ignore a rush of pleasure. Her appreciative display skittered through his mind – followed by a dose of disgust at his blatant interest. Despite that, he continued to watch until she climbed to her feet. He stared as she raised her arms over her head in a stretch, then grunted when she bent over stiff-legged to retie her left boot.

The woman had a fabulous ass.

Through the glasses he followed the swish of her backside as she walked down the trail. The moment she disappeared from sight the same impulse he'd encountered at the diner last night seized him again. Gripped by a desire to follow, he obeyed.

Rising from his place of concealment he loped after her.

15   Chapter Fifteen

HARLAN SIGHTED THE science camp through the trees. The cluster of painted buildings evoked a sense of nostalgia, reinforced by the fact the place hadn't changed much in appearance in the decades since his adolescence. He steered his car along the curvy road and marshaled his thoughts in preparation.

Seeing Maggie Thompson always upset his equilibrium. Although most people knew her as a distinguished scientist today, he and Maggie shared a personal history that stretched back to adolescent awakenings and awkwardness. She'd moved on, made a life for herself, but Harlan never really had.

He marked his arrival by the colored strips of paper stapled to every visible tree trunk and wrapped around countless bush stems. The field station specialized in the study of regional flora and fauna. Harlan figured the tags helped newcomers learn to identify local plants. Or, more likely, given Maggie's cantankerous disposition, the labeling served as a form of punishment for wisecracking students.

Five large dome tents formed a half circle beside the mess hall. Camp chairs and small tables mirrored the shape in a relaxation zone around a stone firepit. Three plywood lean-tos overflowed with sawn and split wood. Evening campfires were common even in midsummer.

Maggie stood outside the bunkhouse. She caught the movement in her peripheral vision and turned her head, following his progress as he pulled in and parked. Her brows lowered into the customary scowl it seemed like she reserved just for him.

His pulse jumped.

He engaged the emergency brake and scanned the vicinity. The facility was a relic from the public works program era. After decades of training fire crews and forestry personnel, the camp was abandoned and fell into disrepair, the road chained closed. The lack of vehicle access hadn't kept out local kids or determined tourists. By the time the university system expressed an interest, not a window remained unbroken. Nimble fingers had stripped away any object of value. The university's offer to float repair costs in exchange for the use of the buildings appealed to park management. Unpaid graduate students provided the labor.

Harlan shook his head. Circumstances hadn't changed much in the intervening years. Every summer brought a new batch of eager pupils.

He cut the engine and darted a quick look at the woman.

No one pushed his buttons like Maggie. She never missed an opportunity to bait him. True to form, she'd turned and presented her back to him. Tall and auburn-haired, she was wiry and muscular with sharp angled features. The stiff line of her shoulders amused him. The petulant act reinforced his nephew's assertion that Maggie cultivated a secret crush on Harlan.

The idea buoyed his heartache. At first he'd brushed off the suggestion but during the last year he'd noticed his hangdog expression often plucked an unexpected soft response.

Harlan took that as a hopeful sign.

Twenty years ago Maggie's Toyota truck had bounced into camp. With the fervor of a new graduate, she'd put her local knowledge of the region to good use and developed a master plan to revitalize the dilapidated field station. She'd charged forward with the finesse of a locomotive veering off the rails, applying for grant monies and making improvements. She produced results and results mattered. Her unprecedented success triggered a landslide of support from university administrators and precipitated a changing of the guard. In fact, the way he'd heard the story told, a majority of the senior faculty in the department opted for premature retirement rather than be pinned under Dr. Thompson's unrelenting thumb.

Harlan suspected Maggie's former colleagues still woke from the occasional nightmare of working in her division. The scientific community esteemed Margaret Thompson but they didn't have to like the woman.

She intimidated the hell out of him too.

Glaring through the windshield he frowned at the people gathered around the camp. The place was crowded for midday. Scientific types tried his patience. In his experience, the group split into two sets, both guaranteed to annoy. The first half talked to him like he scarce understood grunts and snorts. The rest believed prime-time television reflected law enforcement reality. This bunch was sure to harbor elements of each and at least one individual boasting personal legal experience – usually from the opposite side of the bench. At a minimum, one always fancied himself an anarchist and gave a speech.

Harlan rolled his shoulders and prepared to face Maggie. When he hadn't seen her for a while, he felt like a kid who'd gone to bed a gawky teenager with acne and woke up middle-aged, weighed down with responsibility. He'd also escaped the small town life. He'd been a cop in Butte until Bill Johnston dropped dead from a heart attack and the mayor called him, asking for help. The instant promotion had been heady but he'd considered it a temporary position. Someday, he'd head back to the big city. Then the next year his sister became a widow. Harlan had found a new role in his nephew's life and settled in.

A decade passed before Maggie came home.

He climbed out of the vehicle thinking about their history.

Over the years he'd paid his respects at her mother's funeral and answered her call to evict a delinquent renter from the old family house. Once, he'd even bumped into her at the nuptials of a mutual friend. He still spent hours scrutinizing every moment in her company from multiple angles until each shone with clarity, preserved in his memory like tiny flowers encased in amber. His infatuation had matured and solidified into a deep and unvoiced emotion.

He slapped his hat once against his leg and plopped it on his head.

Maggie continued to ignore him as he walked in her direction. Research remained her first desire. She published at a voracious rate, contributing articles to both academic journals and popular magazines. Harlan read everything she'd ever penned, even had a scrapbook of reviews tucked in his desk drawer.

The Porcupine Bluff facility enjoyed a healthy endowment these days. The rough camp exterior disguised a magnitude of expensive scientific instruments. But Harlan surmised Maggie could receive the equivalent of the national defense budget and still complain about having insufficient funds.

Not many people noticed Maggie's return to Riverside.

Harlan remembered the day it happened. The sight of a moving truck parked outside her house sent his pulse skittering. Fence-talk said Maggie had tried on marriage in college. Behind her back, the more unkind gossips around town called her the graduate school black widow. Harlan debated if that meant the unlucky fellow had expired or been consumed. Either way he figured matrimony with Maggie would challenge any man, even a strong one. Harlan wanted very much to test his strength of will.

"Where the hell have you been, Harlan?" Maggie's voice drew the attention of every person present.

Harlan flushed.

She traversed the distance on long legs and met him half-way across the volleyball court. She stopped, crossed her arms and stared. In truth, she gazed down because she topped Harlan by an inch. Tall women didn't put him at a disadvantage, he was too confident for that, but Maggie's green-eyed glare compounded his discomfiture.

His lips parted to speak.

She beat him to it, "What are you doing about this Harlan?" She slapped her palms on her hips, accentuating her trim waist with the aggressive stance. "This is unacceptable. There's analysis to be done and people being paid to do research just standing around."

He flinched at her strident tone and curled one hand in a conciliatory gesture.

Maggie stepped into him, took a deep breath, leaned close and bared her teeth. "I cannot tolerate delay." The words gritted out through her tight lips. He inhaled but she plowed on.

"This kind of disruption can ruin months, even years of work. I'm not the one who stands to lose if the park service doesn't let us get back to doing what they've approved. My students need these opportunities or some of them won't graduate."

"NPS personnel are conducting an investigation."

She dismissed Harlan's placid tone with the wave of one hand.

"Yes, and that's important, but I'm talking about problems caused by your nephew. Robbie has suspended permits without explanation. He claims it's some Forestry Department decision. My time and resources cannot accommodate the government's habit of bureaucratic waste. I adhere to their regulations. Our work here is important. Involving us in these unrelated concerns borders on ridiculous. Damn it Harlan, do something." Maggie glared down the bridge of her nose, her angry tones a warning for students to keep at a safe distance.

Harlan squinted into the sun. She always maneuvered him into the least advantageous position. She should have been a cop. When she inhaled to respond, he hurried to speak.

"Now Maggie, I have nothing to do with your outfit here."

She threw both hands up.

Harlan caught one and she let him hold it. He wrinkled his brow and set out to placate her, listening to the spate of words that flooded out of her mouth.

"Gunther's study was due to complete this year. Next winter he would've published his results." She sniffed and stood silent for ten seconds. "His was groundbreaking work. Such a shame. I'll have to finish it myself and that's wrong."

He'd heard she'd identified the body as one of her graduate researchers.

Her voice trailed away, chilled fingers wrapping firmly around his. She tried to hang on to her anger, but her tense shoulders relaxed and a smile lurked at the edges of her lips.

"Don't you cheer me up, Harlan Groates," she complained. Her face slackened into softness and her eyes glistened. She squeezed his hand before she withdrew hers. "It's a damned waste, Harlan. Gunther was a fine young man."

Harlan acknowledged this uncharacteristic public display of sadness by looking away. The academic enclave had gathered in a semi-circle behind her. As a trained observer he noted the distribution of individuals, how they clustered together. It was a disparate crowd. In addition to the full crew of students in residence, Maggie had taken on a handful of eco-tourists who'd thrown top dollar across the table for the opportunity to be treated like undergraduates.

He aimed his most earnest expression at her, "You know the park people have jurisdiction. There isn't a thing I can do to have your permits reinstated."

Emotions in check again, she sent Harlan a dirty glance. Her chin began to jut out.

He recognized that look and soothed her. "No more than a couple of days and they'll let you get back to business."

She said nothing.

He shuffled his feet under her stare. "I guess I could give Rob a call and ask, if you'd like."

One of the first-year students sidled up next to Maggie. His round eyeglass lenses flashed in the sunlight.

"You the local Five-Oh?" he asked in a thin reedy voice.

Maggie rolled her eyes.

Harlan's mouth tightened in a hard line. The anarchist had shown.

16 Chapter Sixteen

DESPITE THE FACT he enjoyed risky behavior, Savio
ducked off trail as soon as he heard voices. After stalking the elusive female down to the parking lot, he
found her conversing with a ranger. At first he'd been alarmed
she might report his presence but he caught a flash of her leaning against the fender of a bronze colored car and relaxed.

Not wanting to press his luck, he made his way back up the
path and took a circuitous route to return to the mine. The
trudge warmed the chill from his body. To his surprise he enjoyed walking the narrow game trail amid the dappled light fil-
tering through gaps in the canopy of pines. The air cooled in
the shadows and proved invigorating. The climate was a stark
contrast to the temperate warmth of Mexico but he much admired the large pine trees. Palm flattened against the massive

trunk of one, he craned his neck to see the top and almost lost his balance.

Moving forward, he approached the entrance with caution. The site looked undisturbed.

Mackenzie's absence didn't surprise him. The man would show up at some point to do daily maintenance. The waste bucket sat unemptied. The distilling equipment continued to hiss and sputter, red phosphorous dripping through and collecting in the overflow receptacle.

Except for the apparatus and chemicals taking up one side of the main tunnel, a quick search produced nothing. The set-up had been positioned close enough to the entrance to dilute fumes but the accumulation of vapor smelled more noticeable today. The smell, which was an odd mix of ammonia and something reminiscent of skunk, choked the interior. The thick air stung his eyes. Outside he sucked in a deep breath No peculiar odor lingered but the acrid stench burned the sensitive lining of his nostrils.

Savio checked the progress of the drug. In his estimation this batch might finish sometime tomorrow, the next day at the latest. Once the ephedrine he'd brought from Mexico completed being converted into a salable product, the party would end and everyone would move on. So far he'd managed to connect Mackenzie and Remy but he suspected the involvement of a third participant. With the quantity of compound being manufactured, Mackenzie must have more than one distributor.

He considered several options to resolve the situation. The first was taking out Mackenzie himself, an action for which he carried no official authorization. An anonymous phone call might suffice – turn the men into the local authorities, but Savio wasn't quite ready to move on. Putting Mackenzie in jail while he elected to stay in town might prove problematic. On the other hand, he could do exactly that and hop a flight to Los Angeles in time to submit his report on the fiasco in Mexico. But that meant forgoing the pleasure of seducing the pretty senorita – not his preferred option.

Years of military service had once earned Savio a hard reputation. Enemies and allies alike had called him callous, heartless, and ruthless. On more than one occasion he'd been accused of savagery, all in the name of patriotism. He delivered results and slept easy at night. At least he did as long as the PTSD didn't kick in. Now he wondered just how much the private sector work had softened his ragged edges.

Letting Mackenzie continue his business sat wrong with him, especially since Savio had been the one to deliver Benito's package. He'd provided the materials and allowed the man to create the deadly concoction in order to identify and eradicate the local players. Might as well let that run its course. Afterwards, if he allowed the methamphetamine to release into the world, well, that was on him.

Not acceptable.

He preferred to create no collateral damage. The suits who sat behind the desks frowned upon unnecessary civilian loss. The drugs must be removed. Either he relieved Mackenzie of the completed end-product or did something to halt its distribution progress through the food chain. These guys might be dangerous but they were greedy and that made them the kind of men who had weaknesses to exploit.

He exited and walked a distance down the path before lighting a cigarillo. The curls of sweet tobacco smoke soothed his senses as he listened to the silence. After half an hour, he slipped back into the gloom of the manmade tunnel and found a comfortable position where a breeze carried fresh air inside.

With almost two hours till nightfall, he adjusted the hand-gun in his underarm holster and buttoned his green woolen shirt halfway up. He didn't have long to wait before Mackenzie appeared.

"I wondered when you'd show up, Mendes." Mackenzie shrugged off his backpack and pulled off his sweatshirt. "Jesus, it stinks in here."

"*Buenas tardes, senor.*" He motioned to the bucket. "Complete your chores first and then let us talk about our business."

17 CHAPTER SEVENTEEN

ROSE HAD NOT expected to run into Ranger Saxton when she reached the parking lot. The man took one look at her and knew she'd been snooping.

With a face grown thunderous, he ignored her greeting. "What you are doing is risky." His voice turned hard. "You need to stay out of this investigation."

Her temper flared. "Yellowstone needs to honor their agreement and issue my research permit."

"You're interfering in a potential crime scene. Spend the day somewhere else or your permission to conduct a study of any kind will be permanently withdrawn." The ranger's tone had an unmistakable snap.

Rose glowered back. "I don't have the resources to hang around until the park decides the dead guy didn't die of typhoid."

The ranger frowned. "Typhoid?"

"I'm using a figurative example."

He stared at her. After a long moment he sighed and leaned forward, creating a sense of conspiracy. "Look, I appreciate you're caught in a tight place, however you cannot continue to put yourself in harm's way trying to help *the professionals.*"

Rose flushed.

Before she could respond, he continued, "Whatever you're researching has to do with local history, right?"

She nodded.

"The Riverside Library has a private collections room with publications on the region. Check it out. You might discover new information."

Rose didn't try to disguise her doubtful expression. She'd already done a truckload of research.

"Or, enjoy the facilities," he suggested, trying another direction. "Take a few days and indulge in a vacation. Experience the sights. Yellowstone is an amazing place."

Rose stuffed her hands down her pockets. She understood his reasons. She did. She also hated to wait and nobody enjoyed being told 'no'. Scuffing her foot in the gravel like a twelve year old she admitted defeat. And she despised that too.

"Yeah, okay."

The ranger gave her a stern face. "You better not be holding out on me."

She stared at him, eyes narrowed to unblinking slits. "If there's a logical reason for why you think I'm involved in any of this, give me the lowdown."

He smirked, "I got nothing."

"So, how'd the guy die?"

"I can't share information about an ongoing investigation."

She rolled her eyes.

"Do you want to add anything to your original statement?" He asked her as he hunched his shoulders forward and stretched his back.

She glanced over but no hint of humor showed on his face. "Yeah, you should consider the cause of death as unknown and let me get to work."

To her surprise, he chuckled.

They parted company in what she assumed could only be considered a truce.

Rose stole a final glance around as she pulled out of the paved lot. Though she saw no sign of anyone else she experienced a jolt of expectation as if she was about to shake something loose. She needed to up the ante. Determining a way to do exactly that without putting herself at risk was the problem.

She drove directly to town, chewing on her bottom lip. Progress had slowed. She was no closer to figuring out how events had transpired at the thermal pool. She reviewed the facts as she knew (guessed) them and tried to follow the logic. She likened it to watching blips on a radar screen, one thing reasonably led to the next. She reasoned that if the deceased had expired of natural causes then she would be the only person wandering the landscape looking for clues. She wasn't. Thus the appearance of her handsome admirer from town this morning pretty much clinched his involvement. The odds of his presence being unrelated to yesterday's events approached a point of statistical absurdity. She set those details on the back burner for the moment to consider who benefited from the death.

What purpose, if any, did the dead man's demise serve?

She sighed. She had no idea. This was grossly inefficient. Cops on television talked about opportunity but in this case virtually anyone who happened to wander past could've killed the guy. That narrowed things down. Not.

Moving on.

Next, she considered the issue of motive but again she didn't have a clue. No wonder law enforcement personnel acted so cranky.

Time ticked away. Frustrated by her lack of success, she changed her mind and instead of returning to the White Horse, she headed for the town library.

She'd planned to visit both that and the historical society during her stay in Riverside because she knew such places offered local insights about a region. She could consider just moving her research to another part of the park, if they were amenable. Since they were the ones balking at letting her start on her first choice, they could probably negotiate a new location without the usual advance planning. Besides, there must be hundreds of mine sites scattered inside Yellowstone's boundaries, the place was huge. Fortunately, she might be able to locate exactly the information she needed – thanks to Ranger Saxton's helpful suggestion.

An hour and a half later she stood at the end of the now-familiar boardwalk, surveying the same stretch of landscape again.

She visually charted a route up the open expanse, her finger marking an imaginary line from the direction the black-haired blue-eyed centerfold had traveled. If she drew a path to where she'd found the body, the hiding place of her handsome devil sat right in the middle.

She twisted her lips into an ironic smile. Bingo.

Time to act.

She shuffled her feet nervously. Her plan had seemed far more practical when she'd darted out of the library twenty minutes earlier.

Ranger Saxton deserved a high-five for making the suggestion. She'd struck paydirt in the local history section of the Riverside Library. A drawer of old maps contained unexpected treasure. The librarian allowed Rose to handle the delicate drawings as long as she wore a pair of cotton gloves and didn't remove anything from the special collections room.

Carefully spreading the antique charts on the scarred surface of the old oak table, she'd immediately identified numerous hardscrabble mine enterprises inside the current park environs. Most dated from the mid-nineteenth century. She'd studied the entire stack of hand-drawn documents but one in particular held her attention. Not only did the timeframe perfectly match her research but the mine resided in the rocky hills above the place she'd found the dead body. At first, she'd thought it was the same locale she'd already marked on her map but closer inspection showed it was not.

The faded script hand-written on the map identified the location as the Vigilante Mine. Seemed legit to her. She'd snuck a picture with her cell phone.

Now she returned to search the area. She hoped to locate the site and take a quick look. If it proved a good fit for her needs, she'd mark it off the list and move to the next one. She'd keep doing that until she had the requisite number of comparative sites for her study. By the time she completed her clandestine survey, if the moratorium on her permit was still in place, she'd seriously consider an alternative research site.

She climbed over the fence and set off. The landscape offered nothing new. She crossed the open area without incident and pushed toward the woods. Huffing by the time she reached the tree line, she discovered it was much denser up close.

Pine needles crushed under her boots gave up an intense fragrance. She skirted the low-hanging branches of trees and maintained her sense of direction by checking for landmarks until she could no longer catch a glimpse of the terrain.

At last, she set aside her reluctance and entered deeper into the forest. The elevation climbed. She stumbled over a faint path, little more than a rivulet of powdered soil. The line of tracks worn into the ground indicated someone besides deer had been traipsing along this trail. Even with her novice tracking skills Rose could recognize a sneaker imprint in the soft compost of a million decayed pine needles.

Gripped by exultation and swept away by satisfaction, she veered onto the track and pursued the shoe pattern. Fairly certain the path ran parallel to the tree line, she adjusted her direction in what she hoped was the correct trajectory to carry her back toward the infamous thermal pool.

Her heart started to hammer even before her mind registered the sound. She stopped and listened. Her ear had detected the thump of footsteps behind her. She floated off the trail without conscious thought and knelt in the deep shadows behind the trunk of an Engelmann spruce. The instinctive reaction to hide frightened her most of all. Flattened against the tree, she pressed her knees into the mulch, trying to disappear into the gloom.

A single thump sounded – a flash of movement between the trees. She tucked her head down and stopped breathing.

The man passed without hesitation, his footfalls a soft drumbeat of little impacts.

She darted a look by lifting her face and caught a glimpse of a tall figure in a ball cap. Seen in profile, his cheek was covered with the dark shadow of beard.

The stranger kept moving.

Her relief palpable, fear pounded through her body and her breath came shaky for a minute. She had no business impersonating a backwoods explorer. Although she wanted to get to work, Ranger Saxton's words echoed in her head. Was she putting herself at risk? Hikers filed through every national park. Perhaps she acted foolishly. Maybe she should leave this business to the professionals.

Rose kneeled, counting by fives until her pulse rate slowed. Minutes passed before she peered down the way the man had come. Nothing but silence. The path he'd followed curved back into the trees and climbed out of sight.

She needed to make a decision.

Her real goal, and the reason she'd traveled to Yellowstone, hovered beyond her reach until the people in charge learned what they wanted to know. Who knew how long it might take to discover the outcome of the suspicious death. Sneaking around looking at mine sites resulted in a no-win situation if she got caught. Gleaning enough data to support her theory while she waited for her permit to be re-established only proved profitable so long as she didn't get booted off the premises as a result.

But that wasn't even her primary concern, was it?

Fear of getting caught by Ranger Saxton hadn't driven her to hide among the trees.

Her current activities fell outside her realm of experience. If a killer ran loose around the woods, being smart meant scuttling her ass back to the car. Being stupid sent her onward.

Stupid won.

She left the meager shelter of the shadows and crept up the path. The sky lightened. A sharp turn brought her into a small clearing and she stopped short.

Fragments of words came in two different cadences. Conversation. The stranger wasn't far ahead and now he had a friend.

A slim chance existed that a back country hiking trail bordered the western edge of the park. Maybe the voices she'd overheard belonged to legitimate hikers exchanging civil greetings. The man she'd seen had worn a daypack.

She crept forward and saw the first pile of rocks. Not the typical tailing deposited by a large scale mining operation but a hand-built cairn of stones. The mound consisted of rocks piled up one piece at a time by industrious hands over months or years of ore harvesting.

In her experience the more plentiful the debris, the longer someone had worked there. In Nevada she sometimes used the scale of the rock piles as predictors to evaluate which site offered the greatest possibility to produce items like glass bottles, equipment, and personal objects. Mines that played out too quickly yielded little cultural information. She sought those glimpses of daily life in the litter, collecting and analyzing the remnants. Long gone occupants dropped lots of garbage. Short-term outfits seldom offered up enough artifacts to meet her needs so she looked for the sites where men had labored for extended periods of time.

The lure of tailings pulled her onward.

She edged another ten feet up the path. Three more visible stacks of stones attested to a sizeable hand-dug tunnel nearby.

She heard no voices now. The people she'd overheard had either stopped talking or moved out of earshot.

Sidling forward, she almost missed the mouth because the entrance was screened by young trees. Then something bizarre caught her attention. A pattern of rock, like an empty streambed, flowed from the interior. The array puzzled her experienced eye. The stones looked indigenous to the region, matching the geology of the area, but someone had troubled to lay them out in a position a bit too evenly spaced to be the natural result of erosion.

Why do that?

She leaned down to inspect the rock pavement.

No evident tracks.

Even if someone walked on them she doubted the passage of feet would be visible. A shiver of nervous energy tightened her back muscles.

Blood pressure increasing with every step, she approached the outlet. A pungent smell, sulphurous and acrid struck her nostrils. Her nerves jangled.

Cognizant of danger, she swallowed a mouthful of saliva and moved cautiously toward the dark oblong of the entrance. The noxious odor became denser. The path ended here.

She hesitated.

The opening seemed to exhale silence. Tension ratcheted up her spine. Her shoulders felt like wooden blocks. One more step brought her to the edge of darkness. An echo of noise rolled out as she stood poised to bolt, a ripple of laughter.

A jolt of adrenaline-laced fear zipped through Rose. The sound of a warm masculine voice, so at odds with the backdrop, caused her brain to fumble as she tried to align the two.

Without a doubt, the mine was in use.

Any time the public had access to historic mining sites, disaster resulted. She'd worked one summer trying to seal off dangerous shafts and pits. Even if this endeavor had approval, it should be in hiatus. Like hers.

Another murmur drifted up the tunnel.

Rose's scowl morphed into a shiver. She pivoted on one heel. A rock rolled underfoot. She flung out her arms and recovered her balance but a squeak of sound escaped her lips. Abandoning any effort at subterfuge, she leaped away with a clatter. She darted through the trees, ignored the path and plunged down the hill, almost falling twice before panicked instinct took complete control.

She ran.

Arms pumping, her shoulders muscles screeching with tension, she waited for a shout or the report of gunfire, the sharp impact of a bullet.

Nothing happened.

Halfway across the plain, Rose realized her head-long flight led directly to the thermal pool. She slowed, continuing to pick a route over the uneven ground. She dodged the silvery-green foliage where her admirer had hidden and aimed for the viewing platform.

For once she wished Ranger Saxton waited for her there, a disapproving expression stamped on his square face.

She clambered over the low rail at the boardwalk and spun to contemplate the hill. Her heart thumped hard under the palm she pressed to her chest. After a second she leaned over, braced her other hand on her thigh and tried to catch her breath, her gaze searching the landscape.

From where she stood the mine entrance was invisible but she sensed the watching eyes.

18 CHAPTER EIGHTEEN

A S USUAL, WINSLOW Deveraux arrived early but a crowd had already begun to collect. Folks looked forward to the socials hosted by the Ladies Auxiliary. He ducked out the rear cupola and descended the stairs, pausing to stretch on the bottom step. The sun had sunk behind the mountains but full dark had not yet fallen. A lone bulb lit the area, creating a dull yellow glow that crept out onto the lawn.

He inhaled a deep breath with appreciation. There was a crisp edge to the evening air. Twilight was the perfect time to smoke his solitary cigarette of the day, an indulgence for which he preferred privacy.

He swiveled and peered up the concrete steps but no one had followed him outside. He enjoyed smoking but the public unpopularity of his only remaining vice guaranteed there was never a lack of well-intentioned folks ready to offer him a lot of unsolicited advice.

Damned busybodies.

At the age of seventy-two, he didn't much care about the detrimental effects of cigarettes on his health.

He ran an appreciative palm along the painted metal stair rail. In his opinion, modern architectural details lacked the sturdiness of previous eras. The Ladies' Auxiliary had formed during the first Great War. A mother and daughter pair, spurred by the unknown fate of a young soldier had galvanized into action and created the chapter to support the town's servicemen. His memory blanked as he failed to recall their surname. Didn't matter, he decided, the womenfolk had established an enduring tradition of cheerful letters and packages of baked goods mailed to remote outposts and exotic locations. Hell, prior to his own enlistment his mother had already been involved.

He tapped a smoke out of the rumpled pack and returned the remainder to his shirt. Extracting a weathered book of matches from his rear pants pocket, he rocked up on his toes and rolled down on his heels, letting the nicotine anticipation build. His regular two-mile morning run took a shade longer than it had five years ago but the twinge of guilt he experienced about the cigarettes didn't sway his intent.

He planted the butt between his lips and struck the match. The odor of sulfur from the flare coated the inside of his nose as he sucked air through the paper tube. He savored the sweet pungent plume of tobacco. The slow exhalation of smoke and the rush of chemicals carried a sense of homecoming unchanged since his youth.

Winslow descended the last step and turned to eye the blocks forming the foundation. Like gigantic bricks, the stones decreased in scale as the rows grew in height. He felt connected to the structure. After his enlistment, he'd enjoyed the packages and letters. Even after his mom died they had never stopped coming and that simple kind act established a thin lifeline to the town he'd left behind.

He suddenly recalled that Lark was the surname of the women who began the whole business. Now he remembered how the story went. Private Lark came home at the end of the war. Liberated from a prisoner-of-war camp, his return proved a bittersweet surprise. Like too many others, he quavered from shellshock and suffered from the same ill health of a bitter old drunk. Eventually he convalesced, recovered as much as men do from such things, and became a respected town leader.

The original Ladies Auxiliary had been housed in the fire house. In an ironic twist, the place burned to the ground in 1969. A coffee pot left plugged in after a community event was blamed as the inciting incident. By then Winslow had been long gone but the story had been dutifully related in letters. Antiquated wires sparked a conflagration and the wooden structure flamed up before the volunteer department mustered.

He'd sent a donation to help fund the recovery effort.

He inhaled and blew out a puff of smoke. The place had been rebuilt in 1970 but folks continued to refer to the building as *new*. Rumors about the source of the fire circulated until the arson investigator pointed an official finger at the forty-cup coffee urn. Unable to determine who forgot to unplug the device – and in the tradition of small towns everywhere – blame bandied about for decades.

Winslow considered introducing the subject tonight just to see who bit.

He figured the current structure, rebuilt with local volcanic stone, would prove much harder to burn down even if someone took the notion to leave an appliance plugged in. The designers had probably kept such in mind when they finalized the plans.

The collection of photographs lost in the inferno measured the real tragedy of the fire. The snapshots featured local soldiers extending back in time before WWI. Many families in the oldest pictures had no living descendants. The disaster pained the town's collective history. In his youth, Winslow had admired the men with boyish faces and old-fashioned uniforms and experienced their loss in a personal way.

Matches returned to his pocket, he drew on the cigarette.

Lucy Abbot drifted into his consciousness. He exhaled a cloud, trying to decide whether or not he should avoid the persistent woman tonight. She'd gone out of her way to greet him almost as soon as he'd stepped through the door. Not a good sign.

Nelsen had observed, an amused curve on his lips, that she'd been waiting for someone's arrival.

Winslow frowned.

Not to put too fine a point on things, but now that he ruminated, Lucy had also greeted him in the cereal aisle last week. He'd said hello and stopped to chat. Some might construe that as an indication of interest. He hadn't. At least, not until Nelsen clucked his tongue and shook his head. With a flash of panic Winslow recalled Lucy mentioning her widowed status.

He was a marked man.

Delmar was in desperate need of a wife. Perhaps Winslow could deflect interest in his direction.

Bending down to grind the cigarette butt into the concrete walk, he noticed someone leaning against a tree trunk in the shadows toward the back of the lot. Winslow frowned. At the close of summer, the Ladies' Auxiliary sponsored an outdoor potluck on the lawn under those trees. Winslow had attended many such parties over the years and no one ever slept beneath the aspens. Somehow, the sight was disquieting.

The cigarette began to stink. The heat of the cherry burned into the filter and became uncomfortable. He dropped it and stamped on the smoldering stub, retrieving it with a ginger grip to slip the flattened remnant between the plastic sleeve and the paper wrap of the cigarette package.

His gaze danced to the still form under the tree. No need to raise a ruckus if the fellow was just tired. He'd better take a closer look-see.

Winslow stepped on the grass and hopped to the left so light from the bulb washed across the lawn before him. Only a few steps farther and even in the dim illumination he knew the futility of checking for a pulse. Necks didn't bend that way.

He edged forward until he saw the face.

A stranger.

Unsurprising really. Riverside produced few corpses. Natural causes and vehicular incidents claimed their quota but aside from the interesting story of the late Widow Kavanaugh and her three husbands, things stayed quiet.

He'd found a corpse.

After a brief pause to look around, he took another step. A fellow didn't sit down under a tree and experience a spontaneous break in his neck. The sole sign of injury was a thin trickle of dried blood marking the hairline right above the forehead.

Winslow trotted back across the yard. He climbed the steps, his mind already working out what to say when he called the police.

He recognized the dispatcher's voice as soon as he answered the line. He'd known Greg Flannery his entire life. He explained what he'd found behind the building, keeping his tone even and speaking low and slow.

"Well now, that'll put a real damper on the Ladies' hard work tonight," Greg replied.

Winslow's mouth turned down at the corners. The old handset telephone rested on the corner of the wooden desk and he fingered the stacks of papers atop the scarred surface as he pressed the receiver to his ear. He avoided unwanted attention by refusing to meet anyone's eyes.

"Is anyone else aware of the situation?" the dispatcher asked.

Winslow swiftly scanned the busy crowd of chatty towns-folk. He recognized each face. "No. Well, I suppose whoever did him in knows. Everyone here is just enjoying themselves."

"Are you sure he's deceased?"

"Near as I can tell, but I didn't walk up and touch him. I don't believe anyone could bend their neck like that, not even those Chinese acrobats who performed in West Yellowstone a few years ago."

Both men fell silent.

"I recall that was some prime entertainment," Greg said.

Winslow agreed.

"Tell me the details again. I need to write it down on the report form. Sheriff Groates is busy with a problem right now so I'll call a deputy for this DB."

"What's that mean?" Winslow's query was soft.

"Dead body."

The old phone receiver grew heavy in Winslow's hand. "You don't say." He listened to papers rustle and heard the clank of a displaced coffee mug.

Tim grunted agreement. "Okay, I'm ready, go ahead and tell me again."

Winslow repeated the story.

He finished speaking and disconnected, taking a moment to prepare himself to keep this secret as long as was practical.

When he turned around, Lucy Abbot stood six feet away, a feral smile curving her coral lips.

19   CHAPTER NINETEEN

ROSE PARKED IN front of the inn. The dash clock showed the afternoon *hors d'oeuvres* period had passed. She prayed for leftovers and a big fat glass of wine to settle her nerves. Reminded that the Victorians believed alcohol a proper treatment for shock, she was jittery enough to qualify for dosing.

The moment she plowed through the front door, Remy sprang to his feet.

Had the twerp been lurking at the bottom of the stairs? She silently cursed but he pounced before she could duck behind the coat rack. She so did not need this.

"I was hoping to see you and here you are." His wide smile displayed dimples and a chipped front tooth.

Well, that's not creepy at all.

His long survey made her skin feel tight, like she'd been sunburned. The knapsack slid off her shoulder. She caught and slung it down to rest at her feet, the practiced movement buying her a few seconds of time to reconnoiter. She cast about for other guests in the empty space and struck out.

"Great," she muttered under her breath. "What's up, Remy?"

He ignored her lack of enthusiasm.

Remy was one of those guys who needed no more encouragement than an occasional grunt of feigned interest. She sidled past him and approached the table where Lily Ingram set out snacks for her guests.

Bless her generous hostess for overstocking the nibbles. She made a mental note to add the owners of the White Horse Inn to her Christmas card list. They deserved a gilt-edged seasonal greeting with a matching fancy envelope.

She attacked the plate of appetizers with gusto, almost moaning with delight when the tiny puff pastries filled with warm squishy cheese and herbs practically melted in her mouth. She consumed half a dozen as Remy stalked her around the parlor.

He talked nonstop, jerking after her, tall and so narrow he seemed insect-like. When he paused to inspect the offerings, Rose took advantage of the pause and darted to the opposite side. She grazed while completing three full circuits, finishing the pastry puffs and clearing the dessert platter of rolled-up cookies.

She filled a glass with the contents of an open wine bottle and swigged down a mouthful of Gewürztraminer. The alcohol hit her stomach and spread warmth through her body. Yep, those Victorians knew what they were talking about.

Remy stared at her. "There's a social event tonight, a dance, you wanna go with me?"

Caught unprepared by the invitation, Rose stonewalled. Mellowed by an infusion of carbohydrates and alcohol, she splashed more wine in her glass and took another swallow. Curious about Remy's fledgling stalker traits, she wondered if he'd been watching for her return. She drained the goblet, issued a vacuous smile, kept ahold of the half-empty bottle and surged forward.

"I'm just on my way upstairs, Remy. I've mucked about in the dust all afternoon and need to clean up. I'll talk to you later, okay?"

He moved aside but followed her up the stairs.

At least he paused at the top of the staircase and didn't follow her down the hallway.

"This is supposed to be quite the shindig," he called out as she unlocked her door.

Rose considered turning him down flat. "I gotta clean up and relax for a few." On impulse, she peeked at Remy.

His woebegone face got to her. So he creeped her out, in a praying mantis sort of way, but she had no plans to sleep with the guy anyhow. Maybe she'd earn St. Peter points for charity to the needy.

"Yeah, okay. Meet me downstairs in forty-five minutes."

The instant the words left her mouth she realized her mistake. Now he'd think she'd just been playing hard to get. She escaped inside, the bottle raised to her lips.

A shower improved her mood. Undecided between the comfort of a dress or jeans, she elected for the-more-clothes-the-better option. She'd bet a dollar Remy was a toucher. Multiple layers could be employed to deter the most persistent of feelers, at least she banked on that strategy for the evening.

Groomed, she re-entered the bedroom with a twenty minute reprieve and began to organize her work materials. She affixed a map of Yellowstone to the wall behind the door with painter's tape. The blue strips stood in sharp contrast to the honey-toned walls. The western side showed numerous notations she'd already made. Now she grabbed a pen and noted the location of the Vigilante Mine.

Her project was ambitious but since the majority of potential sites would prove useless, she'd marked every one she'd thought sounded promising. Amidst a futile search for sticky notes, she unpacked the coyote skeleton and admired it for a moment. Eventually she found a stash of office supplies in the box with the sheep. She eyed the map as she tore the wrapper from a cube of the multicolored squares.

Usually her research protocol involved locating mines, selecting promising locations, sampling the environs, and then conducting field survey for data collection. In this case, and because she had limited access, she'd had to sort based on guesswork. She located the thermal pool and used a violet highlighter to connect the site to the approximate location of the Vigilante Mine. She stepped back to assess her work.

She'd have to alter her approach. Her normal methodology meant accessing a network of databases to check catalogued soil and rock information. That proved impossible and not just because Riverside presented connectivity challenges. Her efforts to find Yellowstone records produced spotty and incomplete results. Too much investigation accumulated a mountain of documentation from a century of studies. Doing her own field inspections would probably prove more efficient. Without the valuable ability to cross-reference locales with topographic features, she was reduced to undertaking a visible inspection of each and every site. Lucky she suddenly had extra time in her schedule, right?

Stupid park service rules.

The lack of wifi in the White Horse Inn disappointed her. She desperately needed a high-speed link. Laptop positioned on the table in the turret, she logged on through her cell phone. Three bars on the signal indicator offered a midrange hope of success.

The connection failed.

She tried again, studying the row of business fronts across the street while the computer attempted to establish a link. No luck. During the minutes she was distracted by the view it cycled twice more without success. After three efforts she abandoned the process altogether.

Like a prisoner waiting to go before the judge, she checked her travel clock and discovered time was up. With a sigh, she headed back downstairs.

20 CHAPTER TWENTY

SAVIO HAD NO finesse for spying. The sort of nonsense found in B-movies and dime-store novels was inefficient and ineffective for gathering intel. In his mind, his colleagues sneered with contempt at the spectacle of him sitting on a low bench in front of the ice cream parlor with a newspaper spread over his lap. Their jeers of derision echoed in the back of his head, not unlike the reverberation of the bombs that rousted him from sleep that morning. He pushed that aside for the moment.

In addition to feeling stupid, not one headline he'd read during the previous twenty minutes had passed into memory. He struggled to concentrate but *she* clouded his judgment.

Just then she flitted into view and his gaze seized on the movement. The woman exposed voyeuristic tendencies he didn't know he owned. Every time he laid eyes on her another modicum of restraint evaporated. He brooded over his situation. A scenario played out in his imagination, on where he strode across the street and wrapped his arms around her, bending down to kiss her full lips. Since he was fantasizing, he went ahead and slid his hands down to cup the perfect globes of her ass. At least then, when the senorita knocked him flat on his back, he'd have satisfied some measure of his curiosity.

The experience might be worth the risk.

Two firm shakes of his head did little to restore his concentration. Her discovery of the site was unfortunate. She must know any human activity or presence at the old mine was unauthorized, a fact supported by her headlong flight down the rough terrain. She'd moved like a startled deer bounding over the rocky hillside. But, although she'd fled, it appeared she hadn't called the authorities. Her corresponding silence puzzled him. He needed to determine her degree of involvement. Already curious, now that she'd shown up at the door of the mine he felt she must be confronted.

But he feared that wasn't the primary reason for his intense interest. He frowned down at the printed lines of type. She intrigued him, incited his curiosity. Already, she had proven a titillating infatuation.

He shifted on the hard bench and shut down that thought. Mackenzie hadn't realized there had been an intruder. Lucky for all concerned.

Savio folded the *Bozeman Daily Chronicle* and stood up. Twilight had fallen, dimming the light enough that his ruse was likely to draw undue attention. One foot poised to step toward the street, he saw the stained glass door of the inn swing open and lurched to a stop.

The *senorita* appeared on the stoop.

He clamped the paper under his arm and shifted sideways behind the questionable shelter of a wood column. Exposed, caught like a rank amateur. He shook his head as more imagined howls of laughter from his colleagues elbowed around inside his skull.

She bounced down the steps and his breath hitched with every tread.

Remy trailed in her wake and resentment ripped through Savio. His aggression level peaked at the sight of this rival in the company of the dark-haired woman. The reaction was potent enough to knock him back a step but Savio refused to examine this visceral response. Instead, he stared at the girl.

She set off down the sidewalk with her hands tucked into her front pockets. Her elbows poked out in rigid points.

Savio's lips curled up in a satisfied smirk, his combativeness draining away. Her awkward posture stymied Remy's every attempt to sidle in close. Even so, he vacillated about as the pair disappeared up the street. Following them seemed like the best idea but he resisted, unwilling to cede more ground to what was swiftly developing into a full-blown obsession. He was still standing there when the couple returned a short time later.

No, he thought, *definitely not a couple.* He retreated into the deeper shadow of a doorway.

The woman forged up the walk to Vic's restaurant, on a mission to get inside. Her companion followed. The bastard blocked his line of sight, raising Savio's ire because he missed watching the girl's ass bounce up the steps. The mismatched duo slid into a booth along the front exposure of windows.

Convenient.

A swift visit to the second floor of the old boarding house sprang into possibility. He might not have another opportunity to duck in and search both rooms. The idea enticed Savio across the street.

In less than a minute he'd circled the building and pushed open the back door. Inside, a pair of elderly ladies perched in front of the parlor fireplace, knitting needles in hand. They paid no attention when he crossed the common area and mounted the staircase. Adrenalin coursed through his system. He felt sharp-edged, like a finely honed knife blade.

Upstairs he found picking the lock on her door tantamount to foreplay. With an audible click the mechanism released and he entered.

The disarray stole his breath. The senorita was industrious. Stacks of paper spread across every flat surface. A large map covered an expanse of wall, with sticky notes tacked in multiple places. But the bones first claimed his interest. Skeletons piled up in tidy mounds on antique tables, a contradictory and disconcerting sight.

Savio strolled to the windows and peeked out. The man and woman still sat at the table in the diner. He tilted his wrist and checked the time. He calculated an estimate and set the alarm. Then he began to survey.

The contents did not reflect the typical tourist.

Baffled by the skeletal material, he poked at a pile of bones, recognizing only that the teeth belonged to some species of small carnivore. A fast scan of titles from the books scattered on the rug indicated most offered environmental and historical treatises about the region, though several slim volumes referred to early ore mining practices. He selected one at random and discovered the heavy monograph was a guide for establishing the production dates of glass bottles.

This stuff, the *senorita*, all of it and her, fascinated him.

Turning to the wall, he assessed the notations on the map but made little sense of the marks. A quick peek out the window showed them still at the table. He dragged his attention back to her belongings. He flipped up piles of research, the content fanning the flames of his infatuation. He found zero evidence of drug trade. This suggested her involvement was secondary.

Relief flooded him, a tingle that morphed into something different when his casual inventory of her personal items revealed a penchant for matching lingerie. The sight of pink satin undergarments sent Savio out the door without remembering to check the security eye first.

Lucky for him no one waited in the hall.

He relocked the heavy mortise mechanism with noticeably less nimble fingers and turned to approach the man's room. The latch twisted easily. Probably the cheapest accommodations in the inn and rented the most often.

The woman's living space reflected a unique personality. Just in a brief time gave him a sense of complex dynamic individuality. By contrast, in here he perceived a slack identity, a mind with few personal interests. Two shirts hung on hooks above a compact chest of drawers. A mound of dirty clothes lay piled in one corner. An empty duffel bag and a backpack crumpled into another. An assortment of magazines littered the foot of the bed. A quick sift showed the publications consisted of typical male-oriented fodder of automotive, sports and music content. No surprise there. He expected nothing less from one of Mackenzie's buddies.

His search produced little of interest until he flipped over a piece of paper on the bedside table. The page was torn from a small notepad, the logo of the White Horse Inn emblazoned along the top. He'd seen the same thing in his own nightstand.

The senorita had scribbled notes on hers, lines of mysterious references to publications he could scarcely decipher. Sheets from the notepad had been stuck between the pages of her books, mixed in with a plethora of business cards, most of them bearing the name of Rose Brashear.

Standing beside the bed, Savio read the single word that had been written dozens of times over the surface of the note paper. The repetition indicated this information was important to the author. The characters ran in every direction, in small script, large block letters, and illegible scrawls. The word "rose" had been penned so many times it smacked of some disturbed interest.

Savio's neck prickled. He replaced the paper, disliking the connection. He hadn't confirmed the girl's identity but Remy's creepy tribute suggested a link.

The timer beeped.

He took one last looked around. Like the senorita, no evidence indicated Remy participated in drug trade except Savio knew the man was acquainted with Mackenzie.

Back out in the hallway he unlocked and entered his own room. A quick search showed his meager personal possessions arranged in a neat row on the shelf in the closet where he'd left them. He unbolted the window casement and raised it a few inches. Escape routes a pro forma requirement in his line of work, he could be up and outside on the roof before the interior door hit the wall.

Despite the early hour, he pulled off his boots and stretched out on the bed. Setting his phone alarm for just before midnight, he shut his eyes and indulged in a little more fantasizing.

CHAPTER TWENTY-ONE

ROSE TRIED TO recall the breathing exercises her mother taught her clients to reduce stress. A lousy fifteen minutes of Remy's attention made her previous worst date a real winner. The quarter hour mark inched past at a glacial pace and she debated about bailing without an excuse. Everything in life being relative, the next altruistic impulse she experienced would serve to remind her of this evening.

He'd been waiting in the foyer when she descended the stairs. He hit her radar as insincere and that served to reinforce her regret. She knew the signs of a man on the prowl. As the solitary unattached female in residence, she won the attention award. Lucky her.

Maria had been right. She should have worn a wedding band. She'd have to call her best friend after the evening ended and allow her to say, 'I told you so.' After several years of cock-tail waitressing, Maria swore well-placed jewelry offered the most effective passive defensive gesture against overly friendly guys.

"And if they ignore the ring, then you know they're a complete schmuck," her friend had told her.

But Rose hadn't listened.

Sucking up her nerve, she took the offensive approach and barreled past Remy. She bustled out the door and hopped down the steps to the sidewalk, maneuvering to keep him at a distance.

Twilight settled over the street, casting deep shadows. In the company of another companion she might have found the evening downright beautiful. A few bright stars flickered over-head. The town was picturesque and the cool air comfortable against her flushed cheeks. Rose tried to relax and enjoy the walk but the third time she had to sidestep off the curb to avoid the grasp of Remy's hand at her waist, she lost patience.

"Look Remy, I don't know you. Please stop trying to touch me." She didn't enjoy being fondled by a stranger. Her helpful memory chose that instant to supply an image of the guy she'd ogled outside Vic's restaurant.

Remy jerked his head back as though she'd slapped him. "Sorry."

They continued for longer than a minute in complete si-lence. Rose strangled off a sigh. His voice had sounded sullen. She opened her mouth to try and lighten the atmosphere when he stopped walking. He stared at their destination, a building made of giant stone blocks that squatted behind a row of trees.

"Aw hell, everybody's older than dirt."

She saw he was right.

Uh-oh.

Old people enjoyed slow dancing. Ballroom moves required getting up close and personal with her date. Not happening. She made a sudden change of plan. A cup of coffee and a slice of pie appeared a whole lot more appetizing than Remy's arms and a dance floor.

"Appreciate you offering a waltz and all, but I'm afraid I'm going to bail on your small town social program and go to Vic's for pie and coffee." She rotated one hundred eighty degrees on the sidewalk. "You in?"

"I'm with you," Remy said and faced the same direction.

The return walk was much less fraught with tension.

Rose marched up the stairs and into the restaurant, completed a visual sweep of the interior and found Vic's pretty much deserted. Disappointed she couldn't slide in beside her buddy the sheriff or any of her new ranger friends, she dropped into the first booth by the window.

Remy followed her.

For a second she thought he'd try to squeeze onto the seat beside her but she didn't leave room for an invitation. As soon as the waiter appeared she ordered and waited while Remy made his selection.

Still on the offensive she directed conversation away from herself. "So why are you in Montana?"

She gave the coffee an experimental sip, plucked two creamers out of the bowl and doctored the brew.

He shrugged. "I passed through a couple years ago on the way to Cody. I had a job lined up in Wyoming but the radiator in my car busted just before the last exit. I rattled into town and discovered I couldn't get it fixed till Monday. When I called and told the foreman I'd got delayed, he said there was no reason to come in."

"Rough." Rose could commiserate. She'd had her share of car trouble.

He swallowed and his Adam's apple bobbed in his long neck. "I spent a few days here while the shop did the repairs. Riverside's a cool place. The White Horse Inn rocks." He slurped up coffee. "Things turned out okay. I got a job in Billings and been working steady ever since. I save up my vacation days and come back every summer."

At least he had gainful employment going for him, she thought. "What kind of work you do?"

"I'm union for a medical supply company that stocks home equipment, a big national corporation with lots of branches. Mostly, I sort shipments and repackage materials into smaller quantities for redistribution to outlets and customers. It's a pretty sweet job. It feels good knowing that what I do helps people."

A flicker of unexpected respect fluttered through Rose. She couldn't remember the last time she met someone who admitted they enjoyed their basic service-oriented employment. She admired that.

Then Remy stroked his boot up her leg and ruined the moment.

She pulled up her feet and sat cross-legged, repositioning herself on the maroon vinyl upholstery. Out of reach of roaming appendages, she glanced behind the counter and the cook she'd talked to the previous night caught her gaze. He waved at her, then pointed at Remy and screwed his mouth into a disapproving shape before offering a thumbs-down motion.

She bit the inside of her cheek.

Oblivious to her body language, Remy missed the exchange. He went on talking about his classic car. She listened, letting his voice drone on as the server brought their order. Halfway through her dessert, her attention was drawn to the clanking bell. Pouring sugar over her too-tart berry pie, she looked up and almost dropped the dispenser. Tension tightened her shoulders.

She'd been toying with a half-baked plan of claiming the next unattached male who passed through the door when the whole 'boyfriend' idea screeched to a halt. The man she'd seen in the forest today had just entered the diner. He wore the same ball cap pulled low over his forehead and sported a full beard. Her central nervous system flooded with a jolt of fear-induced adrenalin. The response baffled her because when she thought about the fact she'd almost stumbled into a hiker on a path outside the Vigilante Mine, the event shouldn't be frightening.

The guy paused in the glare of the light, his profile on display and her thoughts stalled. The newcomer paid no attention to her. He walked straight to the counter, sat down, and ordered the special.

Rose tuned out the rest of Remy's conversation. Her mind swam with different scenarios. Unused and abandoned mine shafts had a long history of alternate usage. The one she'd seen today was a hand-dug hardscrabble enterprise. The remote site offered no practical access. In such an environment, the only natural explanation led to something secretive, clandestine.

Whatever.

In an attempt to ignore her curiosity, Rose refused to care. The activity at the mine forged one more link in the chain that locked down her research study. Nothing else mattered right now.

Finally realizing she wasn't paying attention, Remy asked if she wanted to go. She offered a half-hearted apology, pleaded fatigue, and stood to leave. He paid the bill while she hovered near the exit.

The bearded man surveyed them with casual, desultory interest.

Rose declined Remy's offer of a stroll and crossed the lawn to the Inn. Inside the parlor she turned down his suggestion to cozy up in a chair in front of the fireplace.

"I'm exhausted. If you'll excuse me, Remy, I need to get some rest."

"Maybe later?"

Already started up the stairs, Rose barely restrained her impulse to roll her eyes. Next he would insist on showing her the etchings in his room. She pretended she hadn't heard his question and fled up to the second floor. This time he had the good sense not to follow.

CHAPTER TWENTY-TWO

HARLAN WALKED INTO the station, his mind focused on pouring himself a cup of the vile coffee every new shift brewed. Mug in hand, he paused to ask the dispatcher for an update but just then the telephone rang and the man behind the counter held up a finger.

Harlan thumbed through the pile of messages while he waited.

The dispatcher's attentiveness caught his attention. "I'll call the Coroner's people and tell them to send out the ambulatory unit." His speech was a clipped static cadence.

Harlan froze. What had happened now? He caught the man's eye and frowned.

"There's a body behind the Ladies Auxiliary," he whispered.

As Harlan listened to the summary of details, he thought about the context of recent events. People died every day. There was no reason to think this death wasn't the result of simple natural causes. Except for the fact the DB was propped against a tree behind the L.A.

The dispatcher hung up.

Harlan asked, "Did the caller mention an obvious cause of death?"

"Winslow said he didn't want to get too close but he thought the man's neck was broken."

Harlan scrubbed a hand across his chin, heard the rasp of beard growth, and exhaled a sigh. That pretty much ruled out normal expiration. Another corpse found in a weird location suggested a killing spree even if the first one happened miles from here.

"Folks are going to be concerned."

Murder generated public outrage. Fueled by anger and irrational fears, gossip created more trouble on top of that. The Township of Riverside boasted a populace comfortable with firearms. The last thing Harlan needed was an angry mob ready to form a vigilante posse.

No way to keep this quiet.

Harlan barked out a series of commands as he formulated a plan. "Send Deputy Williams to the scene." He moved toward the rear of the station and called over his shoulder. "Did you get a preliminary identification?"

"Winslow didn't recognize the guy."

Harlan peered into his office. He needed the crime scene kit. "Go ahead and call the coroner."

The old-fashioned rolodex rattled as the wheel spun.

He snatched up the nylon bag with his field camera and yanked open the cupboard. "Which one of these has the trace kit?"

"Lower shelf."

He grabbed the tackle box off the bottom and slammed the cabinet door. Unsatisfied by the gesture, he kicked a chair on his way out.

As a rookie he'd learned investigation basically meant information gathering. Interviews, scene examinations, photographs and video, even sketches logged in minute details that might make or break a case. Each item and person of interest was mined. The presence of death both intensified the work and increased the risk of error. By now a chain of events was being established by Deputy Williams.

He was out the door and parked in the loading zone less than three minutes later.

People milled about on the front steps. Based on the laughter and the smiling faces, those present appeared unaware of the drama unfolding behind the building.

He pulled out the tackle box and slammed the heavy door on his truck. Driving his personal vehicle removed the stigma associated with a cop car parked out front. He patted his shirt pocket with one hand as if he'd forgotten something, using the delay to let some partygoers pass by. Then he headed around back.

Winslow descended the steps just as Harlan rounded the corner. He jerked his head and Harlan swung his gaze in that direction until he reached the body. Deep twilight disguised the form. In full dark the dead man might have gone unnoticed until the next day, perhaps longer.

Deputy Williams approached.

Harlan's radio crackled.

A voice squawked over the speaker. "The van's en route but the coroner is out the far side of the county. Hold on –" Garbled conversation rumbled in his ear while he waited for Greg to return.

The dispatcher continued, "Deputy Chan says he'll canvas town unless you need him."

Harlan answered an affirmative and squelched the radio.

Winslow came to stand beside him.

Silence draped over the pair for a moment.

"This is more dead bodies than we've had since Irene Kavanaugh decided she'd rather be a widow and her brothers-in-law tried to stop her."

Harlan nodded, his lips set in a tight grim line. He asked Winslow to step aside and went to work.

Photographs were taken and the grassy lawn was combed for any piece of potential evidence. Their task produced scant results. Collection bags were inventoried and readied for transport to the office. Most of the material would probably prove extraneous debris, but every investigator knew that trash sometimes equaled paydirt.

The news broke and brought spectators outside. The dance went quiet and the crowd dwindled.

An hour passed. Then another.

Harlan's shoulders drooped as the night wore on.

The coroner arrived two minutes before ten o'clock, having driven sixty miles across Gallatin County from the site of a fatal car crash. The man put aside his obvious fatigue to examine their scene. The cursory legality of filling out paperwork felt anticlimactic after the tense wait.

Once the coroner signed the release, they prepared for the removal. Technicians wrapped the deceased in clean linen. The sheet preserved trace evidence and reduced the chance of cross-contamination or the introduction of foreign materials. Next they placed the bundle in a bag and strapped the form to a gurney. They wheeled it to the open doors of the van, pushed the cart inside and transferred their burden to the lower shelf. They collapsed the stretcher and stored the conveyance underneath.

Fatigue weighed heavy as Harlan watched the transport vehicle depart. The dead man carried no wallet so there went the simplest means of identification.

The final stragglers left.

Deputy Williams stifled a yawn.

"I've finished most of my preliminary report. You want me to leave it on your desk tonight?"

Harlan stooped to pick up the kit.

"No, morning is fine. Get some rest before you submit for the record. We'll scan the fingerprint cards into the system and hope for a match."

The deputy slipped the camera inside the nylon bag. "Did you place the man? I don't think I've seen him around town."

Harlan tried to imagine the slack features animated with life. He shook his head. "He's a stranger to me. Might be a visiting relative though. We'll know soon enough. The phone'll ring when someone realizes he didn't come home."

CHAPTER TWENTY-THREE

SAVIO SUPPRESSED THE twinge of common sense that suggested his next act bordered on foolishness. He slipped out the window and darted a look into Remy's space. The man sprawled on the mattress, asleep beside a pile of magazines. Flushed with anticipation, Savio crept toward the woman's room. He took a cautious step in front of a pane of curved glass and jerked to a stop.

The casement sat pushed all the way up.

Every window reflected opaque blackness. Even the neon aqua glow of the travel clock was absent.

Hands wrapped across the sill, he leveraged his weight on his palms, bent down and listened.

Not a stir of air.

He leaned inside and sniffed but scented nothing. Instinct howled and he froze. A moment later he registered the tiny click of a round being chambered.

No one ever got the drop on him.

"Why are you stalking me?"

The question surprised him less than the feminine voice. The soft tones were *hers*. Relief rushed through him in a wave.

"You are not dead." He winced at the bald statement. "I feared the worst."

Her tone was dry. "How comforting."

Savio stood motionless. He picked out a few details in the darkness and pinpointed her general vicinity but little else. "My apologies, it was a thoughtless comment."

Light pierced the night, casting the room into sharp relief.

The move was a clever calculation, blinding him until his dilated pupils shrank to an appropriate size. Once they did, he saw the woman sitting on the floor, her back to the bed and a table lamp at her side. An antique settee sat shoved against the wall next to the entry. She wore snug jeans and a tight tank, a flannel shirt hanging low off one shoulder. Her hair was clipped high on the back of her head. Flowered socks adorned her feet.

The Luger P08 in her hand aimed dead center on his sternum. The bluing on the distinctive steel barrel, the color of India ink, gleamed in the light.

She appeared as calm as he. "You may as well climb the rest of the way inside."

Admiration filled him. "Who *are* you?"

Hers came flat. "I'll ask you the same."

Savio displayed his expensive white teeth. His father had insisted on orthodontic treatment when he yet harbored the fantasy his son would enter the political arena. "I am most definitely an admirer."

She watched him through serious dark eyes, the gun held in a casual grip. "Climb in before someone gives thought to why your ass is hanging outdoors."

Her wrist secured against her knee, she looked quite comfortable with the sidearm.

Laughter threading his tone, he asked, "Are you going to shoot me?"

"Maybe later. Right now I'd rather talk." She continued to aim at him as he glided through the window. She indicated he take a seat in the alcove of the turret.

He obeyed, selecting the upholstered chair farthest away. No sense in making her nervous.

She tilted the lampshade so light pooled in a circle on the rug.

They stared at each other.

Savio studied her face, noted the absence of earrings, then the interesting lack of jewelry of any kind. Up close her complexion was smooth and flawless. Her dark eyes stunned him, the color deep as bittersweet chocolate, rich and warm as she returned his regard. Older than his estimate, she was still years his junior. At least he wasn't lusting after a co-ed, a realization which brought him a modicum of relief.

"You must cease interfering," he told her.

Eyes narrowed, she angled her chin toward him. "Did you kill that man?"

Savio's heart jumped in his chest. He debated whether or not to ask which guy she meant but instead he chose to shake his head.

Resting her shoulders against the mattress, she accepted his negative response with a blank face.

He doubted she believed him. That it mattered brought a jolt of surprise. His words soft and curious, he addressed the obvious. "Tell me why you have a gun."

She canted her head to the side opposite his, her lips softening. "It's a precaution when I'm in the field." She contemplated him with an odd half-smile. "Do you want to hear a secret?"

He nodded. He wanted to know all her secrets.

"You're the only person I've held at gunpoint."

"I am flattered." His smile was coy. "There, now we have shared a first together and are friends."

Her expression was eloquent.

Urging her to set the pistol aside as if he could encourage her actions through mental strength alone, he sought to keep her talking. "I can tell you my business will soon be concluded."

She stretched her fingers but didn't put the Luger down. "Are you some sort of cop?"

It was an astute question. He shook his head again. "I do not employ with any law enforcement agency."

"Lone wolf, eh?"

Lips curling in an appreciate smirk, he responded to her smile with a tsking sound.

Her gaze settled on his mouth for a brief moment. With an elegant gesture he swirled a finger at the piece she held. "You have a very fine gun. It looks to be an antique."

She nodded, rotated the handgun to display the sleek design. "My granddad's. He picked it up in the thirties."

He whistled in appreciation.

"So who do you work for?"

The question caught him unprepared and he experienced another of the inexplicable urges to respond. The sensation shocked him to his hardened core.

She wafted a hand. "I figure if you only had personal interests at stake you could have done away with me on several occasions."

He studied her smooth features, lifting one eyebrow just enough to indicate a query.

"How about yesterday when you ducked behind the trees at the thermal pool? That was an opportune moment." The antique gun remained steady.

Savio experienced a shiver of discomfort. Astute fell short of the mark. He'd questioned why she hadn't seen him, when in fact, she had covered her reaction and continued to prance around for another ten minutes. A spark of anger erupted in his chest at her foolish behavior. Clearly, he had underestimated this dainty woman.

He took the defensive. "Who is *your* employer?"

To his surprise she waved her hands around wildly, the barrel aiming in random trajectories.

"I work for Riverbend University. And you," she pointed the Luger at him like she was jabbing the air with a finger, "are keeping me from conducting my research." She dropped her hand and glared at him.

Her frustration was evident. Chest heaving, an action which he much appreciated, for one instant he thought she might throw the firearm at him.

"You are a researcher?" Had she known the dead man after all?

Her dark head inclined in agreement. "After I found the guy in the water, the park shut down every research study in the area." She tucked a loose tendril of hair behind an ear. "I want you guys to move out, give yourselves up, kill each other, confess or disappear." She huffed out an exasperated breath. "Just go away so I can finish my work. I need things back on track."

Savio knew a sense of déjà vu. He dismissed the idea at once because he'd never had such a crazy conversation. Then she flicked out her tongue to moisten her lower lip and he grappled with a flood of desire.

24 Chapter Twenty-Four

ROSE THOUGHT HER late night visitor looked stunned.

"Don't act all high and mighty." She pointed the gun at him again. "I don't care what you do as long as it doesn't affect me, which is the problem. Go. Somewhere. Else."

He quirked an eyebrow and motioned toward the Luger.

She lowered her hand to the floor, pointing the barrel at the rug.

"No concern for what is taking place at the mine site?"

Christ, the man had a sexy accent. His voice was like silk rustling over her shoulders. Rose scowled at him.

"Oh, I care. But right now I'm compartmentalizing. My number one priority is getting back to work. Time and resources are limited. Your undertaking eats into both."

He didn't flinch under her glare. "Tell me more. This is fascinating."

She rolled her eyes but she couldn't deny she was enjoying herself.

"I was here first," he pointed out, aiming his cinema-worthy smile at her.

Rose was affronted by his claim. "I hold the moral high ground."

His teeth flashed again. "What if my actions are not illegal?"

She pierced him with the disdainful sneer the comment deserved. "Then why hide in a mine? You need to go." Rose cupped a hand around her jaw to indicate facial hair. "And your buddy, the guy with the beard."

His posture stiffened. "You are alarmingly astute. I am amused, *Querida* but he would not be." The timbre of his voice dropped at the end, indicating the gravity of his warning.

"Mr. Beard sticks his face through the window I shoot him."

The stare he returned made her wonder if she'd have the chance to fire a bullet. Maybe loading the damn thing was a good idea. She was playing so far out of her league.

The man let his gaze run leisurely down the lines of her body and she stifled a shiver. He leaned forward, eyes locked to hers.

"Not that I am unhappy with the preferential treatment, but I wonder why you are not afraid of *me*?"

Rose sat motionless as color warmed her cheeks. Of course he noticed the blush. The firearm dangled from her fingertips, forgotten. He accurately interpreted her response and his smile heated.

"Now *that* is most interesting." He waved toward the companion seat in the turret. "Care to join me so we might explore this development?"

She inspected him through hooded eyes. "I'm peachy right here."

They'd reached an impasse. Attraction simmered just below the surface. If she couldn't get him to open up with more details, she guessed she could always try to finesse it out like a femme fatale. She blushed scarlet.

His answering smile was slow.

Panic danced in the back of her mind. *What should she do?*

He must have seen her indecision because his sultry expression vanished, replaced with curiosity. "Tell me about your research."

His sudden request took her off-guard but she snatched at the reprieve. She didn't miss the fact he was toying with her, controlling the situation even though she held the weapon.

Mouth curved in a dubious pout, she obliged. "I catalogue artifactual remains from nineteenth century mines."

He indicated a desire for more information. "What purpose is there in this?"

Rose returned his frown. "In order to create a profile of living conditions, I search for the presence of certain products. Specific indicators tell me about the standard of lifestyle. By comparing the artifacts from a number of sites within a designated time range, I make conclusions regarding the quality of life and the access to items of comfort the general workforce enjoyed." She tucked a stray lock of hair behind her ear.

He listened with rapt attention.

"This is usually the part where the listener falls asleep," she said.

He grinned and her mind blanked. Good heavens, he was a sexy beast. She rattled on while she tried to reduce the rapid beating of her heart. "My work here is a comparative control for a study I recently finished in Nevada. This project means nothing to you but I've got a lot riding on the next few weeks."

The man nodded. When he spoke his voice took on an unmistakable warning. "You must not become any further involved."

Rose offered no indication his words made an impression. They did but she worked hard to hide the fact.

Her features tight, she curved her lips into a wan smile. "I guess I should tell you I left a message on the District Ranger's private line a few hours ago. I'm guessing they'll investigate the Vigilante Mine first thing in the morning. You might want to thank me for the advance notice."

He stared at her for a long moment before inclining his head. "You are generous, especially under the circumstances."

She flicked a pinky finger at the window, indicating the open square of night through which he'd arrived, and then turned her attention to his dark clothes and his relaxed posture in the chair. His hands were clasped in front of him, his elbows resting on his knees. He looked comfortable, confident and at home.

The opposite of her.

She'd paddled too far from shore and feared the sharks were circling ever closer.

"Why lurk outside *my* window? You don't strike me as the typical voyeur." She stifled a yawn.

"Perhaps, like the good Samaritan, I try to do right for strangers in need." His voice sounded doubtful, self-mocking.

"Working on a merit badge, eh?" Her sarcasm provoked a gentle laugh.

His smile widened at the responding shiver of her shoulders. She found it difficult to concentrate on his speech because her concentration kept slipping to his mouth.

Sinful lips.

"I represent a consortium of interests concerned with the contraband trafficking of illegal substances through Mexico."

His confession surprised her. She mulled over his meaning for a moment. "Okay, so you're not law enforcement but you act like one. What are you, part of a private security task force or something?"

He seemed annoyed, lifting his shoulders and letting them drop without further comment.

She was unsure if she'd guessed right or if he'd overshared. The pistol hung loose between her hands, the barrel pointed up at the ceiling as she gently rocked the grip with her fingers.

"So what shall we do now?" she asked.

He stared at her. "I will say thank you for not shooting me."

Amused, she spun the handgun around her finger like a cowboy in an old western movie and winked. "You're welcome. Anyway, it's not loaded."

His voice went soft and his eyes narrowed. "You play a dangerous game."

She wiggled her eyebrows. "Now don't get bent. Danger practically oozes out of your pores."

He said nothing but the look on his face was odd.

Was he speechless?

Rose stretched her legs out and arched her feet, the pink and white daisies on her socks flexing with the motion. "I figure you could have disarmed me at any point in the last twenty minutes, if you wanted to. Frankly, I was out of ideas until you showed up yesterday evening." She twisted her features into a scornful face. "Reading the newspaper, really?"

He winced.

"You're far too handsome to blend into the local population." She saw he liked the compliment.

"Misplaced trust can be reckless, *Querida*. But I confess it warms me inside to know you are not immune to my charms."

She wasn't fooled by his amused tone, danger was just an accent to his physical presence. "I fear I've made other mistakes," she said.

"Such an error could prove fatal." His fixed stare bored into her.

She shrugged.

He frowned, clearly taken aback. "You are too unconcerned."

Rose mimicked his expression. She pulled her feet underneath her and sat up on her knees, leaving the gun on the floor. She opened her arms in a wide gesture; the palms of her hands faced the ceiling. "I have limited options. I can spin my wheels chasing shadows, scramble for other potential research locations, and wait for Uncle Sam's representatives to give me the go-ahead in bureaucratic years. Or," she emphasized the pause with a finger poke to the air, "I take the proactive approach and lure one of the bad guys into my cool lair."

Mirth softened his lips in a crooked line.

In an aside she leaned forward, "That would be you."

He shook his head. "Sounds like a risky proposition."

Her smile felt apologetic. "Guidance counselors always claimed I'd meet a sticky end."

He fanned his hands out in mimicry of her position. "All right, I will accept the status as villain. You have caught me in an artfully spun web, what are your conditions?" He glanced over at the wall map before returning his attention to her.

She wondered if he'd noted how she'd marked the mine and the thermal pool. Flourishing a hand in an imperial gesture she told him, "I want you to cease all nefarious activities."

He looked disappointed. "This is the extent of your demands?"

She ignored his sardonic tone and shook her head. "Of course not, I'm just getting started."

He raised a quizzical eyebrow. "What if I have business yet to finish?"

"Stop."

"Or else?"

She narrowed her eyes at his blunt tone. "Don't make me buy bullets."

He chuckled. "It is unwise to brandish a gun without ammunition."

She fluttered an index finger over her shoulder in the direction of the bedside table. "I fudged a little, the bullets are in the drawer."

"I fear for you, *senorita*." He indicated the end of their exchange with a slow shake of his grim face. "Your unloaded firearm concerns me. Others would capitalize on such opportunity." He laid one hand over his chest and held out the other in a stop motion, rising slowly to his feet. He smiled down at her. "I must go *Querida*. Do not get up. I will let myself out."

Based on the fact his attention kept slipping down to her chest, she assumed he had a clear view of her cleavage. She hoped he enjoyed the glimpse of her new flamingo pink bra. "You're going to just walk downstairs and out the main entry?"

He grinned at her scandalized inflection.

"That's so brazen."

He winked at her. "To the contrary, that is the normal and expected way to depart."

She tilted her head back. "Next time knock."

His face smoothed into a cold blank mask. "Lock your window. I am not the only one who might come looking."

Rose spoke after a moment. "I can fend for myself."

He studied her for an extra heartbeat. "Brave."

"Desperate."

"Research must be a tough business."

She pursed her lips. "You have no idea."

Chapter Twenty-Five

ON IMPULSE SAVIO curled his fingers in a come-with-me motion. "Bid me a proper farewell?" To his surprise she reached out and slipped her hand into his.

He tugged her to her feet and discovered her head just crested his chin.

The perfect height.

She raised eyes of rich mahogany as her fingers wrapped through his. Desire thrummed up his spine. He pressed his lips against the inside of her wrist.

She shivered, her eyelids dropping a fraction.

Reason vanished. He bent his head to kiss her. She stretched up on her toes, whispered a fervent 'yes' just before his eyes fluttered closed and their mouths met. She was all softness and heat, opening to him like a flower to the sun. He tickled his tongue against her lower lip and she answered with a purr of satisfaction and deepened the caress.

Stepping close she pulled her fingers loose to fist both hands in his shirt.

His palms wrapped over her shoulders.

The kiss was slow, languid and wet. Passion clouded his thoughts. Need twisted in his chest. Desire knotted in his abdomen.

When they drew apart he rested his forehead on hers. Eyes shut he savored the sensation of her body pressed along his length.

"*Asombroso.*"

Her voice was breathy, "I don't know that word."

"You are amazing." His thumbs brushed the sensitive ridges of her clavicles. He opened his eyes to see that hers were round and dazed.

Her fingers still clutched his shirt, she squeezed him and gave a little shake, "Is this your normal method of information discovery?"

He huffed out a laugh. "I have never used this approach before."

"It's working dandy," she said. "Is there anything else you want to know?"

His mouth found hers again, searching and hungry. The second kiss was more intense, deeper and hotter. They detached with chests heaving.

"I am much intrigued," Savio admitted, gasping for air. Hands settling on her hips, he continued in confessional rush, "I experience oddly proprietary thoughts too."

Rose shuddered out a shaky breath. "Is that a bad thing?"

He looked disconcerted at her response.

She grinned, emboldened. "You're looking at me like I'm not normal." She tipped her head back and forth. "Okay, maybe not. Right now I've got a truckload of happy endorphins flowing through my bloodstream and – I'm just being honest here – some seriously excited hormones." She winked at him. "You affect me."

"Exactamente." He echoed that entire sentiment.

She exhaled a regretful sigh. "One more time but then you really have to go. I'm low on willpower and don't want to wake up with regrets that might ruin an otherwise pretty awesome memory."

He pulled her tight to his chest, one arm circling her shoulders and the other wrapped around her waist. "Then I must make this one count."

A carnal expression bloomed on her face. She melted against him. Her body curved into his, a perfect fit. The slow languid heat of their first kisses was washed away in the scalding intensity of this one.

He slanted his mouth across hers, stunned by the slick stroke of her tongue. Need rocked him. He wrapped a hand over the back of her skull, snatched off the clip and tossed it away. With a grunt of tactile pleasure he speared his fingers into her mass of hair and clenched the strands. Her tresses tumbled down in a thick pile, the silky mane still damp from her bath. She tasted of mint and was fragrant with the scent of flowers.

Her arms wrapped under his to mold his shoulder blades. One of her legs went up to wrap behind his calf. She whimpered against his lips and the raw need in the soft intonation triggered some primal response.

He groaned into her mouth and leaned over, wanting closer. She couldn't miss the extent of his interest; his body was heavy and thick where he ground his hips against hers. He kissed a hot trail down her neck. Her chin tipped up. She let him support most of her weight while he laid kisses down to the hollow of her throat.

"Ohmigod," she muttered.

He shook away the sensual fog but couldn't focus his vision. "I should go now. Understand that we are not done with this." His voice was so thick with desire he didn't recognize it.

She shivered and he pulled her upright. She nodded, her gaze also unfocused. "Definitely unfinished. I think I have more questions but I can't remember them right now."

He brushed aside her hair. The beautiful rich deep color swept down past her waistline in a solid waterfall. He noticed his hand was shaking and could not recall ever being this out of control. Never had it felt sublime to clasp someone in his arms, so right to hold *this* woman. The realization alarmed him.

"*Querida*, I must leave." He traced her swollen lips with his thumb.

Lips parting, her eyelids grew heavy and dropped half closed.

Savio's resolve faltered. He swallowed hard.

She slid her palms down his ribs to rest at his waist. "Nice washboard," she said. She took a deep breath and stepped away, lifted her gaze. "You must exude potent pheromones because I've never kissed a complete stranger."

He grinned. "I think we can no longer claim we are strangers." She smiled and he was struck dumb for a long second. The image clicked like a snapshot in his memory.

One delicate eyebrow rose in an arc. "Well in that case, we should also say goodbye." She wrapped her fingers behind his neck and pulled him down, setting a more frantic pace.

The uncontrolled intensity consumed them. He didn't remember moving but a chair pushed into his calves. His precarious balance collapsed when she shoved him again. He fell into the cushioned seat. She climbed atop him, her knees straddling his thighs. Holding his cheek and chin, she feasted at his mouth.

Palms spread across the perfect roundness of her buttocks, he groaned. She flexed into his touch then pulled back to look at him through glazed eyes.

"So bold," he rasped out on an expulsion of air.

She locked fingers over his shoulder muscles. "You're so hot. Like some crazy aphrodisiac."

"Tell me your name." He squeezed her backside, gloating when she arched into him. He was desperate to touch her skin. His entire body buzzed with desire.

"Rose," she whispered.

Savio's hands clenched. It was *her name* Remy had written with repetitious obsession.

At that moment a soft knock tapped at the door.

The woman stilled and frowned down at him. "Are you expecting someone?"

He flicked the tip of her chin with a finger. "This is *your* room, *Querida*."

She dismissed the reminder. "At this moment I know you better than anyone for hundreds of miles around and you don't even have a name."

He caressed her once more before grasping her firmly at the hips. "I am Savio," he said and leveraged her up on her feet.

He rose to stand beside her. Loathe to release her, he slid his hands down her sides and turned her, patting her pert behind as he pushed her toward the entrance.

"Use the peep hole."

She padded across the rug, the white daisies on her socks bright in the shadowed room. She peeked through the tiny lens as instructed.

He crowded in behind her. "Who is it?" he breathed beside her ear.

"One of the guests," she told him, her tone indicating disapproval. "Remy's pretty slow about taking a hint."

Another muted cuff rapped on the wood panel.

Savio remembered how Remy had slipped down the hall the previous night. Had he knocked on her door then too? Surreptitiously checked the lock while she slept? Although he'd spied through her windows, the idea of Remy sneaking out to do the same outraged him.

Rose gasped when Savio pulled her out of the line of sight and spun her around. "Has he bothered you with unwanted attention?"

She laughed softly at him, amused by his display of machismo. "He's just a tad creepy, too free with the touching."

Without thinking, Savio jerked around and flicked the mortise lock over. He yanked the door wide and planted himself in the portal with an aggressive stance. In his peripheral vision he saw Rose's mouth gape open.

"Yes?" Savio hid his agitation behind a calm tone.

Remy squawked out a shocked noise of surprise.

"You are confused, my friend." His smile felt unpleasant, as he said, "You have mistaken this room for another." He shut the oak panel on Remy's startled expression and latched the lock.

Rose leaned against the wall with a curious look on her expressive face.

He stared at her, his jealousy scarce drained away, at a complete loss to explain his behavior.

"So chivalrous," she said, a wicked smile heightening the angle of her cheekbones. "Thanks for the intervention, I think. If I develop a reputation as a loose woman as result of your testosterone display – a distinct possibility in a town this size – at least I'll be the envy of others since you're so damn sexy."

"Should I apologize?" He knew he sounded aggressive and made an attempt to tone it down.

"Would it be sincere?" She raised one eyebrow.

He stroked her cheek. "Not in the least."

She rubbed against his palm. "I suppose that being the object of envy has certain appealing fringe benefits."

He took a step forward. "Since we are in the spirit of making confessions, I will state that this is one flower I desire to have untouched."

Rose lifted her brows in mock surprise. "Even by yours truly?"

Savio tugged her close. "Of course, I do not include myself."

"Of course," she echoed, wrapping her arms around his neck.

CHAPTER TWENTY-SIX

THE PHONE RANG. Rose burrowed under the pillow and let voicemail pick up. Thirty seconds later the cell jangled out another melodic series of beeps. With a groan, she rolled over and flailed around until she knocked her gun off the table but succeeded in grasping the phone. She mashed three buttons before she croaked out an unintelligible greeting into the speaker.

"Wake up, my princess."

Her eyes flew open. Savio's warm voice caused a stomach flutter as recognition took hold. All the sexual tension of the previous night vibrated through Rose again, provoking a more sonorous murmur.

"Much better," he said.

After a final kiss that seared her lips numb he'd closed the window and left, instructing her to lock the door behind him. She'd obeyed, listening intently but never heard his footsteps descend the staircase.

Afterwards, she'd crawled into bed half-clothed. Slumber had seemed elusive, her body clenched with frustrated need. Eventually she had slept, the gun on the bedside table and ammunition in the nightstand drawer lulling her into what she guessed was a false sense of safety. She shut her eyes and fell unconscious.

"Did you rest well?"

Her body responded to his silky words, flames stoking the fires hot. "Hopefully, no better than you."

His soft laugh did funny things to her innards. "Do not shoot yourself with the bullets I put in your gun."

With the phone pressed to her ear she peered over the side of the bed to where the Luger lay on the floor. She edged open the drawer to the night stand and noted her ammunition was indeed missing.

"Seems pointless to lock up with you around."

"We all have our skills." His amused tone, punctuated by the sound of background noise, indicated he was somewhere out-of-doors.

"Don't you sleep?" His muffled laugh was almost lost in her stifled yawn. "I can't believe you broke in a second time and didn't wake me up."

"You have no idea of the restraint I found it necessary to apply."

With a shiver of half frustrated hormones and half fear, she wondered exactly why he'd made such effort. "Well, next time bring donuts and coffee."

"I will remember that."

She shivered at the promise in his voice. "Did you call me at this ungodly hour for a reason?"

"It is not early. I waited until eight o'clock. Regardless, you must have patience today. Show discretion. Your Park Service friends are already busy."

Ah, her message had brought investigators to the mine. "You don't seem upset about the situation."

"I am not. In this outcome we are agreed."

"I don't recall disagreeing with much of anything last night," she muttered only half to herself. Except for the fact she'd simmered with unexpressed passion after he departed, she wasn't certain what had possessed her.

"My most enjoyable evening in memory," Savio said.

Rose swallowed. "Either you're starved for attention or I made a positive impression."

The rumble of a passing vehicle confirmed his exterior setting. "You forged a most indelible imprint, one I anticipate renewing at the soonest opportunity. Please stay away from the park today, *Querida.*"

The intensity in his words filled her with heat, their tone an endearment. Her toes curled down as her thigh muscles flexed. The man's voice practically instigated an orgasm. She blinked at the ceiling and did a mental head shake.

"Okay. I'll agree to be a busy little tourist today. And just how will you occupy time while I'm shopping and eating?"

His tone chilled. "I am working." There was a soft clunk as he adjusted something, then an audible click and the rich timber of his voice resonated down the line again. "Details must be cleared up."

She figured he had plugged in a hands-free device. "And what exactly is your job?"

A roar of exhaust echoed. "Currently fulfilling my half of our partnership." His words sounded glib. "You are a sound sleeper, *mi flor*. I very much like your choice of night clothes."

Rose rolled over in bed and propped herself up on one elbow. Her face flamed. She wore a tank top and a pair of pale pink panties. She forced her fuzzed mind back to their conversation. "I must be mentally deficient because I seem to have forgotten my side of this agreement."

Amusement sounded evident in his shallow exhalation of laughter. "We can work out the details later."

"Great." She infused the single word with disgust.

"It will be my most sincere pleasure." He laughed the rich chuckle that did funny things to her insides.

Rose kicked the covers off her overheated legs. "I wasn't going to mention the goosebumps sprouting all over the exposed parts of my anatomical bits but you've gotten me riled up."

A wistful sigh drifted from the phone. "Now I will spend the day remembering how warm and flushed you looked in bed. I much regret leaving you alone."

Her limbs went heavy and her mind lethargic. Rose had to clear her throat before she could speak and then the words tumbled out in a little breathless rush. "Well, it's difficult to issue invitations when unconscious, but hey, thanks for not killing me in my sleep."

He made a sound part pleasure and the rest question. "In future, I shall endeavor to waken you. Please spend today in the company of others." The line went dead.

Rose turned the cell over. The screen display said private number.

Figures.

Next time she'd hang up on him. She dropped the phone on the quilt; her eyes coming to rest on the map adhered to the wall. Today she'd find a café with a high speed internet connection, add copious amounts of real cream to expensive coffee, and catch a caffeine buzz. She'd work on her research project and maybe sift through information about foot deformations. Those strange footprints at the death scene bugged her.

Forty-five minutes later Rose unlocked the driver's side and tried to shove her bag across the seat. Clunky and misshapen from her laptop, the weight pulled at her arm and she lost the phone wedged between shoulder and cheek. She mashed her hip against the chassis and caught the cell, activating the speaker button in time for the modulated tone of the voicemail to inform her of one new message.

A second later her mother's voice bleated out in the cold air.

"Sweetling, your father and I are so sorry to hear of this tragedy. I confess we're at a loss – was it someone you knew in Montana, perhaps from school? Do tell us where to send flowers. Call us any time. We're here to comfort you. We love you." The recording ended with a cheery beep.

Accustomed to her parent's ability to breeze over details, she stood frozen trying to sort out the misinformation until the computer-generated voice repeated her modulated request to delete the missive or save it for later review. She deleted, deciding on a follow-up call. Just not right now.

Bagel crammed between her teeth, she retrieved the coffee cup from the roof and climbed into the driver's seat. She fluttered a hand at the old men on the bench in front of the market, pleased when they all waved back. Yep, just another exciting Tuesday morning in Riverside.

Rose completed the drive to West Yellowstone without incident. A steady stream of cars passed in the opposite direction, probably headed for the park. As the crow flew, the distance between the two towns couldn't be far but the paved route featured hair-pin turns and gooseneck loops and made the eight miles seem like forever. The evidence of a recent rock-fall, pushed onto the shoulder, stretched for a quarter of a mile.

When she passed a sign marked Gallatin County, she reduced speed.

The community, a mix of small hamlet and tourist glitz, nestled in at an elevation 6,663 feet above sea level. According to the signs sprinkled along the road, the place was intimately linked to the Yellowstone facilities. If Riverside served as the hub of housing for park personnel, West Yellowstone encapsulated the epicenter for public attractions. Literal herds of tourists gathered at designated points, waiting for shuttle and van transports destined for the interior.

Rose tried to concentrate on the scenery but her mind kept wandering to the previous night. This morning her lips tingled, tender and almost bruised from Savio's physical onslaught. Parts of her anatomy ached every time she reviewed the way events unfolded. The naughty voice in her head muttered and pouted because she'd held back.

West Yellowstone cared about visitors. Summer brought heavy tourist crowds with their much-needed cash infusions. Tourism was clearly the economic mainstay. A plethora of shops lined the streets. In Riverside the number looked out-of-place for the size of the community but here the overabundance shocked. The sheer volume of tourists produced another jolt. By comparison, Riverside seemed insulated. The western gateway to Yellowstone Park reminded her of the Main Street of a nature-oriented Disneyland.

On her first pass through the downtown Rose noted no less than three cafés with high speed internet.

Score!

She chose the Elk Point Coffee Shop on the corner of the busiest intersection. She settled in a velvet chair near the window, pulling a small table around in front to serve as a workspace. She logged into the wifi and began to surf for information.

The mining-related databases she relied on for her Nevada research were regionally specific. Now she looked for details in company archives and government collections but results proved paltry. She'd had this problem at home when she'd tried to mock-up a preliminary plan. Since Yellowstone had become a protected area so long ago, there simply wasn't the same kind of information available. At the end of an hour she had stuck colored sticky notes to every surface in reach but her queries hadn't been overly productive.

Rose turned her attention to the footprints where she'd found the dead man. After a couple of false starts on arch shapes and pre-natal development she narrowed her parameters and discovered a condition called clubfoot.

She looked for images. The number of startling photographs she located on the internet proved healthcare professionals around the globe did not provide consistent early treatment intervention. After studying several examples, she sipped at her cappuccino, feeling vaguely elitist.

Subject abandoned, she spent the next half hour cross-referencing Montana, Yellowstone, Riverside, and murder. Her efforts returned a handful of lurid news articles featuring tragic events within park boundaries. Most read as the sad result of poor judgment exercised by folks who needed mental health treatment or drug and alcohol intervention.

Rose slouched in her chair and stroked the plush avocado velvet. Her glazed eyes reflected in the shine of the clean glass. In two hours of coffee house squatting she'd produced nada. She stretched her arms and rotated her neck. At least she'd caught a caffeine buzz. Needing to move, she packed up and left.

Back at her car, she dropped her stuff on the passenger seat and shrugged out of her flannel, tossing it inside too. She rummaged a packet of beef jerky from the glove box for lunch and leaned her belly against the door. Sun streamed down, making her lethargic. She rested her forearms on the roof. The metal was almost too hot to touch but the heat on her skin felt delicious.

A cadre of motorcycles rumbled past.

She climbed inside the car. Slouched down in the driver's seat she paged through the park pamphlets, considering the possibility of undertaking one of the scenic drives. The light strung over the intersection changed color and a stream of pedestrians stepped off the curb. Sitting a couple of car-lengths down from the crosswalk, she noticed two men as the crowd thinned. A chill knot formed in the pit of her stomach as she watched Remy and the bearded man walking side-by-side.

She slid lower in the seat.

Yesterday evening the pair had been only a couple of yards apart in Vic's Restaurant. They'd ignored one another, even when Remy stood at the register and paid the bill. Now they looked as though they were well acquainted, like on a first-name basis.

They appeared deep in conversation, arguing about something. Both wore tense expressions. She had the distinct impression of anger humming just below the surface, probably because park personnel had responded to her phone call.

Logic suggested both men must be involved in this business. *Who wasn't?*

Fortunately they crossed the busy street in the direction opposite from her car.

The warmth she'd soaked in from the sun seeped away, leaving her chilled. Unnerved by her discovery, Rose started the engine. The proximity of the western entrance to Yellowstone offered a long return route to Riverside. She had no real plans for the day and hanging around had lost its appeal. Since she'd agreed to stay outside the mine area and the thermal pool – a promise extracted from yet another participant in this debacle, she might as well remain off everybody's radar.

Given her current cranky disposition, she decided to drop in at the regional office and chat up Ranger Burnside, see how the man was holding up under the strain.

Rose showed her tattered letter of receipt at the entrance and refused the stack of materials pressed into her hand. They must have a huge printing budget.

This ranger discouraged her from taking the Grand Loop drive, suggesting an earlier start for the 140-mile trek. Since travel anywhere inside the boundaries sped along at thirty miles per hour, and usually less, she agreed. Steering in the general direction of Riverside, she exited at the side loop which – according to the map – reconnected to the main route not far from where she wanted to end up.

The environment was different here.

Leafy deciduous trees lined the rocky banks of a clear stream and a smaller variety of evergreen with feathery soft multi-branched tips dotted the landscape. The scenery was softer and less harsh but maybe only because she hadn't seen the crumpled body of a man in this setting. So far this section of road had been deserted. She rounded a curve, the mid-day sun lighting the ground with gold, and glimpsed a slice of exposed dirt on the hillside.

Rose slammed on the brakes.

She immediately recognized a mine tailing. The telltale stain of residue spilled down from the black blob of the opening. Excited, she reversed her car thirty feet down the shoulder, a slightly wiggly process, and pulled into a hard-packed unpaved lot surrounded by a log-rail fence.

From the parking area, two trails split in opposite directions. There was only one vehicle present, a burgundy mud-streaked Ford Explorer with Idaho plates. Rose pulled into the empty space on the left.

Practically itching with the desire to explore, she decided what Ranger Burnside didn't know, wouldn't hurt him.

CHAPTER TWENTY-SEVEN

NOT TWELVE HOURS earlier Savio had confronted Remy at the door of Rose's room in an uncharacteristic outburst of jealousy. Now Remy was hot on her heels again.

He'd considered the possibility Mackenzie had skipped town with the contraband drug product but his gut told him the guy had gone to ground. The man's debt with the Almeida Cartel still represented a threat.

He understood Remy's personal interest in Rose. She'd knocked him off-kilter even before they'd met face-to-face.

After last night's unexpected descent into sensual exploration, he was anxious to be held at gunpoint again. The connection linking Remy and Mackenzie worried him. Remy's lurid attention in the senorita, her focus on the mine, and Savio's own personal business dealings with Mackenzie might blow up in his face.

He scowled and adjusted his helmet. He found even the suggestion unacceptable.

The motorcycle idled as he sat on the shoulder weighing his options. Providence decided his course of action. Burdened under heavy packs, two hikers trudged out of the woods and climbed into the dirty Ford Explorer sitting in the graveled lot. A few minutes later the vehicle drove off.

Now there were no potential witnesses.

Savio's legendary self-control appeared to have deserted him. The upside to confronting Rose in an isolated location was the relative safety in being so many miles distant from Riverside. If Mackenzie concluded his business in the next few hours, making good on his promise of payment, Savio might coerce both men into departing sooner than originally intended. With the drug production site a lost cause, they had no reason to remain.

The benefits of that were twofold. He removed any potential threat to Rose and freed up time to indulge his fascination.

Soon the park would reinstate her work permit. By then he'd be back in Los Angeles, on to the next job.

He debated several options.

He could force Rose into the role of unwilling prisoner. A risky idea she was liable to reject out of hand. Not even fighting a grin, he considered how that created a tertiary problem in stepping up his seduction campaign. Or, there was the option of keeping her with him at all times. He'd never been inclined to stick like glue to a female but now he found this idea unexpectedly titillating. A poor choice though because it placed her in the line of fire. He questioned his ability to tune her out and monitor their surroundings. She offered too much distraction.

A sigh escaped him. He couldn't safeguard Rose around the clock.

In the end, his training won out. Stranding her for a few hours made her safer. Just long enough to resolve his business with Mackenzie. He steered across the road and parked, using her car to screen his motorcycle.

He might convince her to leave for a day. Even an overnight trip to the far side of the park put safe distance between her and the increasingly desperate men.

He walked several minutes, peering through the trees until movement drew his eyes up the terrain.

He shook his head. He'd wondered at her destination but once she left the trail he lost sight of her in the dense under-growth. Now she climbed straight up a steep wall of dirt. Rocks and clumps of loose scree showered down behind her. As he watched, Rose slipped inside a dark gash in the hillside and dis-appeared from sight.

He cursed softly. The opening could only be another mineshaft.

He picked up his pace. The woman must have a death wish. The ground in this entire region was unstable from all the seis-mic movement. Concern fueled his progress. Technically, he supposed she'd done what he'd asked. Tourists visited to ex-plore the wilderness.

He cut through the undergrowth and scaled the slippery scree to the mine entrance. His breathing came hard by the time he finished the climb but it might have been as much from fantasizing about her thigh muscles as the physical effort. No wonder he couldn't concentrate.

A quick glance into the interior showed a mere half circle of dirt and nothing but darkness beyond.

He ducked inside the entry and crouched, allowing his pupils to adjust to the gloom. His respiration sounded loud in the silence.

She must have gone deeper.

She had.

He moved forward, fingers crawling over the wall. He heard her before he spied the glow. Turning a corner he saw her. She hummed low, whispering the words to some tune as she shined the light on the tunnel floor. Rose wore earbuds, the white wires billowing out at the sides.

He shook his head, not even bothering to hide the sound of his passage. He caught her by surprise, coming up behind and slipping one arm around her slim throat. He yanked her back against his body.

She reacted with a tiny shriek of shock. That and she dropped the cell phone she used as a flashlight, the headphones pulling from her ears as it fell.

Savio took advantage of her shocked immobility and clamped his fingers over her right wrist, bringing her arm down and holding the elbow tight to her side.

She collapsed, going pliant in his arms and words exploded from her in a breathless rush. "Hells bells, Savio, you damn near scared the pants off me."

A delightful thought.

Every point of contact along Savio's body vibrated. Those minor touches aroused him unbearably. "Already you know me?"

She made a happy sound. "You smell good. *Buenos dias,* partner."

He nuzzled the side of her throat and she uttered another pleased noise, one that tightened his groin.

"Tell me something, if you were just going to follow me around today, why did I have to leave town?" She stretched to give him improved access.

Clever female.

"Perhaps I am not the only person monitoring your whereabouts?" he offered.

She nodded. "I'd have done better staying in Riverside. I saw Remy with the bearded man."

He wrapped her even tighter in his embrace. "I know." His whisper produced a full body shiver.

She gripped his forearm hard but she didn't fight. "You were on one of the motorcycles that kept cruising through town?" She snorted a disgusted sound. "I should know to listen to my own body."

He liked that telling admission. He clasped her right hand and wove their fingers together, resting his cheek on the pillow of her hair.

"Ah, *Querida*, you are so clever. This is why I cannot let you return to Riverside." The longer he spent in her company the more rules he found ways to break.

Rose swallowed audibly. "Ever?"

His shoulders shook with silent laughter at the outrage in her tone. "Not for such a long time as that. You should know I do not want to hurt you." Her rigid posture loosened. He inhaled near her ear and smelled the scent of evergreens. "Did you dance with the trees?"

She choked off an uneven laugh. "Not exactly. I tripped by the creek and fell into a bunch of saplings."

Savio began to rock their hips in sync, the fluid motion mimicking a dance movement. Back and forth they stepped, right and then left. "Everything about you pleases me."

She relaxed another fraction in his arms. "Are you flirting with me?"

His smile broadened. "I must be."

"Hmm. Well, I guess that's an improvement over the alternative."

He murmured agreement and slowed the tempo.

"Look, I don't want to ruin the moment because I really am enjoying this little interlude but I'd appreciate an assurance that this won't end badly for me." She matched his movements. "I'd settle for an affirmation of nonviolence. In truth, I'd be relieved with some sincere verbal support for my continued wellbeing."

"Your wellbeing weighs on me," he said with sincerity. Her trembling response and throaty sound of relief encouraged him. "Will you cooperate with my plan?" He exhaled the words beside her ear, delighting in her shiver.

"To be honest, Savio, I don't usually accommodate people. For you, I'll make a real effort. Tell me what to do."

Did he detect a further softening in her tone? "You must remain hidden for today. Things have come rapidly to a head. I want you someplace out of reach of the bad guys."

She went still. "You mean stay *here*?" Her voice softened, the tone uncertain, but he heard the distinct emphasis on their present location.

"It is only for a little while," he soothed.

She repeated his words, a bare echo of sound in the silent place.

Savio bent down, kissing the nape of her neck. He reveled in her softness as she arched into him.

I knew she would be like this.

"You want to leave me in this mine?"

Her husky whisper made him impatient. He rumbled an affirmation, pushing aside the collar of her shirt to lay out a line of kisses.

Rose leveraged to one side and strained up on her toes, lifting her backside to push at his groin.

Savio groaned. His arms slid from her waist to grip her hips. He found it difficult to focus.

She lifted one booted foot and braced it on the wall, grinding into him and murmuring deep in her throat.

His lips worked along her clavicle.

Balance shifted, she pushed off hard and slammed them across the narrow tunnel. Using her upper body as a bludgeon, she snapped his skull against the rock-filled dirt surface.

The impact stunned him motionless.

She darted away.

Sneaky female.

No wonder he was so attracted. He launched behind her.

She ran fast.

One hand reached out, he caught her near the mouth of the mine and spun her into a crushing embrace. They skidded to a halt, crashing into the rough tunnel surface. His shoulder took a new battering hit but he forgot the pain when Rose struggled. Arms trapped at her sides, she clutched his ribs, scraping her nails into his skin. He found the contact exhilarating.

Rose ceased movement with a jarring suddenness and stood quiescent.

Their combined breaths filled the space.

"Well it was worth a try." She spoke in a conversational tone. "How's your head?"

"A little dazed or I would have caught you sooner."

She peered back down the shaft and then up at him. Her chest heaved but she sounded calm. "You're too fast for me."

He grinned. "I admire such honesty."

She gave him dazed regard. "That isn't fair."

He returned a quizzical look.

"First it's the physique of a Roman statue, then the movie-star perfect smile and now a make-my-toes-curl sexy laugh." She scowled. "What gives?"

He frowned but when her gaze dropped lower, he understood. Attraction, she felt it too. A powerful heat flushed through him.

Eyes narrowed and fingers digging into the skin at his hips, Rose raised her face and parted her lips.

He silently cursed.

Cognizant of the risk, he lowered his mouth to meet hers. Her tongue swept across his with searing wet heat. He wasn't aware he'd loosened his grip until her fingers speared into his hair and twisted the angle to deepen the kiss. Her aggression excited him. Suppressed ardor poured through his veins. His stance splayed wide, he settled his hands low on her waist, gripping her hipbones and squeezing. His stomach clenched when she moaned. This wasn't feigned desire. She might have tried to escape a minute ago but now Rose leaned in, framing his face with her palms and kissing him with furious energy. He responded with abandon until she slammed his cranium into the wall.

Savio grunted. He managed to not break his hold, pushing her off to put an arm's length between them. In the process he avoided her head-butt and his vision cleared enough to see her face.

She panted, her eyes wide and her lips turned up in a wick-ed smile. "I like this game," she taunted.

Savio's control snapped. He jerked her against his body and took her mouth in a punishing kiss.

Rose snaked one hand around the back of his neck and pulled. The other clenched over his shoulder. She climbed up his front, a thrum of sound vibrating from deep inside.

One arm strapped across her ass, he lifted her until her legs wrapped around his waist and slipped a hand up her back.

They separated mouths, gazes locked.

"Your lip is bleeding."

Savio leered at her. "You are worth every drop of pain, *Querida.*"

28   CHAPTER TWENTY-EIGHT

ROSE ADMIRED HOW the man kept taking her punishment and coming back for more. Nothing like sending mixed signals.

Savio evaded another blow with ease.

He seemed amused and excited by her responsiveness. He licked a hot wet trail of kisses down her throat, sliding a palm between her breasts until it came to rest on her belly.

Her insides melted again.

"Ah *Querida*, you tempt me. So carnal." His voice caressed her.

"You're really going to leave me here?"

He must have heard her note of disbelief because he met her gaze. In the dim light from the entrance he looked serious "I want you safe. Just for a few hours, only long enough for my business affiliates to complete their transactions."

She refused to hide her belligerent expression. "Don't expect me to aid and abet you."

Liking mines didn't mean she wanted to be left stranded inside one. As holes in the ground went, this one was dry and empty but she had no intentions of spending any great length of time here.

"I promise to return and rescue you before morning." He laid a long-fingered hand over his heart.

Rose snorted and rolled her eyes. She wanted to give a dismissive wave but he'd trapped her hands again.

Smart man.

"You might get shot, arrested, deported, or eaten by a bear before then," she complained. "I could be stuck here until the park service runs a trace on my abandoned vehicle and discovers I've been missing for a month."

He raised one eyebrow. "Surely not so long?"

She huffed out a dissent. "Clearly, you've not worked with government bureaucracy."

Savio laughed hard enough he had to bend over to catch his breath. He released his grip and stepped back, effectively blocking her access to the exit. When his mirth finally passed he held out a hand.

"Come *Querida*, let us be friends once again."

She eyed his advance warily. "I'm feeling decidedly less friendly."

He watched her with open amusement.

She frowned at him. "Why are you doing this? Not that I'm unappreciative of your concern but let's face it, this is a lot of effort to go through for a stranger."

His expression went blank. Head cocked to one side, he studied her. The look brought to mind a raptor eying a small tasty mammal in the Cretaceous period. Maybe she shouldn't have pointed that out.

He winked at her. "It puzzles me too."

Another flush of heat rolled through her. The man had the ability to reduce her resistance to nothing in a matter of seconds. How did that work? She wished she had the same effect on him.

He shrugged out of his woolen button down and offered it with a conciliatory smile. "For additional warmth."

She snatched it from his hand. "Aren't you the old-fashioned gallant? No one has ever given me the shirt right off their back before." She drew it on, his dark glance narrowing as she did the bottom two buttons. Let the sexy bastard freeze.

She sniffed the collar and a shiver ran up her spine. For god's sake, goosebumps burst on her arms. "You smell all sweet and smoky."

His eyelids went half-mast. "Now my scent wraps around you. How enticing."

Without warning Savio invaded her personal space. His hands circled her waist and clasped at the small of her back, his lips nuzzled near her ear, and she responded enthusiastically.

"I do not want to stop touching you," he admitted, a little breathless.

Rose rolled her eyes. "At least I'm not the only one." She pressed her body against him. "I won't deny you're a handsome devil, 'cause what would be the point?"

She dug her fingernails into the soft tissue above his hips, right along the waistband of his jeans until he grunted from the pain. His teeth closed over the curve of her neck and she fought not to moan.

It was difficult to keep her tone light when her throat was constricted by lust. "You might not have noticed but I find you somewhat attractive."

His tongue flicked against the curl of her ear and her knees wobbled. His inhalation was shaky. "Your desire humbles me." He leaned back to stare at her with intensity. "As soon as events permit we will resume this conversation."

She presented her hands as if waiting to be handcuffed and raised her eyes at the ceiling. "I'm telling you now this is going to bite you on the ass."

He dropped a kiss on her temple before stepping back to open a small distance between their bodies. With a practice motion he unclipped a woven bracelet from his wrist and flashed the grin she'd been expecting.

"I take full responsibility for my actions."

Rose hadn't paid attention to the strap but now she saw with amazement how the army green cord unraveled into a shocking length. "That's cool, I want one." She met his gaze. "Do you always carry bits of rope in case an emergency restraint situation pops up?"

He laughed aloud and coiled the line around her wrists with careful attention, securing the bindings with minimal discomfort. When he finished, he held up his keys. Attached was another braided fob.

"Always."

She made an unpleasant moue. "Just so we're clear, buddy, I consider this abandonment. Leaving me tied up in a mine causes resentment. You might want to re-think this. The next time we meet I plan to put as much hurt on that gorgeous body as possible."

"Anticipation fills me." He pointed at the floor and helped ease her into a seated position. "Ankles together please."

Her mouth set in a stubborn line she obliged, straightening out her legs and leaning against the wall.

His movements were practiced but he looped the rope over her Levi's, a fortunate slip, since she never laced up her boots all the way up her ankles.

"I see you have some experience with this, eh?"

He paused to smooth a knuckle over her cheek. "You can escape *Querida*, just not too soon."

"Promise?"

He drew two lines across his heart. "I *will* return for you."

"I'd consider that so much more romantic if you weren't the one leaving me here in the first place. You know you can trust me, right? I'll promise to stay in my room at the inn or tag along in your back pocket. I'll even agree to do whatever you say." She batted her eyelashes and tried to appear enticing.

He smiled appreciatively. "Unfortunately, I do not believe you."

She scowled and shifted position. "My butt is already numb."

Her rancor amused him. He laughed as her angry gaze slid over his body. "I am compelled to ask what you are doing?"

"I'm marking the best parts for damage."

Another laugh burst from him. He crouched down and kissed her until she responded with mindless passion. "You are glorious," he whispered in her ear.

Then he walked away and left her in the darkness.

Rose listened until his footsteps became softer. She pursed her lips. They still tingled from his kiss. She'd sent off a thousand mixed signals in the last five – okay twenty – minutes. The instant Savio grabbed her from behind, her adrenalin spiked, the result of a hormone rush rather than the flush of fear-induced heart palpitations. Nevermind she had zero logical reasons to expect her sexy nocturnal visitor to show up in a mine – her body knew him instantly. Chin dropped to her chest, she squeezed her eyes shut. There was no word to describe her bizarre behavior.

Even her work buddy, Jonathon, the king of bad relationship decisions, would find himself tongue-tied by her antics. After he stopped laughing.

She counted to one hundred, each breath measured with icy control. Having spent many hours in dark spaces, the mine didn't terrify her in the least. Of greater concern was her need to pee. She let a good ten minutes pass before bracing the heel of her boot against the dirt floor and digging in. The sneaky bastard might return to make sure she was incapacitated but she dared not wait any longer.

The cord was snug but she worked it, repeatedly arching her foot and twisting the ankle until it began to give. Minutes later she peeled off the boot, the coils slipping off at the same time. She wiggled her toes. The concentrated effort had warmed her and now the woolen shirt felt overly warm. The second shoe followed a couple minutes later. If she'd laced her boots in the regulation manner, she'd have been stuck here indefinitely.

Freeing her arms offered more of a challenge. She tried rotating her elbows together before rolling her fists in opposite directions. The motion pinched the delicate skin at her wrists but the movement loosened the bindings a bare fraction. The cord he'd used had no noticeable stretch. Concentrated effort resulted in abrasions. She blew on the stinging bruised flesh and promised herself to give the man what he deserved.

No more than twenty minutes after Savio deserted her, she approached the light at the end of the tunnel.

CHAPTER TWENTY-NINE

WINSLOW WATCHED A gust of wind push a candy bar wrapper down the sidewalk into the gutter. The bit of plastic fluttered in the breeze. Summer had always been his favorite season. As a child he'd run outside every morning to feel the warm sunlight pouring over the treetops like liquid heat. Inundated by an avalanche of memories, he sat brooding until his gaze wandered across the street.

He didn't know what to make of the girl's identity.

Sometimes fate delivered right to your doorstep, revealing unexpected treasures under the most improbable of circumstances. Yesterday's discovery blindsided him. At first he'd dismissed any possible connection. The idea seemed ludicrous – but he'd seen her name written in the hotel register. Coincidence might explain why he and Rose Brashear shared the same middle name.

When he commented how many people did, Delmar barked out a laugh and elbowed him in the ribs.

"At least two, you numbskull," he said.

At least two.

Winslow had lived without relatives too long to add up the years. Self-conscious, he patted his shirt pocket to make sure the photograph was still there. Last night he'd dragged out the boxes of old snapshots and sifted through the piles until he located the one he wanted.

Delmar interrupted his reverie. "Any news about the fella you found behind the Ladies Auxiliary?" He twirled the toothpick across his teeth with his tongue and waited for a response.

Winslow snorted. "I called the station and asked if they'd learned anything. The guy who answered wouldn't crack. He passed the phone to Deputy Williams and she said she couldn't tell me even if they had, which they hadn't."

Delmar huffed with amusement.

Winslow rolled his shoulders and studied the sky. Another squall was working up thunderheads but looked likely to blow off.

"The deputy has grit. I enjoy that about a woman," Delmar said. His face took on a faraway look.

Winslow never met Delmar's wife. Persistent rumors claimed she'd been a real battle-axe. According to Nelsen she'd lived up to the legend but after four decades of marriage, being widowed almost destroyed Delmar. After being despondent for years he was finally showing signs of recovery.

Delmar grunted a sudden appreciative sound. "Deputy Williams' granny had grit too." He chewed on the toothpick and rolled his eyes toward Winslow. "Hell, the old dame had a granite backbone. Hard as nails. Put three husbands in the grave before she was thirty. They don't make women like her anymore."

Winslow considered this for a minute. "Sounds intimidating."

Delmar snickered. "Hell, yes. Strong females intimidate you pansies. That's why you never got married." He ignored Winslow's rude gesture. "Handsome woman, stacked in all the places it counts." His grin displayed the gap between his front teeth. "She was a widow of a certain age back in my youth."

Winslow faced his companion and raised an eyebrow.

Delmar nodded. "Bet your ass. Not like we enjoyed a lot of choices then." He sighed. "It was a long time ago. Things were different, easier and simpler."

"True enough," Winslow said.

Delmar agreed.

A loud exhaust rumbled. A truck rolled past and the driver raced the engine, speeding away, the roar impeding conversation for a moment.

"There's ugliness in the world today."

Delmar reflected on his statement and then disagreed. "You're wallowing." He nodded with a superior nod. "It happens. Nostalgia, I'm told, is a sign of old age."

Winslow gave him a dirty once-over. "I'm arguing for a philosophical underlying decay of society." He ignored Delmar's skeptical expression. "I liken it to tooth rot. I reckon today's world suffers from bad teeth. Need to pull out the rotten ones or the poison spills over onto the healthy."

Delmar mulled over the idea. "Okay, I changed my mind, I like your analogy."

A dusty bronze-colored car rolled to a stop and parked under the two-hour time limit sign. He recognized it belonged to the young woman who shared his name. He thought she appeared a bit more dirty and disheveled than usual.

Winslow and Delmar tipped their caps but she scampered up the walk and entered through the stained glass doors without noticing.

Delmar jerked his head after the girl. "Decide what to do about that?"

Winslow shook his chin in a negative. "I can't figure out how to approach the subject. I might be wrong, you know."

Delmar leaned forward to check the street toward West Yellowstone. "You don't really believe you are though."

Winslow peered in the same direction. He frowned as a car appeared. "No, I don't think I'm mistaken."

The automobile sped closer, the driver failing to decelerate even when he reached the shopping district. The low-slung vehicle whizzed by the market, tinted windows too dark to see inside. A single occupant or a full entourage of people could squat behind the blacked out glass. A buzz of noise, chased by a series of thumps, reverberated from the interior. Powerful bass beats emanated through the sheet metal of the doors, the rear window flexed in response to each throb. They followed the car until it turned down a side street.

Winslow pursed his lips. "Tooth rot."

CHAPTER THIRTY

ROSE WAS PISSED off, mostly at herself.

Disillusioned by the fact she'd gotten affectionate with a man callous enough to *tie* her up and *leave* her in a mine, the worst was realizing she'd sign on for a repeat engagement if opportunity arose. Her attraction burned so hot she scarcely avoided third degree burns.

She parked in her customary place and jogged across the lawn.

Inside she experienced relief when Remy wasn't lurking behind the newel post. She charged up the stairs and dashed down the hall. Key pulled from her pocket, she unlocked the massive old lock and flung open the wood panel. The interior appeared unchanged. Afternoon radiance spilled through the mullioned windows. Rainbows of light shimmered on the ecru paint, caught and deflected by the decorative leaded-glass inserts. Rose took in the detail in seconds as she stepped over the threshold. The room looked just as messy as when she'd left this morning. The sound of paper crinkled underfoot. Leaning down, she swiped up a crushed receipt, hooking the heavy door with her foot and pulling. The panel swung shut revealing a woman crumpled against the wall.

Rose screamed but the sound came out as no more than a hiss of high-pitched air.

Collapsing on her knees beside the recumbent form, she recognized Ranger Neet. The familiar park service uniform helped with the identification because an ugly dark bruise crept over the woman's forehead and covered one entire side of her face. Nellie's left eye was swollen completely shut, the puffy tissue separated by a wet line that weeped bloody fluid.

Rose stopped flapping her hands in the air. Taking a deep breath she tried to recall her first-aid training. Number one, is the victim breathing? She looked and saw the ranger's chest move. Check. As she watched, red-streaked saliva trickled from Nellie's mouth and followed a trail down her chin.

Afraid she might be doing more harm than good, Rose eased Nellie's slumped form down to the floor. She stifled a curse, having no idea what to check next.

Duct tape plastered the woman's lower face, one end adhering to the short sandy hair by her ear. Sweat and mucus had coated her lips and cheek with a debris field. Rose pried at the adhesive on one side, worried about Nellie's ragged breathing. The tape lifted, yanking out tiny hairs. The painful process produced no reaction.

Rose seized on the idea of calling an ambulance. She started to rise up on one knee but Nellie wheezed.

She rolled the ranger gently onto her side and her arms and legs went limp, her torso slipping down to the floor. Panicked, Rose dropped to her knees and tried to pull Nellie upright. Her head lolled against the rug but her breathing sounded better. Rose counted off one shaky breath after another until she got to ten. Slowly letting the woman's body relax, she let go and crab-walked over to the nearest window.

Unlocking the sash and shoving it up in a smooth motion, she leaned out and yelled for help.

Utter silence answered. Not a bird twittered or car exhaust rumbled.

Wood creaked as the men across the road rose from their bench. One trotted to the edge of the boardwalk and stepped down.

The other joined him.

Both stared up at her with concerned faces.

Rose hollered for assistance again.

As soon as the old guys charged into the street, she moved back to Nellie. Footsteps clamored inside the Inn. In less than a minute, the two elderly men plowed through the door. One uttered a terrible cry of distress when he saw the scene.

Rose wanted to lift Nellie's head on to her lap like they did in movies but feared restricting her airway. Each breath sounded more labored than the last.

The man with the crew cut said something. Rose didn't listen, too busy helping Nellie breathe, inhaling and exhaling as if she could force air into the woman's lungs just by doing it herself.

Gentle pressure on her shoulders pulled her aside. She tried to object but the second old guy held her in a surprisingly firm grip. She watched as the first one ran practiced hands over Nellie and palpated her scalp and neck with careful touches. His fingers came away red. Not horror-movie gross, just dark enough to make her stomach lurch.

Her companion caught the reaction and turned her from the scene, aiming toward the opposite side of the room. She thought he told her his name but she failed to remember, unable to tear her focus from Nellie.

"I should call someone," she said. She had no idea where to start.

People crowded in from the hallway. Bodies spilled inside and finally blocked her view. After a time, the uniformed professionals arrived and soon departed with the injured woman. Someone mentioned a helicopter life flight.

Rose listened to the voices with growing detachment. The urgency to complete her research study paled beside the battered body of the ranger. From her vantage point near the window she let her gaze rove over the furnishings. Not an item appeared out of place. She couldn't even find a smear of blood on the floor to show such violence had been perpetrated.

Gooseflesh rippled up her arms.

Why was Nellie here?

Who had done this terrible thing to her?

Intellectually, she'd known these people were dangerous but for the first time she really grasped the idea that her interference equated with poking a stick at a wild bear.

Rose shivered.

Now that she'd seen the violence firsthand, Savio's words haunted her. He'd wanted her safe in a remote location until the danger passed. Had he suspected they planned to come for her? Instead of hiding her in a secret place, why not just call the police?

Why hadn't she?

Even after the majority of the mob trickled downstairs, the old guys remained. Grateful for their presence, she took comfort in not having to be alone while she waited to give yet another statement to the local law.

In the privacy of her bathroom she found the scrap of paper still clutched in her hand. Shock made people stupid, she thought, and started to throw it in the trash. She paused and looked closer at the address. The receipt came from a fuel station in West Yellowstone. She smoothed the wrinkled folds on the sink edge and studied the details. The auto-generated payment stub issued by a self-service pump showed today's date.

Nellie wore her work uniform. She might have driven out the west park entrance, pumped up her gas tank, and then returned to the White Horse Inn to talk to Rose.

It wasn't beyond the realm of believability.

Rose hadn't filled up that morning but she knew at least three other people who could have. The time stamp exempted Savio. He'd been locked to her lips during the critical period. That left two remaining applicants and one of them slept just down the hall. Consumed by a wave of anger, she wondered if hitting Remy with a baseball bat would get her arrested.

CHAPTER THIRTY-ONE

SAVIO BLINKED. THEN he swore at the sight of Rose's car parked in front of the White Horse Inn.

The *senorita* had slipped one by him.

He slowed the motorcycle and pulled over as an emergency vehicle entered the north end of town, lights flashing. The van with the candy cane stripe careened to a stop across from him and Savio's breath hitched. His thoughts turned instantly to concern for Rose.

The commotion in front of the inn caught his attention for the first time. The double doors stood propped open and a gathering of people milled around the entrance. Rolling the rear tire back against the curb, he parked the bike and stripped off his helmet. He threw his jacket across the seat and abandoned caution, crossing the street. An upward glance at the second-story showed nothing, the angle of visibility too sharp. After a moment he strolled away from the flurry of activity. At a casual pace, Savio scanned every person in sight before he ventured back to where he'd parked.

He admired Rose's resourcefulness. He especially liked that she was both clever and sneaky. The way she'd played him at the mine had bordered on devious. Among her many other attributes, he appreciated her superb emotional control and bravery.

A frustrated breath whistling out between his teeth, he kicked a pine cone off the sidewalk.

Attraction clouded his judgment. He should have kept her with him, instead of leaving her in a dark hole in the ground. Hindsight. Had he removed Remy and Mackenzie from the beginning, events would have unfolded in a different way. He needed to stop making excuses. No longer just working the job, he continued postponing any real decision about his life. He was still in Riverside because of Rose. Uncharted territory for certain.

He'd offered his shirt to make her more comfortable, tucked her car key deep in her pants pocket so it wouldn't be lost, and even left her cell phone in her possession. Many courtesies had been extended and accepted.

Savio scowled.

The woman made him soft. *Him.*

Then she had the exasperating gall to arrive back in town *before* he did.

Several figures appeared in her window and a surge of panic bubbled below his calm surface.

Rose might even now be injured.

Savio clenched his hands and stared. When he caught a glimpse of her, relief flooded through him with such force he swayed. The figures shifted and he saw Rose tuck her hair behind her ear. Distress apparent, she rubbed a hand across her forehead and nodded.

By now the production location was compromised, leaving Mackenzie balls-to-the-wall. At this point another body on the ground mattered little. Had the man tried to do something to Rose? Options narrowing by the hour, the danger level escalated in a corresponding fashion. The longer Mackenzie stayed around, the greater the odds of connecting him to the drug-production site in the mine. But if Mackenzie skipped town he forfeited his agreement with Savio, the representative of the powerful Almeida Cartel.

Tough choice.

Elude the authorities or make yourself a mark for the courier representing the Almeida family's business enterprises.

Savio decided to revise his plan.

Mackenzie wasn't stupid. A smart man stockpiled his remaining supply of narcotics before cashing out his deal. He had rendezvoused with Remy in West Yellowstone today.

Savio wondered why.

Had the men made a final exchange, drugs for cash? If so, Remy might be on his way out of Dodge. Either man could slip away without explanation or excuse, just pack up and head out, a tourist at the end of his vacation.

The emergency crew emerged onto the porch. Savio's heart struck a hard double-beat when he spied the form strapped to the stretcher. His gaze darted back to the upstairs window. Rose still conversed with someone inside her room.

Curiosity piqued, even from this distance he could see the figure was small, a female, but the woman being rushed to the ambulance was not his.

His?

Savio backed up and collapsed on a bench. The word reverberated on a loop. Even as alien as the idea had first struck
him, already he liked claiming her as his own.

"Mine," he breathed aloud. The affirmation resonated from
deep within.

An obscene phrase, half profane and the rest prayer, spilled
out of his mouth in Spanish. When it came to Rose, the force of
his desire was a persuasive physical energy. The memory of her
body pressed against him, of her unrestrained passion, raced his
pulse. The game had changed. His focus had shifted. Now, he
faced the challenge of convincing her to give him a chance to
explain his behavior. Mouth twisted into a wry smile, he
acknowledged how leaving her tied up in the mine didn't count
in his favor. Her warning took on a new dimension.

He pulled out his phone and dialed Mackenzie's number,
taking it as a promising sign when the man answered.

"The mine is crawling with Park Rangers and U.S. Marshals." Mackenzie's voice sounded terse. "We have a problem. I
told my client to grab his shit and get out. Instead, the stupid
fucker went ballistic on some woman in town. If he's caught,
it'll lead back to me."

Savio's arms felt heavy.

He'd been right to delay Rose's return to Riverside. In the
end, stranding her in the mine hadn't mattered. The time he'd
spent kissing her made the critical difference. He lifted his gaze
to her room but no figures stood displayed in the window now.

"How is that my problem, *senor*?"

Mackenzie sputtered. "If Remy gets busted, he'll spill his
guts to make a deal. I go down, you don't get paid. You don't
deliver the money to Almeida, we both die badly."

Savio shoved down a flare of savage satisfaction. Mackenzie
had just given up Remy's name. He kept his tone even, the

words clipped. "I know about the mine. I am also aware that before the rangers rode in, you cleaned out most of the product." He paused to let the information sink in. "Now, tell me what your client has done."

The muscles in his face tightened as Mackenzie relayed the story Remy had told him.

Mackenzie's voice went thin with anger. "The crazy bastard got worked up over some broad, going on about her all damned morning. Look, this kind of shit is bad for business. Suspicious, he thought she was a cop or something. He went to search her room and she walked in on him. He must have panicked. Either way, he said he dropped her."

The end-result sent someone on an unexpected ambulance ride.

Savio enjoyed the relief of knowing Rose was safe at the moment. He chewed on the inside of his cheek. Even Eduardo Almeida, a monster by his own admission, did not approve of striking women or children. He happily produced and distributed substances by which they might kill themselves but he never considered himself guilty of direct violence. The guys at the top of the food chain relied on personnel for the dirtiest work. In Mexico, he'd observed men like Almeida cultivating fear in their minions. He used that to his advantage now.

He had underestimated Remy's compulsive behavior once – he would not do so again.

"Where is Remy?"

"He called me a few minutes ago from West Yellowstone, said he wanted to meet up and make the exchange. I told him I can't risk it now."

Ah, so Mackenzie still had the product. His wariness in meeting up with the client who'd broken the golden rule and drawn the attention of law enforcement was understandable.

Savio considered options. Rose was surrounded by police. Who had Remy injured?

He climbed to his feet.

Time to twist the screws a little tighter on Mackenzie. "Your client must be stopped before he draws more attention to us. I will take care of it." He didn't have to say the rest.

"I had bad premonition about this whole thing," Mackenzie spat into the phone. "Shit is out of control."

Savio let a heavy accent seep into his words. He wanted to remind the man of his Mexican associations. "Do not excite yourself, *senor*. Leave this task to me. When I contact you be prepared to make the exchange. You may do with Remy as you please. Have my product ready so we can conclude this business."

He ended the call.

The motorcycle abandoned outside the mercantile, he jogged down an alley. The short cut led one block over to the seediest public house in Riverside. Right now a beer and some bar food, seasoned with a dash of gossip, offered the best promise of extracting the information he wanted. As soon as the excitement of recent events passed, locals gathered to share the experience. All Savio need do was wait. After he knew the details, he'd be able to formalize a strategy. Tempted to turn over both men to the local cops, he hesitated. Such an act might compromise his remaining time with Rose and he wasn't quite ready to leave Montana.

She'd capably demonstrated she could fend for herself. Savio trusted the *senorita* to continue doing exactly that for the next few hours.

Chapter Thirty-Two

ROSE FELT TOO calm. She watched Winslow's gaze slide across to Delmar but the other man only shrugged, indicating his uncertainty.

The second old guy turned his watery eyes, colorless as a rain-washed morning sky, toward her and asked what she thought the most obvious question.

"Why was Nellie in your room?"

She rotated in a slow pirouette. "I don't know."

Winslow reached out and swiveled her around by one arm until she met his gaze. "Who attacked the ranger?"

She echoed her previous statement.

Delmar mimed throwing back a jigger. "She needs a tot of whiskey, for the shock."

She thought alcohol sounded like an awesome idea.

Winslow glared at the other man. "Get her some water." He steered her toward a chair.

She let him.

Delmar fetched the glass from the bathroom sink. "Spirits'd be better," he muttered over his shoulder but he thrust the tumbler into her hand and made sure she raised it to her lips.

Rose drank as instructed.

Winslow pointed at the door.

Delmar responded with a probing look before disappearing into the hall.

Rose drained the water and set the empty tumbler on the doily-covered table with a muffled thump. "The answers are here somewhere." She stared at the center of the room. There had to be a reason Nellie came by today. And, an equally valid explanation for why someone had hurt her.

Rubbing her palms down her thighs, she rose to her feet and began to pace.

Winslow waved to get her attention. "Please," he indicated she should sit down, "I'd like to share something with you."

Gaze locked on eyes the same color as her own, she sensed his tension. Did he have inside information about all this? She sat.

Winslow studied her. "You've just had a great shock but while we wait for Harlan to arrive, I thought I'd tell you a story."

Not bothering to hide the puzzled frown on her forehead, she nodded. Her agreement pleased him.

"Back in 1939, the train depot in West Yellowstone linked us to the outside world."

Rose stiffened. Her grandfather had visited Riverside that same year. Curiosity stirred. *Why* share this history?

"The railroad brought visitors, many of them, and like strangers in an unknown place misfortunes occurred. One such event earned the park a special notoriety when a wealthy young socialite disappeared."

His narrative faltered for a fraction of a second as she jerked upright.

She uttered a muffled curse. She recognized this story. She'd heard about the search for the heiress. The one who reappeared, married to an Argentinian millionaire six months later. A man with whom her parents had expressly forbid her to socialize – the same guy who'd done business with Rose's grandfather.

Even as all this information scrolled through her memory, Winslow continued speaking.

"If you face north down Main Street, that empty lot half-way to the curve is where the Comstock Hotel once stood. My mom worked in the kitchens and helped outfit rescue crews. The night after the woman's disappearance, a man arrived amid whispers hinting at an unsavory past. His name was Archimedes Bannion."

Rose raised a hand and interjected. "Anybody acquainted with my Granddad would consider the term *unsavory* to fall quite a bit short of the mark."

Winslow closed his eyes. His voice went hoarse. He repeated her words, "Your granddad?"

She nodded.

"Well, Mede Bannion stayed on, even after all the other searchers gave up –"

A hard knock interrupted Winslow.

Delmar had pulled the door shut when he left but the mechanism had failed to latch. Now the wood panel flew open and bounced into the wall. Plaster cracked where the knob struck.

Harlan Groates stood in the doorway. His rumpled clothing punctuated the hard grim line of his jaw. He appeared older than the last time Rose had seen him.

The sheriff nodded a greeting at Winslow but he directed his attention to Rose. "I need to ask you some questions."

Rose hunched. The image of Nellie's ruined face contrasted sharply with the smiling woman who'd helped her return to the parking lot after the shock of finding a dead man.

"Any news yet?" Winslow asked, leaning forward with a hopeful expression.

Harlan's scowl hardened into deep folds, "She's been airlifted to Bozeman. Until they get her to a hospital with imaging equipment, they can't tell the extent of internal injuries."

Rose had trouble collecting her thoughts. Uncertain if anything she knew was worth sharing, she debated speaking up. The damage done to Nellie could not be undone. Guilt weighed on Rose because she had knowingly withheld information that might make a difference. Events from the last couple of days jumbled up with the story Winslow had been telling her, somehow relating to her notorious grandfather. Too much stuff jammed in her mind. She rubbed her temples again, unable to focus.

The sheriff's radio crackled with a coded message. He held up a finger, wrested the receiver from his shoulder and responded. Retreating, he pulled the door closed behind him.

His departure left a vacant space in the room.

Rose locked gazes with Winslow. He told her this story with deliberate intent. She recognized the signs of nervousness. The big reveal was soon to come. She fervently hoped he didn't reveal her grandfather had killed someone all those years ago. Although the idea existed within the realm of possibility, she felt a smidge brow-beaten today and anticipated taking the news poorly.

"I'm not unappreciative of your storytelling skills, Winslow, but could you summarize and get to the climax? Frankly, the suspense is killing me."

He paused for a moment, nonplussed. "Okay, more to the point, shortly after you arrived in town I paid a visit to Anton and Lily. They own the White Horse Inn." He waited until she nodded to confirm she made the connection. "Anton noticed your signature when you signed the register and he realized we share the same middle name." His gaze held hers.

It took a second for the meaning to sink in but then genuine surprise rocked Rose. She hadn't expected this revelation. Her memory leaped back through the details of the story. Her grandfather had been in Riverside in 1939, a fact she'd already known because she'd seen the photographs in the photo albums. One reason she'd settled on researching in the western side of the park included revisiting a place he'd once spent time. But there was more to this story, a familiar refrain she'd heard told at family gatherings over her lifetime. Her granddad had traveled widely and everywhere he'd stayed, he'd left behind a child, sometimes two.

She held the old man's gaze. "Let me guess, Mede Bannion was your biological father."

Shock widened his eyes.

She smiled at him, "And that makes you my uncle."

"I don't have any proof to show you." Winslow brushed his fingers through his hair, the motion carried nervous energy. He plucked an old black-and-white photo from his shirt pocket and passed it to her. "This is all I have."

She took the picture. Her grandfather, young and tall and handsome as the devil smiled at the camera. One arm wrapped around a small dark-haired and dark-skinned Native American woman, the lens had captured a glimpse of his charismatic personality. The background showed the Riverside Train Depot. She'd seen a similar picture in the photo album at her grandparents' house, one which hadn't included Winslow's mother.

Rose stood up. Even though the man was a complete stranger, she went to him. Perched on the arm of his chair, she leaned down to give him a one-armed hug.

"I loved my grandfather but sometimes I think he was a selfish bastard. Welcome to the family, Uncle Winslow."

He clumsily returned the embrace.

Words muffled against his shirt, she said what now seemed obvious. "I should have noted the resemblance to your brothers."

Winslow echoed the last word. "Brothers?"

The tightness in her throat made Rose's voice shrill. "You *must* come out to the coast and meet everyone."

Winslow's arm tightened in response.

The rattle of the door knob interrupted the embrace. Rose turned her head to find Harlan Groates frozen in mid-step. His mouth gaped open. She imagined her unsteady perch on the upholstered arm, half-sprawled across Winslow's chest probably registered as something different in the man's mind. What exactly, she didn't dare contemplate. If she wasn't careful she'd make a name for herself in this town yet.

Harlan stammered out an apology and backed out of the room.

Winslow snickered, his breath tickling Rose's ear.

"Oh man, this is going to confirm my bad reputation." She bounced off the chair arm with a snort of laughter and swiped away moisture from her eyelashes.

Winslow pointed at the door. "Let's go explain."

Downstairs, Harlan said without preamble, "Nellie arrived in Bozeman but it looks grim." The bags under his eyes looked heavy and dark as bruises. "The emergency crew performed CPR until they arrived at the hospital. Now, it's touch-and-go."

Winslow's mouth tightened into a thin line.

Rose went numb. The shock of this news hadn't completely registered before a surge of hope overwhelmed her senses. Her brain kept repeating the part about getting Nellie's heart beating again. A distant critical voice suggested the wave of grief she experienced was melodramatic considering she'd barely been acquainted with Nellie. Her conscience snapped back with an observation that the ranger might have taken the abuse intended for her. The woman being inside the *Clementine Room* lent credence to this supposition. A minor change or two in the chain of today's events and Rose could be the one in the helicopter.

They gathered in the parlor.

For once Rose found her appetite lacking and the Danish plate sat untouched. Coffee cleared her head and solidified her resolve. She discarded any lingering thoughts of evacuating Riverside. Knowing she had a brand new uncle in town brought her a weird sense of security, a desire to see things through. Now she was no longer alone. Nellie's situation made leaving impossible. Rose couldn't walk away.

Harlan offered subdued congratulations after hearing about the familial connection but conversation quickly turned to the crime.

"Nobody has reason to hurt me." Rose insisted.

Liar, liar, pants on fire.

Harlan cast an apologetic acknowledgement at Winslow and jabbed a finger at her. "That may not be true. You found the first body. Maybe you saw something at the scene?"

She frowned, trying to think through everything she'd learned – or thought she'd learned – in the intervening two days and if any of it mattered.

"Or somebody thinks you did," Winslow offered. He gave her appearance a once-over. "You don't look much like Nellie, at least not to me."

Rose stopped ruminating and thought over what he'd said. She chewed on her lower lip. "Actually, Nellie and I are close to the same height and build. Our coloring is different but it isn't unbelievable she could be mistaken for me."

"Was Nellie in uniform?" Harlan asked.

"She had on a beige shirt and green trousers. At first glance she might not appear to be wearing official clothes. I bet her jacket and hat are in her truck." She pushed up from the table to resume pacing.

Winslow eyed her progress with concern.

Harlan swirled his coffee mug on the oak surface, the ceramic bottom scraping over the polished wood. "The attack makes no sense. Nellie posed a threat only if she had potentially dangerous information. We don't even have a reason for her to be inside the Inn. Did she intend to meet up with you, Rose?"

Rose jolted to a stop, staring at him. She shook her head. "If Nellie dropped by unexpectedly, maybe she was mistaken for me – or she recognized someone here. But neither of those ideas explains why she was *inside* my room."

CHAPTER THIRTY-THREE

S AVIO LOST HIS balance and pitched sideways against the wall, catching himself with one palm and steadying his forward momentum. He didn't feel drunk but his body did not obey his directives.

In retrospect, he would weigh the wisdom of this act tomorrow, but tonight his judgment was sufficiently impaired. He didn't care. The moment he'd laid eyes on the gorgeous creature, his self-control had sustained one serious rupture after another.

He'd hit rock bottom.

Camped out in the local watering hole he'd wrestled with his personal issues in the relative privacy of a high-backed booth – and arrived at the first epiphany of his thirty-five year history. He lived an empty life and worked in a profession devoid of personal meaning.

Momentum had carried him from one risky venture to the next. He thrived on the rush of adrenalin danger brought. The incident that left his flesh scarred also severed the anchor keeping him grounded. After the military turned him out, he'd drifted. The lines between the good and bad guys kept getting blurred. Professionals in his line of work accepted the odds, knew life ended by violence too often.

Which made his exquisite awareness of Rose Brashear even more bewildering. Savio Mendes had fallen prey to a civilian.

One hand sliding along the wall, he passed his room and went to *hers*. He rapped his knuckles against the wood. The noise sounded loud in the quiet of the old inn. He looked down the hall. There had been no lights on in any of the upstairs windows when he'd crossed the street.

He knocked again, louder this time.

She'd told him to knock. The memory made him grin.

Rose opened the door and his mind blanked. She wore a pair of stretchy pants with a matching tank and a somber expression on her face. The tip of her braided hair licked at her waist.

"At least you knocked." She yawned on the last word. She leaned against the edge of the frame and waited.

"I am sorry I left you this afternoon." He had nothing else to say. His brain had gone fuzzy.

Her expression didn't change at first and then a tiny frown creased her brow. "Have you been drinking? You smell like booze."

He nodded and almost lost his balance. Bad idea. She reached out and grabbed his shirt, steadied him until he found his footing again. Not such a bad idea after all.

"I wanted to know you are safe," he blurted out.

And I want you in the worst imaginable way and in every conceivable position.

She rolled her eyes. "Come inside." She pulled his arm, tugging him into the room.

He stumbled forward. Impossibly, the interior sat in an even greater state of disarray. She noted his glance.

"It's a bit messy, I've been working."

Everything about her turned his life chaotic. The woman derailed his purpose and that fact did nothing to dissuade his interest. He studied the outline of her face and an unfamiliar ache tightened his chest. He frowned. Her left wrist showed an angry red abrasion, the result of his handiwork.

He winced. "Ah, no, *Querida*," he touched her skin with a fingertip, "I am shamed by my carelessness." A quick check of her other wrist displayed a similar mark. "I am remorseful." He splayed a hand over his heart and sent her a soulful look, "you have literally driven me to drink."

Her features softened and her silky mouth relaxed. "A sure and certain sign of guilt. Apology accepted." She yawned again. "I'm beat. You're baked. If you wanna stay, keep your clothes on. I'm in no mood to navigate regret, alcohol, and mixed signals tonight."

He shrugged out of his jacket but his boots proved overly complicated.

Rose climbed into bed and curled on her side facing away from him.

He sidled up to the mattress and studied her. So lovely. So confusing. He pulled the covers up and turned off the bedside lamp. Then, fully clothed, he laid down beside her.

Savio usually abstained from drinking. Booze was the great leveler. In the military he'd witnessed the results of over-consumption. Alcohol contained the power to equalize adversaries, reduce reflexes, distort judgment, defeat trained preparation, and violate personal ideals.

He was living proof.

Tonight he'd broken one of his own rules. One drink led to another. The more he'd consumed, the closer he came to grasping some grand design in all his turmoil. Alcohol proved the perfect catalyst for introspection. He'd reviewed his romantic desire for Rose with an almost clinical detachment, concluding a single sexual encounter did not promise to satisfy his needs. Prolonged exposure and unlimited intimacy might.

He eased closer to Rose, her warmth a beacon, and closed his eyes. He inhaled her familiar scent and a sense of recognition overwhelmed his numbed thought processes. His body turned into hers without conscious intent.

He sighed, the exhalation releasing tension.

During his binge he'd accepted three successive truths. The first, he craved being with the woman. That she was affected by his physical presence helped balance the scale but not enough to feed his desire to know more. This brought him to the second truth; he wanted to discover everything about Rose. Every stupid and irrelevant and fascinating detail. All of them. His battered bachelor ego still trying to cope with that realization, the third revelation stunned him almost sober. He was committed to continuing his association with Rose after his Montana business concluded.

At which point his need to see her became critical.

Nevermind the clock approached midnight.

Nevermind she was angry with him.

Nevermind how confused he felt over this fascination.

He wanted her. So here he was – the kind of stalker television movies were made about.

Rose scooted back against him, the bedcovers creating an artificial barrier he disliked but accepted. "Go to sleep," she mumbled.

Her words and the silence pulled at him, his eyes growing drowsy.

"Rose –"

She shushed him. "Tomorrow," she whispered.

Hours later a creak of sound woke Savio. His senses fired, internal alarms ringing. Another small noise from the exterior brought him alert. Ambient moonlight displayed the silhouette of a man on the roof outside. Savio recognized the narrow shoulders and mop of hair. The intruder was Remy.

He nudged Rose awake.

34 CHAPTER THIRTY-FOUR

WARMTH CURLED ALL around Rose. In her sleeping mind the muscular arm across her waist become Savio's. The breath on her nape became his. Pressed against his heated body she undulated and jerked awake.

He really was curled around her in the bed.

She remembered the brief and bizarre conversation, him showing up smelling of booze, contrite and disarmingly charming. Being clasped to his hard-muscled chest felt nice. Her sensitive nose picked up the faint smells of sweet smoke and the stronger odor of alcohol but beneath both was something else, a scent more masculine and unique that caused an instant recognition.

Savio.

Oh, god, he smelled good. She experienced an almost visceral primal response, purring a sound of contentment that brought an answering rumble from deep in his chest. Oh yes, something elemental worked between them.

Rose blinked. Why had he wakened her? His entire form was tensed. She felt pleased by this discovery until she realized she was unable to move from under the heavy weight of his arm. She frowned. His torso and one leg had her half-pinned to the mattress. She inhaled sharply but he spoke first.

"Be still, *mi flor.*" His voice breathed the words right into her ear. The note of warning seeped into her awareness even as his warm lips pressed on her skin. "We have a visitor."

A flicker of shadow at the window made her righteous outrage stumble. Her brain noted the movement, understood the motion indicated someone stood outside on the porch roof. She mulled this over for two seconds.

"You're in bed with me, so who's creeping around out there?"

"We will soon know."

She forced herself to hold still, trying not to betray her alertness. The dark room interior, lit only by a pale wash of moonlight from low on the horizon concealed everything in shadows.

"My gun's in the drawer," she reminded him.

His hand traced down the curve of her hip in a caress and a gentle squeeze on her thigh silenced her.

"Promise you will stay here?" His words, a bare breath of air tickling along her hairline made her imagine he'd beamed them inside her head. Savio tensed and she swore his muscles practically vibrated.

"You just want to play hero." She jerked when he pinched her backside.

"Do not shoot anyone, especially me." Savio breathed out, nipping the side of her throat before he slipped away. The mattress dipped as his weight departed.

Rose went taut as the muffled noise of a casement being slid up came from the window. She frowned. She'd checked every latch before retiring for the night, confirming each one locked and secured. Yet one of the curved glass panels had just been opened.

There was no audible sound, no sense of movement. Savio stood beside the mattress one moment and not the next. She remained unaware he'd crossed the room until a sharp thump, followed by a resounding thud, echoed in the silence. The slither of cloth sliding over the sill was drowned out by a man's grunt of discomfort.

The noise broke her stasis.

She flipped over and scrambled out of the covers. She heard no din or scuffle, none of the slapping sounds of fists on flesh like men involved in hand-to-hand combat did in movies. She fumbled for the bedside lamp. The silk shade clutched in one hand, she grasped for the switch with the other. Finally, she located and flicked the slide bar. Nothing happened. No incandescent glow burst through the darkness.

"Dammit!"

Desperate to understand the silence, she abandoned the lamp and scurried for the wall switch. One snap flooded the space with illumination, the blaze blinding her.

The room was empty.

Her pupils adjusted as her gaze danced back and forth. The interior looked undisturbed. Not a single body lay tossed in a heap on the floor. No blood spatter stained the walls. There was absolutely no indication a struggle had taken place. Even her papers and work-related materials, strewn about in a terrific mess, looked normal.

She rubbed a palm over the back of her neck. A careful investigation showed no trace of Savio Mendes. A half-circle depression in the pillow next to where she'd laid her head was the single mark left by her bed companion.

She scrubbed at her face.

Had she dreamed the entire thing?

Nope. One of the five windows sat wide open. She wrapped her arms across her chest and hugged herself. She'd closed and locked all of them.

This had been no dream.

A shiver of fear danced up her spine. If Savio hadn't knocked on her door, the intruder might have caught her unprepared. Like Nellie had been. She didn't have to imagine what came next.

Unmindful of guests in the room below hers, Rose stomped her foot. Of course she hadn't fabricated the fight. Her imagination could do much better. An erotic dream about the sexiest man she'd run across this millennium would not end with a physical tussle that left her alone in bed.

She walked over to inspect the casement.

The window was pushed fully open. She peeked outside.

The roof lay empty.

She pulled the frame shut and inspected the mechanism. The latch sat in the closed and locked position, both the swivel bar and the receptacle attached. Two screws stuck out the bottom, the matching holes in the sill dry-rotted. Nothing adhered to anything permanent. When pushed down, everything appeared secure. It had never occurred to Rose to tug the thing up.

She did so now and discovered the window moved with bare effort and a minimum of sound.

Goosebumps broke out on her extremities.

The chill crept deeper inside her. If the intruder had entered her room, she might have gotten her gun out of the drawer. Would have if she'd been awake, which she hadn't been.

Rose half-laughed aloud. She pressed her fingertips to her temples, trying to suppress the wildly inappropriate emotions for the man who'd crawled into her bed fully clothed. She was the one having naughty dreams featuring him as the main attraction. If this behavior persisted she'd feel obligated to pay double occupancy rates.

She tightened the bulb leaning loose in the socket – another example of Savio's habitual adjustment of the environment – and switched the lamp on and off twice to make sure it worked. She shivered. Angry as she had been about him leaving her in the mine, finding Nellie had revised her feelings regarding that little adventure.

Rose turned on every light. Then she retrieved her gun, checked to make certain it was still loaded, and retreated to the bathroom. Behind a locked door, she skipped bathing and dressed quickly.

Vexed and frustrated, she forced her attention to her original goals. She'd come to Montana to complete a survey. Refocusing on her research offered the best illusion to gaining control over events. So far she'd found a dead guy, had her project derailed, gotten involved with a man who might very well be a professional killer, and discovered a lost relative.

At least the thought of Uncle Winslow made her happy.

She checked her cell. Nothing.

She dropped the phone and walked over to look at the map on the wall. Instead of wondering what was happening with

Savio, she should figure out a workaround for her study. Rather than worrying about complications with her personal life, she needed to focus on her professional future. She'd start by comparing the list of potential mine sites she'd discovered during her stint in the local library with her original sequence. With a final plan in place, she could estimate how much time to dedicate getting a thorough look at each locale.

Her internal pep talk came along well until the devilish little voice whispered that her permit was on hold. A dalliance with the sexy bastard presented an innovative way to fill her empty hours. Circumstances dangled an ideal distraction in front of her and already preoccupied with Savio Mendes, some self-indulgence was in order.

Rose had to admit, her subconscious was persuasive.

She waited for the angelic counterpoint to pipe up and spout reason, but that self-righteous goody-two-shoes never showed. She pictured Savio, with his perfect white teeth and black hair, smooth brown skin and athletic build and sighed.

Holy-Mother-of-God, she'd just *sighed*! Ridiculous.

Okay, so she didn't blame the respectable part of her unconscious for remaining silent, even virtuous girls know a good time when they see one.

Rose veered into the bathroom. Freud would be thrilled with her innermost yearnings. Mouth frothing with toothpaste, she censured herself in the mirror. Savio was sigh-worthy but he might also be a dangerous man, a criminal of the sneakiest sort. Except he'd demonstrated a sense of honor and gallantry, especially when it came to her wellbeing.

It didn't hurt that his physique *was* divine.

She counted to twenty in three different languages while she finished brushing her teeth, forcing her brain to concentrate on other things. Anything.

After exiting into the bedroom again, she triple-checked for intruders, bodies, explosives, and aliens before flopping on the bed. She stuck her face in Savio's side of the pillow and inhaled. She caught the faintest trace of a scent. Languid warmth stole through her and weakened her limbs.

Oh yeah, she had it bad.

Now the night spent slumbering beside him seemed like a lost opportunity. Inhaling a deep breath, she pushed away disappointment. Next time, she promised, no sleep. She realized with a start, she wasn't worried about Savio. It had never crossed her mind that he lacked complete control of the situation.

The sky lightened. Daybreak arrived. Rose yawned. Was the hour too early to expect coffee brewing downstairs? She'd bet the proprietors woke at dawn.

Determined to be productive, she set about cleaning and organizing. Documents pushed into piles, books boxed up and stored in the closet, she'd just flipped over a page to scribble a note on the back when her phone sounded.

She raced over and swiped the screen. *New message from unknown number* greeted her eyes. Her heart rate accelerated. She tapped the line and brought up the text.

Rise and shine my angel.

A smile arced her lips. She typed quickly.

You okay? Catch the bad guy?

No immediate response came back. After a few minutes she noted the time and forced herself to go in search of her host.

Mr. Ingram fixed the problem of the phantom window with foul-scented epoxy. He filled the stripped-out frame holes with pink goo and explained the process in excruciating detail. The stench forced her downstairs.

She descended to the first floor without meeting anyone and collected a cup of coffee. She grabbed three Danish off the pastry dish on her way out to the porch, her steps increasing in speed as anxiety built. The message beep sounded while she was crossing the foyer and she was anxious to pull the phone from her shirt pocket. Outside, she tapped the flat panel and read another text from Savio.

His jaw bruised my hand – have I earned forgiveness?

Rose grinned.

Such a smart ass.

She liked that. Teeth nibbling at her lower lip, she typed, and hesitated a second. No go-backs, she thought, and pushed send.

Be brave. I'll kiss it better tonight.

Chapter Thirty-Five

SAVIO KNEW HE took Remy by surprise. A strike just below the hairline, his palm slamming hard against the man's forehead, knocked him away from the window and onto the roof. The blow brought a savage satisfaction to Savio's suppressed emotions. Catching the bastard sneaking into Rose's room fed his outrage despite the fact Savio had done exactly the same thing. Maybe because he didn't like the mirror the action held up to him.

With Rose safely tangled in the sheets of the bed, Savio slipped outside and shoved Remy's prostrate figure over the edge of the porch.

Remy hit the ground hard, breath exploding from his chest, a stricken whine of desperate need for air choking in his throat as he tried to inhale and couldn't.

The sound made Savio smile as he prepared to jump down. He dropped down, breaking his fall by rolling to the side and slapping the lawn with his forearms. Even so, he felt the jarring of abused muscles. He bounced up on his feet as soon as he found traction and went for Remy again. Collar firmly gripped in one hand, he half-dragged Remy around the corner of the White Horse Inn while the shocked man still tried to kick-start his diaphragm and suck air into his stunned lungs.

Once out of view of the street, Savio employed a grappling technique and it used to steer his captive.

"I told you it was the wrong room and yet you keep coming around," Savio said, the word grated out in a low voice. He shook the man's collar but Remy had not yet recovered his breath.

The memory of Rose pressed against him in the warm bed pulled at him and he wrenched Remy's elbow until the action produced a squawk of objection. "Twice now you have interrupted a pleasant interlude."

A guttural groan escaped Remy.

"This makes me unhappy." Savio punctuated each syllable with a sharp jab to the captive man's kidneys.

Remy's legs buckled, his breathing failed again, but still Savio forced him along. He pitched him up against a battered Monte Carlo backed into one of the parking places behind the inn.

Convenient enough, he thought.

The faded red paint was splotched with primer black smears. He fished in the man's pants pocket and extracted a key. Pushing Remy through the driver's door, Savio climbed in after him and shoved him over into the passenger side of the compartment. He cast a baleful look at his prisoner.

Remy wheezed out his first words. "Come on, man, she's not important."

Savio hit him again.

"Such an attitude toward females offers a grim future."

Remy shouted out a muffled curse. Blood spurted from between his fingers where he'd wrapped a hand across his face but he made no move.

"You are the not important one, *senor*." He shoved the key in the ignition.

Savio knew he possessed more misogynistic opinions than feminist advocates found endearing, but he detested men who demonstrated a complete disregard for the opposite sex. Even an asshole like Remy had a mother to respect.

The car's outward appearance suggested a pile of junk sheet metal but he was pleasantly surprised when the engine turned over and purred on the first attempt. Savio slipped the gearshift into drive and paused to aim an icy stare at the man on the seat beside him.

Remy responded with a puzzled expression and a belligerent. "Fuck you."

Savio snapped his closed fist against the side of Remy's face. The hard impact stung the back of his hand but filled him with satisfaction. "Continue the insults and Mackenzie will collect only the parts of you that are left."

Dazed, Remy sputtered in a breath. A new trickle of blood from his split lip joined the stream from his nose. A bruise already flushed his abraded cheek. One hand pressed to stanch the flow, he cradled his twisted arm across his chest but held silent.

Savio pulled the car out on Main Street and turned south before flipping on the headlights. "Consider yourself a lucky man," he spoke in a conversational tone, "things could be much worse. Had you succeeded in hurting the little *senorita*, shooting would no longer be an option." He canted his head toward Remy. "Bullets are swift and relatively painless compared to the damage I can inflict on a body."

Remy sulked, eyes trained on the floorboard. "I didn't know she was in the room."

"Surely you do not think Rose anywhere but in her bed at five in the morning?" Savio injected skepticism in his tone. If Remy foolishly suggested she had been elsewhere, he'd earn another tap to the cheek.

The man wisely lapsed into silence.

Savio checked the rearview mirror. He steered with his left hand in case Remy decided to be heroic and lunge for the wheel. He'd put enough hurt on the younger man that he figured he could incapacitate his prisoner and still maintain control of the vehicle.

Remy seemed unsure how to react to his current predicament. Every so often he frowned, his confusion evident, but he remained silent until the need to vocalize overpowered sensible precautions.

"Rose said she didn't have a boyfriend."

Savio disliked even hearing the man utter Rose's name. But since he and Rose had yet to reach an understanding about their status, his proprietary feelings might be considered extreme. Under the circumstances he opted not to punch him again. Besides, his knuckles already hurt.

Instead he raised one eyebrow. "That is good to know. We have not discussed such things as yet."

Remy just looked more confused.

Savio waited until they reached a straight stretch of road and then he swiveled his gaze to Remy. "Your business concerns continue to interfere with my plans. What exactly did you intend to do in the *senorita's* room?" He watched Remy swallow hard enough his Adam's apple slid up and down the column of his throat.

"Nothing," Remy muttered.

"Come, let there be honor among liars. We are both in the trade. What interests you so much? She is pretty, yes?" Savio studied the man's body language while he kept the road in his peripheral vision.

Remy sneered at him and shrugged.

Now that Savio wanted the man to talk, he chose to be reticent.

He chided Remy. "You must understand something, Mr. Boothe. I do not tolerate a lack of response." Savio let anger reverberate in his voice. "When I request information, you answer. When I issue a directive, you do not hesitate to obey."

Remy's cocky expression melted away. The sheen of sweat covered his face.

Savio met his gaze and returned a hard stare. "Choose to be uncooperative and I inflict physical suffering. This is the way we play this sport."

Color drained from the other man's complexion.

Savio smiled.

Remy's head dropped forward. He shrank into his body until he appeared more like a teenager than a thirty-year old man.

Savio returned his attention to the road. The urge to empty his bladder became a need. Here was another aspect of alcohol consumption discouraging his amusement with the activity. They'd already reached the outskirts of town and were surrounded by wilderness. He needed a place to park, somewhere unlikely to attract attention. It was time to contact Mackenzie. He was ready to conclude their transactions and make the exchange. But first, he wanted to check in with Rose.

He typed the text and sent it, pleased when a return response came right away.

Mackenzie ignored the call from Savio but he answered Remy's number on the second ring.

"*Buenos noches, senor.* It pains me to know you no longer accept my calls." Savio infused his voice with humor. He smiled at the sharp intake of breath on the other end of the line.

"Mendes. Since you're calling from Remy's phone, I'm guessing you have him?"

Savio allowed the pause to stretch out before speaking. "You have something that belongs to me. I am prepared to offer Remy in exchange, although honesty compels me to confess he is somewhat damaged."

His status as a courier for the Almeida network still working in his favor, Mackenzie wanted to clear the slate. Injuries sustained by cartels in the war-on-drugs never proved mortal.

"I'm ready to meet the terms of our bargain," Mackenzie assured him.

"Allow me to suggest a neutral locale. Between Riverside and West Yellowstone there is a wide pull-out with an excellent view of the prairie." Savio described the location and ended the call. He wondered if Mackenzie traveled alone.

The sky lightened as he steered the car along the western loop of Yellowstone Park. He admired the dramatic contrast of natural features, fascinated by the herd of buffalo grazing on a hillside. Remy sat sullen and unresponsive when he pointed them out. The sun rose high, spread over the expanse of hills and spilled across a frosted carpet of grass and made it glitter like a pavement of gemstones. It was an astonishing sight.

Remy, finally provoked by Savio's commentary on the odd but elegant moose cows, spoke. "Why don't you just let me out now? Then you can watch the fucking wildlife on your own time."

Savio cocked an eyebrow in response. He didn't even bother to shift his gaze. "No matter the trials in life, you should learn to enjoy the moments you are given." He smirked. "The ride might come to a sudden and abrupt end at any time."

Remy huddled close to the door.

Savio sent another text to Rose.

The route ate up two hours. They passed leisurely through West Yellowstone, approached the rendezvous point and spotted Mackenzie parked along the shoulder one mile outside the town limits. The position of his vehicle nosed in from the wrong direction suggested their arrival had been expected from Riverside.

Savio studied the scene.

He slowed the car and pulled off the road. The natural drop created a panoramic vista for photographs. The place offered easy disposal of unwanted bodies, if it came to that.

Remy sprawled as far away from Savio as the interior allowed. The second half of their drive through the park had been silent, except for Remy's labored breathing. An inability to hold his tongue resulted in two sharp blows to the solar plexus which convinced him to be quiet.

"It is just as well Mackenzie has a use for you, Remy. I am about out of patience." He shifted the car into park and looked at the set-up. He wanted Remy as cover. Nothing else offered much alternative. If they opened fire, a shield was his best option.

Mackenzie leaned against the rear quarter panel of his truck. The same backpack Savio had carried from Mexico hung over the man's shoulder. The bright red canvas was the color of ripe tomatoes. A second man, dark haired and powerfully built stood on the passenger side. His charcoal wool slacks, heavy knit pullover and leather boots indicated casual wealth.

Savio assessed the stranger. He noted the weapon pressed against one thigh. The pose *could* have been more aggressive but the posture demonstrated he was not a rank amateur.

The elusive third party.

He ordered Remy to climb out of the car. Savio slid across the center console and followed.

Mackenzie shook his head at Remy's battered face. "I told you to leave town." He turned to nod at Savio.

Keeping the unknown man in his peripheral vision, Savio was prepared to leap behind Remy should he need a protective screen.

The potential for violence inched higher.

"Whatever difficulty exists between you and Remy isn't my problem." Mackenzie raised one hand in a gesture intended to calm. "I'm getting out of Dodge. Let's just finish our business." The silence lengthened. "After today I don't want to see either of you again."

Savio hoped that was true. It was impossible to tell if his adversaries realized how unstable the situation might become.

"This is the guy I told you about." Remy jabbed a finger towards Savio. "He was in the woman's room the other night." Remy lunged forward, scuffling over to rest his arm on the fenderwell for support.

Savio let him go.

The third man took a step back, his gaze swiveling from each player.

Tracking the movement, his own pulse rate edging up, Savio shifted sideways to reduce his available body mass. He tried to make himself a smaller target.

"This guy?" Mackenzie pointed at Savio. Oblivious to the increased tension, he swiveled to cast a curious look at Remy.

Remy bobbed his head.

"The woman is a pretty diversion," Savio lied. "I politely informed Remy to defer his interests elsewhere. He did not."

Mackenzie clamped his mouth shut in a tense line.

Remy shot a defiant glare at Savio. "There are maps of mines and documents all over her room."

The silent partner stood with his gun pressed at his side but his eyes continued to dart to each speaker as words were exchanged. His gaze settled on Savio. "How much is the female worth to you?" he asked.

Savio stilled. Rose did not figure into his exchange. As far as he was concerned, negotiations were ended. The implied threat in the man's question tipped the balance and fired protective instincts Savio didn't know he possessed.

Head tilted to one side, his features hardened into an intimidating glare and he took several aggressive steps toward Mackenzie. "Give me the money or the finished product, *senor*. Eduardo Almeida requires one of the two." His voice was an eerie sing-song.

Mackenzie dropped the backpack and retreated, searching behind him for the door handle without taking his focus off Savio. "Almeida paid for everything inside. Take the product. We're done here. I'm leaving." He motioned for the third man to stand down.

Slowed by Savio's repeated thrashings and the fifteen foot drop from the second floor of the White Horse Inn, Remy stumbled on unsteady feet.

The unnamed man did not speak again but he retreated down the side of the truck.

Savio took a step forward and the others fell back. The distance between the sides increased. He snagged the red pack and circled behind Remy's car.

The trio climbed inside the black truck. Plumes of gravel fanned out from under the tires as they sped away.

Savio felt no need to take unnecessary chances. He crouched behind the Monte Carlo and waited for his heart rate to return to normal. After the adrenalin rush passed he inspected the interior of the backpack. Inside he found a dozen clear plastic cylinders, each packed with pink tinted powder. The cache contained multiple batches of high-grade methamphetamine. A glossy label wrapped around the tube read Orange Sport Drink Mix.

The ruse was convincing. Mixed in with camping equipment the contents appeared unremarkable. He hefted the weight. The pack held a lot of street value. Now he had to figure out what to do with the stuff. He needed to keep the poison out of the system.

An idea unfolded in his mind. He re-secured the drawstring top, flipped over and sealed the velcro closure. He deposited the bag in the trunk of Remy's car, climbed into the driver's seat and made for Riverside.

There was no guarantee Mackenzie wouldn't circle back but Savio doubted he'd try to take the drugs.

The drive past the White Horse Inn was unnerving but to his relief, nothing looked out of place. The windows to Rose's room were empty, as was the front porch. Her car was parked at the curb. She must be close by.

Savio drove slowly through town, turning on the street behind the police station and crisscrossing the neighborhood until he found what he was looking for. Not far from the civic center was the impound yard. He cruised Remy's car around the block twice as he tried to decide if this was the best choice after all. No one was inside the fenced area, so he parked outside the chain-link gates and picked the padlock as quickly as his skills allowed. In less than a minute he swung them open. Jumping behind the wheel, he idled inside and left the vehicle in a far slot, the key in the ignition.

He closed and re-locked the eight-foot fence sections. With a casual pace, he strolled across the street and disappeared down the first alley. Officially, he was almost off the clock. The job was done. He'd identified the bad guys and neutralized the illegal stimulant. Without dumping it in the landfill someplace, he'd left the drugs hidden in the trunk and parked in a secure lot. Maybe he'd drop a dime and call in an anonymous tip once he was safely back in Los Angeles, just to make certain law enforcement realized the drugs weren't drink mix powder.

Now it was time to retrieve his phone and make the call he'd been postponing all week.

Chapter Thirty-Six

From her seat on the porch, Rose spied Winslow walking toward the White Horse Inn. He raised a hand and waved.

She bounded down the steps and met him at the curb.

"Good morning, Rose. I thought you might like to join me for breakfast this morning?"

"I'm always ready to eat," she said and fell into step beside him.

She kept up a steady stream of questions, asking about his mom and his years in military service. When she finally sputtered to a stop he started.

"What are you doing in Riverside?"

She explained her research premise and the reasons for the delay. "I'm on a tight schedule to complete this survey." She grimaced. "I can do it, if the Park Service ever lets me get started. Riverside seemed like a logical choice since I could combine working in Yellowstone with my desire to visit a place where Granddad spent time." She glanced up at him. "Somebody should have realized the possibility you were here. I mean, everywhere Granddad went, he left a kid behind."

Her words sounded harsh but she didn't apologize. It was the truth. A stranger had contributed half of Winslow's genes. It was nothing more than a happy accident they were related.

Winslow steered her toward a dilapidated storefront with a hand-lettered sign reading 'The Caribou Pit Stop.'

The interior looked delightedly disreputable.

Rose scuttled gamely inside the dim bar where they sat at a tiny round cocktail table. She sank deep in the fake cognac leather upholstery and experimentally rolled across the floor on shiny brass ball-feet.

She grinned at Winslow. "This is so retro it's cool all over again."

He glanced around. "I guess the place needs a décor overhaul." He focused on her. "So what's your research about?"

She leaned back to allow the server to set down a plate of assorted toast points and a crock of butter. "I'm trying to demonstrate how mine workers lived a different life than popular history suggests. We have these images of dirty half-starved guys with grimy faces. True enough, in one sense, but they earned a decent living at a time when the entire country was run by back-breaking labor. They labored hard and they enjoyed the results."

She stopped talking to peer inside each of the trio of tiny jars with spoons sticking through the lid.

"I recommend the pot roast and eggs, unless you're one of those vegetarians?"

Rose shook her head. "Not me, I'm carnivorous."

He told the server what they wanted as she slathered warm raspberry spread over a piece of buttered toast. Stuffing the wedge in her mouth, she rolled her eyes and made appreciate noises.

"How much do you know about your, uh...dad?"

"Not much. Mom said he didn't stay put long."

She nodded. True enough. "Do you want to hear some stories?" She waited until he indicated yes and then she began to talk in earnest. "Things got censored due to my tender ears but I've managed to piece together most of the big picture. Before he married, Mede Bannion's life revolved around women and shady deals."

Rose paused to pour cream in her coffee and sip. "Don't get me wrong, I loved and admired the old rascal but I try to balance myth with reality. He was generous with his wealth. Not so giving with his time. Only God keeps tally on the kids he abandoned."

Winslow winced and she felt sympathetic.

The server set down two thick ceramic plates.

Winslow pointed at hers. "Eat first."

Rose obediently shoveled food for a few minutes. Thinking about her Uncle Achmed, she realized Winslow was a year older. She paused and calculated.

"I think you're the oldest child."

He looked surprised

She thought he should appear alarmed but he didn't, not yet.

"Congratulations, Uncle Winslow. You just became the head of the family. Uncle Achmed's been in charge for all these years and he'll be happy to turn the reigns over to someone else."

Winslow set down his fork and caught her gaze. "For a kid who grew up one generation removed from the reservation, I'm having a difficult time imagining a brother named Achmed."

Rose nodded. She couldn't imagine what he must feel like. Deprived of the love and attention of a parent was bad enough but being denied access to siblings and extended family sucked.

She finished eating in silence and slumped back in her chair, cradling her mug. "Thanks for inviting me. That was awesome. If I don't start exercising, I'll be rolling down the street in a week."

Winslow laughed. He picked up his cup and settled back in his chair. "Tell me about my dad."

Rose asked the waiter for a refill.

"If one word best described Mede Bannion, it would be contrary. His mid-life crisis ended in monogamy. The stories I most like are the ones from his youth, before he became slightly respectable – which still leaves a fair amount of unexplored material to work with.

"Granddad traveled extensively. He disappeared for months into the heart of one wilderness and reappeared in another. Part of the charm of those years, at least for me, is that they occurred in an era when rules were fluid. Overseas travel today requires all sorts of things like inoculations, papers, and permissions. Mede went where he wanted and did what he desired with a devil-may-care attitude and a wad of cash. If rules existed, he avoided or ignored them with impunity."

Winslow shifted in his seat. "He sounds like an ass."

She grinned. "One of my favorite stories concerns his attempt at an illegal excavation in the Valley of Kings. He didn't stick a shovel in the ground before the guards showed up. Egypt was just as political back in the 1940s as it is today and he found himself forced to talk his way out of another tight space.

The idea that Granddad could possibly discern a clue missed by trained Egyptologists and generations of local looters, well, it's absurd." She studied his face. "His command of Arabic was lousy but as an accomplished grand-stander he boasted and blustered long enough for the others to slip away in the darkness. The guards, uncertain what to do with the loud foreigner, sat down to discuss possibilities."

Winslow shook his head, amused.

"He shared his cigarettes and then his tea. The men were devout Muslims and never drank liquor but the brew was laced with brandy." Rose gave a sage nod. "When the next shift took over the guard post, he accompanied one of the guards home and met the first of his international brides. The father insisted his unmarried daughter was a fine woman but unsuitable to the men of the village.

Granddad later boasted it was because she had a mind of her own. They wed and had two children. Achmed emigrated to the U.S. after their mother passed away. Hessa married a well-positioned bureaucrat and still lives in Luxor."

"How many siblings do I have?" Winslow asked the question slowly.

Rose bit her lip. "A lot. Uncle Achmed is the oldest – well, not anymore – I guess. Next, is Aunt Fatima, who is from Istanbul. After that is Uncle Giang, from Vietnam. There were two sisters from China who died in an epidemic. A return winter visit to Egypt produced Hessa."

She paused to let him take in the information. "Your dad got caught in France during the war and begat the French brood: Jean-Paul, Jean-Claude, and Jean-Michel." She ticked them off on her fingers, her smile a little lopsided. "Lest you think he settled into a routine, the boys all have different mothers."

Winslow closed his mouth.

"I know about a daughter in Morocco and another one in Ireland but I've never met them. My mom is the youngest of the nine children from his marriage to grandma. On more than one occasion a surprise arrival has landed on the doorstep."

Rose watched closely but words appeared to fail him. "Drink some coffee," she suggested.

He did.

Remembering what Delmar had suggested yesterday, she asked, "You want a shot of whiskey?"

He insisted he didn't but he looked a bit shell-shocked. They rose to leave, meandering back downtown and gazing through shop windows.

By the time they returned to the White Horse Inn she'd explained the basic relationships.

"So, most of Mede Bannion's children also raised families." She linked elbows with him and looked up, squeezing his arm. "That means you've inherited scads of nieces and nephews. I promise it'll get easier once you have faces to go with names. Swear you'll visit California."

He smiled but said nothing.

She tugged at his arm until he stopped and looked down at her.

Holding his gaze, she said, "Just FYI, Winslow, but when the family finds out you exist, they'll expect to meet you. They'll want to see you. If you don't come to California, they'll come to Riverside."

CHAPTER THIRTY-SEVEN

ARLAN'S HEAD POUNDED. Each thump echoed loud in his eardrums. He glimpsed a cloud along the horizon line and focused his concentration on the puff of white rather than the pounding of his vascular system. It didn't work. His ribs hurt. He tried harder, trying to remember what the cottony fluffs in the bright blue sky were called.

Cumulus.

Remembering felt like an achievement until another spasm stole his breath. Against his will, his focus was forced back to his body. Each battered palpitation pulled at his chest muscles. He drew a deep shuddering inhalation and expelled it, trying to concentrate on repeating the process. Inhale. Exhale.

Breathe in.

Breathe out.

These were symptoms, Harlan realized. Something had happened to him. A severe trauma. The frightful shortness of air frightened him. He gasped. The pressure in his torso pained him. The accompanying cold sweats and dizziness made him lightheaded. He tried to frown. These bits and pieces were bad enough by themselves but when he added all the symptoms together, the result spoke ill for his odds of survival.

Well, goddamnit.

His analytical mind returned to assessing his state. He smelled something burnt and remembered the groove that plowed along his skin and the hole in his shirtsleeve. Yes, the first bullet burned through his uniform and tore into his upper arm. The projectile perforated the fleshy bottom of his bicep, landing across the road with a solid thunk. He assumed it was imbedded in the butt of the old cottonwood stump.

The wooden thump echoed in Harlan's mind. With detached clarity he registered the welling of blood from his wound. Not so bad. Messy, but a pressure bandage would stem the bleeding. He moved on. The emotional part of his brain began to relive the moment, shouting and reeling from the rush of adrenaline caused by his altercation with the men. The details were still fuzzy but he remembered the dusty black Ford F-150 veering onto the pavement and racing away.

Harlan tried to reassure himself that his injuries were minor. The first shot had been something small, probably a .22 caliber. Pulling together his scattered thoughts, he attempted to review what he knew about ballistic trauma. Stop blood loss. If he bled out, shock wouldn't matter.

Stickiness spread down his left arm and trickled over his armpit, emphasizing the growing numbness around the impact site. Neither of the two bullets struck in a critical area. Not sure where all his organs were, he decided no major component of his central nervous system had been blow apart. Gunfire to the brain or spine brought a swift death. Usually.

Panic gripped him but he simply didn't have the breath to freak out.

He needed to know how much time elapsed since the exchange of fire. He coughed, tried to inhale. A crackling wet din filled his ear canals, like bronchial congestion in the chest.

That's a bad sound.

A bleeder in at least one lung. Tissues torn and damaged by gunshot sucked up the surge of endorphins his body released in an effort to minimize shock to his system.

He exhaled. For an agonized fraction of a second, he couldn't draw fresh air. That moment of paralysis brought the panic response he'd been fighting. Then he inhaled again and the incredible pain lessened. His fear did not.

He passed out.

Awake once more, he was uncertain he'd really gone unconscious. Was he bleeding out? That was the most common result of untreated gunshot. Fluid pooled under his shoulder, he assumed it was blood. Hopefully his organs failed before his brain experienced irreversible damage from loss of oxygen. He blinked. Another cloud floated into his peripheral vision. Warm asphalt heated his palm. He flexed stiff fingers.

Harlan clutched his sternum. Every movement inserted hot coals carefully and precisely in the entrance wounds. He persisted, searching for his revolver with his right hand. It was no good. The gun landed somewhere out of reach. He concentrated on breathing, counting down from ten. He turned his head an inch and his eyes settled on the still form of another person. The man he shot. The body lay twisted in a strange angled position, his feet protruding in an unnatural way.

How did these events come to happen?

He racked his brain, piecing together the sequence. He'd pulled his borrowed cruiser onto the shoulder and parked behind a truck. The stop was routine, like dozens he'd made over the decades. A broken down vehicle on the side of the road. In empty country with swift-changing weather conditions, lives sometimes depended on such courtesies. His actions were predicated by a lifetime of experience and a career spent assisting people.

Two men were busy changing a tire. One was in the process of hoisting the flat into the bed. Harlan remembered him as thin and young with a scraggle of auburn beard covering most of his chin and a cigarette clamped in the corner of his mouth. The second man, also bearded, crouched beside the wheelwell tightening the last lug nut. He rose to his full height as Harlan stepped out of his vehicle.

Harlan recalled glancing up to the cab.

A third figure climbed out of the rear seat through a half-sized suicide door. Before he'd returned his gaze to the guy with the tire iron, a popping noise sounded and a sharp sting bit his arm.

Amid the shouts and curses Harlan reacted. He drew his .38 revolver and rotated. A second report echoed and a bullet zinged over Harlan's uniform hat at the same time. He fired twice in swift succession. The young perpetrator went down silent, a crumpled pile of clothes and limbs on the graveled shoulder.

He'd stumbled backward, shocked as much by firing his weapon as by the impact of actually being shot. Everything moved in slow-motion. That was one thing Hollywood got right. The tire iron was flung forward, spiraling through the air. The bar fell short, bounced off the road surface and skipped across

Harlan's boots. He staggered but stayed on his feet, registered no sense of pain.

He'd levered his aim sideways, surprised to find his gun already in position. The bearded man bent low and scrambled toward the cab. The last assailant raised his firearm. The retort of Harlan's .38 barked at the same moment the barrel kicked up in the other man's hand. A bullet hit Harlan low in the chest and tore through his skin like a fiery brick.

He didn't remember falling on the pavement but he'd continued to fire his sidearm, emptying the cylinder on instinct. He thought a bullet caught his target in the lower back as he climbed inside the truck. The impact spun the assailant around and slammed him against the open passenger door, his gun clattering to the road. Maybe. By then he'd been close to blacking out, the world gone grey and purple, filled with shadows.

He'd heard the engine crank over, imagined the driver pulling his wounded companion inside before violently stabbing the accelerator. The vehicle swiveled as the screw jack slipped from under the axle. The rear tire spun until they caught traction on the loose gravel. The big four wheel drive bucked onto the asphalt, the tires squealing as they found purchase on the pavement. He looked up to see the truck careen across the lane into the direction of oncoming traffic before the trajectory corrected. The passenger door swung wide once and slammed shut.

Thankfully, they didn't reverse and finish him.

The bullet imbedded in his chest hadn't splintered out his back, at least he felt no exit damage. Probably another .22 caliber. He took stock of his physical condition. He still lived. He hurt. He couldn't draw a deep breath.

Trying to force his sluggish body to respond, a whimper trickled up Harlan's throat. He swallowed it. He concentrated on rolling to one side. He wanted to face the man he'd shot and he didn't want to drown in his own fluids if he passed out again. The pain grew with each passing second. Until today, he'd never drawn or fired his gun in the line of duty. Surprised his aim even found the mark, he chalked that fact up to reflexes and survival instinct.

Time inched past. He tried to remember why he wanted to turn over. So tired. Too tired. His mass grew heavier, each breath shallower in the draw. He relaxed and his vision came to rest on the red-haired man. He was sprawled with his face turned away from Harlan.

I killed someone, he realized with a pang of regret.

Spurred by panic, he rolled over. The flash of pain blinded him for a moment. Cheek crushed against the pavement, he cried aloud. Every nerve-ending screamed. As a kid, he'd gotten hit in the head by a baseball. The impact hadn't knocked him unconscious but he'd seen stars. The same sensation gripped him now except his lungs burned like fire. He raised his arm, recalled his hand no longer held the gun, and stared. Blood saturated his shirt-sleeve. He mulled over the source of the wetness.

He fought the loss of consciousness, feared the shadows behind his eyelids. Despite his efforts to remain awake, he lost ground. Just before his eyes closed, he wished he'd called Maggie.

CHAPTER THIRTY-EIGHT

BOREDOM DROVE ROSE across the street to the bench in front of the market. She hadn't been introduced to Delmar's companion but when she walked up, the pair just slid apart to make a space for her to sit.

Cars drove past. Nobody spoke. Unsure if she was interrupting some time-honored introspection, she busied herself with calculating the combined number of years they'd existed on the planet. After several false starts she concluded they reached somewhere near the bicentennial end of the range. Impressive. The quiet which had at first been uneasy became comfortable.

She imagined a life spent in contemplation from this bench. It was an unfathomable idea. Besides, the exercise proved foolish because she couldn't conceive not wanting to know what lay beyond the boundary of town.

It passed the time though.

Dark clouds drifted overhead. The afternoon lengthened and the sky darkened.

Rose hunched her shoulders and stared in the same direction as the old men. They squinted together when a car drove past. Most featured loud music and arm-flailing teens. All of them swirled dust into the air and earned a disapproving, if silent, consensus.

They sighed in unison every time a stray beam of sunlight filtered between the goldenrod leaves of the aspens and lit their shoes, warming their toes.

The tensions of recent days eased. Rose decided lotus posture on the town bench was a cool occupation. Too bad it didn't include a paycheck. The casual viewer might inform themselves about the comings and goings of the local populace simply by paying attention. Faces and cars already seemed familiar. She bet her companions could tell her the names of every person in sight. If she hadn't invoked the code of silence, she'd ask one of them for a demonstration. Instead she amused herself by inspecting people's timepieces as socio-economic barometers. One old woman wore the same ugly brooch pinned to her sweater that her Aunt Fatima never left the house without. The giant face lit up bright as a flashlight. More than once it had been borrowed to fish Lego's out from under the coffee table. Nelsen didn't wear a watch and Delmar's vintage pocket clock predated her dad's birth.

They frowned in concert as a black truck sped down Main Street. The knobby tires stirred up a mass of leaves and dust. All Rose glimpsed was a person slumped against the passenger door before coughing spasms overcame her. Delmar covered his mouth with an old fashioned bandana bleached salmon from laundering. Nelsen closed his eyes until the gust of wind swept

past. Rose snorted and wheezed. She made a threatening gesture at the driver but the truck was long gone by then.

That summed up their last bit of excitement until the Air
Raid Siren went off. The noise blared so loud, Rose jerked and
fell off the bench. While she squawked and flopped on the
ground, Nelsen and Delmar jumped upright on nimble feet.
Each man grabbed one of her arms and hauled her back up before they surged down to the sidewalk. They hurried one block
west. Rose stumbled along behind the two spry old guys.

Delmar headed directly for the honking diaphone mounted
on the top of the courthouse. Other people made their way in
that direction. Before they reached the steps, a shiny new fire
engine and an ancient ambulance careened around the corner,
headed out of town.

Her stomach lurched. Emergency personnel and the antiquated alert system signified a major event. Two bodies already
graced the coroner's roster. Nellie had been badly beaten and
might yet die. Rose swallowed. A man she believed was Remy
had tried to enter her room this morning. Her knight in tar-
nished armor had still not put in an appearance since waking
her up in the wee hours of the night, stinking of booze and un-
chaste thoughts. Oh wait, that last part had been all her.

The diaphone bleated. In the pause between pulses she
caught snatches of conversation. Nothing made sense. Alarm
signals alerted communities of dangers like tornados, floods,
fires, or air raids but none of those circumstances seemed likely.
Even after the blasts ended, her ears still rang.

Delmar and Nelsen abandoned her on the sidewalk and
loped up to the doorway. They fell deep into conversation with
a white-haired old man. She stood at the base of the stairs as
more people arrived, taking turns scanning them and the gathering crowd. She saw expressions of concern on many faces. It

didn't take a genius to figure out the diaphone warranted a true emergency. Speculation grew about what disaster had struck.

Savio leaped to mind – just not necessarily as victim. He'd been conspicuously absent most of the day. And his track record was questionable.

Low-voiced comments circulated. The hushed voices and shocked faces sprinkled through the crowd told her that whatever had happened was bad. She sidled up to a group in time to overhear a thin woman with a time-ravaged face say into her cell phone, "What do you mean somebody got shot out by the turn-off to Newcomb Ranch?" The man beside her jerked like he'd been buzzed with a cattle prod. He grabbed hold of the woman's arm and demanded she identify the victim. Rose leaned in too, tilting her head to catch the conversation while she watched her escorts disappear inside the building. A cluster of more old men followed up the steps in their wake.

The lady flapped her hand for silence and listened intently. She raised her face and closed her phone, clutching the device tightly in her hands. "Harlan Groates was involved in an exchange of gunfire out on the interstate."

The bare facts echoed in Rose's mind like a looped recording. Her almost-friend, a nice man who'd pulled over to help her out even when she hadn't needed assistance, had been shot. Shocked and numbed by the violence, she stopped listening for a moment. An image of him slapping his hat against his thigh as he thanked her for her patience repeated in her memory.

Someone asked if he was dead.

Rose spun on one heel. She hadn't even considered the possibility he wasn't. Shamed, she listened. Her throat closed up tight and scratchy as another voice said he'd still been alive when the emergency team arrived. She leaned against the pole, the diaphone finally falling silent. Sound seemed muffled in the absence of the mighty booms. She sifted through fragments of details, eavesdropping on conversations until she gleaned the bare facts.

The sheriff got shot out on the highway. Allegedly there was one other person killed and some indication a vehicle had departed the scene. A passing motorist called 911 and an emergency unit dispatched from West Yellowstone. First responders arrived and identified Harlan and phoned the station. He'd been unconscious and bleeding from a chest wound.

He lived. That was a good sign, surely?

Nausea twisted up her throat and Rose fought not to vomit. She swallowed against the burn of guilt. At least one victim was known to her. She prayed she couldn't identify the rest of the participants. Someone suggested Harlan's current condition as critical might be upgraded to serious when he reached the hospital.

Rose stopped wringing her hands and made a conscious effort to drop them to her sides. The other man, she heard, had been declared DOA. Rose stumbled and repeated the phrase. Spoken aloud, the words fell eerie and final. She shivered.

The news scared Rose but it clearly pissed off the people of Riverside.

The normal friendly demeanor of the town turned somber. She could easily visualize shops signs being flipped over to the closed side, children collected from summer school activities and taken home. Even the teenagers acted subdued, filing down the sidewalks in small clusters as they disappeared into the residential areas.

Though no one treated her differently, Rose felt like a true outsider for the first time since she'd ventured into Montana.

Rumblings of anger built once the shock passed. The sheriff was a well-liked man. Her arms wrapped around her waist, she remembered the glimpse of humor and genuine care she'd seen in Harlan Groates. She exhaled a shaky sigh and offered up a sincere prayer. She desperately wanted him to survive.

When the crowd dispersed, she turned toward the J&L storefront.

Her personal concerns increased as she retreated. She hunched over in sick anticipation of someone pointing at her and somehow holding her responsible. Unreasonable or not, she held herself culpable for some percentage of this most recent crime. She'd not shared information. The guilt didn't dissipate.

Even in a tertiary way, she couldn't argue that she was uninvolved. She had been the one to find the first body. She carried on a flirtation with a man who demonstrated repetitive criminal behavior. Inside her room was where someone had attacked the ranger.

With startling certainty she claimed a degree of culpability in this latest catastrophe. The idea repulsed her.

The most experienced lawman in Riverside lay shot on a deserted highway. Okay, that sounded melodramatic but in Montana even interstates qualified as isolated roads.

She paced the cracked sidewalk in front of the store and tried to clarify the chain of events from a logical perspective. Nothing came to mind so she went inside.

Grabbing a random assortment of food and drink items, she tossed a composition book and package of roller-ball pens in her red plastic basket. Rose was drawn to writing instruments the way some people were attracted to the tactile pleasure of crisp dollar bills or the cold smoothness of shiny just-minted coins. Just having a new package of pens helped put the world a step closer to the correct axis.

Her steps slowed as she approached the checkout counter. If the shooting of Harlan Groates related to other recent illegal occurrences, reasoning out what motivated at least some of the parties could help law enforcement. She latched hold of the idea because it relieved a sliver of her guilt.

Chapter Thirty-Nine

THE PICKUP HURTLED along the outer loop road. Rob swore his blood pressure spiked every time the truck crossed the yellow line to swerve around slower-moving tourists.

He empathized with the driver's desire to pass other vehicles but the way the guy darted in and out of lanes indicated a bad disposition. He also understood poor frames of mind. As of late, everyone he knew suffered from a similar condition, himself included. But rules were rules and he was a law enforcement ranger. He twirled his hat to the passenger seat, flipped up the visor, and commenced pursuit.

The truck disappeared around a corner at the same time he got caught behind a traffic jam. He slowed to avoid a rear-end collision, impatiently drumming his fingers against the steering wheel. The asshole sped further away while he waited for a car loaded with Florida visitors to haphazardly navigate onto the shoulder. There wasn't quite enough space to pull two cars off the road where four already sat parked. He shook his head in frustration. Thousands of determined tourists had rolled the vegetation into a form of hard-packed adobe pavement. Ignoring their blatant disregard for the posted signs, he steered the park service vehicle past a late model Cadillac and stabbed the gas pedal. He rounded the turn and found the focus of his pursuit had vanished.

Rob let the car slow. He surveyed the empty pavement ahead. Even at maximum speed the guy he pursued couldn't pass out of sight. That left one option, his quarry had gone off-road. Only two places offered the possibility of disappearing fast into the landscape. The first turn-off was impenetrable. He knew because he'd authorized the placement of a dozen boulders to block the tight path between an outcropping of rock spars. No way did the width of a truck squeeze through such a barrier. The second passage featured a rough track leading into the high country. Rob approached an opening in the side rail fence intended to restrain visitor access and rolled to a stop. Tread marks led across the painted line. He whipped the front end around and aimed for the narrow gap bounded by steel railings. The sedan pushed aside undergrowth. A burst of salty odor rose from the pungent sagebrush. Two sets of defined tire tracks ran ahead.

Rob grabbed for his radio and called in his location.

The rutted dirt slowed his progress. The car sashayed sideways as the tires slipped and lost traction in the thick mud. The truck's tread had clear advantage, their wide heavy knobs muscling through the sludge. The trail proved easy enough to follow but the road conditions grew steadily worse. He jerked the steering wheel to avoid a boulder on the slick track and winced when the rear fender crunched against the stone. He scowled, cursing under his breath. That would cost him an hour of paperwork.

He cornered the huge rock. The truck sat mired in a bog. Deep mud had swallowed the oversized wheels. Rob slammed on the brakes. His car slid in a slow skate across the surface of the ground until it came to rest against another mass of stone. Muscles tensed, adrenalin flushing through his body, he tried to take in the scene. The first thing that struck him was the driver's side door standing ajar.

With relief he visually traced the sloppy trail leading away from the stranded vehicle until it disappeared up the bank and into the trees.

He slammed the gear lever into reverse and pushed down on the gas. The car did not move. Mud spun in arcs off the rear tires. Snowmelt and runoff created a pocket of standing water as if nature had designed it to capture unsuspecting travelers. He'd also been caught by the soft muck. Now his service sedan provided the sole available cover.

He hadn't followed some yahoo wanting to get his truck muddy. The driver abandoned his vehicle upon hearing Rob's approach. Off-roading in the park carried a stiff fine but not enough for the typical tourist to scratch off the cost of a ride. He followed the exit route with his eyes again. A firearm could be aimed at him right now. The thought made his shoulders twitch. The car offered minimal defensive value but it was better than nothing. He slumped down, thinking. He needed to check the truck interior. Although someone had fled the scene, a cornered criminal might double back and try to remove a lone pursuer. He used the radio to call in his location. Dispatch took his brief description of the situation and alerted backup.

Rob knew he should wait in the car. He had no desire to trek over the treacherous mud and expose his body as a potential target. He did it anyway.

He crawled out the passenger door, the awkward task rewarding him with solid ground. The fugitive's path led up the steep embankment, a trail of blobby footprints disappearing into the scrub. Rob hunched over, listening intently. He'd come too far from the main road for vehicle traffic noise. Not even a bird sang out a discordant note. A little spooked, Rob picked a careful path forward. The truck's tires had kicked up wide swaths of mud and the metal frame, glopped thick with hunks of muck, obscured the registration plate.

Rob crept along the side of the Ford. He caught the sound of the engine, the low rumbling of exhaust. He craned his neck to check the interior. Not close enough to see inside. Thankfully, the rocky berm was solid underfoot but the slow progress wracked his nerves. Scruffy branches caught his pants. Fat meadow burrs clung to his socks. At least they were still soft. By late summer those same prickles would dry and harden until sharp enough to draw blood. To Rob's over-heightened senses they felt like lumpy bugs and he had to suppress the urge to stop and scratch.

His service revolver in one hand, he clamped his wrist with the other to steady his hold. This left his balance more precarious and as he drew even with the cab he searched the tree line above the small ravine. A trickle of water flowed down a rocky abutment and pooled in the declivity of the dirt track. The Ford's front end had slipped down a half-exposed rock and listed to the left as a result. From his elevated position on the bank, he spied the top of a man's head and right shoulder.

Rob drew aim and barked out an order.

No response. He edged closer. The hair rose on the back of his neck at the sight of fine red droplets spraying the interior window. Blood spatter. Unable to tear his eyes away from the body slumped in the seat, Rob's other senses screamed at him to check his perimeter for safety. He ignored the demand and took a deep breath, listening again, trying to detect any sign of human movement.

His radio crackled.

The noise made Rob jump. One foot slid in the sloppy terrain and he fell. Landing with a leg extended, awkwardly supported on his side, he was amazed he hadn't discharged his firearm. The figure slouched in the passenger seat, almost invisible. That produced a new jangle of alarm in Rob. Blood pressure ratcheted up, adrenalin so pumped up that he darted a quick look inside.

The man hadn't moved.

The receiver squawked again. Rob dropped his arms. He couldn't maintain a discharge stance for an extended period of time. As the last rush of adrenalin drained away he felt foolish crouching in the mud. He climbed back to a standing position and limped around the truck bed. Scrutinizing his surroundings every step of the way, he sidled up to the driver's door. Inside, a dead man stared out of sightless eyes. The stranger's face angled toward the rear-view mirror, blood plastering his torso and exposed hand.

Rob didn't check for a pulse. He needed no further proof the guy was dead.

He stood for a moment, studying the scene. The deceased wore fine clothes. His palms were free of calluses, the nails clean and neatly trimmed. Rob figured he'd spent his days in a place of comfort. The fabric covering his chest shone wetly, saturated with dark stains. By the amount of blood, he guessed the man had bled out.

Rob backed away.

He tromped through the muddy water, the shortest route to his car. Mud caked his boots, coated his legs and reached up to his knees. He stretched inside the passenger window and snagged the radio, called dispatch. The silence was broken by a flurry of broadcast responses as park personnel galvanized into action. Rob counted off another two long solitary minutes before the first backup arrived.

40 CHAPTER FORTY

ROSE PEELED OFF her boots and sagged on the bed. The message light on her phone didn't glow. Still no word from her favorite criminal. Worry gnawed at her. Not about him lying dead in a ditch someplace but his potential involvement in today's disaster. She heaved a frustrated sigh, torn between desiring to know and not wanting to confront the truth.

She ate a container of yogurt hoping to soothe her stomach. She couldn't stop worrying over the situation, so she made a list of events occurring since her arrival. All she succeeded in doing was covering a page with random information. No inspired epiphany. She slashed a line from corner-to-corner and tried again. This time she tumbled around the idea of her personal involvement. Not to be completely narcissistic and put herself at the center of the recent crime spree, she was involved in more than one way.

At any rate, it wouldn't hurt to consider the possibility in the privacy of her thoughts. The details took too long to write so she recorded each main event with a word or two and doodled along the edge of the paper.

Nothing new there.

Trying again, she drew a series of columns on a fresh page and titled one with her name. Underneath she wrote 'arrive in park.' The second she marked 'events' and beneath she listed: 'find body,' 'catch sexy intruder,' 'discover uncle,' 'help Nellie,' and 'Harlan shot.' In the third section she scribbled 'bad guy' and underneath detailed: 'leave corpse,' 'hurt ranger,' and 'shoot sheriff.'

That didn't clarify matters. She tossed aside the notebook. What a pointless exercise.

She drank some spritzer and rolled over to stare at the ceiling. Step-by-step she retraced her route until she came to the discovery of the dead man. Then she backtracked even farther, returning to the main highway. She relived her first meeting with Harlan Groates.

She tried to recall with all her senses.

The grasslands turned to forest, prairie grass replaced by evergreens. A rock outcropping signaled the single change in geology. From there pine trees spread out in uniform invasive waves.

Her phone beeped.

Adrenalin surging, she burst off the bed and snatched it from the table. She swiped a finger up the screen lock and identified the caller.

Disappointment rocketed through her.

Unprepared to talk to her mom, she ignored the call and set the phone down.

She returned to remembering.

An abandoned car trailer had sat beside the highway, the sides rusted into lace by the lengthy Montana winters. A collection of hubcaps shoved between strands of barbed wire by some concerned local created an impromptu modern art display. She'd slowed to admire the accumulation of shiny disks and discovered the dip in the road which produced the unintended offerings from speeding motorists. Every so often a rodent skittered across the asphalt.

In her memory the air tasted sweet and clean, unforgettable after the city smog. The landscape sparkled, fresh from the rain spilled by a thunderstorm in the hour before daylight. Sunlight burned bright and the sky sat clear of clouds, not yet warm enough to roll the windows down. Nothing discordant stood out.

She remembered the few vehicles with clarity. A topaz car whizzed past with loud musical reverberation. A pickup truck overfilled with baled hay lumbered in the opposite direction. A semi passed while she'd inspected the deer. A sedan had come next, just before the cop car. The memory made her think of Harlan again and she wondered how much of a police force remained in Riverside.

Rolling over on her side, she pulled the notebook in front of her. On a clean sheet she tried a new approach. She capitalized the word 'mystery' at the top and underlined it twice, stuck the end of the pen in her mouth and contemplated. She scribbled items below the heading:

Body #1 = found at the thermal pool

Body #2 = discovered behind the Ladies Auxiliary

Rose reviewed her paltry list. The police interviewed suspects and collected information until they amassed enough raw materials to forge connections between suspicious circumstances or link people. Without access to that kind of data she must approach her inquiry like an intellectual exercise. Good thing she was an academic.

Anyone could solve a mystery. For decades network television had offered up proof on a weekly basis, murder and mayhem unfolding from the point-of-view of the viewer's couch. Private detectives and Columbo and Ironsides, Monk and the lady on Murder She Wrote solved mysteries every week. Somehow they stumbled across solutions. All those brainiacs excelled at identifying criminals. Perry Mason even got the guilty person to confess on the witness stand, a relief for viewers because it removed any kernel of doubt regarding the villain's guilt.

Rose liked that certainty but television proved a poor imitation of real life. This sleuthing business was tough. Protagonists never had enough information. Witnesses always glanced away at the opportune moment. Most leads culminated in dead ends. No wonder people enjoyed a good murder mystery. Each fact added up. All the necessary clues affirmed the reader's pleasure with an occasional red herring tossed in for confusion. Solution tied up with a bow at the end and no questions left to ask.

Hah.

Rose frowned at her list. She penned a notation about the locations of the bodies. Solving crimes clearly involved making decisions based on information from which the general public was excluded. Who knew what law enforcement had discovered during the investigation process. Like her own field, most criminal cases required people with specializations. She considered calling her campus lunch-buddy for advice. Jonathon had served as a consultant on several investigations, had recently accepted a position working alongside investigators. He might offer helpful advice.

She didn't pick up the phone though. He'd yell at her for sticking her nose into what was arguably not her business. True enough, except she felt involved.

Besides, considering how Riverside found itself short of personnel at the moment, she didn't think they'd mind if she volunteered an hour or two of her personal time.

Removing herself from recent events might change the way things looked.

She tossed out the trash and tried to clear her mind of preconceived notions. False assumptions usually led down the wrong path.

In her own research she had browsed through publications and sorted photographs that ultimately proved unrelated to her project, resulting in a huge waste of time. The same must be true of criminal investigations. Quality control demanded she consider all possible data, as well as reject individuals whose participation was insupportable. To her way of reasoning, 'a mystery solved' aligned with 'a research problem answered.'

Archaeological excavations often unearthed the unexpected. Experts like her interpreted the past via artifactual remains but doing so required contextual knowledge about the objects recovered, as well as the place and time. Results didn't necessarily equate with accuracy. Conclusions were just opinions, albeit reasoned ones.

Again, the same thing must apply to solving crimes.

Archaeologists never attempted to unlock the secrets of ancient tombs without proper tools and preparation. Lack of forethought resulted in destroyed data. Once lost, the physical remnants of yesterday could not be retrieved.

She needed a plan.

Lower lip caught between her teeth, she scribbled on the page. Her research design must assess every aspect of the mystery. The trouble with this method revolved around the possibility of presupposition. A detective visiting a crime scene who assumed he already knew what happened, needn't work hard to prove his theory. Students often succumbed to this pitfall and proved their fieldwork in the classroom before they set foot in the research environment.

Preparation was critical. The discovery of who killed the two men made a good starting point. Assuming they had been murdered. Had the dump sites been selected for a specific reason or had they been opportunistically chosen?

That circled Rose back to her first topic. If she began with a premise of linked deaths, there must be a corresponding link between the deceased men. To her knowledge, no evidence indicated they were acquainted.

Pleased with her progress, she narrowed her focus. Unrelated subjects might be connected in a webbed network. She didn't personally interact with a lot of other anthropologists, but the ones she did know had their own connections. When she had a question, or needed a recommendation from a subject matter specialist, she tapped into the network. Applying that same idea to her current puzzle, and presupposing the two victims had been known to one another, who knew them both? What common circles did they rotate through? Which spheres of influence overlapped between them?

Rose grunted, hunched over the notebook. Her pen scratched over the surface, script large and sloppy as ideas flowed out in waves. The time had come to consider resources, find people to interview. First-person accounts lent credibility to a theory. They also often produced new directions to investigate. She needed primary and secondary sources. The first established effective research parameters and the second provided backstory. Local speculation offered numerous ideas but actual participants shared the real drama. A tickle of information swirled in the back of her mind. She already had an appointment – she refused to term it a date – to meet Savio tonight. Ruthlessly crushing the buoyant sensation just thinking about the man produced, she planned the interview to provoke answers regarding her suspicions. Nevermind the flutter of excited butterfly wings in her chest. Nothing good came easy, she reminded herself.

Since Savio only seemed to show up in the middle of the night, she'd have more luck leaving out a list of questions and hoping he answered them on his next visit.

The goal of groundwork was to affirm factual and relevant information. Her assumptions and unconfirmed conclusions demonstrated the faults in her research design. Weak arguments produced weak results.

She'd once witnessed a panel of tenured reviewers deconstruct a candidate's anemic premise in moments, leaving years of labor cast aside in a pile of shredded conjectures. Failure to defend their dissertations had ended the careers of many promising students.

Rose realized documentation did more than provide visual validation. A strong thesis lashed together the lines of an argument in the same way steel spikes speared railroad ties to the earth. Known for viscerally defending her position, Rose needed to poke around and find new avenues to pursue. She decided to begin with the research station at Porcupine Bluff, the place her dead guy called home.

CHAPTER FORTY-ONE

CROUCHED IN FRONT of an ancient computer in the Riverside Library, Savio pieced together facts extracted from various news outlets. His plan to re-enter the grid required knowing as much as possible about the events surrounding the takedown of the Almeida Cartel. He found little to flesh out what he'd witnessed in Mexico City. Until he'd reasoned out a motivation for Henri's strange behavior and Cole's sudden personal interest, Savio refused to trust either man.

The satellite phone remained shut down, secreted away in the locked storage compartment on his motorcycle. He'd removed the battery in order to make himself untraceable. Even then, he wasn't one hundred percent certain it had done what he hoped. Technology became ever more complex. Fingers shoved through his hair, he sighed. Tomorrow he'd decide who to call. For now he left the device turned off, not ready to let them pinpoint his location.

Rose's message about suspicious activity inside the Vigilante Mine brought Mackenzie's business to an abrupt conclusion. Law enforcement rangers swooped in and scoured the mine clean.

Moving around in public felt risky and Savio sensed he operated on borrowed time.

He scanned the headlines of a Mexican newspaper. The internet made access to information almost too easy. Seemed a shame they had missed catching Mackenzie but at least the man skipped town with Remy.

Savio rubbed a hand over the back of his neck. What a fiasco yesterday. He should have told Rose to stay at the inn and read a book. For Christ's sake, they'd *all* been skulking around the six square blocks of the downtown.

His intent to keep the *senorita* safe had failed. Despite his efforts, Remy singled her out.

In truth, he wasn't happy with his results thus far.

He'd neutralized Mackenzie.

Remy's unwarranted attack on the female ranger complicated things. Savio caught himself clenching his fists again. Each time he imagined Rose as the intended target, a wave of rage enveloped him.

He checked his burner phone.

Nothing.

He left the library, walking down the residential side streets to return to where he'd parked the motorcycle. Uttering an oath against a repeat of his behavior from the previous night, he entered the bar. At almost four in the afternoon, only a trio of guys sat at the counter. A different server popped caps off bottles and replenished the patrons' glasses.

The door barely closed in his wake before he overheard mention of a shooting.

What shooting?

Savio slid into a dark booth and gestured for a beer. He listened with avid attention while he waited.

Muy interesante.

When the drink came he ordered a plate of hot wings and settled in for a longer stay.

The bartender switched the television to a local channel and everyone focused on the small screen.

The reporter didn't share much but Savio had a good idea of how to fill in the blanks.

He guessed the trio hadn't traveled far this morning. At some point after they parted company, a shootout occurred between Mackenzie and his goons and the local law. A cop took two bullets and there was one confirmed death.

Which one got himself killed?

Based on the blurry distant photograph of the scene, Savio identified the corpse being loaded into a body bag at the site of the shooting as Remy. Mackenzie was a much bulkier man and the stranger who'd been present at their morning exchange wore his black hair cut short. The report of a second victim at a different location stirred angry speculation among the crowd. The lack of information made it impossible to know if the two events were related but Savio hoped Mackenzie bit the dirt.

A line of white text scrolled across the bottom of the screen.

He squinted to read it from such a distance. The breaking news revolved around a fugitive-at-large warning inside Yellowstone.

The second body had been discovered in the park. Now a fugitive ran in a mad dash for the high country and Savio bet his money on the runner being Mackenzie. He was more the overland type than his polished amigo.

Desperate men committed desperate acts.

While he ate, the news replayed familiar images and reported the same information. He only half-listened, his mind processing what he'd learned.

Given the circumstances, law enforcement had to connect the activity at the Vigilante Mine, the shooting on the highway, and the fugitive giving the rangers a workout. Not that multiple criminal enterprises must be related but too many incidents in such a short time defied the odds. Even if later proved unrelated, veteran investigators would consider them interlinked now.

Pulling out the cheap disposable phone he'd purchased yesterday, Savio typed out a text to Rose and pressed send. Then he called the local airport and made stand-by arrangements for a midday departure tomorrow. It didn't matter where he went, so long as he flew the coop.

He'd give himself one night to get the senorita out of his system. The image of her sitting on her knees, her pink bra strap slipping out from under the tank top and the Luger in her hand, flashed across the inside of his brainpan. He shifted on the seat. Christ, just thinking about her made him hard. He checked his phone again. No response yet.

Savio climbed the stairs to the second story of the White Horse Inn. Even though he hadn't paid for another night's lodging, no one's attention followed him as he strolled through the downstairs. The amount of trust displayed by the general populous sometimes disconcerted him. He knocked on the door of the *Clementine Room* but Rose did not answer. Not surprising since her car remained absent from its regular spot out front but he observed the courtesy before picking the lock.

Inside he discovered her cell phone plugged in to the charger and experienced the first panic attack of his life. After he regulated his breathing and calmed down, he thought the situation through. His message from this afternoon showed up as unread. Like him, Rose seldom left her phone behind when venturing out. He opened the drawer and found the Luger stowed inside.

Dread consumed him.

Shoving down panic, he logically concluded she needed to recharge the battery as it still sat plugged in on the bedside table and registered a full charge. She might not carry the gun all the time. The night he'd crawled through the window she'd told him she didn't.

He tried to figure out where she'd go. Probably into the field in defiance of park restrictions. Or following up on a clue.

Either offered a distinct possibility. Given how many times she'd returned to the area near the mine, this posed a reasonable explanation. He thrust away the one idea that kept returning to prey on his fears. When he finally allowed the thought to unfold in his mind, his stomach ached with the same hollow intensity presaging a PTSD episode.

Mackenzie could have taken Rose.

Unlikely, but the possibility existed.

That morning he'd exchanged Remy for the drugs and the third man – the stranger – had questioned Rose's worth. Savio's intense reaction indicated her value was great.

He forced himself to work through the evidence.

Remy represented a risk. He'd attacked a woman, a law enforcement agent, an action guaranteed to invite scrutiny. Mackenzie willingly turned over a large chunk of drug in order to clear his debt with the Almeida network and recover Remy.

Savio chewed over this idea, liking the synergy.

Mackenzie could have killed Remy, shot the sheriff, and high-tailed it out of town. With no identity attached to the second body he didn't know for certain who ran loose in the park but a desperate man might take a hostage. It might be Mackenzie or one of his confederates.

Remy was dead.

Mackenzie had disappeared.

But, so had Rose.

Had she been abducted? If so, Savio could still retrieve the drugs and use them for leverage. He got up and paced across the room. Careful to avoid the wide expanse of windows, he peered out at the street.

With her car missing, the reasonable conclusion was she simply drove somewhere. A safe destination in mind, she left her gun behind. That should make him feel better but it didn't. He glanced over at her phone. Why not take it – unless given no choice? At the rate people wandered in and out of the White Horse Inn, it wasn't a stretch to believe someone strolled in and took Rose back out with him.

He whipped out his cell and dialed Mackenzie's number. The phone rang five times before an automated voice came on the line and directed him to leave a message. Inconclusive. The man had ignored his calls before. Trying again, he got the same result.

Fuck.

Savio checked the street every twenty minutes.

He racked his memory for snippets of conversation, any information to narrow down a potential destination for Rose. The Vigilante Mine was off-limits. Park service personnel denied access to anyone not wearing a uniform and he didn't think she'd go that far. Besides, she had no reason to return there or the thermal pool.

Which brought him full circle to imagining Rose and Mackenzie colliding in the back country.

Savio paced the room. The last message she'd checked arrived after nine that morning. He scrolled the list of missed calls. All came from names entered in her contacts. No strangers.

In the bathroom he washed his hands and face, eyeing the clawfoot bath tub, imagining her surrounded by mounds of iridescent bubbles. He scrubbed a hand across his chin and stumbled into the bedroom. The sight of the bed produced a series of disjointed impressions and memories from last night. He'd inhaled Rose's fragrance until his senses swam with desire. In her sleep she'd pressed against his body and he'd struggled to restrain himself. Now he wished he hadn't.

A wine bottle on the table in front of the windows drew him over. He sighed when he found it empty.

An hour crept past. Then, another.

He burned off his surplus nervous energy with a hard regime of push-ups followed by sit-ups. All the exercise pumped up his anxiety levels. He longed to run but jogging through town in full view of the suspicious public eye seemed unwise.

Instead, he completed an extended stretching routine. Twice.

Dusk lengthened. He left the lights turned off. Finally, to distract himself, he picked through Rose's research, reading her notes and studying the map.

Another glacial hour ticked away.

Worry ate at his gut, making it impossible for him to relax. For a man who once napped during an armed conflict while gunfire rattled overhead, the fact he couldn't doze because a woman he barely knew had driven off somewhere was inexplicable.

He dropped his head in his hands. Maybe he should stack this up as yet another symptom the doctors warned him he must face. Sooner or later a panic attack at an inopportune moment would finish him. Done. *Finito.*

Rose's phone beeped.

Curiosity piqued, he reached over and picked it up.

A memo filled the screen.

Buy condoms and wine.

He read the message and his gut twisted. He hoped to god she meant the reminder for tonight. Without a tickle of guilt to his conscience, he scanned the data folders on her device. The address book identified numbers by names. A few cryptic entries listed as Chinese, Pizza, and Mexican he concluded were take-out options. The video folder was empty but he spent a long time perusing pictures. He scanned hundreds of snapshots, mostly landscapes of open terrain, roads disappearing into horizon points. Some featured piles of bones, desiccated skeletons of unidentified animals. Others showed expanses of dirt but try as he might, he saw nothing in them. If they documented anything important he failed to see the focus. Numerous people appeared and he wondered about their identities.

One series of pictures raised his hackles and that ridiculous sense of possessiveness reared its ugly head again. In the first photograph Rose stood with her arms twined around a man's waist. Snugged against his hip they both smiled for the camera. The next was almost a duplicate. The man wore the same suit and Rose filled out the same skin-tight dress. The couple posed at some fancy event and she looked exquisite in the deep blue color and sexy spiked heels. Her companion towered over her, one hand splayed possessively at her waist.

Savio jabbed the advance button. The next picture caught him off-guard. The photo featured two men, so identical in appearance he'd thought them a single individual. In this snapshot the trio appeared with Rose seated on a leather couch between the twins. The dress left no doubts about her lush figure and her artfully arranged hair spilled down in a cascade of curls from some elaborate clip on the top of her head. Her tiny proportions emphasized the height and broad shoulders of her companions. Middle Eastern in appearance and handsome as djinn, they sandwiched Rose between identical black Armani suits. Brilliant white teeth flashed at the camera, her animated face eclipsing the two men.

Savio scowled at the picture.

He tried to get a handle on this weird reaction. Never had he wanted a woman like he did Rose. Sure, he'd desired plenty of women but always with a take-it-or-leave-it attitude. This one was different and he didn't understand why. At last he set aside her cell and seated himself on the settee with his back to the bed. He stared at the cold fireplace and introspected. In the end, he reached no epiphany, found no conclusion. He pushed stiff fingers through his hair, torn by dual desires to wrap the woman in his arms and shake her until her teeth rattled.

42 CHAPTER FORTY-TWO

THE SCIENCE CAMP impressed Rose by its sense of isolation. The deserted enclosure was eerie when she parked across from the central plaza. The buildings arranged around the square space were reminiscent of a playground in a strange rural schoolyard. Several cars sat in the dirt lot. One grungy SUV displayed a large official decal.

Rose climbed out of the car and stepped across a log barrier. She called a hello.

No response.

She walked into the plaza area. Seats sawn from rounds of tree trunk dotted a fire pit in an oval arrangement. A covered barbecue, halved from a fifty-gallon drum, was set to one side on a stone platform. The compound offered basic necessities with a touch of comfort thrown in. Right now the place creeped Rose out.

"Is anyone here?" she asked again, louder.

An inarticulate shout responded, followed by the bang of a door. Rose turned to face a tall red-haired woman advancing from one of the buildings. The lines on her forehead told Rose the frown was normal rather than a sign of personal disapproval.

"Is there news?" The woman's voice was scratchy with strain.

The puzzled expression on Rose's face must have indicated confusion.

The woman came closer. Dark shadows ringed the underneath of her eyes. "Didn't Rob send you?"

"My name's Rose. I drove in from Riverside to ask a couple of questions."

Her face darkened. "You a reporter?"

Rose wilted at the display of ferocity and stammered. "No ma'am." The denial and the formal address slipped out in an automatic response.

The fierce expression deepened into a scowl.

"I found the body," she blurted.

At this admission the woman paused and focused her attention on Rose in a way that indicated mild interest. Shoulders slumped with weariness; she turned and walked back toward the building she'd exited. "Come inside Rose. It's damn cold out here and I just made a pot of coffee."

Rose trailed behind.

They entered one of the camp structures, the interior decorated with an accumulation of materials acquired over many years of use. Two taxidermied specimens, an antelope and a petite fierce bird, hung above a Franklin stove. Narrow trestle tables and benches filled the space. Through an open door she spied cooking appliances. A table was pushed flush to the wall and housed two coffee pots. One was a large metal industrial urn, the kind that percolated sixty cups, and the other a small drip machine. The glass carafe of the Mr. Coffee sat two-thirds full of dark liquid. A bulletin board hosted an assortment of announcements, fliers, and informational sheets. A schedule tacked up beside the current page of the calendar showed a number of slots with names written beside them.

Rose sat on a bench.

The woman filled a second mug and handed the fresh cup across to her before sitting down and staring in her direction. "My name's Maggie Thompson. I run this place."

The surface of the coffee swirled with the oil slick of strong brew. "I feel bad about the man who died," Rose said.

Maggie appeared to accept her awkward words at face value.

Sipping the hot liquid, Rose tried to figure out how to explain her purpose. "I don't want to intrude, just help. Somehow."

Maggie nodded as though she understood. "I appreciate the desire but have no idea what you'd do." She dismissed Rose with little interest. "Are you a wildlife biologist or a conservationist?"

"Anthropologist."

She made an affirmative noise.

"They train us to believe we can do anything," Rose said.

Maggie shifted on the hard seat of the bench. "In my undergraduate anthropology class the professor acted like a total nutcase, climbed on top of his desk to demonstrate primate social characteristics. The antics worked. I remember that though I've forgotten his name." A genuine smile curved her lips.

"Thanks for the coffee." Rose enjoyed the warmth of the strong brew spreading through her body. She hadn't felt cold until now. "Coming out here seemed productive but I don't know what I expected to learn." Her words trailed off.

"Hear any news?"

"Only that the gunshot wounds were serious." She stopped when Maggie's narrowed eyes locked on her.

"I thought the ranger was beaten?"

Rose nodded her head. "Yes, she was." The shooting figured so prominently in her thoughts it took her a moment to organize all the events in her mind. "Sorry, I assumed you were asking about the sheriff's injuries."

Maggie's face drained of color. She dropped her mug and coffee spilled in a hot stream over the scarred wood.

Frightened by the sudden terrible change in the woman's appearance Rose rushed to explain. "He's alive."

"What happened?" Maggie grasped at the edge of the table.

The words spilled out of Rose's mouth. "Harlan Groates was shot during an altercation on the highway sometime this afternoon."

The woman grabbed Rose's hand. "Where was he hit?" Her voice cracked with emotion.

"Once in the chest and somewhere else." Maggie's fingers had gone icy cold but her grip did not lessen. Rose tried to remember how to treat shock. "The emergency people took him to West Yellowstone. Someone said he was flown by helicopter to a hospital. I'm sorry you didn't know."

Maggie struggled with her composure. She revived from the shock and withdrew her hand to straighten her back.

"Are you okay?" Rose asked.

She nodded. "Just need a minute to pull my head together." She pressed her palms to her cheeks and swore softly, "Damn you, Harlan."

Rose recognized an undertone of emotion and guilt over her crass delivery of news that had clearly been a blow gripped her harder. "Can I do anything for you?"

Maggie gave a shaky laugh. "Don't tell anyone I almost passed out. I'd never live down the jokes." She bent over and placed both palms on the tabletop. "You said a helicopter transport flew him somewhere, right?"

Rose hummed an agreement.

"That means they called for a life flight. He'll be transported to the closest major medical center in Bozeman." Maggie straightened. She never broke eye contact. "Give me two minutes to lock up and then if it wouldn't be too much imposition, you can drive me to the hospital." Maggie walked over and flipped the coffee pot switch to the off position. She scrawled a message on the dry erase board menu next to the kitchen door.

In the car Rose realized she couldn't locate her phone. There went her idea for looking up hospitals. "I'm sorry, I must have left my cell back at the Inn."

"I'll do it," Maggie said and pulled a battered Nokia relic from her pocket.

She located Harlan with a single call. The hospital was ninety miles away in Bozeman. They departed without delay. Intimate with the terrain and familiar with every feature of the region, the drive was punctuated by Maggie's rambling one-sided conversation. Stuck in a car with a complete stranger, Rose learned a lot of enlightening information about people she didn't know. She understood the talkative chatter was cover for

Maggie being buzzed out of her mind with worry so she let her talk, responding when appropriate.

Maggie coached her through the maze of intersections in Bozeman. The city looked like a metropolis after Riverside. A population of tens of thousands might not seem huge but the state of Montana was a big place with few folks. The closer they got to the hospital, the terser Maggie's directions became.

"Drop me off here," Maggie said, pointing at the emergency entrance.

Rose let the woman out and drove around looking for a parking space. She lucked out and squeezed between two large trucks. One more dividend paid to her economical automobile. She worried about being able to find Maggie once she'd gone inside the grey building but her concern proved groundless. The woman's voice carried. The desk closed at six so Rose followed the voices. She pushed open and peeked through a set of double doors to find one of the night staff.

Maggie didn't waste time on niceties. She demanded entrance to the critical care unit.

The red-faced clerk repeated his denial. He offered what sounded like a spiel about medical information only being accessible to members of the immediate family. Rose figured he'd probably said it hundreds of times but the lack of sympathy in his demeanor sat wrong with her. He was kind of an ass about it.

Not that Maggie was much better. She inhaled and started chewing him out.

Rose backed up a step. She refused to get caught in the feeding frenzy.

The walls fairly quaked when Maggie declared Harlan her fiancé. Her angry tones brought a flurry of people from all directions. The flustered employee continued to recite institutional rules until a harried man in a rumpled suit scurried up to the counter and intervened. A muted conversation took place. Eventually the irate clerk handed Maggie a visitor pass with a strained smile and allowed access.

Rose trailed in her wake and nobody stopped her. Based on this demonstration, she suspected few people found the courage to stand up to Maggie Thompson. She grinned for the first time that day. Harlan Groates had no clue what his future held.

They sat alone in a small room amid an awkward jumble of chairs and tables and waited for Harlan to survive surgery. Maggie settled into a blank reverie, her mind obviously elsewhere. Rose meditated on the ugly wall color. She debated whether the dim fluorescent fixture cast amber light and turned the turquoise walls a sick shade of institutional puce or if the unfortunate hue had been intentionally selected. Perched in silence, she found her thoughts kept returning to her mysterious paramour. There was a good possibility Savio had departed for parts unknown. The idea produced a hollow sensation in her chest and she opted not to think about him for a while. Grateful to bring Maggie to Harlan, the continuing guilt she experienced over not sharing information that might have made a difference to how events played out, was somehow balanced in a small way.

She studied the two paintings adorning the walls. The first featured a man astride a tractor in a sunny field of grain. The composition evoked nostalgia for the simple life but it depicted a visual lie. Rural farming equaled hard work. The second picture was more of an assemblage with a bundle of dried colorful flowers attached to an old fence post inside a shadow box. The style wasn't appealing to her but it had a nice countrified aesthetic. Plastic sleeved information sheets about hospital protocol posted near the door served as the only remaining distraction. The place lacked even the litter of magazines found in reception rooms around the world. Having exhausted the entertainment possibilities in the room, Rose slumped in her chair and returned to indulging in speculation about her nighttime visitor.

She considered how he might figure into this tragedy. If instrumental in the event and thus in some way responsible for Maggie's anguish and Harlan's pain, by default she shouldered a portion of the load. Guilt flared hot for a moment before she doused it with a bucket of common sense. There was no point in regret. Roads not taken went places she'd opted not to go. Holding herself responsible for events in which she hadn't directly participated was narcissistic. And, since she was halfway down this avenue already, she might as well figure out where she wanted it all to end up. Besides with her and Savio tangled up together in a bed.

After an hour more people entered to sit in a private huddle. No one shared grief.

Rose got up and stretched. She wanted to walk but being restless, even on their designated side seemed rude. Maggie watched her with hooded eyes, following her movement as Rose completed a slow circuit from the man riding the tractor to the double-paned window.

Maggie's spoke, her voice hoarse. "Tell me again what you heard in town today."

Rose repeated the information and when she'd finished, Maggie nodded once and fell back into her own thoughts.

Left to amuse herself, Rose tried composing imaginary setdowns for Savio. The number of his offenses was increasing. He still deserved payback for abandoning her at the mine, for attempting to break into her room, and for being unconscionably sexy. She thought far too much about his black hair and blue eyes, the hard stream-lined body. Despite her best efforts, stray moments from their nocturnal snuggle interfered with her concentration and she reveled in the memory.

43 CHAPTER FORTY-THREE

ROB COORDINATED HIS team of mixed law enforcement representatives. The men were focused, professional. He witnessed none of the jockeying for position
that characterized some multi-jurisdictional operations. Every
grim face turned to the back country, aimed in the direction the
fugitive had vanished into the landscape. Rob considered the
possibility the runner was an experienced outdoorsman. He'd
known where to exit the main road to access remote stretches of
the park. Disappearing into a stand of trees didn't require skill
but moving across an open expanse under the watchful eyes of
experienced trackers did. If the perp had extensive knowledge of
the environs, that made the task of capturing him even more
difficult.

The man moved fast. They'd already been forced to expand the search area twice. There was simply too much land to cover, even with a lot of trained personnel.

Their best bet was to throw a wide net and tighten the outer perimeter until they ran their quarry to ground.

In the hours between his pursuit of the truck and the subsequent discovery of the corpse inside, Rob learned about his uncle's life-threatening injuries. Worry chafed at him. Guilt weighed down his shoulders. He wanted to be at the hospital rooting for the man who'd been like a father to him. Instead, he worked the job, feeling in his gut that this fugitive was responsible. The idea of catching the bastard brought a jolt of satisfaction. Rob clenched his jaw, his cheek flexing, mouth aching. He tracked down the bad guy while doctors worked over Harlan's bullet-riddled body. Being here was hard but right.

A helicopter circled overhead. The chopper maneuvered in wide sweeping passes. As night drew closer, the effectiveness of the aerial unit declined. Soon they'd resort to searching on foot. Given the fugitive's armed and dangerous status, they had made the decision to reject waiting for daylight. If their positions were reversed, Rob might expect personnel to play the safe end and wait. If it was him out there, he'd push hard now to escape.

Rob's recommendation for pulling in two of the best trackers in the western half of the park had been granted. Both men had stripped down to their leanest garb as they listened to the brief. Each carried a radio, a sidearm and a canister of bear repellent as they set off through the brush.

The helicopter's powerful search beam lighted a swath of brilliance as Rob bellowed the order to begin. Searchers fanned out in an arc across the landscape.

Fugitive apprehension was always risky. They had no way of knowing how far a desperate individual might go to achieve his end. The wooded environment created additional challenges. The rugged terrain held hidden dangers. The farther they progressed into the isolated wilderness, the greater the probability of confronting an aggressive predator. Rob knew what a bear could do to a man. And, as the pun intended, the sight was grisly. Only a single species of venomous snake lived in the park and although encountering one of them in the upcountry was slim, the concern plagued Rob's mind. So much could go wrong. During his tenure as a park employee, Rob had encountered a snake only twice. Both times he'd found them by looking for the squiggle of lines in the dirt that showed their passage. Something else Harlan had taught him how to do.

Rob forced his uncle out of his thoughts and concentrated on his duty.

His navy and gold nylon bag carried water, nutritional gel tubes in place of rations, and wet weather gear in case the threatened squall broke. Extra ammunition and emergency medical supplies rounded out the kit. When the old timer had handed him the pouch, he'd told him to write a note to his wife and stick it in with the contents. "Ain't diddly squat gonna keep you alive in there," he'd warned.

A voice crackled over the radio. "Aerial has positive sighting."

Rob grabbed a pen and marked the coordinates. He requested confirmation. The location came back as two miles due north.

Tense moments passed before a new comment sputtered static. "Subject dove for cover."

"Good enough for government work," Rob muttered. He traced a circle on the map with an orange highlighter. In the next five minutes he relayed coordinates and issued detailed instructions to teams. They had established a perimeter around the fugitive's last known location. Time to squeeze the circle closed.

They lapsed into silence. Routine communication created noise so conversation was limited. Close in, the men would coordinate formations with hand signals. Rob understood that while park personnel were experts in dealing with the drunk and disorderly crowd, they lacked critical skills in the area of fugitive apprehension. Armed standoffs simply fell outside their comfort zone.

He climbed into the all-terrain jeep reserved for extreme off-road access. He motioned for Paul Clements to join him. He handed over the crumpled map after the man dropped into the passenger seat.

"You know the remote parts of this quadrant better than anyone. Navigate me to the mark." Rob shifted into gear and stabbed the accelerator. The jeep bounced over the rough terrain. "I want to take this bastard down."

Despite the failing light and the jarring ride, Clements buckled his seatbelt and studied the route. When they arrived at the first split in the track, he pointed to the right. After another half mile he did the same again.

Rob let the vehicle roll to a stop and peered through the windshield. "I don't see a road."

"Use to be. Go slow. Make a new one."

He sent Clements a skeptical look but steered onto the path. Five minutes later the Jeep crawled along, still faster than Rob could walk but not by much. The axle ground over rough surfaces, skidded across rocks and bent down sapling trees and tall shrubs. His shoulder muscles burned with exertion.

Finally the old ranger indicated they should stop. He pointed up a steep-sided slope. "There."

Rob released the steering wheel. The helicopter shined the powerful light down on the side of the mountain. Under the searching glare, he finally picked out the figure darting from one scrubby patch of growth to another.

"Call in our position."

Clements nodded and reached for the receiver.

Rob trained the flashlight beam at the ground. Without the sweep of headlights in front of him, staying upright in the topography and trying to move with any speed presented a challenge. His progress slowed. Fifteen minutes travel brought him within sight of the spectacle. The fugitive was a big man. Muscular legs pistoned as he pushed up the hill, a trail of turned rocks and upended clumps of new growth marking his passage. He had to be exhausted after being on the run for hours. The searchlight exposed clouds of vapor erupting from the man. The chopper circled overhead. Despite knowing he would go down, he still struggled.

More personnel arrived.

The net closed.

The tactical team from the U.S. Marshals Office appeared out of the gloom. Instructed to lay out a warning shot, without hesitation the sharpshooter raised a rifle to his shoulder, adjusted his grip on the elaborate grain of the wood stock, sighted along the line of the barrel and fired.

Rob heard the boom and crack of the report at the same time, the sounds too close together for him to differentiate. A plume of dirt kicked up near the runner's leg and the man collapsed. He went down as if knocked out by the heavy fist of a prize fighter.

"Is he hit?" he asked.

The sharpshooter shook his head. "Nah, he just figured out he's playing with the big boys. Gave up."

The fugitive, arms still wrapped protectively over his face when the first responders reached the location, offered no resistance. He was escorted down, stumbling from exhaustion, his wrists manacled in shiny restraints, Rob wondered if this man shot his uncle. He found no opportunity to ask before the U.S. Marshals took their prisoner into custody.

Chapter Forty-Four

ROSE EXCAVATED A tattered newspaper page from the bottom of her bag and penned President Polk into the crossword with an internal crow of triumph. The door opened. A woman from the other cluster of occupants darted to her feet, but sank back onto her seat when the doctor turned his attention toward Maggie.

He approached with one hand outstretched. "Ms. Thompson?"

"I'm Dr. Thompson." She returned the shake.

He ignored Rose. His face settling into tired lines, he spoke only to Maggie. "Mr. Groates' condition is stable."

The statement didn't comfort Maggie. "What does that mean?"

He pressed his lips together in a somber line. "His current heart rate, oxygen saturation, and blood pressure are solid and his vital signs are steady within standard ranges. This is excellent news, particularly given his class III hemorrhage."

"How much blood loss?" Maggie asked.

"He required multiple transfusions." The doctor pulled out a chair and sat down. He placed his hands flat on the tabletop. "Let me explain."

Rose hunched in her seat and listened.

"This type of injury is complicated and messy. He came through surgery well but faces a lengthy convalescence. His wounds are the result of two separate gunshots." He demonstrated by pulling up his sleeve and folding his arm, squeezing and tugging the loose skin at the bottom of his bicep. "This muscle mostly provides strength for rotational movement of the forearm. The bullet passed through and out, which is good. The entry and exit sites are cleaned and packed, expected to heal and close in a comparatively short time. The greatest concern with this manner of tissue damage is the amount of muscle restriction occurring through atrophy and retraction."

Maggie leaned forward. "What can be done to minimize loss of movement?"

He fiddled with an instrument in the pocket of his smock. "That's an astute question. He'll need to stretch and follow a strict therapeutic follow-up. The recovery of full range of motion and arm strength will take work and dedication."

Maggie stated what Rose had just been thinking. "The second wound is the more serious."

Dr. Hunter gave a curt nod and tapped his chest. "A .22 caliber bullet entered about midway. The projectile crashed through the cartilaginous structure and fragmented into surrounding tissues. The tip of the xiphoid was broken off by the force of the impact. The sliver of bone lacerated muscle near the lining of the heart."

Rose swallowed.

Maggie's face tightened until her angular cheekbones stood out like blades.

The doctor raised a hand in a halting gesture. "A similar event can result when a person administers CPR and their hands are incorrectly placed or they over-compress. I've seen those injuries heal fine. The major damage has been caused by fragments of bullet ricocheting around his chest cavity. Small pieces bounced off his ribs and hurled through muscle and lung tissue." He stopped and waited while Maggie swiped at her face and took a breath.

He glanced at Rose for the first time but Maggie laced her fingers together and clenched her hands into a ball, indicating she was ready for him to continue.

"None of the debris entered the spinal column. This was my primary concern but there's no evidence of damage. That's the best news of all. Mr. Groates did sustain two punctures to the pleural lining of his anterior lung before the main fragments came to rest." He paused to give Maggie a chance to ask for clarification but she apparently didn't need it. "The patient is facing a lot of different issues. Blood loss, soft tissue trauma, the entrance wound and subsequent bullet fragmentation leave him in serious condition."

Dr. Hunter laid one hand over Maggie's fists. "He's out of surgery now but he'll stay in ICU for observation until he is fully conscious, probably for a while to come. With this much damage, pain management is problematic."

"How long do you estimate his recovery?" Rose asked.

Maggie looked over at her like she'd only just realized she wasn't alone in the room.

The doctor prepared to rise. "I can't answer that question. Healing is largely dependent on his motivation. Even the treatment adds another level of trauma to his system. Sensitive tissues have been probed, stretched and manipulated, excess fluid drained. He's in good shape for someone his age but the interior landscape of his body is permanently changed. He's already recovered seventy-eight percent of his lung capacity, a positive sign."

Maggie's smile was shaky. "He's hardheaded."

"My professional opinion is guarded but optimistic." He pushed back his chair and rose to his feet. "I'll take you to him now."

Rose was surprised when Maggie grabbed her by the elbow and steered them both into the secure area. The central station was ringed by glass-walled cubicles that separated patient spaces from the epicenter of technology.

The first room had a large sticker with a numeral one stuck to the glass. Harlan was visible through the window. He lay on an elevated bed, wires plugging him into screens and machines. His skin appeared pale and waxy. He stared fixedly at the ceiling.

Maggie stumbled, righted her posture and pushed forward, leaving Rose to hover near the doorway. Inside the room, she laid a gentle hand on Harlan's arm and mouthed a thank you back over her shoulder. Maggie clearly did not intend to leave Harlan's side again and Rose had been dismissed.

She was happy to escape. Seeing Harlan in this condition made her uncomfortable, like a voyeur. She didn't even know the man and his own family had yet to appear. She felt intrusive. Mumbling a self-conscious reply, Rose scribbled her cell number on a scrap of paper and tucked it into Maggie's pocket before she left.

The ICU ward doors were swinging shut when she glanced back and saw Maggie standing with the almond colored phone pressed to her ear. Her eyes were focused on Harlan's still form.

No one questioned her as she exited. The place was creepy after hours, empty of personnel. Even the emergency room was quiet. She hurried faster as she approached the outer world, breathing deep of the refreshing night air once she burst outside.

Her car waited like an old friend. She sat inside the dark interior and just breathed in and out, waiting for the image of Harlan, grey-faced and supine on the hospital bed to meld with her memory of the lawman walking toward her backlit by Montana sky. The two images wouldn't mesh. Anxious to make the two-hour drive, she started the car and retraced the route from the freeway, searching for an open gas station.

Rose huddled deeper into Savio's shirt and tightened her shoulders against the cold breeze. The sluggish pump filled her tank but it trickled in with glacial slowness. Her Levi jacket hung in the closet back at the Inn, doing her absolutely no good. She cursed the weather. July in Sacramento tipped the daytime thermometer into the high nineties and hovered in the low seventies at night. Montana felt damn near the freezing point. She glared with undisguised malevolence at the clerk inside the comfortable glass-enclosed kiosk.

He ignored her. White earplugs connected to an MP3 player, his head bobbed in rhythm to the beat of bass. The ass flipped through the pages of a magazine while she shivered out in the elements.

She shoved away the snapshot of Harlan and the chirping equipment. In her memory he laughed with suppressed amusement during her interview with Ranger Saxton. She wanted to think of him as whole and healthy, a good omen for recovery.

The visuals in the intensive care unit just didn't jive with her recall of the fit older man who'd distinguished himself by the duty and responsibility of his office. In the hospital he lay amid a field of beeping monitors, rust and saffron flashing lights, and a squawking alarm that issued strident tones until a nurse slapped the keypad and reset the timer.

Rose shivered.

Maggie had seemed assured that things would be fine but Rose remained unconvinced. Harlan's drug-induced paralytic state appeared dire. His empty gaze, eyes staring at the ceiling haunted her.

The numbers on the vintage pump flipped over with metallic clicks as her mind played back the night. Today had packed in twice as many hours as the normal. When the gas finished flowing, she shoved the nozzle into the hook and climbed into her car. She switched the heater to high and pulled into the city traffic. Years of offensive motoring served her well now. After two false starts, she backtracked and departed Bozeman with a sharp acceleration.

She swore the return route took three times longer though she drove faster than the posted speed limit and the clock marked the travel time as the same. Rose figured she'd hit a wall of sorts. Exhausted, battered by strain and stress, she reeled under the culmination of too many shocks. She entered downtown Riverside fifteen minutes before midnight and could have cheered with relief. The hour seemed later. This was not how she'd envisioned spending her evening. That thought just bought Savio to mind and put her back on that merry-go-round. At least she'd probably find a message on her phone.

She'd been out of the loop all day. Caught up in the drama of Harlan and Maggie, she had no idea what else had been going on. Was there news on Nellie? How about the two dead men?

Or should she count three now, with the man killed on the highway during the confrontation with Harlan? She sighed and rubbed the palms of her hands against her eyes.

Rose pulled in and parked in front of the Inn. Twelve hours earlier she'd sat in companionable silence with Nelsen and Delmar on the bench. Too much had occurred since then for her to process. She floated in a disassociated, surreal haze.

She left the car in the no park zone. The chances of a ticket were close to nil and she was past caring anyways. A bright pool of light glowed from the lamp in the front yard and lit the street. She scrutinized the porch, examined the bushes around the structure, and plotted her route. She was taking no chances tonight. After a quick sprint, she'd soar up the stairs and leap into her room, brandishing the can of knock-off Mace she'd purchased from the head-set wearing malcontent at the gas station.

Strategy prepared, she exited.

A car turned onto Main Street and began a slow approach. Stiff from lack of movement, she didn't bound over the lawn in reality like she had in her imagination. Oncoming headlights flashed and illuminated her as she staggered up the steps to the walkway. She reached the porch, dashed forward and found the knob refused to twist in her hand.

The front door was secured for the night.

Mr. Ingram had told her every room key also unlocked the double-keyed locks on the entrance. Rose dug the brass implement from her pocket and shoved it in the hole. The mechanism released and she flung it open.

The crunch of tires sounded from the street. A car had pulled in behind her Ford. She didn't look back. She pushed it shut and as soon as she heard the latch she flipped the mortise. Then she fled across the foyer. Taking no chances, she stomped firmly up the center of the staircase, each rapid step accompanied by a squeak of floorboards. She rounded the corner and peeked toward her room. The dim bulbs in the tiny candle-shaped sconces lit the empty hall.

Rose crept along the carpeted runner, the pepper spray clutched in her right hand. She inserted the key to the *Clementine Room* but before she could turn the lock, the knob twisted against her palm.

CHAPTER FORTY-FIVE

TOO MANY HOURS of waiting had drained Savio's adrenalin reserves. He'd flop on the mattress only to bolt upright again a few minutes later. Finally, the sound of a car pulling to a stop outside took him back to the window. He spied the front end of Rose's vehicle and his heart accelerated. Where had she been all this time?

He crossed the rug and waited until he heard sounds of her passage through the house.

When she inserted the key in the lock he opened the door. He saw her startled expression, witnessed the fear slide across her features before recognition set in.

"Jesus Christ, Savio, are you trying to give me a heart attack?" She pushed inside before there was barely enough room for her to fit through, punching his shoulder as she did.

He closed the heavy wood panel behind her. The frustration and amped-up energy in her voice told him she was as much on edge as he. Rose was spooked, ready to bolt.

"Where have you been?"

She huffed out a breath, leveling an angry glare at his harsh demand.

Savio cursed low. This was not how he wanted their interaction to go. He reached for her.

She darted back and held up both hands in a stopping motion. "Don't touch me."

He halted. A muscle twitched in his cheek. "I was concerned by your long absence." He took another step forward and studied her.

She was pale, her cheeks drawn with fatigue.

She set her things down on a chair and a canister of pepper spray, its distinctive shape evident in the light from the hall, dropped to the floor and rolled away.

His gaze followed the cylinder until it came to rest next to the kickboard. His temper spiked. Did she believe it necessary to protect herself from him? He glared at her through narrowed eyes.

She stared back, stone-faced.

He deliberately gentled his voice when he spoke again. "You have no need to fear me, Rose."

"I don't believe you."

Her words hit him in the solar plexus and stole his breath as effectively as a gut punch.

She wrapped her arms across her abdomen and hugged herself.

He frowned. "Tell me what has happened."

Rose sighed. "Everything is wrong." She pointed at him and then her chest. "You. Me. Us."

Holding her gaze he walked over and she let him wrap her in an embrace. Securely banded in his arms, she sighed again and the sound worried him. Their bodies pressed together, his worry drained away. Her dark hair was untidy and he buried his face in the shiny spill and inhaled.

Rose went still in his embrace. "Did you just sniff my head?"

Her puzzled tone made laughter burble up inside him. "Indeed."

Her back stiffened and she sank an elbow into his ribs. She turned at his grunt and he caught a flash of teeth. She was grinning.

"That you are safe relieves me," he told her and slid his palms down her body. There was a telling hitch in her breath. She was not immune to him.

Rose dug into his ribcage again. "Back off buster."

"Your elbows are sharp," he complained. He'd sport some bruises tomorrow. Exasperated he leaned close, mouth hovering above her ear. "Stop struggling. Talk to me."

"Now you want to *talk*? I'm ready for all the explanations you can offer. Tell me exactly what is going on and how deeply you're involved."

Ah, she was angry with him. Deep emotion was good. He need only turn it to his advantage. Lips quirking with amusement, he licked her earlobe. "Very well. What would you like to know? Since we are being honest I will confess how much I want to kiss you again."

Her laughter was harsh. "Not likely." She punctuated each syllable with a rake of her nails down his legs. "No more liplocking until you tell me what I need to know."

He shuddered against her. "But you are so stimulating."

Rose chortled with inappropriate amusement. "This is not foreplay, you whacko."

The pictures he'd found on her phone flashed across his mind and he was unable to stop the accusatory question. "Who are they?"

She ignored his out-of-context query and said something quite rude.

"Language, *Querida*," he chided.

Rose writhed her lower body as she tried to punish him with another elbow jab.

"Ah, do that again," he whispered in her ear.

She stilled at once, resembling a plank of wood more than a warm angry woman. "Uncle," she said, her voice tight.

"*Que?*"

"That means you let go and I get to breathe."

The wheeze in her tone relaxed his hold a fraction. He brushed his lips against her temple. "I apologize, but you are strong. I have worried about you, *mi flor*. All day my mind has been filled with catastrophic accidents, terrible events that stalked you while I waited impotent in the shadows of your room."

She whistled before responding. "Melodramatic thing, aren't you?"

Rose inhaled deeply three times and he began to wonder if he'd squeezed her too hard. Before he finished the thought she bucked her hips and broke loose, twisting around in his arms. Her spine pressed to his belly, Savio tried to hang on to her but the position was awkward. She lifted her legs and let her suspended weight drag at him.

She inched down his body, increasing the stress on his grip.

He growled when her elbows marked the front of his thighs. More bruises there in the morning. He admired she was such a scrapper. She didn't know how to fight, not really. He'd need to remedy that in the future. Savio locked his fingertips together below her breasts and jerked her hard against his torso.

Air whooshed out of her lungs and her feet dropped to the floor, restoring his balance. He pulled her up and pressed a kiss against her neck while huddling close to protect vulnerable areas of his anatomy. He released her seconds before her instinctive flight response kicked in and she began to fight in earnest.

"*Querida*, please do not struggle. You will cause yourself injury." His words came out in Spanish. Distracted by the pleading note in his voice, he didn't move fast enough.

Instead of stepping away from him, Rose slammed her cranium back against his face.

Her hair got tangled in his mouth and choked off his exclamation of pain. Blood spurted from both nostrils. His sinuses burned from the impact. He grabbed her by the shoulders but her head bludgeoned him a second time. Cartilage snapped.

Rose twisted away.

Warm fluid poured from his nose. Strands of her long tresses wrapped in sticky lines around them both, leaving behind thin wet trails of red.

Across from him, Rose gasped beneath a drift of tangled umber, her lips parted and chest heaving. Eyes wide, her gaze locked to his. Blood coated her left cheek in a thick smear. Tendrils stuck to her forehead, also soaked with the viscous flow.

Savio thought her beautiful.

Seconds passed as they stared, then her eyes narrowed to slits. She aimed a wild blow and swung at him.

Savio caught her fist and grinned when she grunted out a frustrated noise. He stroked his fingers over her clenched hand, remembering how in the mine she'd vowed to damage the more delicate parts of his body.

Dark eyes glowered at him. She looked ready to deliver on that threat.

"Were you there? Did you shoot him?"

He understood the context of her question. She wanted to know if he'd been part of the shooting that claimed Remy's life and left the local lawman injured.

He shook his head. "No, *Querida*. I swear I was not."

She softened the smallest fraction.

With a groan he released her hand and snatched her under the arms, pulling her up to his waiting mouth. This need overpowered all others. He kissed her with abandon. The taste of blood added a coppery flavor. The kiss stripped away her anger. Passion overwhelmed and crumbled her remaining defenses. A fierce sense of recognition swept through him the moment her resistance vanished.

Rose melted into him.

Tongue tangling with his, an utterance of pleasure thrummed from her throat until she reared back and slammed her forehead into him.

He took the hit hard on his cheek, turning in the final second to avoid the impact against his injured nose.

She danced out of range.

The force of the blow stole his breath, stunned him momentarily. He gasped out a word as soon as he could pull air back into his lungs.

CHAPTER FORTY-SIX

R OSE STAGGERED BUT kept her balance. Had he just said she was magnificent? To her amazement Savio shook his head and stayed on his feet. She'd barely slowed him down. She backed up and stumbled on the rolled edge of the rug, windmilled her arms and almost recovered before falling.

He lunged for her.

In a frozen moment, time stalled. She experienced an unwilling appreciation for the aesthetics of the visual, registering the grace in his movements, his elegance of motion. Getting one foot under her, she stopped herself from falling flat on her back and pushed off. For some ridiculous reason she came up swinging and landed a perfect right hook.

The dynamic changed instantly.

Savio hit the wood floor, sounding like a sack of concrete dropped from a forklift.

Rose yelped. She shoved her fist in her armpit but the instinctive gesture produced no useful effect. Every one of the twenty-seven bones in her hand ached as if they'd shattered on impact. She experimentally opened and closed her fingers, flexing her palm. Everything moved correctly.

He wasn't even unconscious.

Shit!

"How hard do you need to be hit?"

Savio stared up at her, his face twisted in a fierce growl. Blood streamed down his chin and still she found him handsome. He pushed off with his hands.

Rose pivoted and tensed her leg to shove him away.

A fist pounded on the wall. Someone shouted from the hallway.

Savio flung out an arm and swiveled toward the opening door.

Rose ignored the newcomer.

Savio continued to move into her path. His attention drawn to the intruder, she planted her boot into the side of his head with a solid satisfactory thunk.

He dropped like a stone down a well.

She swiped the back of one hand across her mouth and looked over at the entrance to the *Clementine Room.*

Two uniformed policemen stared back at her. One held a gun.

"Hi," she said. Her breath sounded shaky. She bit down on her tongue to stifle a burst of hysterical laughter.

The cop holstered his weapon and stood over Savio's unconscious form. The second officer escorted her into the hall and asked her questions.

Discretion seemed her best option. She had no idea what to say. With no means of explaining recent events, she didn't try. Everyone assumed her too distraught to talk, so remained silent. She let them form their own conclusions. Voices talked on her behalf, she just nodded and mumbled.

Mrs. Ingram cleaned the blood off Rose's face and tended her swollen fingers, chattering nonstop as she wrapped the injured hand with practiced movements. She fetched a bag of frozen peas, bundled them in a kitchen towel and offered her the frigid parcel.

"Maggie Thompson alerted the Riverside Sheriff's Office to watch out for you. Those nice young men came to make sure you'd arrived back safely."

Rose acknowledged the two officers but murmured a meaningless response and tuned out. One minute faster or slower on the return drive from Bozeman and she'd have missed the cops radar altogether. The same was true if she'd parked behind the inn instead of bucking the rules.

The policemen had spotted her scurrying up to the front door. Her furtive actions brought the dutiful public servants inside to investigate. They roused the Innkeepers and entered the premises. She assumed the police had been explaining their presence while she and Savio had wrestled upstairs.

"Did you invite Mr. Mendes to your room, Rose?"

Mr. Mendes?

Rose shook her head absently. She considered trying to explain this was a big silly misunderstanding but drew a blank about explaining his presence.

"I think this is just some kind of mistake," she finally said.

Mrs. Ingram patted her shoulder. "I'm sure it must be, dear, if you say so." She paused to give Rose a chance to add input, continuing when she said nothing. "The police have arrested him but it's up to you to press charges."

Rose jerked and made a negative motion. What the hell did they plan to arrest him for on her behalf? She had assaulted him. He wore the bruises, the broken nose, and the blood-covered clothes.

The policeman asked questions. She answered in one-syllable words. He pressed for details until she became offended by their personal nature.

"No. Stop it. Nothing happened. You aren't listening, I think he got confused and entered the wrong room. I don't know. I'm tired. It's been a sucky day. Can we do this tomorrow?"

Her last question appealed to Mrs. Ingram's maternal instincts.

The cop finished with her.

So exhausted she could barely think, Rose allowed herself to be led downstairs. She dutifully drank what Mrs. Ingram put in front of her.

The policemen descended a short time later with the prisoner in custody. Any trace of grogginess had disappeared from Savio's step. Held between the two uniforms, he floated down the wide staircase with a sensual quality Rose admired.

When he noted her in the shadows, a red flush suffused his damaged face. His mouth curved into a smile displaying straight perfect teeth, white as the best Akoya pearls. The visual was marred only by his misshapen swollen lips and the coat of blood drying on his chin. The vivid sapphire of his eyes sparked in the dull light of the parlor lamps. Momentum carried him along even after his gaze caught hers and he slowed to stare at her.

Rose arched her brows in query.

The man had the audacity to wink at her.

A jiggle from one of the policemen discouraged words but Savio never broke eye contact even as they forced him out the door.

Rose stared back at him until the stained glass panel closed.

The Ingrams fluttered around her like she was one of their kids. She had to convince them she wanted to return to her room and finally they gave in.

The clock had passed one in the morning before she shut everyone out and approached the bed. The useless pepper spray sat on the bedside table, thoughtfully replaced by one of the cops. She opened the drawer and discovered Savio had stowed his personal effects neatly beside hers. His handgun nestled next to her Luger.

She found the sight charming and rubbed a hand across her forehead to check herself for fever.

She roamed the room, looking for other objects. His jacket hung in the closet beside her two flannels. His footwear sat beside her spare sets of shoes.

Bizarre.

Rose unearthed his wallet from his left boot. She pounced on the leather bi-fold. With no more than a slight sense of naughtiness, she opened it up and perused the contents. Not much to look at. Inside she found a credit card of the pre-loaded kind and two international calling cards, also prepaid. The few receipts showed unimportant incidentals. A single business card and a California driver's license made up the balance. Both of the latter caught her attention. Surprised to see the name of Savio Mendes on the stiff plastic rectangle, she decided that didn't mean it was his real identity.

She copied all his data into the address book of her phone and noted the pink organ donor sticker with approval.

The business card she turned over several times. The number written on the back made her frown even as telltale warmth crawled through her veins. Printed below the distinctive university logo she read her name, title and contact information. She had dozens of the things stuck in books as place-markers. The numbers and letters scribbled on the reverse she recognized as the registration number for her car.

Most women would find it creepy. Rose was flattered.

Tonight she had confirmed the existence of Murphy's Law. Everything that could go wrong had. The first guy she'd found attractive in forever, she'd physically pummeled into submission before letting him get arrested. She should have cleared up matters. In retrospect, she might have admitted she brought home a guest and their interests got a little out of hand. She blushed, imagining the expression on Mrs. Ingram's face and squirmed.

Tomorrow morning she'd figure out some way to make this right.

Odds were, Savio felt a bit less enamored with her now anyhow.

Awesome.

CHAPTER FORTY-SEVEN

WINSLOW WAITED WHILE Anton carried the phone to his niece. It tickled him to think about Rose as his blood relation. He'd been surprised to discover she was already downstairs and hoped the scuttlebutt he'd heard this morning proved overblown.

Voices murmured and then came a clatter as the cordless receiver was passed.

"This is Rose Brashear," she mumbled.

He'd bet his most recent poker winnings her mouth was filled with Danish pastry. "Good morning, this is Winslow. I understand there was a bit of a ruckus last night. Are you okay?"

Rose gave an audible swallow before her voice came warm across the line. "I'm fine Winslow, but thanks for calling to check on me. I'm off to the Sheriff's Office in a few minutes to sign my statement."

Winslow tucked the phone against his shoulder and struggled to find the right words but he couldn't decide what to say.

"I'm getting pretty adept at cop-speak." Her speech sounded muffled like she'd covered the speaker with one hand.

Winslow rubbed his forehead. "This hasn't been a great visit for you."

"Nonsense. The Danish are divine."

A smile tugged at his mouth. The girl had a determined shiny outlook on life.

"Want to go with me to the station? They have the bad guy in custody. I kicked him in the head. Well, I guess it'd be more accurate to say he hit his noggin on my boot."

Winslow processed this new piece of information and frowned.

"Did I overshare?" Rose spoke around a mouthful of something.

He exhaled loudly. "I'll wait across the street. Bring me a couple of Lily's pastries."

Winslow held the door open for Rose at the Riverside Sheriff's Office. This was the second time he'd been inside the building and both visits had occurred this week.

The rectangular space consisted of a main workroom with offices lining the right side and access to the two jail cells through a door on the left. The small lobby was split by a protective glass wall that stretched from side-to-side and extended to the ceiling. A slide window with a lip of countertop centered in the expanse served as the public information portal and reminded Winslow of the drive-up at a fast food restaurant. He'd wager the space hadn't changed much since being built some-time back around the turn of the twentieth century.

He steered Rose toward a side door where they could enter the inner workings and pressed the buzzer on the wall. He'd come here to sign his statement the day after he'd found the body at the Ladies Auxiliary.

Rose waited beside him as Officer Williams approached.

Winslow said good morning.

The woman returned Winslow's salutation and directed her attention at Rose. "So this is your niece?"

Winslow did introductions.

"The prisoner is in the lock-up." Deputy Williams' voice was inflexible as steel. She buzzed them through the security door and pointed Rose to a table where a typed statement sat beside a ballpoint pen.

Rose read the paperwork. She skimmed a finger down the center of each paper, flipped the pages and stared at the wall for almost a minute before she spoke. "The cop wrote down pretty much what I remember telling him."

Winslow glanced down at the statement. "If you don't have anything more to add, you initial the bottom of each page and sign at the end."

Rose's pale cheeks had taken on a strawberry stain. She sat in curious stillness for a long moment, the pen loose in her hand, before she began to scribble.

The deputy returned from answering the telephone and handed Winslow a paper cup of coffee.

"What's the story on the prisoner?" he asked.

She shrugged. "He's got no identification although the In-grams provided the name he used to check into the White Horse Inn." She darted a sharp look at Rose's gasp.

"He was a guest?" she asked.

Winslow watched a funny expression cross his niece's face.

Deputy Williams nodded. "For a couple of nights. He checked out yesterday." She gave Rose a quick appraisal. "He won't speak, even refused medical treatment. Excellent self-defense, by the way. Are you sure you don't have anything to add?"

When Rose didn't raise her face or respond, Deputy Williams turned and met his gaze. She shook her head at his unvoiced question and a huge weight fell from his shoulders. Rose's seemingly normal behavior after such a frightening experience had worried him. His anger and impotence over the attack was mollified by the knowledge she'd been spared the trauma of sexual assault.

Rose cleared her throat and glanced up, a frown wrinkling her forehead. "No, I've got nothing to add. This was all some weird misunderstanding. He was in the wrong place and I over-reacted. Yesterday was stressful. You should probably release him. I don't want to press any charges."

Winslow laid a comforting hand on her shoulder.

Deputy Williams resumed her cop face. "The prisoner's fingerprints don't appear in any database we run them through but they should. The man in that cell is dangerous."

Rose lifted her gaze.

Winslow watched a tiny frown crease her brow as she shifted position in the chair and rubbed her ribcage. He wondered if the display of pain was unconscious or calculated.

"What do you mean?" he asked.

The deputy's eyes flicked from him to Rose and back again. "We ran him through every database, including Interpol, but nothing flagged."

A quizzical expression formed on Rose's face.

"He's a professional. You got on his radar." She glanced at Winslow again. "That's a place you don't want to be."

Rose focused on the paperwork.

Deputy Williams prompted her with another question. "You said you'd seen the prisoner before, right?"

Winslow didn't know this. He wasn't happy about what that might mean.

Rose nodded and exhaled a shaky breath. "I saw him outside Vic's on Monday. I remember because I had an appointment to pick up my research permit."

Winslow squeezed his niece's shoulder and Rose smiled up at him.

Ignoring his hard frown, the deputy coaxed her to go on.

"There isn't much to tell. He waited at the sidewalk while I drove out of the parking lot and we made eye contact. We didn't speak. Last night he showed up in my room." Rose blinked up at him. "Maybe it's just one of those random weird things?"

He patted her shoulder.

Deputy Williams waited until their attention returned to her. "He singled you out for a reason."

Winslow didn't like the implication that Rose withheld information. He eyeballed his niece.

Was she holding back?

Rose pursed her lips. "I have no logical explanation."

"How about an illogical one?"

Rose grinned and spread her arms in a wide gesture of innocent denial. "I can proffer dozens but each makes about as much sense as any conspiracy theory." She turned to face him. "Would it be entirely unbelievable he intended to declare a grand passion for my affectionate self?"

Winslow huffed out a laugh at her plaintive tone. "Hope springs eternal."

Rose snickered. She handed over the paperwork and slowly straightened. "I'm achy and sore."

Winslow kept one hand on her arm.

Deputy Williams frowned. "How are you feeling?"

Rose demonstrated her stiff fingers. "Better than I deserve. I punched him in the face like a total dumbshit. I thought all the bones had snapped but once the swelling went down Mrs. Ingram decided they hadn't. She wanted me to go to the 24-hour-clinic in West Yellowstone but I couldn't face the drive." Rose smirked up at him. "It's too many damn miles."

Winslow was unconvinced by the diagnosis. He thought her fingers still looked puffy and inflamed and preferred she go to the clinic but he grinned back and steered her toward the door.

Deputy Williams raised a hand to halt them. "The preliminary coroner's report indicates the man recovered from the thermal pool died of natural causes. The autopsy showed he suffered from a heart condition. The family confirmed he took medication."

"A heart attack?" Rose asked.

The deputy shrugged. "Apparently."

Rose shot her a puzzled frown. "How do they explain the antler?"

Winslow frowned. What did an antler have to do with anything?

Deputy Williams shook her head. "That remains part of the ongoing investigation. The toxicology reports will take weeks yet, and may show something completely different. So far, the man wasn't murdered. The medical examiner said he experienced a massive cardiac spasm."

Winslow steered her toward the exit again.

Rose peered over her shoulder. "Could I see the prisoner?"

Deputy Williams stared at her like she'd sprouted a second head. "For what reason?"

Winslow wanted to know that too.

Rose shrugged. "You said he's not talking. He's going to be released soon though, right? You don't really have anything to hold him on if I refuse to press charges. I think he's harmless, just a kook who confused my room with his."

Winslow couldn't remember the last time he'd heard such a lame excuse but Deputy Williams appeared to be considering the request.

"What's he been charged with?" he asked.

The deputy's attention remained riveted on Rose. "Right now, the prisoner is a person of interest in just about every-thing, not the least of which is explaining his presence in your niece's room at the White Horse Inn."

Rose made a noise he thought sounded suspiciously like a snort of laughter.

The deputy sighed. "And that means we can only hold him for a specific period of time." She turned her attention to Rose. "Steel bars separate the lock-up from the visitor area, but there's no protective screen. If you want to do this, safety is imperative. That means you don't approach the cell at any time and you follow my exact instructions."

Rose nodded. Two bright spots of color stood out on her high cheek bones, a sharp contrast to her pale face.

Winslow pressed his lips together but said nothing.

48 Chapter Forty-Eight

THE JAIL CELL looked like a scene from a movie production set. Rose was reminded of reruns about the old west she'd seen televised all during her childhood. Thick metal bars stretched floor to ceiling along the fronts of two cells. Centered in each was a large door with an ancient lock mechanism. She'd wager this one posed no real challenge. Even she could pick the antique mortise.

Not that she would try.

Not really.

Savio's cell contained a simple frame cot covered by a woolen blanket, nowadays probably woven from some hypoallergenic synthetic product and a flat pillow.

The effect was stark.

The stainless steel commode and wash basin jarred her senses. They seemed out of sync with the interior, a blend of different centuries. Not a single exterior window allowed a glimpse of the present era inside. There'd be no tying a rope around the bars to pull them out by pony power.

Not that the idea had crossed her mind.

Not really.

Cheap light fixtures mounted outside the units cast a jaundiced glow over both halves of the room. The second cell replicated the first in a mirror image. A solid wall separated the two spaces leaving neighboring inmates to pass objects freely back and forth at the front of the shared divider.

Rose wondered what happened if the Riverside Sheriff's Office ever held more than a pair of prisoners in custody. Maybe they doubled up and brought in bunk beds. She pushed the thought out of her head. Only one was occupied today. Her eyes found Savio at once but she tried to subdue the wild escalation of her pulse by finishing her inspection of the interior. She failed. Every nerve ending in her body was focused on him where he stood in the center of the space like an old-time outlaw.

Except for the fact he still wore socks.

Rose paused a few feet inside the door and stared at him with intensity. Regret rolled through her. The discovery of the dead man at the thermal pool complicated her research study but here was the true source of the disruption in her life. In another place and time, under different circumstances, she would enjoy their interactions much more.

Savio lacked his normal groomed elegance. The bridge of his nose was discolored by a dark bruise, his longish hair tousled. He wore his own clothes sans footwear.

An internal sigh fluttered inside her like moth wings flapping against a window pane. She took another step forward.

"Keep to the wall side of the yellow strip," Deputy Williams reminded.

Rose lowered her gaze to the colored stripe on the concrete floor. She wondered if the state employed some complicated formula to determine the average range of motion of an adult and then painted the sunny strip a corresponding distance away.

Savio smirked when their gazes connected like he sensed the random thoughts bouncing around her skull.

She eyeballed him boldly. Acquainted with her for mere days, the man seemed to understand the way her mind worked. She wanted him to see she'd change the circumstances if she could.

His face was washed clean of blood but a line of bruises bloomed along his jaw.

She winced inwardly at the harm she'd inflicted then changed her mind. *Scratch that noise,* she thought.

Savio Mendes was responsible for his own actions. He'd tied her up, abandoned her in a mine, and then found fault in her lack of appreciation for his efforts. He passed through her room like it featured a revolving door. True, he'd routed an unwelcome visitor and she felt grateful for that intervention, but the man got what he deserved.

Rose slapped both palms on her waist.

The prisoner responded with his full attention.

After his arrest she'd experienced the smallest twinge of regret for the amount of damage she'd delivered. Perhaps a bit of a pang registered after she'd realized he'd waited on her return for hours. Actual remorse made an appearance after she'd read the texts on her phone. One particular missive had been sweetly persuasive. She'd reviewed it numerous times, a flush of color sweeping up to her hairline. If she hadn't displayed such emotional volatility nine hours before, the police might have interrupted a very different activity altogether.

And they wouldn't be staring at each other through steel bars this morning.

Savio stared at her intently, a curious smile hovering around his finely crafted lips.

Her breaths shallowed as she studied him. The dratted man noticed and his grin widened. She folded her arms across her stomach, an action which pushed her breasts up, and smirked when his gaze followed the movement.

"So, how're things with you?" Her voice came out polite, her tone even.

"I am well, thank you. Your arrival has much improved my morning."

He sounded sincere but she rolled her eyes. Last night she'd overheard one of the reserve cops characterize Savio's mannerisms as effeminate. That perspective baffled her. To Rose, he exuded masculinity; his every movement a controlled force. Even motionless he mesmerized. She knew the risk of proximity to the man. He was dangerous to her equilibrium. The excitement level in her life had escalated with Savio's arrival, blood humming through her veins.

Head canted, she stepped forward, her gaze locked to his. She all but heard the crackle of electricity as magnetism flared between them.

CHAPTER FORTY-NINE

SAVIO WONDERED WHAT information Rose had withheld from the Riverside Sheriff's Office. He studied her, automatically searching for weak spots, knowing she was out of her element.

Rose must have requested this meeting. The deputy operated too much by-the-book to suggest a victim go face-to-face with a prisoner. His gaze drifted down her body, a slow luxurious treat. His memory, though not photographic, worked perfectly and memorizing every detail satisfied an undefined hunger. The stretchy fabric of her scoop-neck shirt, the soft hue of pink carnations, hugged her torso and displayed a hint of cleavage.

His body responded.

The dark denim of her pants was stiff and new, the color of a stormy Caribbean sea. The tight fabric smoothed down her legs, a forceful reminder of what it felt like to slide his palms over her hips. His nostrils flared. The pale denim shirt she'd thrown on as a jacket had been laundered until soft and supple, a faded memory of the original rich indigo tone. The palette was a perfect complement to her natural beauty. The sleek steel-toed boots with which he now shared an intimate acquaintance, shone with an oil buff.

He'd never been so enticed.

The tip of her long braid flipped at her waist as she swished forward. He ached to wrap the length around his hand and pull her hard against his battered ribs. Her cheeks flushed and her breath came light and fast. His eyes narrowed. His little flower might be displeased with him but she was here. And she was excited.

Face pulsing with a bone-deep ache, he reached up and loosened his jaw.

She winked at him.

His mouth curved into an amused smile and he dropped both hands to his sides. In the future he would be wary of her excellent right hook. He'd also avoid angering her unless she was barefoot.

Her voice came low and intense. "I have a secret to share."

The words got Savio's attention. He leaned forward, the response earning Deputy William's interest. "Tell me."

Rose's eyes went half-lidded.

His heart rate increased as she offered the same sensual perusal he'd received in the mine.

"I worried your needs were not being met," she waved a hand to encompass the room, "but my concerns are alleviated now that I've seen the facilities."

She played with him and *ay dios mio*, he liked the games. He spread his hands in a wide arc. "The accommodations are rustic, are they not?" He ignored her lack of response and shrugged his shoulders. "No matter, I will not be here long."

She moved until they stood facing straight across at each other. Face solemn, all trace of interest and desire gone, her features looked carved from fine alabaster.

He perused her in a slow sweep. "You are lovely as ever." He willed her to understand his emotional turmoil, a real trick considering he had no grasp on it either.

Deputy Williams stood planted a few feet from the door, taking in every nuance of their exchange.

Savio admired the woman's consummate professionalism, but right now he wished her far away. He wanted to express himself openly.

Rose returned his blatant regard. Her gaze crept up his torso, excited him, even as curiosity compelled him to ponder what details she'd omitted from her official statement. Though heartened by her presence, she also appeared wary before the deputy.

Rose tilted her head.

"The deputies know your name but they wonder why you were in my room last night. I told them it was some sort of misunderstanding, right?"

His flower had shared little with local law enforcement representatives. Instead of responding to her question, he watched her evaluate the distance to the bars. He did the same. How close would she need to come before she entered his reach? He could move swift as an eel and with as much flexibility.

Rose ventured a step forward and shifted her stance until Deputy Williams no longer had a clear view of her profile. The calculated movement intrigued him to an almost unbearable degree. Like a hummingbird, he sipped sweet bits of information but was unable to reach the stamen filled with nectar.

He blew Rose a kiss and tapped his chest with the fingers of one hand. "You and I have unfinished business." The gesture bordered on melodramatic but Rose's reaction satisfied him.

She scowled at him. "We're virtual strangers."

Conflicted by his own desires, he understood her confusion. Attraction simmered between them. He struggled daily with unfamiliar longings – one which drove him to be with the woman and another urging him to take her along when he departed.

Rose's gaze dropped to the floor.

He took a step closer. "Look at me."

She swung her face up at his heavy intonation and the room seemed to narrow down.

"What do you want from me?" The tension in her voice was unmistakable.

A rush of memories boiled through Savio. He flashed on their bodies straining against each other, lips slanting across mouths, tongues dueling with aggressive passion and inhaled a shaky breath.

Rose edged closer.

"I want you to see *me*," he said.

CHAPTER FIFTY

ROSE *DID* SEE him and she struggled to contain her mixed-bag of contrary reactions. Having this interaction in front of an officer was too much to process. Every word she spoke was being assessed for multiple meanings and half the time she had no idea what she and Savio tried to tell each other. Part of her wanted to be angry, furious even, but she wasn't.

She also had a big fat pinch of guilt over his shadowed bruises. When he approached the front of the cell, his graceful movements across the concrete floor were at odds with his battered face.

Deputy Williams stepped away from the door but she didn't interfere.

Savio stopped directly behind the bars.

Rose traced the contours of his features.

After a silent thirty seconds he touched a finger to his cheek. "Not such a soft touch."

Conflicted emotion swirled through her but dark amusement won out. "Your chin roughed me up fine." She raised her hand in an inadvertent rude gesture and displayed the splint straightening her two inner fingers.

A whistled breath escaped his lips. "Please accept my sincerest apologies, *Querida*." His mournful gaze and musical voice were accompanied by a slower cadence of speech and a pronounced accent.

Rose couldn't suppress her shudder of reaction. Propriety demanded she be repelled by this attraction, but the man had just apologized for the injury which she had incurred by punching him in the face. Rebuffing his chivalrous apology made her feel churlish. A vague sense of indignation was the best she could work up, more the product of thwarted desire than real outrage.

Savio appealed to her. She found his intense vitality hypnotic. Intensity might as well be her drug of choice.

She flicked a glance to Deputy Williams. The woman stood silent and alert, absorbing every word, probably recording the entire interchange in digital format.

"The police are curious why you were in my room."

Savio crossed the remaining distance to the metal bars.

She'd never seen anyone move like him. Every step fluid and smooth evidenced his mastery over muscle and indicated more than mere athleticism.

His expression burned with curiosity. "I fear you misunderstood my intent last evening." He regarded her taped fingers and bowed at the waist. "I apologize for my abrupt embrace," he paused and leaned in close, "although in truth, I hold great admiration for the wonderful curves hidden beneath those boy-ish clothes."

Rose's face flamed. The rat gave the impression they'd been involved in an adolescent necking session that spun out of control. Well, okay, sort of.

Savio curled his fingers around a thick bar and rested his forehead against the old metal. "Were the local constabulary not so adept at their profession, we might have spoken at greater length." One brilliant orb stared from either side of the iron strip. "Fortunately, I caught you when you stumbled. You misconstrued my actions."

Rose understood the term dark angel for the first time. Savio's expression was warm and sincere. His tone radiated conviction and the words were utterly false. Uneasiness swelled inside her. The man both chilled and charmed her. He attracted her like mercury drawn to gold flakes. Despite everything to the contrary she trusted him instinctually.

Stupid.

He stretched one hand between the bars, prepared to exchange a shake as if these were normal everyday circumstances. "Allow me to present myself, I am Savio Mendes."

Deputy Williams jerked.

Rose wished she had a better idea what to do. She'd let him know the information the cops wanted and he'd obliged. Did he want more from her?

Savio gazed at her. "Will you not give me your name?"

She puckered her lips and ignored his outstretched hand. He knew it, even had one of her business cards tucked away inside his wallet. But he wanted the deputy to believe they were strangers. Tapping an index finger against her cheek she stared at him for a silent count of ten.

"I think not. It's nothing personal, Mr. Mendes. For a psychologist, you'd be a career-making case but in my profession you're just another nutjob."

Savio grasped the iron bars, threw back his head and laughed. Mirth rolled up from deep inside and transformed his face.

Rose's insides clenched in response. She waited until he regained control.

Calculation glittered in his gaze. "How long do you remain in Montana?"

He didn't *look* crazy.

"Why can't I live here?" she asked, buying time. They had already discussed her work. He knew she wasn't local.

What did he want to know now?

He leaned against a bar and offered her a soulful expression. "Surely I cannot be expected to believe such a rare flower grew in this place?"

His question affronted Rose on behalf of her uncle's hometown. She quite liked the little community. "Riverside is a perfectly respectable town."

He cocked an eyebrow at her tone of insult.

The license plate number he'd written on the back of her business card popped into her mind. "Did you follow me from California?"

He nodded and shrugged at the same time. The gesture conveyed exactly what he wanted it to – possible guilt.

His eyes went half-lidded. "Your beauty affects me greatly."

What game was this?

Savio hadn't known about her until a few days ago.

"That's freaky," she offered. Thank god Winslow couldn't hear this exchange. She tried for bewildered but only achieved breathless as a flood of graphic memories flowed through her mind. She glowered at him. "I don't know you. You're mental."

A heated smile curved his lips. "Most definitely."

Rose grew flustered. Even an imbecile could sense something volatile between her and the prisoner and Deputy Williams was no birdbrain.

"It's time for me to go," she announced.

Savio stood with his attention locked on her. "Fate has brought us together, *Querida*. Remember that fortune favors the bold."

One side of her mouth lifted at his deliberate misquoting of the Latin phrase. "Don't forget the soldier who abandons his ally deserves what he gets." She broke eye contact, caught a glimpse of his appreciative smirk and flounced away.

The deputy indicated Rose should exit first.

Winslow probably waited anxiously on the other side of the door so she pasted on a bland smile.

Savio's voice carried after her. "I will find you, *mi flor*."

The latch shut behind Rose with a snap. Her stomach heaved a little at the sound.

The deputy placed a hand on her arm. "You did well, Rose. Take a deep breath."

Rose nodded, only giving the woman part of her attention. She remained focused on the man in the cell. Savio had provided distraction, misled casual ears. Their awkward conversation had skewed interpretation of the actual events. If local law enforcement harbored any doubts about her story, the prisoner had bolstered her position by making it sound like he'd followed Rose to Riverside as a crazed stalker. Now she was stuck continuing the charade. All those good intentions paved the way to Hell. She'd bet a dollar she'd trudged halfway down the block to stand in front of Satan's house.

Winslow stepped forward. Anxiety radiated from his features. "What happened?"

Rose turned to him. "Nothing."

"Semantic games," Deputy Williams confirmed.

Winslow's lined face was troubled. "Why did he go after you last night?"

Rose briefly met his eyes. "That's a mystery he won't be answering any time soon. He talks in riddles, doesn't make a lot of sense."

Winslow stretched another survey between the two women. "Is the man crazy?"

"Doubtful," Deputy Williams said.

Rose shrugged. She didn't think so either but wasn't so certain about herself.

They left.

Stepping into the lobby felt like escaping. Walking out the door was even better. Winslow pointed out local landmarks and shared bits of gossip as they walked away from the Sheriff's Office. Rose appreciated his efforts at distraction. Her mind whirled with confused images and ideas, all of them centered on Savio Mendes.

When they passed the J&L Market, Rose waved at the customary empty bench. "Where are Delmar and Nelsen?" She tucked her injured hand in her armpit but it continued to throb.

"Nelsen tends his garden in the morning." Winslow jerked his head toward the market. "Delmar's inside checking orders."

Rose puzzled this over. "Delmar works there?"

"He owns the place. He's the Johnston in J&L. His grandfather opened a general store on these same premises back at the turn of the century. I can't remember the partner's name."

"I assumed you guys just sat around on a bench," Rose admitted.

He squeezed her arm. "Well, it's a common mistake."

A beep sounded. Rose pulled her phone from a pocket and saw a new message on the screen.

"My service sucks," she muttered.

Two bars on the signal strength weren't enough to make the cell ring but at least her voicemail had functioned. She autodialed and listened, a smile blossoming across her face.

"I've got to go, Winslow." She bounced up on her toes to kiss his cheek. "Ranger Saxton asked me to come by the Regional Office. My research permit must be ready. That means I can get to work."

51 CHAPTER FIFTY-ONE

WHAT DO YOU mean my permit hasn't released?"
Fists clenched, Rose leveled a dirty glare in his direction. "The guy died of natural causes. How much
longer will your investigation take?"

Rob grimaced. She would know that. "I'm just waiting for
the clearance to come down the line. Until then, I can't do anything."

His polite smile stiffened under her regard. This wasn't going as planned. He watched the woman's face redden, her voice
becoming as hard as Maggie's had been that morning. He'd
snapped out responses like she was his superior officer, setting
the tone for his day. He'd apprehended the man responsible for
his uncle's injuries and caused an avalanche of tasks resulting in
hours of additional paperwork. Rob was tired and stressed, he

knew his features mirrored his mood because this was not the reception he'd hoped for.

"I want to ask for your assistance." He tried to relax his pose.

After a long pause Rose slumped against the counter. "You need a *favor* from me?"

Rob winced at her sarcasm. Her stony face promised no better than her tone but he plowed forward. "I can't take time off from this investigation and Maggie is at the hospital with Harlan until evening." He hurried on when she frowned. "Someone needs to pick up Maggie's son at the West Yellowstone airport in a couple of hours and bring him back to her house."

A delighted trill of laughter escaped Rose. She held up her index finger. "Let's make sure I understand the situation. You need *my* help."

Reluctantly, he nodded.

A second digit joined the first. "You're asking *me* to do something no one else is available or willing to do."

Behind the counter, Rob wilted. He didn't understand how a woman who looked so pleasant could be such a hard case. He nodded morosely.

Rose gleefully extended her ring finger. "You've got something I need, Ranger Saxton."

Rob deflated further.

Her smile increased. She raised her pinky, wiggled them all as though waving and pointed at her chest. "It's time to negotiate. I'll start."

He squared his shoulders. "I couldn't release your permit even if I wanted to. I have to follow park rules."

"No deal then." Rose eyed him. A moment of silence passed and she twisted her lips. "Forget the tough guy impersonation. I've had my fill lately."

Rob didn't know what to make of her flippant response.

She buffed her fingernails against her shirt. "How about I collect your soon-to-be-cousin and drop said waif on the doorstep? I'll even commit time for tourism this weekend if my research permit was released, let's say, first thing Monday morning."

Rob fought to keep a smile off his face. "Did Maggie really tell the entire hospital she was Harlan's fiancée?"

"I bet even the cleaning crew heard her."

He lost the gambit and grinned.

Rose pushed her hands in her pockets and wiggled her brows at him. "So, Ranger Rob, does my permit get a pre-release slip from lockup or do you spend the next three days entertaining the newest member of the family?"

Rob's humor drained away. He scowled at her.

She glowered right back.

He was about to capitulate when she narrowed her eyes.

"I require another concession."

His tone went flat. "What?"

"I want permission to collect faunal specimens inside park boundaries."

He shook his head. "I don't have the authority to approve that sort of thing."

She yawned and raised her gaze to the ceiling.

He counted to fourteen before he abandoned the contest of wills and ground out his defeat in a single word. "Agreed."

She slapped her palms on the counter. "Excellent."

The deal could be worse, he decided. "You can begin research Monday, but not until you come to the office and I sign-off on the paperwork. And the removal of skeletal materials has to be approved by the wildlife conservationist." He stuck out a hand.

Rose shook on the agreement and smirked. "I'd have done it anyways," she admitted.

"The park service will probably lift the moratorium by Monday anyhow," he sneered back.

Cracking her knuckles, Rose glanced around. "Now then, where's Ranger Burnside?" She covered her mouth with fingertips and feigned horror. "Don't tell me the homicidal maniac got him. Or dare I hope he encountered some heretofore unknown strain of flesh-eating viral pneumonia?"

"Don't." Rob couldn't stop his shoulders from shaking. "There is no man more susceptible to suggestion."

Rose lifted her eyebrows and shifted her head a quarter turn. "Nervous disposition?"

"He practically quarantined himself, checking online medical sites for symptoms. I had to send him off to visit Nellie at the hospital." He waited while she cackled with mirth.

"How is Nellie?"

"Improving. The doctors aren't saying much about her making a full recovery. Her left eye isn't responding the way they'd like but overall, things look good." No matter what the end-result, he'd find a place for her on staff.

Rose leaned heavily against the counter. "I'm relieved to hear she's getting better. Maggie said she'd try to see her the next time she visited Harlan. I heard he's getting better too."

He nodded. They both had a long ways to go but at this point he was grateful they'd both lived. At least his uncle was talking now. Holding hands with the woman he'd been in love with for thirty years boosted his recovery in untold ways. The thought made him smile.

"So, what time do I scoop up Maggie's kid and what's his name?" Rose asked.

He checked the slip of paper where he'd written down the information. "Tobias York arrives on the 2:20 flight from either Denver or Salt Lake City. I don't which connecting flight he caught." He lifted wide shoulders. "The planes are small, only seat about a dozen. I understand he's rushing out here to hold Maggie's hand." He laughed at Rose's doubtful frown. "I agree. The sentiment is unlikely but Maggie said he over-reacts."

Rose screwed her brow into a series of lines and showed concern for the first time. "How old is he?"

Rob displayed every one of his large square teeth in an amused grin. "About your age."

CHAPTER FIFTY-TWO

SAVIO FOLDED HIS arms under his head and stretched out on the bunk. The accommodations might be rustic but he'd passed time in less comfortable jails. He closed his eyes so he could recall Rose standing on the other side of the thick steel bars in all her glory. She'd struggled to make sense of his bizarre innuendo, even played along despite the events transpiring between them last night.

That fact soothed some of his incarcerated frustration.

News of Mackenzie's capture cheered him too. Rose was safe. Her shifty behavior left him feeling all warm and toasty inside. Her dissembling with Riverside's finest stroked his ego but Deputy Williams was no fool. As long as Rose went on with her business, local law had nothing on her. Unless she carried a criminal past he didn't know about. Interesting thought.

A muffled outburst interrupted his musings.

Savio shook his head at the shouted expletive. Deputy Chan sported a foul mouth, a sense of humor, and an apparent dislike for practitioners of jurisprudence. The first time he entered the cell area to stare at their only prisoner, Chan cracked off a lame joke.

"Hey Mendes, what do you call a parachuting lawyer?" The deputy waited with a wide grin till Savio quirked an eyebrow. "Skeet."

Chan slapped the wall and disappeared back into the adjacent room. About every half hour, the man reappeared. The frat-house façade failed to disguise he was keenly observant.

Savio liked Montana. Everyone here was *loco*.

On the next visit, the deputy held up an unopened bottle of water as he stood in front of Savio's cell, rocking up on his booted toes and grinning at him through the bars.

"So Mendes, how do you get a lawyer out of a tree?" He waited for a sign from Savio and continued after a twenty second wait. "You cut the rope."

He tossed the bottle. It landed on the end of the bed and bounced against Savio's stockinged foot.

The jokes worsened as lunch neared. As an attempt to get him to talk, it failed. He elected not to. Unless they brought Rose back, which seemed unlikely.

Savio dozed, catching up on his sleep. He knew change was imminent. Twelve hours since his arrest. Once his fingerprints entered the system, the scans submitted to national and international databases, the wait shortened. Digital information was snagged out of cyberspace and his location electronically identified, the efficient machinery of the modern world dispatching his retrieval. The company relied on state-of-the-art communications technology. The reason he'd avoided using his satellite phone. The cops turned it on but without an access code it was useless, little more than an expensive paper weight. On the other hand, it worked like a signal beacon, identifying his current location.

Amusement curled his lips.

After he'd disappeared had his colleagues wagered on his whereabouts? His detainment in Riverside, Montana might net someone a generous windfall considering his last contact originated in the wealthy and deadly district of *La Meridad* on the outskirts of Mexico City.

He was a long way from home.

Savio listened to the raised voices in the room adjacent to his cell. Multiple murmurs were punctuated by exclamations. After another strident outburst he surmised the feds had arrived. No one engendered quite as much dismay to local law enforcement as an agent who handed over the standard writ and uttered some garbled excuse to take the prisoner into custody.

Savio smiled.

Time to pack.

Six hours later his overconfidence in things working to his benefit sputtered out. Federal agents had indeed arrived but when they produced documentation for his transfer, the Riverside deputies acted like possessive toddlers unwilling to share their new toy. They didn't capitulate and turn him over till the close of business, and then they were ungracious, which genuinely amused Savio. That federal agents allowed the delay, indicated a level of inexperience he fully intended to capitalize on. The government should be shamed for sending green recruits on this task. His was never a standard transfer of custody.

Deputy Chan fired off a few final questions at him as the suits escorted him to the car.

Savio ignored the guy.

He understood their frustration. Jurisdiction was one reason he'd joined the private sector. Now he sat cuffed-and-stuffed in the rear seat of the standard issue nondescript sedan while his former jailers glared from the department steps.

He grinned at the pair.

Chan proffered a lewd gesture, probably aimed more at the feds than him. Williams never cracked her professional guise.

Savio slumped back in the seat. He wondered where Rose spent the day.

A hundred miles down the road he questioned whether or not these federal officers even had field agent status. He thought they might be recent graduates but new recruits were typically partnered with jaded careerists. By comparison to the other occupants in the vehicle, Savio's age and experience weighed heavily. The blonde one couldn't even grow a beard, though the brunette might pull it off if he didn't shave for the rest of the month.

Savio tried again. "You gentlemen should release me now and save yourselves a lot of additional work. You lack legal reason to hold me in custody."

Blondie held up Savio's cell and threw him a glance. "Kidnapping? Imprisonment? Any of this ringing a bell? And on federal land, no less."

The agent had been trying to access Savio's satellite phone for over an hour, an impossible effort since the six-digit alphanumeric code ensured millions of possible combinations. The probability of a random correct sequence was laughable.

Savio switched to the patient approach. "You are misinformed about recent events."

Not really.

"Shut it, chum." The dark-haired agent spoke over his shoulder. "We're just the retrieval party. You can plead your case when we get back to Salt Lake City."

Savio sighed. Unaware Montana lacked a regional FBI office, now he was en route to another state. Not even the one next door. He'd missed his flight. Worse, he'd forfeited an evening with Rose. Their situation far from settled, being transferred to Utah ruined his schedule. He should never have allowed the arrest. Feds were notorious for adhering to protocol. Once the system flagged his whereabouts and dispatched a courtesy escort, he'd figured on being able to disengage and go on his way.

Reluctant to leave Rose, he also had another concern. If the retrieval team actually transported him to the regional office, the internal leak plaguing his work in Mexico City might be waiting to wipe the slate clean. Not a position he was anxious to find himself holding.

Besides, no longer shocked by his fascination with the senorita, he wanted a chance to say his goodbye.

Halfway through Idaho the driver flipped on the turn signal and exited the highway. Savio concealed his surprise. These guys couldn't be inexperienced enough to pull into a motel.

They were.

He bit the inside of his cheek to check a grin. Apparently, his unseasoned escorts enjoyed filling out expense reports. Good. They wouldn't mind the additional paperwork when their prisoner escaped federal custody.

Chapter Fifty-Three

ROSE KNEW SHE'D been suckered. Her mood didn't improve when Tobias York walked through the door of the tiny lobby in the West Yellowstone airport and turned his gaze on her. He was tall and handsome, charming and affable, and like Rob said, close to her age.

Tobias left her unmoved. Cold as a block of ice.

His caramel eyes didn't sparkle. His chestnut hair had no raven highlights. His smile was warm and sincere, not filled with wicked sensuality and a hint of menace. She pasted on her professional pleasant expression, thrust the mercenary out of her head again and held out a hand. Tobias laughed at the sign with his name written in block letters, unnecessary with only six passengers on the flight. After introductions he prodded her for a concise report of events as they walked to the car.

Out in the parking lot he stared at her over the roof. "That's a ton to absorb in just a few sentences. If we stop for coffee can you deliver the long version? My treat."

Over monster-sized cappuccinos and a stack of almond bis-cotti cookies Rose told him the story. Tobias plied her with questions about the town and Harlan. Rose spent two hours roughing out the prior week while he sat with his mouth open. He too found amusement in Maggie's official engagement an-nouncement.

"You have no idea of the havoc she's capable of producing." His face became serious. "She and my dad married before I turned twelve and divorced by the time I graduated high school." He grinned at her. "When I was fourteen I bought her a live peacock for Christmas. She kept it."

Rose made a skeptical face. "If that isn't love, I don't know what is."

He laughed and checked his wrist. "Mom said she'd be home by six. We can leave by seven and probably arrive first."

The velvet chair fought her release. Rose accepted his hand and noted there was no telltale tingle of sensation. He pulled her to her feet and examined her taped fingers.

"I'm fine," she said self-consciously. At that moment she wasn't lying. "Just a silly accident." No need to try and explain, he'd hear the gossip soon enough.

Tobias kept her entertained on the return to Riverside. For an elementary school teacher he knew a lot of raunchy limer-icks. Her cheeks ached from laughing by the time she swerved in at the curb in front of a small blue clapboard house.

They had almost beat Maggie home. Parked in the drive-way, she was climbing out of her car. Rose saw the exhausted woman's face light up when Tobias unfolded his lanky frame from the passenger side. He yanked his oversized backpack from the rear seat, bent down and peered inside the window.

"If you have time this weekend, I'd go for some sightseeing. I'm sure Mom will be preoccupied."

Rose agreed, "I'd be happy to oblige." Distraction was welcome.

Tobias charmed her, in a good guy sort of way. Too bad nice guys didn't stir her emotions these days. Loping across the yard, he grabbed his stepmom in a bear hug and Rose drove away with a grin. She'd never expected Maggie Thompson to squeal like a teenager.

An hour later a sonar beep echoed in her room. She plucked her phone off the table and tilted the screen. Maggie's home number showed on the display. She answered.

"I could use a BMO," Tobias said in her ear.

"A what?"

"That's an acronym for bail-me-out. You don't get around much do you, Sunshine?"

Rose tilted her head sideways. "Already done with familial duty? It's not even cracked an hour."

"Are you kidding? Mom has plans to abandon me before dawn. The hospital has some tests scheduled." He didn't sound put out in the least.

"How is Harlan?" Snippets of information floated around town but this was better, a font close to the primary source.

"Stable and awake for longer periods at a time but still not talking. Guess it takes too much effort."

Rose rubbed a hand across her chest in the spot where he'd been so heavily bandaged. She figured Harlan was being smart and storing up strength. He'd need the stamina to face Maggie. Once the man was strong enough, Rose bet she planned to give him hell about getting shot. She said as much to Tobias.

"You've got Mom figured out. So, can I convince you to play tour guide? Don't hesitate to turn me down. I'll be crushed, but will recover in a month or two."

She snorted. "I like the no-pressure sales pitch."

"If you're too busy, I can couch camp." His voice dropped to a whine. "Please don't make me watch network television. Have you seen the drivel they foist on the pecuniary public?"

"Wait." Rose hesitated. "Before things go any further I need to ask you something." Silence rang down the line. "I've never heard that word used in a sentence before. Who are you really?"

The quiet was broken by a long sigh. "I majored in English, sometimes the words slip out. I correct grammatical mistakes when people talk too. Sorry, it's a curse." Tobias spoke like someone giving confession.

"Alrighty then. Get your boots prepped, Cupcake. I'll be over at eight in the morning." She disconnected and felt almost normal.

The sense of normalcy didn't last.

Work couldn't hold her attention. She checked for messages. *Zip.*

In a fit of pique Rose wrote Savio a text, sending it as a response to his final message. She vacillated over what to say until she settled for the truth.

I hate that I can't get you out of my mind.

Safe and ambiguous.

Her disposition improved.

After the fact it occurred to her the police might peruse their way through Savio's phone calls and figure out she'd fudged on the truthful side of things. That was the point at which she reached the *screw it* stage and fired off a whole series of statements.

She had to correct three spelling mistakes before she took a deep breath and slowed her fingers to type the remainder of the second message.

I'm so angry I refuse to think about you anymore.

She pushed send and her mood elevated. Then she proceeded to tell him everything she hadn't said in front of Deputy Williams.

What were you thinking?

Each text led to another and echoed some facet of her frustration. She pressed the keypad.

I can't believe you got punked by local cops.

She dropped the phone and strode over to study her map. She rubbed her face. She'd opted to be alone tonight. Turning down an invitation to dine with Tobias and Maggie, later begging off dinner with Uncle Winslow. Afterwards she'd convinced her hosts she wanted to stay in the *Clementine Room* and escaped upstairs. Now as evening stretched into night she wondered if it was a mistake to remain by herself. She searched the closet, checked the locks on all the windows and for the first time, pulled down the blinds and drew the curtains. She found it difficult to recapture her previous contentment in the space.

She resorted to cliché and ran a hot bath.

While the water filled the antique clawfoot tub she sent another text.

I'm having a soak. You're not invited.

She monitored the heat level and typed a new message.

You're a sexy bastard and a total nutjob.

Of course he wouldn't get the messages because he was in jail but it made her feel more in control to be able to vent her frustrations at him.

Rose yanked a handful of her hair. What was *wrong* with her? Jeezus, she'd lip-locked, loitered around with, and partnered with a frigging mercenary, a bona fide professional private soldier. She tossed her phone on the bed quilt and left a trail of clothes across the floor.

In the bathroom she dropped her bra on the tiles and climbed into the cast iron tub. The ache in her ribs soothed as she settled in the sudsy water. Her nose wrinkled. She might have poured in a bit too much of the freesia scented oil. Forcing herself to review the previous night she didn't shy away from questions about her reactions. Why hadn't she screamed? Yes, she'd gotten caught up in events and struggled hard to breathe, but not so she couldn't call for help. The reason behind her silence was complex and not entirely complimentary. Her conscience squirmed even as her body relaxed in the heat.

Her physical struggle with Savio triggered a response so secret she hadn't acknowledged it until afterwards. Her mind danced away from the idea but she barged in and finished the thought. An intimate shared moment had occurred. She'd experienced a cathartic event as a result of the violence she'd perpetrated.

Oh hell, was she having one of those relating-to-her-captor-kind-of-experiences?

Rose wallowed in humiliation for three seconds then rejected the Stockholm syndrome idea. Savio hooked her interest long before rope got involved. Potent chemistry simmered every time they came into contact, overpowering common sense and tossing aside normally rational behavior. Omitting their conversational exchanges for the cops made giving a statement less personal.

Under other circumstances, she'd enjoy an extended torrid vacation fling. Rose banged her head against her fist. She found Savio Mendes dangerous and attractive – too much of both. Yes, he'd demonstrated criminal behavior. The fact she was more uncomfortable with her attraction to the man than the legal and moral risk he represented didn't escape her notice. Despite having no reasonable explanation to trust him, she wanted to.

Someone needed to point at her and yell crazy woman.

Rose leaned back in the tub.

Savio's spectacular athleticism, the grace in his every step and gesture was provocative and seductive. Those points didn't even account for the perfect smile, shining hair and piercing orbs.

Sucker, she accused herself.

She pulled the loosened tape off her sprained fingers and dropped the splint. The aluminum brace hit the tile floor with a tinny reverberation. Rose rotated her hand. She inspected the bruises. She'd had a bang-up first-time intimate experience with Savio all right. Hot tears spilled down her cheeks. This was not like her. She fought with words, not fists and feet.

The bath lost its appeal. She ached to lie down and pull the covers over her head. A few minutes later she crawled into bed, redolent of freesia. She checked her phone one last time.

No messages.

She bet Tobias never left a girl hanging. She'd also wager he couldn't curl her toes and make her mind blank from desire with just a kiss. She feared only Savio had that power over her. Exhausted from the release of deferred emotion she slipped the phone inside the drawer next to her loaded gun and closed her eyes, praying for dreamless sleep.

54 CHAPTER FIFTY-FOUR

SAVIO TRIED TO loosen his tense shoulders. He flipped down the kickstand and shifted his balance. He'd purchased new clothes, some temporary boots and a substitute jacket but he felt naked without the shoulder holster and gun. To his relief, he found his motorcycle still parked in the alley upon his return to Riverside.

Yellowstone was busy today. A cluster of cars cruised past the narrow pullout where he'd paused to spy. Even though the space was too small to accommodate an automobile, several tourists slowed to consider the idea. He aimed a severe glance toward each driver. Cars couldn't lurk long in the park environs, heavy traffic flow forced the congestion to move.

That was another reason he'd dumped his borrowed vehicle inside the Riverside Impound Facility. At this rate he'd run out of parking places before the Sheriff's Office realized any additions had been made. Remy's car sat at the end of the lot. Presumably the drugs remained stashed in the trunk but he didn't take time to check. Eventually someone would realize it shouldn't be there and search the car. The drugs would be found and disposed of – just one more mystery left unsolved.

He forced himself not to hunch over. The midday stroll through the small downtown strained his nerves but he wanted to retrieve the motorbike and search out Rose immediately.

The number of park visitors had increased in exponential waves since his arrival five days before. A steady stream of vehicles disgorged floods of passengers.

Savio shook his head. Rangers needed stun guns to control this kind of crowd.

It took him an hour to locate her car among the teeming throngs of vacationers. A small GPS tracking device promised to make that an easier accomplishment in the future. He spent another five minutes finding her in the mass of humanity. Had she not made a spectacle of herself performing a dangerous balancing act along the top rail of a fence with camera in hand, it would have taken much longer.

Originally, he'd planned to retrieve his personal belongings from the White Horse Inn this evening, say his goodbyes, and depart. He couldn't wait for dark. Despite the consequences, he'd needed to confront Rose Brashear. His lips curled. Worst case scenario, she might bust him up again and call the cops. The action could become a regular part of their courtship. His thoughts stumbled to a halt.

Was that what they were doing?

He dropped the binoculars and tried to recall his last social engagement. The woman's name eluded him. He pulled up a vague image of a tall lithe female with an upsweep of honey-toned hair, one in a series of elegant, beautiful, and insipid companions.

For the last week he'd been struggling with an unfamiliar emotion. He lifted the glasses and searched again for Rose, found her in a precarious balance at the edge of a bubbling mudpot. Straightening on the seat until his spine went rigid, he swore. Pale jeans and a long-sleeved t-shirt emphasized her curvy compact body. His leg muscles tightened as she wavered on one foot and kicked out to counter-balance. She grasped a camera in one hand and waved the other to help calibrate the pose. He tensed until she staggered back to the platform and her companion assisted her to safety.

On top of everything else, he intended they have a special discussion about her reckless behavior.

The *senorita* did something to him. Each time they inter-acted, she inched deeper beneath his skin. Like a tick, he thought, sucking at his peace of mind, leeching away his re-sistance. Her texts from the previous night served as the coup de grace. For hours he'd itched to get hold of his phone. Every time a text came in, the device buzzed on the tabletop, the two agents taking turns trying to crack the code. Once Savio got loose, he stood in the doorway of the tiny motel bathroom in Idaho and read each line several times. He recognized in her words an element of a familiar conflict. He knew his interest in Rose extended beyond a casual fling and hope began to build that she reciprocated his confusion. Exactly what that meant remained a mystery even to him.

Only a few hours ago he'd bid a distracted farewell to the federal agents, locked the motel door, and driven away in their sedan.

Reckless as a new recruit, he'd headed to Riverside.

Rose hadn't been home.

One booted foot planted on the asphalt, Savio scowled blackly. He'd assumed she was working in the park. He had not expected to discover his romantic interest in the company of an attractive young man. Savio prided himself on not being the jealous type and his reaction to the boy stunned him. When other men scoped out the female on his arm Savio found a perverse pleasure in being envied yet he did not care where the woman spent her next evening. Now some vigilant covetous switch had been flipped on inside Savio. In his opinion, Remy was an unworthy candidate for Rose's affections but this man was young, handsome, and probably backed by an excellent education. A fit match for the *senorita*.

Savio did *not* like him.

Jealousy ate at his insides, a corrosive acid consuming him from within. He adjusted the focus on his field glasses and studied Rose. He tried to view the couple's interactions without the haze of resentment but her body language suggested enjoyment in the excursion. Envy flared up. He wanted to be the one helping her down the wooden steps.

The boy offered his hand at every opportunity, a possible demonstration of courteous manners, but Savio thought him enamored with Rose. How could he not be? She captivated him.

Her conversation was casual with her companion. No more so than Savio's with the waitress who served his lunch at a burger stand in West Yellowstone. Her lack of response cheered him. Cool detachment returned. Her attention wandered and satisfaction filled Savio. He and Rose shared a hyperawareness that made each of them unable to disguise their mutual attraction. In her company, he found all other distractions disappearing into the background. Now he saw that she stared at her feet and gave a tiny visible jolt when the boy spoke.

Distracted, he thought.

Savio pondered the thoughts turning over in her mind. The possibilities were endless. She defied commonplace expectations.

More than one clock was ticking. Local law enforcement would be on the lookout for him. He'd successfully pissed off the feds. His employer must grow impatient with his maverick behavior. Responsibilities waited for him in Los Angeles. Mackenzie was in custody. Remy Boothe and the third nameless confederate were dead. Business completed, he should leave town.

He needed closure with the senorita even more.

Through the field glasses he watched the pair trail behind a ranger-guided tour, following the long boardwalk as it snaked between vivid pools of water. Rose pointed into the distance and her lips moved.

Savio grimly determined he couldn't tail them for the rest of the day. He'd be spotted and arrested. If not, at some point he'd lose patience, storm over and smack the boy for his proximity to Rose.

He'd already demonstrated a serious lack of control. Considering his strong attraction to the woman, the smartest option was heading for California. He dropped the field glasses and set his jaw, resolved to depart. Instead, he rode the motorcycle to West Yellowstone and rented the last available room in a budget motel. After scalding his body in a hot shower he collapsed naked on the sheets and slept.

CHAPTER FIFTY-FIVE

WINSLOW WAS PLEASED when Rose agreed to join the boys for dinner. She'd spent the entire day sightseeing with Maggie's son, enjoying the scenery the rest of them took for granted.

"How was your tour of the park?" Nelsen asked.

She obviously liked Nelsen and enjoyed his dry sense of humor. She responded by waving her fork in his direction as she spoke. "Disappointing. Tobias never tried to kiss me. It's not like I made myself available, but still, a girl has expectations."

Winslow couldn't remember seeing that expression on his friend's pinched features before. He thought Nelsen might be scandalized.

Rose turned to face him. "I think I'm going to have to mark Tobias down as pitching for the other team." She speared a chunk of potato.

Winslow opened his mouth. No words came out. He struggled to find an appropriate response but Rose had moved on.

Delmar wore a funny wrinkled half smile.

"It figures too," Rose stabbed the air for emphasis, "the first pleasant guy I spend time with, in my generation," she encompassed her dinner companions with a gesture, "and he's not interested on the most fundamental level."

Winslow realized they all stared at his niece.

"He could make a pity pass for ego's sake." She forked a piece of prime rib with an energetic plunge and scanned their faces for the expected feedback.

Silence built around the tiny table until it crackled with tension.

Rose frowned at each of them. "Don't you three gawk at me like I said something outrageous. You don't get to turn into a trio of virginal prudes eliciting shock at my forward behavior." She chewed as one-by-one each shifted his gaze away.

She snorted out a cackle rude enough to catch the attention of two men at the neighboring table and Winslow began to find humor in the situation.

"I'd like to point out a new century mark passed a while back." Rose's words came fast. "The Victorians died over a hundred years ago, the Puritans even longer, so you fellows better catch up with the times."

Winslow admired her articulation. When she dropped the fork on her plate and flailed her hands, he grinned. Her voice drowned out Nelsen's shush as she fluttered a hand in his direction.

"Let me recap a few historical landmarks in social progress, gentlemen. Let's initiate with a big one, shall we? At the beginning of the *last* century, women got the right to vote. This was followed up with long outrageous work hours at factory jobs during World War II because all the men ran off to fight each other." She drank some water, shifted in her chair and pointed at Winslow. "Right?"

He didn't attempt to hide his amusement.

She turned and poked a finger toward Delmar. "And, we did it for less money."

He narrowed his eyes and glared back.

"A few decades later hemlines went up and bras came off." She punctuated each statement with a raised finger until her hand was lifted over the table like a stop sign. "Then birth control arrived and the era of the liberation movement, gentlemen. Women get to go to school now and learn to read with the male young'uns." Rose closed her fist and snatched it out of the air with a flourish.

"My grandma was a suffragette," Nelsen offered. His shoulders shook with amusement.

Winslow laughed.

One of the men next door clapped until his companion struck him on the shoulder.

Delmar considered Rose as if he'd never looked at her before. He took an extra moment to digest her tirade before he spoke. "I've got three great nephews trawling for wives." He rolled a toothpick around with his lips and stared at her with a speculative expression. "If you're offering yourself up, that is." He proceeded to rattle off their names.

Nelsen pantomimed frantic negative motions outside Delmar's vision.

Winslow watched Rose jerk her head back and forth between the two men. She was about to make a remark when he spied a uniform at the door and laid a hand on Rose's arm to draw her attention.

Winslow's grip tightened as the deputy approached the crowded table.

The woman stopped next to Rose. "It took me a while to track you down. I'm sorry to say the feds trumped our assault charges and claimed prior jurisdiction." Deputy Williams hesitated a second as she studied Rose. "They transferred custody of Savio Mendes yesterday."

Rose tensed under his hand. Her face flushed but she made no comment.

"The FBI agents were discovered in a motel room outside Pocatello at noon today. The prisoner was not present." She continued to stare at Rose.

Winslow didn't like the implication his niece was somehow involved in this madness. He glowered at the deputy. "But, that was hours ago."

Twin spots of color on her cheeks brightened. "We just received notification."

Rose covered her mouth with one hand and Winslow couldn't read her reaction.

"He killed two FBI agents and escaped?" Nelsen asked.

Delmar turned to face Rose. His voice, mirroring his expression, expressed a mixture of disbelief and incredulity. "You knocked the guy out cold. In my book that makes you a real bad ass." His tone sounded only half sardonic.

Deputy Williams shifted her gaze around the table. "Savio Mendes didn't kill them. He removed his handcuffs and disarmed both men, leaving them incapacitated while he walked out the door and drove away in their car."

Winslow shook his head. A regular run-of-the-mill kind of guy couldn't do stuff like that. His ears felt stuffed with wool. "Are the agents hurt?"

The deputy's mouth twisted into a crooked shape. "Embarrassed. The prisoner handcuffed them together on either side of the toilet. Naked."

Rose made a tiny noise. Winslow feared the muffled sound was a squeak of laughter. Both her hands now covered the lower half of her face and he suspected it was mostly to hide a smile.

His own mouth twitched. At least the bad guy had a sense of humor.

Delmar barked out a laugh. "I bet those fellas are royally pissed."

"Do you believe the prisoner will come back here?" Winslow asked.

Deputy Williams eyed Rose with a thoughtful expression. "I think he might."

56 CHAPTER FIFTY-SIX

WINSLOW WAS PLEASED when Rose agreed to join the boys for dinner. She'd spent the entire day sightseeing with Maggie's son, enjoying the scenery the rest of them took for granted.

"How was your tour of the park?" Nelsen asked.

She obviously liked Nelsen and enjoyed his dry sense of humor. She responded by waving her fork in his direction as she spoke. "Disappointing. Tobias never tried to kiss me. It's not like I made myself available, but still, a girl has expectations."

Winslow couldn't remember seeing that expression on his friend's pinched features before. He thought Nelsen might be scandalized.

Rose turned to face him. "I think I'm going to have to mark Tobias down as pitching for the other team." She speared a chunk of potato.

Winslow opened his mouth. No words came out. He struggled to find an appropriate response but Rose had moved on.

Delmar wore a funny wrinkled half smile.

"It figures too," Rose stabbed the air for emphasis, "the first pleasant guy I spend time with, in my generation," she encompassed her dinner companions with a gesture, "and he's not interested on the most fundamental level."

Winslow realized they all stared at his niece.

"He could make a pity pass for ego's sake." She forked a piece of prime rib with an energetic plunge and scanned their faces for the expected feedback.

Silence built around the tiny table until it crackled with tension.

Rose frowned at each of them. "Don't you three gawk at me like I said something outrageous. You don't get to turn into a trio of virginal prudes eliciting shock at my forward behavior." She chewed as one-by-one each shifted his gaze away.

She snorted out a cackle rude enough to catch the attention of two men at the neighboring table and Winslow began to find humor in the situation.

"I'd like to point out a new century mark passed a while back." Rose's words came fast. "The Victorians died over a hundred years ago, the Puritans even longer, so you fellows better catch up with the times."

Winslow admired her articulation. When she dropped the fork on her plate and flailed her hands, he grinned. Her voice drowned out Nelsen's shush as she fluttered a hand in his direction.

"Let me recap a few historical landmarks in social progress, gentlemen. Let's initiate with a big one, shall we? At the beginning of the *last* century, women got the right to vote. This was followed up with long outrageous work hours at factory jobs during World War II because all the men ran off to fight each other." She drank some water, shifted in her chair and pointed at Winslow. "Right?"

He didn't attempt to hide his amusement.

She turned and poked a finger toward Delmar. "And, we did it for less money."

He narrowed his eyes and glared back.

"A few decades later hemlines went up and bras came off." She punctuated each statement with a raised finger until her hand was lifted over the table like a stop sign. "Then birth control arrived and the era of the liberation movement, gentlemen. Women get to go to school now and learn to read with the male young'uns." Rose closed her fist and snatched it out of the air with a flourish.

"My grandma was a suffragette," Nelsen offered. His shoulders shook with amusement.

Winslow laughed.

One of the men next door clapped until his companion struck him on the shoulder.

Delmar considered Rose as if he'd never looked at her before. He took an extra moment to digest her tirade before he spoke. "I've got three great nephews trawling for wives." He rolled a toothpick around with his lips and stared at her with a speculative expression. "If you're offering yourself up, that is." He proceeded to rattle off their names.

Nelsen pantomimed frantic negative motions outside Delmar's vision.

Winslow watched Rose jerk her head back and forth between the two men. She was about to make a remark when he spied a uniform at the door and laid a hand on Rose's arm to draw her attention.

Winslow's grip tightened as the deputy approached the crowded table.

The woman stopped next to Rose. "It took me a while to track you down. I'm sorry to say the feds trumped our assault charges and claimed prior jurisdiction." Deputy Williams hesitated a second as she studied Rose. "They transferred custody of Savio Mendes yesterday."

Rose tensed under his hand. Her face flushed but she made no comment.

"The FBI agents were discovered in a motel room outside Pocatello at noon today. The prisoner was not present." She continued to stare at Rose.

Winslow didn't like the implication his niece was somehow involved in this madness. He glowered at the deputy. "But, that was hours ago."

Twin spots of color on her cheeks brightened. "We just received notification."

Rose covered her mouth with one hand and Winslow couldn't read her reaction.

"He killed two FBI agents and escaped?" Nelsen asked.

Delmar turned to face Rose. His voice, mirroring his expression, expressed a mixture of disbelief and incredulity. "You knocked the guy out cold. In my book that makes you a real bad ass." His tone sounded only half sardonic.

Deputy Williams shifted her gaze around the table. "Savio Mendes didn't kill them. He removed his handcuffs and disarmed both men, leaving them incapacitated while he walked out the door and drove away in their car."

Winslow shook his head. A regular run-of-the-mill kind of guy couldn't do stuff like that. His ears felt stuffed with wool. "Are the agents hurt?"

The deputy's mouth twisted into a crooked shape. "Embarrassed. The prisoner handcuffed them together on either side of the toilet. Naked."

Rose made a tiny noise. Winslow feared the muffled sound was a squeak of laughter. Both her hands now covered the lower half of her face and he suspected it was mostly to hide a smile.

His own mouth twitched. At least the bad guy had a sense of humor.

Delmar barked out a laugh. "I bet those fellas are royally pissed."

"Do you believe the prisoner will come back here?" Winslow asked.

Deputy Williams eyed Rose with a thoughtful expression. "I think he might."

CHAPTER FIFTY-SEVEN

SAVIO SLEPT ALMOST nine hours. He rolled his shoulders. Rest had been critical before executing an important decision like thrashing the boy who reached for Rose's hand every time opportunity provided an excuse. Repose and distance offered some perspective. The rash acts he'd wanted to perpetrate resulted from jealousy. The adolescent desire still burned but he decided to forgo the regret.

He rubbed gritty eyes with dry fingers. The overheated recycled air in the small room dried his throat and left his voice scratchy. After showering he'd turned up the thermostat too high and fallen asleep.

A huge yawn stretched his mouth until his jaw cracked. He worked his fingers into the hard line of scar tissue around his thigh and hip. It hurt. Muscle spasms and cramps incapacitated his mobility when he neglected therapy. He'd been immobile for much of the past three days, a particularly unwise situation under the circumstances considering his current status as a fugitive.

Ravenous, he postponed eating in favor of finding out if he was the subject of a manhunt. He ignored his rumbling stomach and checked the news. Network television offered nothing but the local reports summarized events from the last week, concluding with an update about the status of the sheriff's improving condition. The report identified the third man in Mackenzie's crew as a mid-level drug distributor from the Chicago area. A picture flashed up on the screen and Savio recognized the face of the courier he'd replaced. Benito had finally been identified and his known connection to the Almeida Cartel revived interest in the investigation.

Excellent, that distracted attention to other things.

Savio watched the television screen as he worked through a stretching routine. He hoped West Yellowstone was large enough to have an all-night diner. This eating once every twelve hours wore on him. He walked nude across the room and flipped off the heater. On his return to the bed he picked up his cell phone, disconnected the charging cord and automatically typed in his access code.

He did a double-take when the screen lit and revealed *new message from Querida*. Sarcasm echoed from the single line.

Are you really gonna stand me up?

A grin split his face. Oh yes, he liked this woman. He checked the sender to confirm her phone number. Legit. He read the text again. The receipt time indicated her complaint had arrived just before midnight. He started to dial but more than two hours had elapsed.

She probably slept. Disappointed he hadn't responded? He hoped so.

That she expected him to visit pleased his vanity. Her obvious pique over his tardiness warmed him. He exerted some of his notorious self-control and squelched the urge to depart immediately. Certain practicalities took precedence.

He pressed the autodial for his voicemail and listened to the series of messages he'd ignored since retrieving his phone from the shocked FBI agent in Pocatello.

The first one was from Henri. "Concerned by your long absence. Contact with current status." The line disconnected smoothly. The even enunciation and military precision of the man's speech did not disguise his immediate superior's displeasure.

When Savio had tasks to prioritize, the order he chose illustrated the importance ascribed to each one. His attraction to Rose clashed with his commitment to his job. His decision to put Rose first no longer knocked him sideways. Once Savio extracted a promise of future contact from the woman he'd get on with the business of flushing out the informer who'd skewed things in Mexico. The leak would be identified, the faulty components removed and the plumbing repaired. He'd make an example of the guilty party, maybe something deadly and messy as a deterrent.

The second recorded message was also Henri. This one had been left after Savio parted company with his federal escort. "I'm anxious to know the reasons for this escapade. Good work in Mexico but why are you in Montana? Contact for debriefing."

The third and final message came from Cole, the principal owner of the company and the man who employed Savio. "I can't wait to hear the rest of the story. Call my direct line when you're ready to come in."

Savio thought he detected frustration in Henri's tone but amusement colored Cole's. He set that aside for the time and focused on the remainder of the night.

He had to act now. Once he returned to Los Angeles a new task would land on his desk. The clock reset and his schedule began ticking down again. A sigh escaped him. Life felt more restrictive today that it had a week ago. He gave himself another twenty-four hours but then he must leave Montana.

A quick shower washed away the vestiges of slumber and cooled his overheated skin. He donned clean clothes and packed his meager essentials. Every parking slot in the motel lot was filled, the rooms silent and dark when he pulled the door shut behind him. He ate quickly, stoking fuel into the furnace of his body. In a short time he dropped a twenty dollar bill next to his plate and set out to see the *senorita*.

58 CHAPTER FIFTY-EIGHT

ROSE RECOGNIZED HIS voice even in her sleep. She swam to consciousness as the sounds became words.

"Wake up my angel." The tender whisper of sing-song brushed the curve of her ear.

"I don't know why I bother to lock up," she muttered.

Her dinner companions had escorted her to the *Clementine Room* and searched for intruders. She was perversely gratified to learn that their gestures were as pointless as she'd figured.

A slight movement on the bed and a sigh of air current fluttered over her cheek. She opened her eyes to find the shape of Savio's head visible against the backdrop of wall.

He spoke, his accent heavy with humor. "In point of fact, you did not lock up. The window is open. But being expected pleases me."

The bathroom light washed the room with illumination.

Rose pursed her lips and wrinkled her nose. "You sound quite satisfied."

His words came melodic even in a tone just above a whisper. He lay on his side, stretched out on the bedcovers, propped up on one elbow. "But I am. You missed me."

She pushed upright. "You're conceited. But yes, I did."

Savio fell back on the pillows and crossed his arms under his head to study her. "I could not leave without a proper farewell."

"Want to retrieve your stuff?"

He reached out and rubbed a thumb along her lower lip. "I have done so. Thank you."

Rose swallowed at the sight of his smile.

He shifted his weight, inching closer to gaze up at her. "I missed you *Querida*."

Her sarcasm was thick but her pulse pounded. "My heart is all aflutter."

"Alas, I fear you do not return my regard." He laughed when her mouth fell open.

Voice fierce and low, she aimed a punch at his arm. "That's rich, you ass."

He caught her wrist and held on. "Careful. You are not recovered from the last blow you landed."

Rose stopped pulling at her hand and canted her head. "You're right. I guess we're even."

Savio tugged hard enough to make her sway forward. "I am only concerned for your wellbeing." He tickled her palm with a finger. "Exhibit A, when I left you in the mine I gave you the shirt right off my back for extra warmth."

Her nervousness drained away as she fumed at his mellow tone. He talked about that like he'd dropped her at a bookstore to browse for a couple of hours. "That seemed reasonable to you?"

He tapped her chin with a fingertip. "Mines are cold places and I had to improvise. Remy had seen the map on the wall in your room and feared you had discovered their enterprise. He decided you must be removed."

Her thoughts began to link together. Pieces fit into the puzzle though she already knew the answer. She sulked at his nod. "You don't expect me to thank you?"

White teeth flashed. "I guess not."

She shifted position to face him. "If you hadn't delayed my return, he'd have hurt me instead of Nellie."

He flourished a hand. "You removed your bindings and returned almost quick enough for Remy to try."

Disapproval vibrated in his tone, but she figured he was equally disgruntled about her escape after he'd gone to such trouble. The silence lengthened after his implied criticism. His censure affected Rose. She was way out of her depth. Why wasn't she screaming? Oh yeah. She'd already answered that question and didn't need to review the process again.

She appreciated all he'd done for her but felt uninclined to tell him so. "What do you want from me?"

"Now *that* is a profoundly interesting query." His response was immediate as if he had just been considering the answer.

Rose wouldn't meet his gaze.

He shifted on the bedcover, his laugh a low murmur as he touched her hair, lifting a long strand and rubbing the texture between his fingers.

"What do I want from you?" he repeated.

She went still. His tone was light but it didn't relieve her tension. "I think you're playing with me."

"How shall I convince you of my sincerity?" His words were a caress.

"Seems risky to believe anything you say." The little voice inside her head whooped with laughter, Rose had done a lot more than take his word on things in the last week.

His hand dropped to rest on his raised knee, his eyes never leaving her face. "That is because you are an intelligent woman."

He was dressed in funereal hues. For some inexplicable reason Rose noticed he wore socks but not shoes.

What kind of killer sneaked into her locked room barefoot?

He followed the direction of her gaze. "Questions, *Querida?*"

"You have no idea."

Savio gave a muted laugh at her bald statement.

Another long moment passed and Rose's internal self-preservation alarm began to emit beeps. The man in her bed didn't move or breathe but she had a clear sense he was weighing some decision. He stood in a fluid movement and reached a hand down to her. His movements seemed sudden after the stillness.

"Come. We will drink wine together and satisfy your curiosity before I go."

She thought she detected the tiniest pause before the word curiosity and cursed her active imagination for supplying an alternative idea. Rose battered down her last remnant of common sense and slid off the bed.

He leaned too close for a moment, inhaling the fragrance of her hair.

Her knees wobbled, indecisive until a warm palm dropped to her waist and pressure guided her to one of the upholstered window chairs. A bottle and two glasses sat exposed in the light from the bathroom.

Gooseflesh rippled up Rose's arms. She recognized the label as her regular brand of Riesling. "I didn't take you for a white wine enthusiast."

He bowed his head and assisted her into the seat. "I seek only your satisfaction."

"I'm not sure that's comforting, Savio."

He hummed a pleasurable note. "We make progress. Names are so very important."

Opening the bottle with a practiced movement he poured the narrow flutes half full and handed it to her, following suit with one of his own. She couldn't fathom why the man had casually brought wine to a late-night assignation while he was currently a fugitive from the law. She might be flattered by the attention.

Rose held up her glass, amazed her hand didn't shake. "To our continued health."

Savio clinked in the typical ritual and offered her a wicked smile. "We must make every moment count for not many remain."

Chapter Fifty-Nine

SAVIO WATCHED ROSE upend her glass so the room temperature wine rushed down her throat. She set the delicate flute down on the table with a thump and pierced him with her dark eyes.

"Statements like that are not designed to put me at ease, Mr. Mendes. This is my room. Continue to make such cryptic remarks and I will ask you to leave."

She was so brave and brash and totally out of her depth. She left him breathless with desire. Savio feared he'd just fallen a little in love. He grinned at her from behind the rim of his wineglass. "Trust me, at ease is not where I imagine you."

That left Rose speechless.

In the reflected light she appeared to study his face. Much of the inflammation had subsided from his injuries, the bruises blending away in the gloom.

"Sorry about the nose thing." She swirled her finger in front of her features.

"Are you?" He poured more wine into her glass, curious how sincere she was being.

"I did warn you I'd be angry." She settled her hands in her lap.

He nodded. That was true, she had warned him, even scoped out the more tender parts of his anatomy. He topped up his glass too.

She strummed her fingers along the arm of her chair. "I am sorry. It's not my nature to hurt people. Besides, I figure it never hurts to apologize. If you killed all those folks I might earn brownie points and if you didn't kill anybody, the manners thing could be worth even more."

A rumble of laughter burst from his mouth. She said the most unexpected things, odd truths that disarmed his composure. She flushed, a touch of self-consciousness brightening her cheeks. He was relieved when her stiff posture relaxed marginally. His mirth was genuine.

"You are delightful, Rose. I have never met anyone like you." He laid a folded piece of paper next to the wine bottle and drained his glass. "This was intriguing."

She reached over and touched the page. Her eyes narrowed and he guessed she realized he'd searched her room quite thoroughly while she slept.

"I see you found our list of theories."

"Some of them are close to the truth. If you like, I can fill in the gaps and satisfy your curiosity."

He offered this casually but he suspected the lure of knowing would be impossible to resist. The idea of sharing information became increasingly difficult every time her gaze drifted to his lips. What he really wanted was to bend her over backwards and kiss her breathless.

Rose studied the glass he twirled between his fingers. "The park rangers caught your bearded friend out in the back country." She looked at him. "He tried to make a run for it."

He shrugged. "So the news said. Judges do not approve of men who shoot law enforcement employees. Even if he did not pull the trigger, Mackenzie will receive a stiff prison sentence. That pleases me."

She rolled her eyes. "More years than say, oh I don't know, maybe a prisoner who escapes from federal custody?"

He toasted her response with his empty flute. God but she made his body ache. Their crazed embraces in the mine had haunted him. The sheer overwhelming physical attraction he felt in her presence disarmed him, dulled his senses.

The silence stretched out between them.

"I am having difficulty considering anything except kissing you," he told her, his eyes locked to her mouth.

Rose touched two fingers to her lips. She picked up the wine bottle and refilled his glass. "I'm flattered but time moves forward."

Savio's gaze flicked to the clock. "So it does. My business in Montana is concluded. Soon I must walk out the door. Before I do, I want this uncertainty settled between us."

Rose responded to his words by going still. She reminded him of a songbird, delicate and alert. "You're here as part of your job, right?" she asked, leaning back in the upholstered chair.

Savio stared at her through hooded eyes. Uncomfortably aware of her skimpy shirt, his gaze occasionally darted down to where her nipples peaked against the thin fabric. He suspected she knew exactly how strongly he reacted to her body.

"I intercepted a courier en route from Mexico. He leaped from a moving car, an unfortunate decision that broke his neck."

Her eyebrows lifted. "The man behind the Ladies Auxiliary had such an injury."

"The same." He held her gaze. "I did not want to leave him along a road, perhaps never to be found."

Rose tilted her head, seemed to consider the information. She crossed her legs and the movement made her breasts jounce. "That was very thoughtful of you." She sounded like she meant it.

"I am uncertain how the man in the water died." He doubted Rose believed his words because most people wouldn't but confession was part of what he'd come here to do. "In order to achieve a desirable level of distrust with my companions, I took the man's car keys and used them as a weapon." Rose winced and he paused to study her flushed cheeks. She looked so youthful, so innocent. "Are you too tenderhearted to hear these things?"

Rose closed her eyelids for a long second but shook her head. "No. I just realized I have to apologize to Delmar about the antler after all." She waved for him to continue.

He twirled the wineglass by the stem. "The man was already deceased so my action, though perhaps wrong, was not deadly." He shrugged off the distinction.

Rose scowled and leaned forward. His eyes dropped back to her chest. "You couldn't have simply called the cops – or the rangers?" She snapped her fingers to draw his focus up to her face.

"Your lack of foundation garments is both distracting and provocative." He pointed at her small sleep shirt. "You are without pity."

She snorted but twisted sideways in the chair and pulled one leg up to circle her arm around a knee.

His mind blanked. She was so limber his imagination ran rampant for a moment.

"*Que?*" he asked after he realized she'd spoken.

"What else?" she repeated.

Savio set his wine glass on the marble-topped table and laced his fingers together, staring at her with a somber expression. "Then there is you." He wondered about the thoughts processing through that complicated mind of hers.

"Don't look at me like I've been out whacking people," she complained. "We're focusing on your illegal activities tonight. You answer my questions and I'll consider answering yours."

He let several seconds tick off before indicating agreement.

She jumped in with a new question. "Explain the footprints at the murder scene."

Savio blinked.

"You know." She wiggled her fingers like multiple legs in motion. "Explain the strange footsteps in the mud around the thermal pool. Some were spaced at odd irregular intervals, as if whoever walked through took a long step followed by a short hop. One of the feet left normal foot-shaped prints but the other was formed with a stump or club foot."

Savio turned his head sideways and beheld her with amusement. "You are so observant, I believe further speculation on your part will bring you to the answer."

"Daylight's coming soon so you should just go ahead and tell me."

He swallowed the last of his wine and put aside his glass. They had other topics to discuss and he was anxious to get to them.

"After I left you in the mine, things rapidly fell apart. Thinking I had secured your safety, I set out to locate Mackenzie and Remy. I failed to do either. By then Remy had attacked the ranger. When I arrived at the inn, you had also returned. You cannot imagine my distress as emergency personnel descended with flashing lights and administered immediate medical assistance. I was concerned about you."

He held up the bottle with a quizzical expression.

60 CHAPTER SIXTY

R OSE IGNORED THE criticism in Savio's tone and held out her glass for a refill. She took advantage of his distraction to admire his lips as he poured the wine. They were fine, lean and streamlined like the rest of him. She did a mental headshake. "I got the sash on the fourth window fixed."

"Good idea. Roofs provide easy access." He sent her a meditative glance.

She shivered. "Don't be creepy. You didn't thank me for the open invitation tonight."

"You should not be so foolish."

"And closing the window would have kept you out?"

He smirked and shook his head.

Rose leaned forward and gestured with a hand. "Operating on the assumption that you might be angry, I had hoped to talk you into a better mood." That was also why she'd worn the smallest tank top in her luggage. The alcohol must have reached her bloodstream because warmth stole through her body. Of course it was the wine.

Savio's silky tone intensified. "What reasons have I to be angered?"

She grimaced. Convoluted syntax. Probably not a good sign. "I did hit you several times." Her uneasiness increased as he continued to stare at her with a blank face. "Okay, I admit I shouldn't have kicked you." She frowned when she realized he still waited for her to say more.

What?

Leaning back, his features took on a menacing seriousness. "You cannot imagine anything else?"

Rose was puzzled. She searched her memory. He seemed unconcerned about the physical damage. "I'm sorry. I don't know what to say." She set down her wine glass, straightened her back and folded her hands in her lap. Her attention didn't waver from his glacial expression.

After a lengthy pause he finally spoke. "Did you never consider I might be distressed to find you in the company of another?"

Her mind sluggishly processed his question. The words made no sense. "What are you talking about?"

"I saw you with him today."

Rose stuttered to a stop. Her eyes widened. Savio had seen her and Tobias in the park? All day she'd struggled to pay attention and act like a good guide while her brain was stuck on Savio and he'd been there.

She gritted out a question, "You're jealous?"

A muscle twitched along his jaw.

"You're kidding." Nope, he wasn't. Warmth bloomed in her stomach. She hopped to her feet and crossed the short distance to stand in front of him.

He swiveled his gaze up to meet hers.

"Really?" she whispered. Completely bemused, she rested her fingertips on his cheek. "I've *never* received a better compliment." Cupping his tensed face, she leaned down and kissed him until his mouth softened and he responded.

Savio's hands landed on her waist, sliding down until they curved over her hipbones. His palms scalded her flesh. His lips were tender at first but the kiss deepened until both of them breathed hard enough they had to pull back and catch their breath.

After a moment Rose squirmed away. She wanted to clear things up before they progressed farther down this particular road.

Savio reluctantly let her go.

She resumed her seat. "Your competitor is the sheriff's lady friend's stepson and just to be crystal, he's not competition of any kind." She waited while he worked out the relationship. "I got sandbagged to show him the sights in exchange for an early release of my field permit." She made a speculative face at him. "Would you react the same way if Tobias was a girl?"

He looked amused. "He is not, so your question is irrelevant."

"That makes you a bigot."

He shrugged but his earlier tenseness was gone. A smile played around his mouth, the sort that promised he had something in store.

She laced her fingers together. "You don't consider this possessiveness of yours a little unwarranted considering the situation?"

"I can say only that you make a strong impression." Hunger showed on his face as his gaze roved over her body. "You might recall I mentioned feeling proprietary that first night after I climbed through the window. Exclusivity was implied."

She boldly surveyed him in return. God but he was hot. "Well don't go getting all bent out of shape when I tell you I have plans to visit with Tobias this weekend."

He arched one brow. "I fear such will not be possible unless you convince me."

Holy shit, she thought her knees might have melted.

"Time's short so I'll accommodate your request but after tonight you're back to knocking on the door like anyone else." She smirked. "And for the record, exclusivity goes both ways."

"Granted."

His swift affirmation brought a blush sweeping up her cheeks. She thought she'd just agreed to go steady with a professional mercenary recently escaped from federal custody. She exerted some effort to get back to recent events.

"Who shot Harlan?"

Savio looked pensive. "The police will determine which gun fired the bullet."

Rose slumped in her chair. "I saw him at the hospital." She liked that he met her gaze without flinching and though her confidence wavered, she asked the question that had plagued her peace of mind. "Where were you when the shooting happened?"

His broody expression returned. "I promise you I was not there, *Rosita.*"

She wanted to trust him but she figured he'd tell her whatever he needed to in order to achieve his objective. "I want to believe you."

He leaned forward. "Occupied with work-related activities, I sat in the Riverside Library doing research on an unbelievably slow internet connection. As soon as I concluded my business, I came directly to you. You were gone." He steepled his fingers and continued. "When you did not return, I feared Mackenzie had abducted you." He broke the stare and rubbed a palm across his chin. "I worried about him trying to use you as leverage."

She'd recognized Mackenzie was the bearded man she'd first seen in the forest and later in Remy's company. His face had been all over the news after he'd been apprehended by the park service. If she could be considered leverage, then the bad guys truly had known she was involved in some way. Rose probably owed Savio more than he let on. She followed the trajectory of his hands as he dragged them through his hair. She might be disconcerted by the vulnerable tenor of his admission but she wasn't nearly as uncomfortable as he.

She sent her companion a meaningful look. "I drove Harlan's lady friend to the hospital in Bozeman. I forgot and left my phone here at the inn. I didn't get back until midnight and, well, you know what happened then."

The lines of his face were as animated as a statue.

"You want me to apologize again?" Her tone sounded disgruntled.

His laughter demonstrated another quicksilver mood change. "We must agree to make no apologies, *Querida*."

She frowned at him. "Well that gets you and your poor behavior off the hook."

"*Exactamente.*"

He raised his empty glass from the inside and wiped it with a clean handkerchief. "The bad men are defeated. Right has triumphed." He completed the same motions with the bottle.

Rose observed in silence. He might have done this a hundred times. "Does that mean you're on the side of law and order?"

In the light from the bathroom his penetrating stare turned solemn. "I think not, *Querida.*"

She'd guessed as much.

His mouth curled into his dark angel smile. "But that does not mean I am one of the bad guys."

Blood rushed through her veins and she smirked. "Of course not."

Savio held out a hand. "Come, we must say our goodnight."

In a déjà vu of their first encounter, she wondered if he caught her frisson of fear as she clasped his fingers and was drawn into the loose embrace of his arms. He leaned close to rub a cheek against her temple. His breath warmed her ear. Instead of corny, she found the motions sensual.

"You smell like sunrise. Scent is underappreciated." His muted tone soothed her nerves as he drew her hand into his and lifted their entwined fingers high overhead. He turned them in a slow double pirouette.

The pieces connected with a jolt. His smooth graceful movements reflected years of experience. His muscular control and incredible agility made sense now. She raised her face. "You're a dancer. Those were *your* footprints near the thermal pool."

He smiled down from a height not too many inches taller, wrapped one hand behind her neck and pulled her tight against his chest, pressing low on her back.

She clutched at his shoulders as he bent her over.

"Dancing is only one of the things I desire to do with you." He said, his voice hoarse, mouth angling towards hers.

He closed his eyes and blocked out a blue so vivid she speculated if he wore colored contact lenses. His entire frame shuddered. The kiss started slow and hot, his lips warm and dry until he dipped his tongue inside her mouth. Heat uncoiled within her as his hold deepened and his taut body pressed against hers. Trusting him to support her, she let go and looped her arms around his neck.

One hand trailed down her side to curl over her backside. "Forgive me these liberties, Rose. I do not want you to forget me."

Her laugh was broken, her breath ragged. "Impossible," she breathed out, tugging at the collar of his t-shirt and wishing it buttoned down the front. She licked the exposed line of his throat, flicking her tongue against the hollow below his Adam's apple.

Savio groaned.

Her words came throaty when he raised her up and clamped palms over her hip bones. "I don't suppose you could stay and visit? The day stretches ahead... and me with zip to do."

Savio leaned his head back, hands pulling her lower body tight to his. "I thought you had plans with the kid?"

A small exhalation burst from her lips at the contact. "Not till Sunday."

He increased the pressure, grinding his hips into her softness. "Want to spend the day with a fugitive from justice?"

She wiggled against him, dropping her hands to his waist to skim her palms up the hard muscles of his chest. "I've heard the hike out to the continental divide is pretty amazing." Her gaze locked on his mouth. "Or we could stay inside."

61 CHAPTER SIXTY-ONE

SAVIO COULD NOT remember a more perfect morning. The air was crisp, so fresh his lungs expanded with every breath. He looked to where Rose was doubled over with her hands propped on her knees and grinned at the sight. She was overheated and disheveled, as if they had just made love. He was anxious to see her that way.

"I actually believed... you'd opt to... spend the day... in my nice... comfortable room." She gasped out the sentence, noisy inhalations punctuating her every two or three words.

He'd pushed hard on the trail, suspecting she'd plodded along without complaint only because she couldn't catch her breath.

She pointed an accusing finger at him. "Not fair. You haven't even... broken a sweat."

Her disgusted tone of voice amused him.

Rose blinked, her gaze drifting over the multihued bruises decorating his face. She swirled a finger along her profile before jabbing it at him again. "This is punishment for that." She sucked in another deep draw. "Oxygen levels have dropped, right?

He chucked her under the chin before shedding the backpack. He waved a hand around the landscape. "This was your suggestion, remember? I just wanted some alone time with you." By the appearance of things, they'd found all the privacy left on the planet. Ascending a trail before sunrise and hiking two hours, they split off the main track and took a thread of a path up a steep incline until they reached this small ridge. Now an expansive vista undulated before them in waves.

"There is nowhere more secluded." She paused for another breath. "If a bear charges out of the forest I fully expect you to vault in front of me like the hero you are and be devoured." She lurched over to him and fisted his shirt, jerking him against her body.

He sucked in air at the contact, heat replacing his amusement. "I like when you get aggressive." Close proximity was a special kind of torture. He grappled for restraint.

"I'm not kidding," she sputtered, her breasts rising and falling with her quick breaths.

He managed to keep his face a study in neutrality but his voice rumbled with suppressed desire. "Seclusion has its dangers."

Rose took an almost normal respiration and smiled up at him. "Oh sure, like that never occurred to me, you know. I guessed going off in the wilderness with a wanted man could be complicated, maybe even prove risky." Her cheek settled over his heart, her arms stole around his waist in an embrace and she relaxed against him.

Mirroring her actions without conscious thought, he marveled at her heat. For a small woman she generated a lot of energy. The steady rhythm of her breathing lulled him into a state of utter contentment. "Does that mean you trust me?"

"Do you really need to ask?" Her hands sneaked under his woolen jacket so she could rub her fingers along his lower back, tracing the contours of muscle through his t-shirt.

Yes, he did.

He wanted to hear the words.

He laid his cheek on her hair and closed his eyes. The warm female in his arms filled him with satisfaction. With the endless landscape stretching out in all directions around them, he enjoyed the sense they were the solitary two people in the world. Nothing had ever seemed so perfect. No woman had ever felt so right.

"Give me coffee," Rose demanded.

Savio leaned back and peered down with suspicion. She appeared serious. "Where do you expect to find such?"

Rose pointed at the pack.

He retrieved the bag for her. She squatted near a patch of ground blanketed by a thick layer of pine needles and unzipped their supplies. From inside she pulled out a slender stainless steel bullet-shaped canister. With practiced movements she unscrewed the lid, poured coffee into the small cup and handed it to him.

He drank. The hot liquid was like pure adrenalin. He sent her a heated appraisal. "You are a woman worthy of devotion."

"As it should always be."

He watched as she withdrew a bottle of water and a folded cloth from inside the pack, wondering what else she had secreted away.

She spread the flannel sheet on a bare patch of ground and crawled on top of it where she began unlacing her boots. She peeled off her shoes and then her socks, setting them neatly to one side before leaning back against a boulder. She patted the ground beside her. He needed no further urging and followed suit, joining her. Barefoot in the chill air, the sun streaming across their resting place, he felt connected. Grounded. Their arms close enough to touch, they stared at the panorama.

Rose tilted her head, staring at the territorial view from different angles. "That's amazing. It actually resembles a spine if you squint." She glanced sideways at him. "I wanted to do this while I was here but I didn't expect to have company. Thanks."

With a simple sentence she'd disarmed him again.

"Now that we're somewhere private," she made air quotes with her fingers, "explain our jailhouse conversation so I know what the hell we were talking about."

He liked how her mind jumped from one topic to the next.

He swapped beverages with her and emptied the water bottle. She refilled the coffee and took a sip.

"I had no idea what information you might have volunteered to Deputy Williams or the cops who interrupted our midnight reunion. Since they didn't charge me with anything specific, they had to release me after the requisite number of hours passed unless you agreed to press charges. That would have complicated things." He bumped against her side. "Thank you for not doing so."

"People will fill in details if you let them." She bumped him back. "With no clue how to explain our relationship, I didn't say much of anything. I'd like to pretend it was to protect you, but if we're being honest here, I was trying to figure out a way to avoid confessing that I'd known what was happening behind the scenes of all this criminal behavior."

He'd guessed accurately. "Always protect your position. Under the watchful eyes of Deputy Williams, a woman who sees all and admits nothing, I tried to elicit details without revealing the extent of our acquaintance." He met her gaze. "I did not know when I might get back to find you and was frustrated. This is better than hunting you down in California."

She peeped at him through dense eyelashes. "Had plans did you?"

Face solemn, he nodded and picked up her hand, laced his fingers between hers. Now was the time to discover if he'd been dealt the right cards. He stared into her eyes. "I want to try this again when your work here in Montana is finished."

Rose didn't hesitate. "I'll mark my calendar for September and expect you to turn up in California."

Satisfaction flowed through him. She too wanted to explore this intense physical response. Then he grew skeptical and frowned. "Your reaction is not rational."

"I know." She wrinkled her nose. "But trying to date in a place where you're Public Enemy Number One offers too many complications. Besides, I'm busy for the next six weeks."

"I keep telling you I am not on any wanted list."

"I bet there are two FBI agents who say otherwise."

He snorted a derisive laugh.

"Prolonged exposure to crazy is said to affect a person's judgment. My relatives are eccentric. My family is a cross between an international music festival, the X-Games and a bar brawl. They're half loud and wonderful, half moonstruck daredevils, and not half bad, most of the time."

He shook his head. "That is a lot of halves."

She shrugged. "Minus the handcuffs, you'll fit right in."

"All set to take me home to meet the family?" He couldn't hide the note of derision in his tone.

"Don't look so aghast." She took the thermos lid and drained the contents, slipped the cap on and scooted closer. "At the moment I'm more interested in us getting better acquainted. You can worry about meeting the 'fam' later. Even though you're secretly mad that I kicked your ass and got you arrested, don't you want to demonstrate how much you missed me?"

He dropped the empty water bottle beside his boots. "Invitation accepted."

He scooped Rose up and dragged her over his thighs, smothering her laughter by leaning her back in the crook of his arm and exploring her mouth in a leisurely fashion.

Holding the petite *senorita* in his arms as the sun inched across the sky filled him with an unprecedented sense of peace. He'd wanted this chance to touch her, to enjoy the slow and thorough discovery of learning her body. He yearned to make her purr with satisfaction, to know she shivered and cried out for him. The contentment he experienced from the sensation of her limbs melting into his was beyond compare. Against the backdrop of the endless green vista he imagined a life completely different than the one he'd lived and it didn't seem like a fantasy. He *needed* to see Rose again, was already certain he couldn't last till September.

From the first moment he'd been in her presence, he'd gravitated toward her. She glowed with an irresistible vitality. The physical attraction was potent, but something undefined and more powerful drove him. The intensity bordered on desperation. Uttering a soft groan he gave into the desire that stripped his control raw.

He pulled at her shirt. "Take this off?"

Rose complied, her nimble fingers shrugging off her flannel and tugging her tank up over her shoulders. She smiled at him with a hint of mischief as she pulled it over her head and revealed the flamingo pink bra.

The satin cups molded her breasts and she plucked at a strap. "Remember this?"

Savio's thoughts pounded with the rush of blood that surged through his veins. "*Si.*" He shook himself and repeated in English. "Yes."

"Did your voice just get hoarse?" She climbed up on her knees and pushed at his shoulder, shoving until he collapsed onto his back.

"You enjoy being in control," he rasped out. When she crawled up his body and straddled his waist, he thought his eyes rolled up in his head.

"I do," she whispered and nipped his ear lobe. "But I think you like it even more."

Dear God in heaven, she might be correct.

She stripped off his shirt, leaving him clothed only in jeans. She inspected the hard ridges of his abdomen, blazing a sensitized path in her wake. When she bent low and traced the length of the scar along his ribs with her tongue, he forgot to breathe. Never had he been seduced with such ferocity. With a series of contortions she wriggled out of her own jeans and displayed a matching pair of pink panties.

His mouth went dry. "You are magnificent," he told her. His hands skimmed over her curves. "So lush." He'd dreamed of seeing her naked but with her softly rounded body displayed before him like an offering, he exhaled in a rush.

He traced a knuckle down her cheek. "Your passion humbles me, *Querida.*" The reality of what they were about to do stole his breath.

She smiled down at him. Straddling his belly, she undid the clasp on her bra and tossed it aside. Her full breasts brushed against his chest as she licked near his ear again. Leaning in close she exhaled a teasing question.

He froze for a fraction of a second.

Could he make her lose control?

Challenge accepted.

In a single smooth move, he folded his arms around her and tightened, pulling her close as he rolled her beneath him. Then he claimed her mouth.

62   Chapter Sixty-Two

ONCE THE SUN came up and spilled light across the world Rose became a bundle of nerves. In the dark of the night she'd been able to avoid thinking about the complications of their situation. Now she near panicked over how to get Savio safely out of the White Horse Inn to somewhere he couldn't be captured and thrown back in jail.

She stroked an appreciative hand down his spine. "Until I met you, I was a relatively law-abiding person."

Savio stowed his gun in his shoulder holster and turned around. He traced a finger down Rose's cheek. "You are not breaking any laws right now." He bent down and kissed her gently. "I will miss you, *mi flor.*"

The tender touch warmed her inside but she concentrated on logistics. He was far too casual about the risk of capture this morning. "I'll be missing you as well. Now stop trying to change the subject and get ready. Winslow's probably already waiting downstairs. The messages he left yesterday said as much."

Savio fastened the bottom three buttons on his flannel and tucked the shirt into his pants. "He is one of the old men from the bench across the street?"

Rose nodded, frustrated by his obvious lack of concern.

He smiled at her. "You go first to distract him."

"What if somebody questions your being inside the house?" Rose demanded. She pulled the hairbrush through her hair and rocked back on her feet from the vigor of the action. Her sensual lethargy from their bed play had turned to nervous concern as Savio made final preparations to depart. Half her problem stemmed from the realization she might not see him again. Despite their future plans, September in California was a long time and a far distance from the magic of this place.

He chucked her under the chin. "I am just another traveler expressing interest in a room." He brushed his lips across her temple. "I like your show of concern." He pressed his forehead to hers and held her for a moment. "You will let me know?"

She flushed. Glad he couldn't see her face; she burrowed against his chest and confirmed she would, her voice muffled. In the bright light of the morning after, she felt bashful about her outrageous brazenness of the night before. After they'd hiked down the mountain and returned to the White Horse Inn, well, one thing had led to another and they hadn't been as careful as intended. Now she played the waiting game until her next menstrual cycle came as scheduled. Or didn't. She hadn't anticipated his leaving to be so hard. In less than a week Savio flipped her world upside down. In only a day he'd turned her emotions inside out.

He stroked her back. "It will be okay, *Querida.*"

She appreciated his attempt to soothe her concern. He'd done that the first night he'd crawled through her window. It had made her knees weak then too.

"I'm sorry I beat you up." She wrapped her arms around him and squeezed, noting his responding quiver of amusement.

He dropped another warm kiss next to her ear. "Between now and September you can consider the many ways to make it up to me."

His words served to distract her, as she was sure he'd intended.

Minutes later Rose left the *Clementine Room*, her overheated blood steaming all rational thought from her mind. She forced herself to concentrate on not falling down the stairs. While that might create an awesome diversion, he'd ruin it by rushing down to help her back up on her feet. Taking each step slowly, she navigated to the first floor on limbs that felt lethargic and pleasantly fatigued. She stumbled out onto the porch and found her uncle waiting.

Winslow jumped up from a chair when she emerged. "Rose, I've been concerned about you." He was dressed in his typical pullover sweatshirt and pressed jeans, precision creases down the front of each pant leg. Running shoes peeked out the cuffs.

She aimed a brilliant smile at him. "Hi, Uncle Winslow. I got your message too late to call you back. Is something wrong?"

"You were gone all yesterday. I was worried." He looked self-conscious.

Guilt flooded through Rose. "I'm sorry. I spent the day hiking and didn't consider how concerned you might be. The park service promised my permit would be released soon." She displayed crossed fingers and hoped he restrained from asking what occupied her until after dark.

His gaze shifted over her shoulder as the door opened again but he brought his attention right back to her. "Do you think it wise to be alone? Under the circumstances, I mean."

Rose caught movement in her peripheral vision as a figure stepped outside. She recognized Savio at once. He wore a tailored leather jacket and carried his helmet. He walked out the front entrance of the inn with a brazen set to his shoulders and a relaxed expression on his face. She fumed. A normal fugitive from justice should slink out the back exit.

She laid a hand on her uncle's arm to keep his attention on her. "I appreciate your concern, Winslow. It was inconsiderate of me to leave you hanging without an explanation but I think Deputy Williams's apprehension is overstated." She hoped he didn't wonder why she chattered with such nervous energy.

Savio walked away, his steps ringing off the wooden planks of the porch.

Rose bit her tongue. The man could move quiet as a cat when he chose. She glanced over as he pulled the helmet over his head and descended the stairs. At least his face was no longer on public view. She turned her attention back to Winslow and tried to concentrate on what he said but all her senses were focused on her lover's exit. A moment later the vibrating rumble of a motorcycle engine roared to life. The sound distracted her. The chance of a last glimpse of Savio astride the bike was too much to resist. She swiveled to watch.

Winslow's voice trailed away.

Savio rolled down the driveway of Vic's Restaurant, his thigh muscles flexing as he reached the end of the drive and braced his feet on the pavement before pulling out on the main road. He idled around her parked car, creeping along in front of the White Horse Inn. He stopped when they shared a clear view of one other.

A long moment passed.

Rose lifted a hand and blew Savio a kiss.

He responded by raising a fist, tapping his chest and pointing at her. Then he revved the engine and pulled away. He was gone a second later. After a brief pause Rose turned to face her uncle.

The old man studied her with a determinedly neutral expression. "I'm going to go out on a limb here and guess you weren't alone yesterday."

Rose lit up the most dazzling smile she could manage. "You not only got the Bannion family beauty, but the brains too. Would you like to have breakfast with me, Uncle Winslow?"

EPILOGUE

S AVIO SETTLED INTO his seat on the tiny jet. He withdrew his billfold and pulled out Rose's business card. Her full name intrigued him, another thing he wanted to learn more about. He turned the paper rectangle over and grinned. The senorita had ransacked his wallet while he cooled his heels in jail. She'd left him a note.

Savio = sexy.

A trio of stars and an initial "R" formed her signature.

He flipped through his phone photos until he found the pictures of Rose. The one he most liked, a close-up three-quarter profile showed her staring into the distance, her eyes focused on the Continental Divide. This picture reminded him that despite the odds, somehow he'd got the girl. Rose had seen him, just like he'd urged during their jailhouse meeting. He stared at the photo for a long time before typing a quick text.

He pushed send as the jet began to taxi down the runway. Switching the flight mode on, he tucked the satellite phone inside his shirt pocket. Once airborne, he closed his eyes and slept all the way to Los Angeles.

***

Rose returned from an enjoyable hour with her uncle. He'd abstained from asking questions about her association with the man on the motorcycle but she harbored no illusions that he would let the topic drop indefinitely. Winslow probably had a plan worked out in his head on exactly how to approach the subject.

She returned to her room, half-expecting an echo of the cold atmosphere from the afternoon she'd discovered Nellie collapsed on the floor. Instead of emptiness, the warm colors emitted the glow of life. She found the space stuffed with memories of Savio and a lingering intimacy. Her stuff scattered around in a familiar jumbled mess also brought her comfort. She noticed her knapsack on the chair and beneath it the shirt he'd given her in the mine. He hadn't retrieved the garment even when the opportunity arose.

A sonar beep clanged and Rose regarded her cell with suspicion. She walked across to the bedside table and scooped up the phone. With the sweep of her finger she unlocked the device and saw the text.

She blinked, read the line a second time and snorted out a laugh. *New message from Savio Mendes.* He'd programmed his damn number into her phone. Rose didn't know what to think about that.

She touched the icon with a fingertip and opened the note.

I will call you tonight, Querida.

Bemused, she stared at the words until the screen blanked. Then she slid open the keypad and tapped out a response. She vacillated for a moment. Embracing her new motto of celebrating danger, she pushed send.

It's poker night – call late. I miss you too.

ABOUT THE AUTHOR

As an anthropologist, Lesann divides her time between academic interests and professional research focused primarily on the American west. Crossing genre lines, she pens both contemporary and historical mysteries, romantic suspense, and even a little horror.

Find out what happens next for Rose & Savio by visiting:
WWW.LESANNBERRY.COM